To Lieut. K. M. [illegible]
from Martha & Milo
Sheldon. 1942.

Clearwater and the Kootenai—on all these timeless streams which gave themselves at last into the Columbia. I rode on waters churned by the big rapids, riled by rocks on earth so long before man that to them he is no more than the passing of a wind along the canyon walls. I rode on waters that would hurl themselves over the precipice at Celilo and past Dalles City, curling a little in their backwash at the ancient basalt, taking up the Willamette in their rolling tide, seeking the Columbia's treacherous ever-changing mouth, scattered with ships and yet so hungry, into . . . the western ocean.

THE END

Clearwater and the Kootenai—on all those timeless streams which give themselves at last into the Columbia. I rode on waters churned by the big rapids, riled by rocks on earth so long before man that to them he is no more than the passing of a wind along the canyon walls. I rode on waters that would hurl themselves over the precipice at Celilo and past Dalles City, cutting a little in their moment at the ancient basalt, taking up the Willamette in their rolling tide, seeking the Columbia's treacherous ever-changing mouth, so surfeited with ships and yet so hungry, into . . . the western ocean.

THE END

SWIFT FLOWS THE RIVER

SWIFT FLOWS THE RIVER

By

NARD JONES

GROSSET & DUNLAP
PUBLISHERS NEW YORK
By arrangement with Dodd, Mead & Co.

PRINTED IN THE UNITED STATES OF AMERICA

TO

JUDGE FRED W. WILSON

OF THE DALLES, OREGON,

WHO KEEPS ALIVE THE STORY OF

THE COLUMBIA

ACKNOWLEDGMENT

THE lives of thousands of men and women now living in the Pacific Northwest have at one time or another touched upon the Columbia in the days of its high glory. Those who know the Great River of the West feel keenly about it; rightly they wish to see that justice is done. I hope I have not disappointed too many of those citizens of Astoria, Portland, The Dalles, Walla Walla, and Lewiston who so willingly assisted. I trust that veteran steamboat men will allow the mutation necessary in a work of fiction based upon actual happenings.

I am especially indebted to the following: Judge Fred W. Wilson, The Dalles, Oregon; J. C. Ainsworth, Portland; Miss Elizabeth Barry, Portland; the late Winlock Miller, Jr., Seattle; Capt. Arthur Riggs, Portland; H. C. Hanson, Naval Architect, Seattle; Richard Montgomery, Portland; Robert G. Bailey, Lewiston, Idaho; W. W. Baker, Walla Walla, Washington; Dr. Stephen B. L. Penrose, Whitman College, Walla Walla, T. C. Elliott, Walla Walla; Milton C. Henderson, Portland; Lieutenant-Commander Frank Higbee, United States Coast Guard, Astoria; Truman Cook, Astoria. I am grateful also to Russell Blankenship, University of Washington, and to Harry Hartman and J. Gordon Gose for suggestions as to the narrative.

Acknowledgments are made to the United States Army Engineers, Portland; The Dalles Public Library; and the magazine *Pacific Motor Boat* for special services and information. The files of the Oregon and Washington historical quarterlies were consulted frequently, and I would like to salute the memory of William Hand, editor and publisher of *The Mountaineer* in the earlier days of The Dalles.

PART ONE

CHAPTER 1

My father was proud of the strange, green land he had chosen as our home. He was fond of saying that if ever we became a State it would be the first added to the Union by occupation and exploration. The notion seemed to have a pleasant significance for him, and although I was not yet aware of the possibilities in this distinction, the idea pleased me, too.

It made my father furious when the Commander of the Pacific Division insisted, from the comparative ease and gaiety of San Francisco, that the Northwest was fit for nothing but an Indian reservation. Our meager little band, set down along the bank of the Columbia at The Cascades Rapids, was not inclined to agree with General Wool. The first explorers by land had come and gone. The traders had arrived both by land and by sea. Migrants from the States were now settling as comfortably as nature and the Indians would allow. When my mother and father and I reached the river in 1855 men and women were already working and dreaming in the shadows of the green gorge. They had no sense of being shut in, and apart, and they did not feel unimportant, for the river came down from a wide country and went to meet the sea.

We heard that San Francisco was really growing to be a sizable place. We heard that to the north settlers had established a town on the shores of Puget Sound, and that east of Fort Walla Walla a settlement had rooted itself in a valley of grass. But these were reports brought in by the soldiers or by private citizenry traveling on the river boats, and could not always be trusted. But with

Astoria, and Vancouver, and Portland we had a more direct connection. Astoria was twelve miles from the mouth of the Columbia. Portlanders had settled themselves on the quieter Willamette at a point where it empties into the Columbia. At Vancouver there was a military post. These towns were west of us, and upriver was Dalles City, a last outpost that stood between us, a vast country known only to those who had come West by wagon train or professed to have trapped and hunted there.

The little steamers *Mary* and *Wasco* plied between The Cascades and Dalles City, while the *Belle* and the *Fashion* landed at the lower wharf boat from the downriver towns. The conjunction of these steamers was the reason for our settlement. At The Cascades the river narrowed appreciably, squeezing in at Hamilton's Island and growing slimmer still at Bradford's Island, until at the blockhouse you could almost throw a stone across. Through this channel, as though provoked at being so suddenly curbed, the Columbia roared too swift for navigation. When the Army wanted to get supplies into the back country it was necessary to transport them from Portland on the *Fashion* or the *Belle,* then haul them along the portage road at The Cascades. At the upper end of the rapids, the *Mary* or the *Wasco* waited to carry the stuff on to Dalles City.

The boats from the west would skirt Hamilton Island and unload at the lower landing near a scattering of cabins. The cargo was then hauled by mules past the rapids to the Upper Cascades where stood Bradford and Company's store in the center of another tiny settlement. There was always plenty of excitement when the boats were in; and, boylike, I assumed that all of it was for my personal entertainment. I was too young then to fully realize the military importance of The Cascades, or to know that my father, working on the new portage bridge, was contributing his part to the movement of the troops and the opening of the back country.

Until that horrible day of March 26, 1856, of which I am about to tell, I never fully understood the dark mutterings of Mike Shea.

Mike Shea was a fine friend for a boy to have, but because he was one of a detail of only eight men under Sergeant Kelly from Company H, and was stationed at the blockhouse a good mile and a half upriver from our settlement, I did not get to see him as often as I wanted.

He was a huge fellow, with brick red hair and a complexion to match it except for the two thin trickles of brown which forever coursed from the corners of his mouth to a point beneath his chin. He detested the post at The Cascades, mainly, I suspect, because it offered little in the way of excitement. But there was another reason for Mike's dislike. The Cascades presented a ticklish military problem, and considering that he was only a private in the ranks, Mike took his soldiering seriously. Naturally valuable materials accumulated at the portage, so that the Army—conscientious Mike Shea in particular—worried about them incessantly. And with excellent reason. Not infrequently the shipments contained arms and ammunition, rich booty to the savages.

Mike and I would sit on the river bank near the blockhouse and watch the *Mary* loading. Often I expressed a desire to be her captain, and this always brought scoffing from Mike. "That steam pot!" he would roar. "If it's a boat captain you want to be you should have seen the ship I took from 'Frisco to Vancouver. But who'd want to be cooped in a floating shack, anyhow?" Nevertheless, just to please me, he'd carve out little boats, and we'd launch them with ceremonies and watch them out of sight. More times than not, the rapids drew them under before our eyes. But occasionally Mike created a craft which, we felt certain, got beyond them and found the Pacific Ocean.

While Mike carved toy boats he talked. I was never quite sure whether he talked to me.or to himself, but I listened eagerly when it was a tale of Army life, or an Indian fight, or how he outwitted the waterfront thugs of 'Frisco. When he began to harp, as eventually he would, on the danger coming to The Cascades settlement, my mind would wander. The idea had once startled me, then as time went on and nothing happened I paid scant attention—despite the fact that Mike grew more and more obsessed with his belief that the Indians were going to wipe us out.

"Yes, sir, Caleb. Your mother and father should be keepin' you close in. You got no business up here at the blockhouse and that's a fact." This went unheeded, for I knew that he liked to have me visit him. There was little enough to do at the blockhouse except play poker and, sometimes, spend a night drinking whiskey toddies and telling Army yarns.

"These vermin," Mike would say, "are brewin' trouble, and that a-plenty." He never referred to the natives except as vermin. To me the Indians had always appeared very peaceful. Although I gave them their distance and disapproved their smell, I admired the quiet villagers with their harmless habits of fish spearing and weaving. It seemed to me that they were happy and contented. I was aware that they differed from the plains savages and suspected Mike of being prejudiced by his experiences in the back country.

In our Indian village a man had not more than one wife, and he shared the work with her. Great respect was shown the old men and women, and in everything except standards of health they measured up well with the rest of us. Their eyes were often in a state of soreness, and many had lost the sight of one from the disease. Their teeth and gums were atrocious due to a diet of soft salmon and dried, sandy roots. It was not unusual to see a native with his teeth worn to the gums.

Once my father had taken me to the Indian village and we had been royally treated. We were asked into a house made of straw matting for a fine salmon feast. First, wood was split with an elkhorn wedge, and a fire made. Then the old Indian, who had helped my father on the portage bridge, put stones into the fire until they were very hot. Finally his squaw brought in a bucket of water in which was a half-dried salmon. Into the water she forked the hot stones, and soon the fish was boiled and taken out of the bubbling water to be set before us on a platter of rushes. Armed with sticks and our fingers, the four of us plunged into the meal, and I have never tasted anything better. When my mother heard of our adventure, however, she was amazed and disgusted. She told my father that she would not have been surprised if Mike Shea had taken me into an Indian hut to eat bad fish off dirty straw, but she had never believed my own father would do such a thing. Of course she did not really mean it, so my father laughed and promised to show her how the squaw had cooked the fish.

It was easy to understand why the neighboring Indians were a somewhat lazy lot. The big salmon were so plentiful that they used the dried fish for fuel. I had seen the salmon drift ashore in such quantities that the villagers needed only to gather them on the beach, split them, and dry them on scaffolding in the sun.

Before that fateful March I fondly believed that these people wanted only to live as they were, and that they were neither envious nor afraid of the whites. But Mike refused to share this opinion. "They're all alike, these vermin. Mix in a Yakima or a Klickitat with the Cascades and one's as bad as the next. You just wait, Caleb, my boy."

Most of Mike's misgivings sprang from a dislike of General Wool. He had no doubt as to the ability of a trooper to handle "Mr. Lo." But those in command were notoriously stupid, Mike said, where vermin were concerned. "Old Johnnie Ellis" Mike called General Wool, the Commander of the Pacific Division. He was too old to fight anything, much less Indians, and he didn't know anything about the country. "Look now! . . . he's sending Colonel Wright to concentrate at Dalles City. Goin' to have him build forts up in the Walla Walla and Yakima country—as if *they* needed them! Why, the minute the vermin get wind of that we'll get Hell a-plenty around here!"

I was not the only recipient of Mike's warnings. In fact, Sergeant Kelly dressed him down in my presence for too much talk among the settlers. Later Mike defended himself to me. "He knows I'm right but he thinks maybe I'll scare the folks. I only figure to give 'em a little warning." Mike spat viciously. "He says I'll put ideas into the heads of the local vermin. Hell, I couldn't give 'em any ideas they ain't had afore this. Yes, sir, there's going to be pepperin' around here, and it won't be long, neither."

CHAPTER 2

On that March morning when I plodded through the rain to the blockhouse, I had no premonition that what Mike Shea feared was coming to pass.

The weather was damp and chill, and my father had told me I had better not come down to the portage bridge to watch the work. "It won't hurt you to do a little reading," he suggested. "How long has it been since you read?"

I had to confess that it had been quite some time. Our only book beside the Bible was *Pilgrim's Progress,* and I had already stumbled through it twice. So, after my father had gone to work, and my mother had departed for Bradford's store to join the other women in a quilting, I soon convinced myself that the rain had let up enough so that I could visit Mike at the blockhouse.

The bank of the river was resilient from the night's downpour, and the trees and brush on the slope above me were so soft and wet that there was no longer any sound as the drops fell. Somehow the rain seemed to quiet the rapids, too, and I hurried along, anxious for Mike's booming, reassuring voice.

It was dark that morning in the gorge, and the rain-soaked evergreen boughs hung low and brushed against my face whenever I forgot to mind my way along the path. The deluge had brought up all the smells that were frozen out in the winter and which dried up in the summer—the light clean smell of cedar leaves and fir needles, and the heavy brown smell of the underbrush, of layer upon layer of decayed foliage and rotting branches which the silver thaws had brought down winter after winter.

There was no sign of life around the blockhouse when I reached it. The heavy door was shut, the narrow windows blanketed from the inside. It stood squat and square, so weathered that it seemed part of the rock-strewn promontory on which it stood by the side of the river. I had never before quite realized how impregnable and formidable it looked. The vertical slits through the hewn logs were ominous. As I approached I could imagine a puff of powder smoke drifting away from the one nearest me.

Suddenly the door swung open and I saw Mike, his huge figure filling the whole frame. The red stubble shone on his chin, and he looked just a little the worse for wear. But he took a deep breath, and when he had filled his lungs with the outside air he pounded his chest with the flat of his fists.

Spying me coming through the brush he called out, "Hallo there, Caleb! You're just in time. Could you be running an errand for us?" The question was purely academic. To do an errand for Sergeant Kelly's men was an honor. Mike produced a canteen from behind the door and held it out.

"We were tellin' stories last night," he said, "and I got a feelin' the boys will be needin' their bitters this morning. Would you fetch this to Bradford's store and bring it back full of whiskey? Tell Larry Coe to put it on my account." A sonorous snore issued from somewhere inside. Mike grinned. "It's the old German. You should have heard him tryin' to match us last night. Claimed he was one of Blucher's Waterloo veterans, no less!"

The reference was a mystery, but I joined Mike's laugh. I knew old Herman Kyle and could at least see the humor of his attempt to keep pace with the tall yarns of Kelly's men.

"Will you do it, boy?" said Mike, waving the canteen.

A sudden quandary presented itself to my mind. To get the canteen filled it would be necessary for me to go to Bradford's store. And in Bradford's store were my mother and other good ladies of the settlement! Nevertheless, I took the canteen, hoping that before I reached the settlement I could plan a strategy which would preserve my standing with Mike Shea and keep me out of jeopardy as well.

I started off, working away from the bank in a slight detour so that my father, working on the bridge, might not get a glimpse of his son hauling spirits for the soldiers. The rain was drizzling out. Small clouds scudded ahead of an early morning wind, and before I had gone very far from the blockhouse the sun burst free. It was a strange, quick transformation for that part of the river.

Passing the Indian village, I noticed a group of savages standing together as if in council, and could hear the drone of their talk even above the sound of the river. This earnest occupation of the natives, so different from their usual manner, filled me with uneasiness. I forced myself to hold my pace until I was beyond sight, and then broke into a run, dragging the big canteen by its canvas straps.

I ran wildly, for suddenly there built up in my imagination an entire band of Indians in pursuit, following stealthily yet with a swiftness which meant my doom. I assured myself that the fearful picture was one with those I had witnessed in my mind's eye on other occasions, and although I kept up my headlong flight, I must have succeeded to some extent in calming my fears. Certainly I was not prepared for the sight that met me when I topped the bank.

There in the middle of the road sat Jake Kyle, the son of old Herman whose tales had amused the soldiers. The look of him, half sprawled, dejected and awkward, was at first puzzling. Then I assumed that perhaps he too had been at the blockhouse and had not quite been able to make it home. I opened my mouth to greet him—but never made the sound, for at that instant his trunk seemed to melt down against his twisted legs. Then his whole body rolled on its side in the mud of the road. His neck was covered with blood, and from the small of his back there stuck up the feathered shafts of three arrows, all within an area no larger than could be covered by a silver dollar.

How long I stood there before I heard the rifle shots, I do not know. They were coming steadily, and perhaps I had not heard them before because of my threshing through the brush and over the pebbles of the river's edge. They seemed to be coming from the hill above Bradford's store, but where I stood the foliage was so thick that I could see nothing of the settlement—and the blockhouse, too, was screened from view. And then, quite clearly I heard a deeper sound—canister shot from the six-pounder at the blockhouse! I had heard it fired on parade, but now I knew that it was engaged in serious business. The attitude of the Indians in the village, the dying Jake Kyle there in the road, the faraway sound of rifle shots and the boom of the cannon, all meant one incredible thing. Mike's prophecy had come to pass. The Indians were attacking along The Cascades section of the river.

Frenzy generated a sort of movement in my palsied legs, and I fled into the woods, away from the river bank, blindly, still clutching at the canteen and banging it crazily against every tree I grazed. But, run as I might, I could not rid my ears of that sound of rifles.

Not two hundred yards from the road I confronted something more horrible than the sight of Jake Kyle in the road. A stack of cordwood had been dumped from its neat pile in a clearing and from beneath the scattered sticks protruded the scarcely recognizable head and shoulders of Les Rooney. His face had been battered with his axe which lay still with the blood upon it. I remembered that with Ed and Roy McManus he had been spending a week in the woods cutting fuel, and I was sure that the two brothers were beneath that pile.

Slowly it dawned upon me that in running through the forest I was inviting an identical fate. I half realized that even if I hid myself I would have to face the savages if they were victorious. Too young and frightened to have thought as yet about the safety of my parents, I knew only that my hope of survival lay in reaching the settlement again. Gasping and trembling, I started to make my way back toward the river.

Near the settlement I got my first sight of the attacking Indians. There was a whole line of them, stretching from the mouth of the little creek to a point at the head of the rapids. Near Bradford's store the slope rose abruptly and they had ranged themselves atop this so as to give themselves the advantage of height in the attack. Naked, they were smeared from toe to head with red clay except for white smears across noses and cheeks. The majority were using bows and arrows with incredible speed, but not a few possessed rifles.

Their attention was concentrated chiefly on Bradford's store for a reason I did not at first fathom, and easily I could have sat there by the river and watched the whole affair. But by now I was fearing for my mother and father and was anxious to reach them. My fear made room for my purpose and I began creeping along the river bank toward the cabins and Bradford's place.

Now I could hear the yells of the savages and the shouts of men in the settlement. Occasionally there would come the chilling, piercing scream of a woman. Here was, I realized with frightening clarity, not one of Mike's half romantic Army yarns, but a fight for life. It was flint lock and percussion gun, horse pistol and pepperbox revolver, bow and arrow, spear and war club—hissing, whizzing, blazing, crackling in furious uproar.

I saw a puff of rifle smoke coming from one of the windows of Bradford's store and knew that this fire from shelter was all that held the enemy in check. A man ran pell-mell across the clearing, the store door opened a little for him—and then, just as he reached out to gain it, he slumped in a lugubrious heap. I saw that man fall, and yet I kept on, heedless of the painted murderers above me. There was not the slightest bit of courage in my course. I simply did not think of death in connection with Caleb Paige. I knew I would have to pass before their fire to reach our house, well beyond the store, but it did not occur to me that I might be hit. Perhaps, indeed, I was safe enough, for a twelve-year-old boy must have presented a very small and fleeting target from the hillside.

The sawmill was aflame and I thought how odd it was that this ill fortune should be happening at the same time as the Indian attack. Not until I saw another column of gray smoke and realized that it came from our house, did I realize that the Indians were using firebrands as well as arrows and shot. I do not know what I might have done after seeing our cabin in flames, but that decision was taken from me, for Jim Sinclair came rushing out, his arms waving wildly.

Sinclair was an old Hudson's Bay man. I had never cared for him for once I had heard my father express a dislike for him. Because Sinclair was a fur trader, my father, I suspect, looked upon him as one who wanted to hold the country back from the honest settler and the interference of government which naturally would follow. He was a very small man, with red-rimmed eyes and a black clipped beard that was like a bandit's kerchief mask, and he wore the buckskin jacket with fringed sleeves. It was by then a bit of an affectation in our section of the country.

Nevertheless, I was mighty glad to see him. He had a weapon in one hand, and as he ran toward me he fired it in the general direction of the slope. Suddenly his fingers were roughly clutching my shoulder. "You little fool!" he shouted. He kept shouting it as he dragged me along toward the store. I tried to hold back, for I believed that my parents must have hidden themselves in our cabin at the first sign of the attack, and it was there I wanted to go. I doubt that my struggle was even noticed by Sinclair in the blaze and crackle. We stumbled over the body of the man who had been killed in front of Bradford's, and in the next second I was literally fired through the doorway ahead of the exasperated trader. He was still scolding as the door heaved shut behind us. "Your father's out there somewhere hunting for you, you damned idiot!" And then he said, to those inside, "I found him mooning along the bank, like nothing was happening. If you ask me, he's an idiot, that boy!"

I did not care what Sinclair was saying, for my mother's arms were around me. She had been at the quilting when the Indians attacked. But my poor father had run from the portage bridge to the cabin, and then to the store. Not finding me at either place he had started out again in search of me. I was sick with shame and fear, but I knew enough not to mention to my mother what I had seen in the woods.

There were about thirty in the store. Lawrence Coe, a manager for Putnam Bradford who was away in the East, had assumed charge of the defense. I recognized half a dozen men who worked for Coe and Bradford, either in the store or on the wharf boats and the portage road. Too, I knew the Watkins family, the Bushes, and the Hunts. Mrs. Watkins had her small baby which, frightened out of its wits, kept up a ceaseless howl. With the Hunts was their daughter, Victoria, a little younger than I, and when I reached the store in the insistent company of Sinclair she had been crying almost as bitterly as the baby. But at sight of me she stopped.

She was a thin, dark-haired child, brown as an Indian, very proud and not given to much talk. We had occasionally played together on the bank of the river, but not as much as I had liked—partly because I didn't want to be accused of preferring the company of a girl, and partly because my mother never seemed to approve of it. I never knew just why until one day I overheard Mrs. Bush and my mother talking about the scandalous way the Hunts were raising Vicky. I could not get the gist of it at the time, and indeed I wasn't particularly interested.

When I saw her there in Bradford's I resolved that she should witness the courage of a man. "Just wait," I said, my voice shaking in spite of all I could do, "wait until Mike Shea and the soldiers get here from the blockhouse. I heard the cannon go off, and they'll be coming here."

Lawrence Coe, handing out arms from behind the counter, smiled weakly at my bravado. "I reckon those nine men in the blockhouse got their hands full enough as it is. I figure there's two hundred Indians out there—plenty to give us all a run hereabouts." Then he went on handing out the guns. By good fortune there were nine United States rifles in the lot, with cartridge boxes and ammunition, left there for trans-shipment to the post at Dalles City.

There was a deliberateness about Coe's movements which contrasted oddly with the hectic antics of the savages on the slope outside. This deliberateness gave us courage; while the Indians were like hysterical children, here was Coe as calm as if we were making preparations for a picnic.

Although Coe had never appealed to me as strongly as Mike Shea, I always liked him. Mike's face was as smooth as a rock in a rapids, which alone was enough to intrigue a boy's interest. Lawrence Coe wore a black beard, like my father, but his mustache was grander. It dropped down on either side of his mouth like silky cascades and was kept meticulously free of both food and tobacco. Tall, muscular, and with a fondness for store clothes from San Francisco, Lawrence Coe was proud of his representation of Putnam Bradford, and held himself a little above the common run of settlers. His speech was slow and his laugh lazy, but he had an alert mind which you could see burning steadily behind his eyes. It was not every man that Putnam Bradford would have left at The Cascades in charge of the portage road and the store, for the contracts with the government were valuable properties.

Considerable had been done in the blockhouse before my belated arrival. The windows had been covered with the rough-hewn shutters which guarded the place at night. The heavy iron bar was in its slot at the inside of the door. The benches which ordinarily paralleled the single counter were ranged now against the wall where I huddled with my mother and the other women and children.

I had liked to visit Bradford's often, but Coe did not encourage loitering and my presence there was only when my mother had sent me on an errand. The place was filled with pleasant and mixed-up smells: gunpowder and cheese and kerosene and the sweet dry odor of flour. It seemed to me that on the four long shelves behind the counter were all that a man would need in the world. Sugar and syrup and corn meal, bacon and beans and coffee. There were candles, too, and soap and lard. Sometimes there were delicacies like dried fruits, shipped up from San Francisco. In the room behind the store, where Coe slept, there were other stores. And down cellar were barrels of ale and beer, and bottled liquors, and sacks of potatoes and onions.

It seemed very strange to be in this big room of pleasant memory and know that it was a fort against death and God knew what torture from the Indians. We were isolated within those log walls, our only connection with the rest of the world would be through the *Mary* and the *Wasco,* and none of us could believe that they would get away to Dalles City before the savages had taken them over and made them useless. The *Mary* lay at the mouth of the creek with the wind hard against her and boilers cold. The *Wasco* was on the Oregon side of the river and we could not tell, from that distance, if she was manned.

Coe had just finished his rationing of the ammunition when the firing of the Indians let off a little. He became instantly suspicious, and his reasoning proved sound. Peering through cracks in the shutters we could see that a party of the savages had left the slope above us and were heading for the *Mary*.

Two men were ashore on the upper side of the creek, frantically hauling on the *Mary's* lines when the first of the savages bore down. The pair did the only sensible thing. They struck out into the woods at the highest speed of which their legs were capable. I saw the fireman come up from below deck, a revolver in his hand. He did not get it to his waist before he was dropped. But a moment later the score was evened when one of the red devils gained the boarding plank and took the load of a horse pistol full in the face. The weapon was fired by a deck hand who stood with feet wide apart on the hurricane deck and seemingly could be struck by neither shaft nor ball.

Only one man aboard had a rifle, and we groaned when we saw him jump overboard, crazily, rifle and all, and disappear in the force of the river. The vessel was partially concealed from us by trees, and as smoke began rising we feared she had been set afire. Our joy was boundless when a few minutes later she began edging out into the stream. The black cloud above her was issuing from her stack! It seemed to us a miracle that she would manage an escape from that vicious horde, but the Indians were at the disadvantage of being in the open and the fate of their brother who had dared the gangplank was a lesson they had absorbed even in their bloodthirsty excitement.

For an awful moment it looked as if the *Mary* would not get away, for there was still not enough steam for her to make headway and she began to drift, her paddles turning idly forward. Hardin Chenowith, one of the crew, ran up into the pilot house, then sank out of sight below the windows. I was certain he had been dropped, for the savages quickly made the pilot house their target and its glass was shattering in the sunlight. In a moment, however, Jim Sinclair began jumping up and down and shouting that the *Mary* was being steered. "It's Chen!" he cried. "Good old Chen is lying on the pilot house floor and steering her!"

It was true. With one of the crew directing him from below, Hardin Chenowith was lying flat on the wheel house floor, taking the *Mary* into the stream with his feet! She nosed out slowly, painfully so to us there in the store, for we knew that our lives must assuredly depend upon the arrival of that puny packet in Dalles City.

She set herself staunchly against the current—and then, above the din of the rifles and the screaming of the savages—her whistle sounded. It pierced through the logs of Bradford's again and again, derisively, and the *Mary* headed diagonally across to where the *Wasco* lay. In a few moments her whole crew was ashore, tearing like mad men at the fence of the Atwell farm near the landing. They literally brought up posts by their hands, and both posts and rails were tossed any which way on her deck for fuel.

Now there began to be signs of life aboard the *Wasco,* too. We were to have two vessels heading for help. Whether that assistance would come in time we had no way of knowing. The miracle of their escape was a good omen, but the savages, angered at the escape of the *Mary,* and knowing that it meant they would have to speed their evil work or fail in it, were bounding back up the slope like the insane pack they were.

However, the attack on the vessel had given Lawrence Coe an opportunity to strengthen our own position. The upper story of Bradford's was reached by an outside stairway, and this Coe and Arne Peterson and Dave Brackett hacked away so that it could not be of use to our attackers. They then hauled down the stove-pipe, enlarged its hole in the ceiling and crawled up, armed with rifles, to secure the upper part of the store.

We were as ready as ever we would be.

The three women, with the baby and the girl and I, had been herded into the farthest, safest corner. But I resented being classed with them, and was anxious to impress Victoria Hunt. If the truth must be told, I was beginning to feel secure. After all, the savages were outside, and the familiar walls of the store were rugged. The goods on the shelves, the familiar outlines of the big pickle barrel, the gently swaying kerosene lamp swung from the center ceiling beam, were reassuring. These were all the handiwork of civilized whites, meant for their use. They were there, ready for tomorrow and the next day and the next.

Yet when I sauntered near a window shutter, Watkins hauled

me back roughly. "Better keep yourself away from them shutters, son," he growled. Immediately afterward he grew practical and handed me a brace and bit. "You can drill some gun holes," he said. With a nail he scratched the outline of one, just big enough to sight along a gun barrel. He kneeled experimentally and poked his rifle against the wall. "Yep," he said, "about level with your eyes is right."

Proud at being given a duty, I fell to work while the men piled more heavy goods against the door, fearing that the savages might attempt to burst it with the butt end of a log. From time to time I could hear Coe and Peterson and Brackett firing from the gable under the roof. I could guess that they were picking their shots and making them tell, for occasionally above the din we would hear one of them yell in grim exultation. The Indians, on the other hand, were firing continuously. Their supply of ammunition seemed inexhaustible, and the thud of arrows against the building was incessant.

My mother sat staring straight ahead. She appeared unafraid that I would be hurt as I turned the drill, and I suppose that a veil of stupor had been drawn mercifully over her brain. The drilling was difficult, for the logs were thick and I had to lean my entire weight against the brace to make any progress at all. It was a small bit and I drilled four holes, close together, and then poked out the chunk and shavings. When I had got the first one through I peered at the hill above. The savages had withdrawn a little, but some were still firing. Others gave their attention entirely to yelling derisively and making obscene gestures. This was a trick which had worked often with the troopers when they had been less practiced in the ways of Indian warfare. Many a fine body of men had suffered heavy losses because they could not absorb pantomimed insults from an Indian. They wanted us to become so angry at their taunts that we would open up our fortress and go storming up the slope. But Lawrence Coe was too wise for that.

Watkins tried a shot from the hole I had drilled and pronounced it satisfactory. I set to work drilling others, in places he had marked. I had just knocked out the third when there was a terrific crashing above us and the whole building trembled. The Indians had dropped a shower of stones onto the roof of the kitchen at the side of the store.

"The damned heathens," muttered Jim Sinclair. "They're goin' to save ammunition and pepper us with rocks."

I knew well how easy it was to do. Often I had stood on the ledge above the store and thrown pebbles at the roof of Bradford's—then dropped behind a bush to peer at Arne Peterson when he came outside, puzzled and angry.

After a second volley of stones, Coe poked his head through the hole in the ceiling. "They're building fires," he yelled down. "We'll have to watch 'em right smart or they'll burn us out."

"They'll knock the place down before they burn it," Victoria's father said. He looked nervously at the women and children in the corner. "If it wasn't for the women and the kids we might try a break and stand 'em off behind the river rocks."

"We'd never make it to the water," Coe told him. He looked very funny, with his head and shoulders poked out of the hole above, and his face growing redder against his black beard. "Throw a bucket in that pickle barrel. If they get a spark on the roof maybe I can snuff it out with the brine."

That was the first time I had thought about water. There was only a lone bucket, half filled, on one end of the counter. The river might as well have been fifty miles away.

Hunt had no sooner pushed the pickle barrel into place and fastened a rope to a bucket than Lawrence Coe had occasion to try his defense. There came a sudden peppering of the roof again, and I looked up the hill to face a dreadful sight. The savages were throwing firebrands now. Hot irons, pitchwood, balls of straw tied around stones—anything that would hold a flame—until the air was streaked with smoke trails. Only occasionally was there a rifle shot now. They were intent upon burning us out, if they could, then doing away with us at their leisure and by what means their excited fancy might conceive. We had only one advantage, but it was important. The distance was at least great enough so that only the more perfect of their flaming missiles reached the roof of Bradford's. The heavier ones fell short, and if a warrior advanced too close with a flaming torch he was picked off quickly by one of the men in the gable opening.

The confusion inside the store had given way to a grim sort of order. While those upstairs acted as sharpshooters and lookouts, we below were never idle. The men had taken up positions at the holes as fast as I could make them. Whenever a fair shot presented itself they would fire. All except Sinclair who had appointed himself to keep an eye everywhere. He stalked about with his pepper-box revolver and a small dipper of brine, peering from shutter cracks and peep-holes, or once in a while tossing a word of comfort to the women. Whenever Coe yelled for brine, Sinclair filled the bucket. The trapper was, literally, too nervous and irritable for the type of warfare we were being forced to fight.

After Coe had hauled up the bucket of brine we would strain our ears for the faint sizzling which would tell us he had doused a burning brand. Fortunately the rain had given the roof a good soaking, and had it not been for this the savages would have set the place afire in a dozen spots before Coe got the brine into action.

No one thought of food except the Watkins baby, and no infant was ever in such excruciating agony. The terrific noise kept him awake and howling until he would doze off from sheer exhaustion. Then suddenly a new noise would arouse him, fear would clutch at his nerves and hunger at his stomach, and he would begin again—yowling until the face was purple and the eyes crimson blotches. The mother, possibly from fright, could give him no milk, and he was beyond the point where he could be appeased simply by suckling at a breast. At last Jim Sinclair, that ingenious busybody, went to the shelves of the store and found a small cask of molasses. He knocked in the head impatiently, tied a small knot in the end of a rag, dipped into the molasses and shoved the knot at the infant's wide open mouth. Peace reigned in that small corner of the store.

Later in the afternoon the ubiquitous Sinclair received another inspiration. He put the women to work, my mother among them. He ordered them to prepare rations from what they could find in the store. Commanded to do something both useful and familiar, they lost much of their horrible paralysis. I saw my mother fall to helping, but she moved as if in a dream. She had hardly spoken two words since she greeted me, and I knew that she was certain that my father had fallen into the hands of the savages. A terrible thought came to me out of a story Mike Shea had once told me—of a woman who had barricaded herself in a cabin against the Indians and lost her mind before her husband and her friends could save her. I wanted to comfort my mother, but I could think of nothing adequate to say, and I knew that if I went to her she might break down all over again and weaken us both.

The food was cooked atop the pot-bellied heating stove—beans, bacon, and a mess of corn meal fried together in an immense skillet from the store's stock. In the haste and confusion the new skillet was not burned out too well, and the taste of it mingled with the food. But nobody cared. The men threw it into their mouths, and then munched salt pork and oyster crackers, more out of nervousness than hunger. We sent food to the men above in the brine bucket and they dipped it out with their fingers. When everyone had eaten what he could, Sinclair portioned out the water, giving the women a cupful each, and the men half a cup. This left hardly more than would wet the bottom of the bucket, and the thought that we were almost out of water began to make me frightfully thirsty.

"If they let up a little tonight," Sinclair said, "I might be able to slip down to the river bank and get water."

Lawrence Coe had dropped below for more ammunition and at Sinclair's remark he laughed bitterly: "We need men right now more than water, Jim. And if I know Indians they'll set afire to other cabins tonight and light things up so we won't dare stir."

It was the first time I realized the struggle might last beyond that day. Somehow I had believed it would end by nightfall—that the Indians would either be beaten and leave us in peace, or we would be taken and killed. The prospect of more of this uncertainty was worse than either. I asked Sinclair how long it would take the *Mary* and the *Wasco* to get back with help.

"Maybe tomorrow some time," he told me, "and maybe not. Most likely not. Depends how far Colonel Wright has gone inland with his troops. He's been ordered to the interior, and when the boats get to Dalles City a scout will have to be sent out after them."

I began to understand Mike Shea's contempt and hatred for General Wool who, in his sublime ignorance of conditions, had got us into this predicament. But I had little time to be wasting in feelings against "old Johnnie Ellis" for Bush, peering from a crack in a shutter at the rear of the store, cried, "There's Caleb Paige!"

My heart whirred in my breast like a frightened grouse, and my mother ran to the shutter and tried to unfasten it. Bush held her back, while I, from a chink in the logs, stared down toward the river. My father was on the lower end of the little island that stood between us and the Oregon shore. He was creeping on his hands and knees from the direction of the half-finished warehouse the company was building. At first I thought he was injured, but then it dawned upon me that he was only seeking to avoid the attention of the savages.

I had often gone to the island to watch the building of the warehouse, rowing over in a little skiff that was the community property of the settlement. My father must have believed that I had gone to the warehouse, and searched there after making sure that my mother was safe in the store. The savages' attempt to capture the *Mary* had made escape impossible for him, but now that they had returned their attention to us he was trying to get across to the mainland.

Cautiously Bush took out the shutter and shouted to my father to stay where he was. "Your son is here," he yelled. Then he lifted me up to the window so that my father could see me. Even as I watched, the dirt sprayed up near where he crouched. The clay-smeared monkeys had spotted him. From above us came the sound of increased firing and they began once more their unearthly screaming. Every man left the rear of the store and got to his post, hoping to divert the attentions of the Indians.

My father had half risen to his feet, as though to make a break for it and swim the river between the island and the shore. Suddenly he clutched at his wrist, lifted it high in a spasm of pain, and I saw the blood course along his bare arm.

From above us Coe's voice boomed out clearly. "We'll get you off later, Paige. We'll get you off later. You can't make it now."

He yelled it several times and finally, to our immense relief, my father nodded weakly, sank close against the earth near a great rock and stayed motionless. How long I stood there watching I do not know. He would be so quiet that I felt sure he was dead, and then, joyfully, I would mark a movement in his leg or arm or shoulder. I wondered if his wound could be fatal, but I didn't want to ask. What Caleb Paige must have suffered in the pain of that shattered wrist I will never know. Surely it was nothing to what he suffered in the long hours that followed. If I had known what he was to endure the next two days I would have wished he had been shot dead with that first ball.

As the day wore into evening Sinclair would occasionally take down the shutter and shout encouragement to my father. Sometimes there would be an answer in the way of a weak signal, but more often he would not move at all. I saw then that he was holding himself behind the rock, for he lay on an incline more precipitous than was at first apparent from where I watched. "When it's dark," Jim Sinclair told me, "I'll go down there and fetch him."

But I remembered what Coe had said about the savages lighting fires at night, and I had a sickening doubt that a man with a shattered wrist could fight against the current of the Columbia at that point. It did not occur to me then that Caleb Paige was down there because he had been searching for me. That came later. And even now, whenever I think of it, I get a queer gone feeling in my breast and my wrist aches as if from an old wound.

True to Coe's prediction, the sun had no sooner set than the savages fired a cabin not far from where our own was a smouldering ruin, and when the blaze was high the Indians retired into the shadows of the slope. Coe felt reasonably sure they would not attack during the night, but nevertheless two men stayed at their post in the gable window.

By now the women were exhausted and dozing, my mother on the floor by the rear window, one arm flung along the wall. She had fallen asleep as near as she could get to my father. The Watkins baby was quiet at last, pacified by the molasses. And Victoria slept on an Army blanket from the store shelves.

We were beginning to suffer from the lack of water, but the

blaze outside made an attempt at the river bank unthinkable. So from the liquor cellar Coe brought out all the stores in the place at that time—two dozen bottles of ale and three bottles of whiskey. He opened some of the ale and poured it into the water bucket. This he rationed out, a quarter of a cupful to every man, woman and child. I was unable to get down all of my share of the bitter stuff, and what I did take from sheer thirst made me so groggy that I went almost instantly to sleep.

When I awoke, the sky was still colored from the blaze outside. We kept no lamps burning in the store and in the shadows I could just make out the figure of my mother seated near the window which looked toward the river. Jim Sinclair saw me rising and brought over a fist full of oyster crackers and a piece of dried beef. I gulped the food gratefully, and took the rest of my ale to wash it down.

"Have the Indians gone yet?" I asked.

"Well," said Jim Sinclair, "the sons o' bitches are restin', anyhow."

Soon again, from the effects of the ale and excitement, and utter weariness, I was asleep on the floor. When next I awakened it was to shouts inside the store and I stirred upwards to see Jim Sinclair, stripped to the waist and holding a dripping cask, being helped through the rear window by Coe and Hunt. He had slipped down to the bank for water, and miraculously returned with both his life and the precious fluid. The men greeted him with great, rough slaps, and inarticulate noises from parched throats.

My mother demanded to know if he had been able to talk with my father. "I could see him," Sinclair said. "He's all right. We'll get him out of there all right. I didn't dare yell over at him or they might have got me."

But when daylight came the Indians renewed their attack so fiercely that everyone, I think, forgot my father except my mother and me. At the first streak of day they started hailing the roof with stones. From that distance, the Indians could not heave stones of a size that would endanger the heavy structure of the store, but they knew in their devilish minds that the incessant pounding would help to unnerve us. Most of their rock fire they aimed at the slighter roof over the kitchen, knowing that with luck they might split it and that every volley against that adjunct to the main building would shake the whole as if an earthquake had joined the attack.

The fear and the ale and the noise began to work on me and I had to make a run for the little pantry which Coe had designated as a relief station because we dare not use the out-house. In that close, confined space I grew violently ill and wished I might die and never come out. But presently, as I leaned with my forehead against the wall, my arms hanging limp, I felt Jim Sinclair's hand on my shoulder. "Better get out of here," he said. "You'll feel better now."

I half staggered into the main room, hoping to hide my white face and my tears from Victoria Hunt. Sinclair guided me to the rear window and lifted out the shutter. "You keep a watch here," he said, "and let us know about your father." I nodded weakly, and sank against the ledge, my nose barely above it, grateful for the air. In the early morning light my father lay on his back, his wounded, blood-soaked arm flung over his eyes, his other hand still clutching the rye grass to keep him from sliding down the bank of the river and in plain view of the Indians.

We had suffered no losses inside the store, but our luck was not to hold out for long. As I stood by the window I heard a cry ring through the room and turned to see Victoria's father straightening from one of the gun holes, his rifle still clutched in his hands. His throat was spurting red from a ball which had come through the opening above the barrel of his own gun. He whirled toward us, a surprised and pitiful and longing look was on his face as his eyes met Victoria and her mother. And then, with a gasp, he fell solidly to the floor.

Mrs. Hunt threw herself on the corpse and could not be lifted from it. The screaming Victoria roused the Watkins baby into its own wailing. And the quick death of Hunt, the hysteria of his wife, and the crying of the girl and baby, began to shatter the morale of the men. Jim Sinclair tore the cork from one of the bottles of whiskey and took a long pull. When the rest had taken a drink, he jammed the cork into the bottle and tossed it up through the hole in the ceiling.

Coe stuck his black bearded face into the opening. He needed no explanation as his eyes lit upon the frantic Mrs. Hunt. He dropped his tall frame to the floor, firmly took the woman by the shoulders and brought her to her feet. "In the back room," he said to Sinclair, nodding at the body of Hunt. "And clean up the floor." He knew that a weakness in that bad moment might tell the tale of the siege.

I tried to comfort Victoria, putting my arm around her as Jim Sinclair had done to me. But she jerked away and began beating and clawing my face with her small hands as if somehow I had been the cause of her father's death. I had to abandon my chivalry and return to my post at the rear window.

On that second day Jim Sinclair began to worry about the return of the steamboats. Every few minutes he would glue his eyes to a shutter crack and look upstream, searching for smoke from the stacks of the *Wasco* or the *Mary*. I am sure that he had really given up hope. We all realized that those aboard the boats might easily decide that we could not survive the attack and that there was little need for a hurried return to The Cascades. Believing us massacred they might even delay their return, dreading the sight they felt sure would meet their arrival.

Despite this, I began to watch for the steamers, too, and sometimes I prayed, asking God to set them suddenly in the river, filled with soldiers who would not realize that they had been moved, boats and all, several miles down the stream by His great hand. But the air above the river remained clear and blue, free from the smoke of a steamboat.

Once I looked across to the island to see my father slipping down the bank. He rolled over and over toward the river and then, striking the cold water, began to struggle ashore again. He had only fainted. But it seemed to me hours before he regained the shelter of the rock. The savages, intent now upon the store, did not notice —or else decided the man on the island could be disposed of when the time came.

Already half of the water had been used by Coe in putting out firebrands on the roof, for he had exhausted the pickle brine. We knew that it would be more than miraculous if one of our party could slip down to the river and fill the cask a second time. Apparently we would be given the grim choice of being burned to death within the wooden walls or collapsing of thirst.

Soon after Hunt was killed, Arne Peterson dropped headlong from the gable with an arrow through his thigh, and the Indians drilled the front of the store so terrifically that none dared go out to see if he could be saved. A few of the more reckless savages ventured to get at the body, but a couple of volleys from the store changed their minds on this score.

Then Bush was struck in the shoulder so badly that he could not hold a rifle. Soon Jim Darby and Simeon Kram and Henry Leigh lay prone along the wall, Leigh never to rise again. And Bush received a ghastly wound when an arrow sped through his upper gum as he turned from one of the gun holes. It shucked out teeth like corn from a cob and caused him to bleed so much that he was too weak for use.

Sinclair was pale, and I could see that he believed the tide had turned against us. The savages were growing smarter and more determined. They had discovered that they needed only to post a few of their best marksmen to watch our gun holes and the cracks in the shutters. At the slightest sign of a movement they would fire, sometimes with the accuracy which had done for poor Leigh and caused such pain to Bush and the others.

Yet those who remained never relaxed, and it was curious how the wounds of the men strengthened the women. So long as they had been protected they had been unlike themselves, but the moment they were needed to dress wounds and comfort the bereaved they became strong and somehow hopeful.

It was in the mid-afternoon of this second day that my father lost consciousness and slid down again into the grip of rushing water. By the merest chance Jim Sinclair saw it happen. His hands clutched the sill of the window, gripped it until they were white, and I heard him whispering "The dirty red bastards . . ." over and over again as my father was carried downstream a way and then, by the utmost effort and suffering, made the bank. Now he was fully exposed to the sight and fire of the Indians.

"By God, I'm going after him!" said Sinclair suddenly. "He's as good as gone if we leave him out there!" With that he was astride the window ledge, and in the next moment had leaped to the ground below. He ran swiftly down the slope, shedding his buckskin jacket as he went. Into the white stream he plunged, facing against the current. Every man on the lower floor crowded to the window, watching him, and then I heard Coe yelling angrily from upstairs. He jumped down to the floor, his face livid. "Get back to your places, you jackasses!" he cried.

But I could stand and watch, not realizing that my mother was just behind me. Sinclair took my father around the waist and they stepped into the river side by side. Then for endless minutes only their heads showed, and at last they had gained our shore—two small, bedraggled figures fighting hard for a stake in the years ahead. On the bank my father fainted again and poor Sinclair, himself near exhaustion, could not support him upright.

And then it happened. The savages on the slope above us seemed to concentrate all their fire on those two unprotected figures by the bank of the river. Instantly the two crumpled like rags tossed in a corner.

"Caleb! . . ."

The name, cried out by my mother, was the most agonized sound I have heard issue from a human throat. Before anyone could stop her, before I could bring myself to realize what she was doing, she lifted herself through the window. Before I could even call for help she was running toward the river, tripping and falling over her long gingham at almost every step. I do not know how many times she was hit before she reached the river's edge. But she got to my father and Sinclair, and sank down with her arms outstretched as if to protect them.

Often in my dreams I have seen that little heap of bodies quivering, and the slight movement of their clothing in the still air, as the arrows and the balls struck them again and again.

CHAPTER 3

THAT night the savages crossed to the island and set fire to the half-built warehouse. Then, in the weirdly dancing light by the side of the river, they stripped the clothing from their three victims and dragged the bodies across to the island.

I was not allowed to watch, and my brain whirled dizzily with imagined pictures of those painted things in the shape of humans, torturing bodies already beyond torture. Soon none of the others watched, either. I saw Lawrence Coe, white-lipped, turn away from his place at the shutter.

"Good God," he said quietly, "what wouldn't I give for a howitzer!"

I saw the men fill with a stubborn hatred there in that room. Until now it had been almost a matter of resigned defense, as if the Indians were particularly vicious children whose pranks must be endured before they were punishable. But now the men were ready to kill and murder, bursting for an attack. Several made the wild suggestion that an attempt be made to smoke them off the island and give our dead a decent burial, but Coe vetoed it. Yet I believe if it had not been for the women and children he would have been willing to lead the expedition himself.

Such spirit as was displayed then, however, had to fade before the realities of our situation. Our losses had been heavy, and the Indians began to suspect this, for they grew more daring. Approaching closer to the ledge they sent their firebrands with greater effect. Arne Peterson had been a quick and excellent shot and was sorely missed in the gable window above. The roof was growing quite dry and thus the danger from fire heightened with every hour.

Worst of all, the ammunition had dwindled startlingly, and when nightfall came at last and the savages let up a little, Coe said, "Tomorrow we must save our fire. Keep a constant watch, and don't let go of a shot unless it's necessary." We were a weary, hopeless lot that night. We knew that from this point on our defense would have to consist mainly of trying to keep from being burned out.

At daybreak the Indians resumed their vantage point above the store and began heaving firebrands and stones once more. As the first stone struck with a terrific impact, Victoria's mother screamed. "I can't stand it!" she cried. "I can't stand that again. I can't! I can't!" She could not be stopped until Mrs. Watkins shook her roughly and slapped her face with blows that rang. I thought it cruel and yet realized that it was also necessary; and when Victoria, in a rage, began attacking Mrs. Watkins, I held her arms tight to her sides until her mother had stopped her hysteria.

By now the store was a shambles. But worse than the disorder were the smells. The fetor from the back pantry, the faint yet unmistakable odor of death, and the smell of undressed and bloody wounds, all were mixed with the acrid air of powder smoke and the steam of perspiration. I have heard it said that a child's olfactory nerves are particularly sensitive; certainly I thought that if the savages did not kill us we must die from the odors in that place.

It was at ten o'clock that morning that shouts went out from the gable window. At first I thought that another man had been hit, or that the roof had taken blaze beyond their control. Then we heard Coe shout, *"The steamboats! The steamboats are here!"*

Watkins ran to the rear window and ripped down the shutter. Surely enough, there were the two little black-plumed vessels, their decks blue with soldiers, and astern of the *Wasco* was a flat-boat on which were tethered dragoon horses! The troopers were ashore almost before the boats' noses touched the bank, and at the same instant a howitzer on the *Mary* sent a heralding shower of grape into the Indians. When the vessels made fast, the savages were of a mind to give the newcomers a fight. But a second blast from the *Mary,* and the imposing avalanche of blue changed their plan and they turned tail to rush wildly up the slope and into the woods. Frantic with joy, we cheered the pursuit. Our men began tearing down the hodge-podge of goods which had barricaded the door. Some were laughing insanely, tears streaking down the caked dirt on noses and cheeks. For that joyful moment, the strain and weariness were forgotten. Everybody pitched in to help and the door was pushed wide just as Colonel Wright came up the bank with his aide.

He was a sturdily built man who wore his uniform well, and to me he appeared the grandest figure in all the world. His broad brimmed hat was pushed back from his forehead, his gauntlets tucked neatly behind his belt. His boots were coated with a dry white dust that must have come from the encampment where our message found him.

Mike had told me all about Colonel George Wright, and I found the man no disappointment. He was a veteran of the Florida and Mexican campaigns, and had been sent out to command the Ninth Infantry—which meant correcting bad blunders made by Major Haller and General Rains, blunders which had caused the savages to decide that even whites in uniform were vulnerable.

A single searching glance told Wright what we had been through. Taking Lawrence Coe's outstretched hand in both his own he said, "Sorry we couldn't be here sooner." He talked in swift, short sentences, as though issuing orders. "We'd started for Steptoeville. Camped at Five-Mile Creek out of Dalles City when we got word from the boats. We were back in town by daybreak. But the *Mary's* engines were in bad order. Only got to Wind Mountain the first day."

"Thank God you're here at all, sir."

"How are things with Kelly down at the middle blockhouse?"

"We can't say," Coe told him. "They must have had their hands full or we'd have had them here."

"The blockhouse should have held. Too bad they weren't with

you. The cannon would have made things different. You're to be complimented, Mr. Coe."

"We've lost five men and one woman. There're several wounded —and a man was killed attempting to reach the store. We don't know what happened outside when the devils first hit, but I imagine plenty."

Wright nodded. "There'll be a detail to do what it can."

It was by listening to the men and soldiers in Bradford's store, during the days that followed, that I picked up what had happened along our turbulent stretch of the river. There had been more of the enemy than we in the store had believed, for the attack took place all along The Cascades, from the lower landing clear to Bradford's. Not less than three hundred red men had been bent upon destroying everything at The Cascades, and taking it over completely. The savages had besieged not only our settlement, but those who sought refuge in the blockhouse as well. The landing at the lower settlement had been completely taken. The portage bridge was burned, the mules killed.

At the Lower Cascades a warning by a friendly Indian that Yakimas were attacking the blockhouse saved some of the settlers. Getting onto anything that would float—bateaux, hastily made rafts, even clinging to logs, they drifted down the thirty-six miles to Fort Vancouver and gave the alarm. There were a few stalwarts who attempted to remain behind and fight it out, but these had at last followed suit. On the way downstream their log raft passed the *Belle* on her rescue trip. Aboard was Lieutenant Phil Sheridan and forty men.

He had no artillery except a small salute cannon, mounted on a wooden base, and borrowed from the captain of a San Francisco steamer lying at Fort Vancouver. With some difficulty he had found shot to fit it and had the weapon set aboard the *Belle*. This, and his forty men, Sheridan landed below the settlement, then sent the steamboat back to Vancouver to seek volunteers.

Meanwhile, according to his nature, Sheridan was not idle. There was no way to get to the savages except along a narrow neck of land, and on a reconnaissance a bullet grazed the Lieutenant's nose and killed the man beside him. The ship's salute cannon kept the Indians at bay, but no direct attack could be attempted.

"So what does he do?" related Mike in delight, "but take his men across the river in a bateau? He had to make two trips on account of the barge wouldn't hold but twenty at a time. Then he hid behind Bradford's Island, close to the other side of the river."

What amused Mike most was that Sheridan had rounded up a party of squaws which had been put on the island for safety during the fight, and made them tow the bateau up the rapids. "And I'd have been giving anything to see it," Mike said. "Them red bellied bitches haulin' the barge!"

There is a smooth stretch of water at the upper end of Bradford's Island, and here Sheridan loaded the bateau with part of his men. The rest went along the bank until they were opposite the blockhouse. There he took the whole command across and was about to surprise the savages when Colonel Steptoe's column of dragoons hove into sight from above—and an idiot bugler blew a blast as if he were on a parade ground! The Yakimas fled, while their allies from the Cascades tribe rushed at once to Bradford's Island to simulate peaceful Indians at home.

"Steptoe and his bugle!" Mike exploded. "He's a fit one for old Johnnie Ellis's army, all right. Sheridan and Wright know what makes the vermin tick, and they got horse-sense to boot! But these parade soldiers—"

With the Yakimas scared from the trap before it sprung, Sheridan could only return to the island and question The Cascades savages. Every Indian swore he had nothing to do with the attack. But Sheridan had taken with him his salute cannon and Steptoe's dragoons. Before this impressive array he lined up the Indians with their muskets in their hands. "So he goes along the line," Mike said, "and sticks his finger into the muzzle of a musket. It comes out black as their hearts. He wipes his finger off, careful, like a gentleman eating ice cream at a church social, and sticks his finger in the next musket. It comes black out of that one, too. The ones he catches like that he sends packing off to the lower landing!"

The difficulty with Lieutenant Sheridan's ingenuity, according to Mike, was that it did not consider those vermin who had been making war with bows and arrows and war clubs. As a consequence, there was the unremote possibility that many of the guilty ones were escaping punishment, and certainly the Yakimas who had filtered through the woods at the arrival of the *Wasco* and the *Mary* were guiltier than any of The Cascades tribe. Mike was for shooting the whole lot of the latter, however. "Why should the government put on a show of a trial?" he asked indignantly. "Them vermin don't know anything about justice and bein' proved guilty before bein' prosecuted. A military trial is just lowerin' the Army in the eyes of the enemy, that's what it is!"

The Indians whom Sheridan designated as culprits did not stay long at the lower landing. Colonel Wright ordered them brought up with other captives to face trial by military commission. The remainder he sentenced to the island with orders that they be shot by either citizens or soldiers if caught on the mainland.

Lawrence Coe acted as interpreter at the trial, and when nine of the Indians were sentenced to be hanged he asked me if I would like to see the proceedings. I was charmed, and indeed it turned out to be a gala occasion. There was not a settler but was glad to see the nine of them stretched at the end of a rope, although we realized there could well be guiltless ones among them. They had testified against one another so freely that Wright had difficulty in knowing where the truth began and where it ended. There was pressure from some of the settlers to wipe out the whole village, but Wright stood against this idea from the first. And there was the knowledge, gnawing inside us all, that most of the Yakimas had escaped without a scratch. Many were the acid comments regarding Steptoe's dragoons and his fine bugler.

On the day of the hangings I trudged proudly to the upper side of Mill Creek with Coe. The soldiers were already on the spot—the Ninth regiment, the First dragoons, the Third artillery, Sheridan's infantry and volunteers, and Kelly's men from Company H. They made an imposing array, and behind them, chained together, were the condemned savages.

The settlers were not long in arriving, although Coe and I had come soon after sun-up. There were women and children as well as men, and few had missed suffering a loss in the attack. The boots of the men were caked with earth from newly dug graves, and the hands of the women were grimy from digging in the ashes of burned cabins. Yet they were quiet and apparently without hatred. Hardly a sound issued from the crowd except for the wailing of an infant and its mother's quieting voice. All stood, neither impatient nor reluctant, watching the care with which a young corporal knotted the hanging rope. He tossed it over the limb of a tree near the creek, then tested it by placing his boot in the noose and swinging his whole weight against the hemp. Old Chenowith, chief of the Cascades tribe, was first to be lifted onto the topmost of two kegs stacked end on end.

Out of the nine he was the only one who had managed to wash off his paint and get himself clothed. He wore his leggins and buckskin coat, but his moccasins were gone and he sported no beaded straps or belts. His black hair was matted and tangled, his face was a dark mask.

Wright stepped forward and said to Lawrence Coe, "Ask him if he has anything to say."

Coe spoke, and Old Chenowith answered promptly. Coe, translating, faced Wright. "He offers ten horses and two squaws to every white friend if he can be spared."

A guffaw went up from a settler in the crowd, and was cut off by a stern glance from Wright. The Colonel turned to Coe again. "Tell him that is not possible. Has he a final request to make?"

Coe delivered the message to the old Indian. Chenowith spoke, his lips scarcely moving.

"He is afraid of a grave in the ground. He wishes to be put in an Indian death house."

The Colonel hesitated a moment. Then, drawing himself a little straighter, he said, "Tell him it will be done."

At a word from Wright, the young corporal adjusted the rope around the old chief's neck. Instantly the savage let out a fierce war whoop, sending chills through the crowd and startling the corporal out of his wits. The old man must have believed, even at the last, that his red brothers would appear from the woods and save him. But in the next moment the corporal had pushed over the top barrel and the chief dangled at the rope's end.

Even then he did not die. His face grew horrible and his thin body jerked. He cried, *"Wake nike quash copa memaloose!"* Coe turned a meaningful glance toward Wright who took his pistol from its holster and shot the savage mercifully through the heart.

More practiced, the corporal hanged the rest with great facility. I watched them spin to the end of that rope and leave the earth—Tecomeoc, Four-fingered Johnny, Captain Jo, Tumtah, and the rest. Vicky Hunt and I had often gazed at them in awe when they came into the settlement. They were Indians, and therefore we kept our distance, but we had believed that The Cascades natives were harmless and obedient.

A little sick, I searched the ranks of soldiers for Mike's friendly face. I found it among Sergeant Kelly's men. He stood at attention, yet looking not quite reputable, and gazing not at the Indian on the gallows but at the row on the ground. He seemed to be saying, "Vermin—they're all vermin, and you can be sure of that!"

Well, I agreed with Mike, bitterly. I wished I could be sure that some of those dead Indians were the ones who killed my mother and father and Jim Sinclair.

CHAPTER 4

The Army had acted with dispatch. It had made the rescue, hanged what culprits could be discovered, and immediately gone to work to prevent a repetition of the affair. A detail of men was put to work constructing a blockhouse at the Lower Cascades to augment the one which had held out against the massacre. It was to be a gallant affair of two stories in the shape of an L, with a look-out tower on the roof. There were to be fifty-two gun slits through the walls, and the foundation logs were hauled to a site which would allow besieged whites a commanding view of the terrain.

But the work of the surviving settlers was more complex, and they could not proceed with the swift organization of Colonel Wright's men. It was a slow, grim business, sorting the dead from the ashes, picking up what was left of those poor unfortunates who had been caught in the open, like Les Rooney in the forest, or my parents and Jim Sinclair on the island.

Lawrence Coe arranged the burial of my mother and father. Wright had set men to building rough coffins, mostly out of scorched lumber from the wrecked portage bridge. Coe procured three of these, and my parents and Sinclair were buried side by side in the little clearing beyond the settlement. Until now, death had visited The Cascades sparingly and in forms that were unspectacular. But as Lawrence Coe and I watched the lowering of the caskets that day we were surrounded by more than a score of little groups like ours, each intent on giving some loved one a decent burial. Pressed and harried, the settlers could not proceed in this with any order. Bodies were interred as they were found, and if the soldiers got behind in the making of coffins then the dead were put away only in shrouds. Markers were simple and hasty, usually a cross, or merely something to identify the mounds until stones could be ordered from Portland, or wood slabs carved and painted.

It was not until a week later that a service was held for those who died in the attack. There was no minister in The Cascades, and some of the women felt that the last rites should be performed by a clergyman rather than an Army chaplain. So a minister was brought up from Portland to hold the services.

The day was gray and drizzling, much like the morning on which the Indians had begun their attack, and I was reminded of that unhappy time as I stood there in the rain with Lawrence Coe. It seemed years now since I had seen Jake Kyle in the road and heard the shots from the middle blockhouse. I was still dazed, and I do not think I fully realized that my parents were gone forever. I know that I was glad to have Coe beside me, for Mike had been kept very busy under Sergeant Kelly on reconstruction work, and during the services he had to stand with the soldiers.

For the services, an organ had been brought up on the *Belle,* along with the minister, and two men held a canvas over both the instrument and Mrs. Leigh who played it. They looked very solemn and tired after a while, holding the canvas, the water dripping down their noses. They were glad when we had finished the hymns and Mrs. Leigh joined the rest and they could simply drop the canvas over the parlor organ.

The minister had recently come West by way of the Horn and his expression and tone were full of amazement at what had happened at The Cascades. He was an apprehensive little fellow, and he had a wisp of blonde hair that stood up comically in the wind as we gathered around him in the clearing. I think he was frightened by the whole prospect—the rather wild appearance of the settlers, the presence of the soldiers, and even the roughness of the country itself. He looked at us, and at the fresh mounds, and then at the lowering sky. He began quoting Scripture almost, it seemed, at random, as if he had to warm up before he could discover what he had to say about people who would choose to live in the wilderness among savages. And at length, after several false starts, he got going.

The ways of God in His wisdom, the little man allowed, were unfathomable. Nobody could hope to understand why He had sent these departed so far from home in order to meet them. Yet we should not condemn those who had brought them to their ends. The minister rolled his eyes a little nearer to Heaven and hoped orally that nobody had struck back in quick wrath. He pretended to know nothing of the hangings, yet he could not very well have missed hearing about them on the steamboat. And then he launched into a sermon on the need for bringing the savages into the fold of Christianity. He said that if the Indians were educated in the ways of God they would not slaughter people with such abandon. It seemed unthinkable to us that he should be ignorant of all the missions which had been built for the Indians, or that there were missionaries who had even blazed trails for settlers who came later. But there he stood in the little clearing, saying it, loud and clear:

"They are children who know not what they do. Can it be possible that this, our sorrow, is visited upon us as punishment for being derelict in our duty toward them?"

The minister paused, then, and the pause was fatal. Suddenly, as loud and clear as the minister's own, there issued the voice of Simeon Kram at the rear of the crowd. "Is it you are saying that these people died because it is all right?" Inside a church, Simeon Kram would never have dreamed of interrupting to ask the minister a question. But when Simeon Kram was out under the trees he felt at home and free to ask whatever questions he chose. What is more, he was angry—and as he asked the question the other settlers discovered that, beneath their respect for the cloth, they were angry, too. A low murmur of approval moved through the crowd.

Encouraged, Simeon Kram went on: "We wanted you to come here so that these people could have a decent burial yet. We did not want you should come to tell us that it is all right for red Indians to kill our fathers and sons and mothers and daughters."

The minister's mouth took on an oval and his mild face turned quite pale. Back in his little parish in the East he could quickly have extinguished a member of the congregation who had the unimaginable audacity to question his word. But here he was lost. He looked at Simeon Kram, and then at the rest of us. Then he reached down and picked up his soggy hat from the ground and started out around the crowd in the direction of the steamboat landing. He was not leaving in indignation or sorrow. He was leaving in plain, unadulterated panic. It had filtered through to him that he had succeeded in insulting a primitive people.

When he had gone, we all looked at Simeon Kram. He nodded grimly and walked to the spot the minister had left. One arm was bandaged. His broad, honest face turned to us. "That is good rubbish gone," he said quietly. "We have done what we could. We have had a minister here for these people. We have sung some hymns for them yet. They were all brave and good, and let us all now kneel down and say to ourselves our own prayer."

Then Simeon Kram kneeled in the soft wet clearing, and all of us followed him. The water ran down my neck as I bent my head forward in imitation of Lawrence Coe. The rain sounded soft on the trees. I felt much better, somehow, about my father and mother now. It seemed to me that they would like what Simeon Kram did better than what the minister had been saying.

In the days immediately following the attack I discovered another side of Lawrence Coe. I had seen him as the store keeper, all business, jovial only in a way that was slightly forced, as though good humor, too, was part of his duty to Putnam Bradford. When we were besieged inside the store I had seen him as the leader, autocratic and seemingly cold and brutal. But now I was to find a whole new facet to his nature. The ashes of the burned cabins were still warm when Coe was making the rounds from the Upper Cascades to the lower landing, surveying what had happened to the settlers, asking where he could help. He made the tour under the guise of an inspector for Putnam Bradford. "I've got to make a report to Put," he'd say. But he did much more than write his employer. He replaced stolen hams, refurnished beds stripped of their blankets, and gave away tools to take the place of those burned or lost.

Whenever he found a household where death had struck there was nothing that the Bradford company could do—and this fact seemed to move him more deeply each time he encountered it. It was the first time I realized that Coe felt responsible for all those families whose men had come to do work at The Cascades.

The loss and suffering that I saw with Lawrence Coe helped me to endure my own predicament. When death strikes singly at a loved one it is difficult to bear in mind that others have suffered bereavement, to philosophize that it must come to all. There may have been a hundred reasons why death was better than a continuance of life. There is no way for me to know what suffering or disappointments lay in wait for my father and mother had they not been taken in the massacre.

But when death strikes as it did at the settlements, there is comfort. I had lost my parents. But there were parents who had lost their children, and there the suffering is greater. Poor Mrs. Hunt had lost her husband and had a small girl to care for. The Utterstroms, at the lower landing, had seen their five-months-old baby drown in the river as they escaped on a raft. Old Herman Kyle had lost all that he had been living for—Jake, his son. Mrs. Leigh, weighted with years, had seen her rheumatic husband fall to his knees for the last time. The Wickton's had looked helplessly from the blockhouse while the savages tortured their daughter in a hundred ways. Sarah Deems, too ill to stir from her bed, had been burned to death in the Deems' cabin. Henry Sillcox, trapped in his own front yard, had turned his rifle on his wife and small son—and had his skull split by a war axe before he could reload and die by his own hand. The little Davis girl was missing altogether and we could only imagine what terrors were being served for her in a camp of the Yakimas.

When I had walked with Lawrence Coe and knew such things as these I could think to myself, "I am not the only one." But there were bad moments. Most of them would come at night, and sometimes in broad day. In a sudden rush of reality I would realize, once again, that my mother and father were gone, that they would never again touch my hand or my cheek or speak to me. It was difficult to believe. It would seem, most of the time, that if I went down to the portage road I would find my father working there. He would greet me with his wide, proud smile, and perhaps he would put his hand on my shoulder, heavily as though I were a man, or rub his knuckles against my cheek and give me a warning about the river or the woods. And if I wanted to see my mother all I need do was to go into the house—a house no longer there!—and call to her. She would come hurrying out of the kitchen, holding her apron up a little from the floor, asking me not to do any jumping up and down because she was baking a chocolate cake.

That was the way it seemed, most of the time. I did not really keep thinking that—but I went about my business as if it were true. Then would come one of those awful moments when I knew that it wasn't true. It was as if a hand reached down and shook me out of a make-believe. Sometimes I tried to face it. Sometimes I would say, "When my father was alive . . ." But it was no good. I could never quite brazen it out.

Twice a week Lawrence Coe would ask me if I had visited the graves of my parents. Mike Shea never mentioned going there And if I suggested it, he would try to change the subject. Mike was a Roman Catholic—at least he had been one somewhere in the dim past—and he really did not believe in grief for the dead. They were better off, Mike tried to convey to me, and besides, he intimated, my grief might be more for my own predicament than for the departed. But somehow it made me feel better to go to the clearing regularly and stand a while before the wood slabs with the names of my parents on them. Coe had carved only their names and the date of their death, for I had been unable to tell him much about them.

I do not know why they chose The Cascades as a place in which to live. I know that my father was a lawyer by profession. But it was not strange that he should be building the portage bridge, for there was no law business at The Cascades, and along the river a man did what he could in order to make himself useful and earn a living for his family. They had come from Southbridge, Massachusetts, and my mother had told me that Caleb Paige helped to build the meeting house, and had drawn up the petition for changing Southbridge from a poll-parish into a town. She said, too, that he was one of a committee of seven elected to compose a town charter. She mentioned these things proudly, and I remembered them.

On the fly-leaf of our Bible was my mother's name—Louisa Ball Benedict, and the names of her parents, Louis Benedict and Sarah Ball. After Louis's name there was written in a cramped hand: *Born in Italy. Parents did not survive shipwreck on way across to America.* The poor man evidently knew as little of his parents as do I, and after the attack of the savages I felt more than a blood kinship with this Louis who has been gone so many years and is buried I know not where.

That Bible did not carry the date of my own birth, or the place. I suppose that the event came during some change in the fortune of my father. Perhaps the Bible was packed away in household goods that were on the move, or upon whose title my father's hold was insecure at the moment. That is the only way I can explain the fact that a pillar of Southbridge was in The Cascades. I am sure that he had reason to seek solitude, and to turn away from a profession he might have practiced in Dalles City or Portland.

Out of all the survivors at The Cascades, only Victoria Hunt and her mother left the place after the attack. They too would have stayed except for the fact that Mrs. Hunt had a sister in Dalles City and, with no man in the family, thought it best to take the child there.

The rest stayed on, not simply because a new blockhouse was built and a company of soldiers assigned to duty there. They stayed because they were a stubborn lot, and to the majority the thought of leaving perhaps never occurred. The savages had killed and raped and burned, true. Most of the homes were in ashes, and almost all the meager possessions the settlers had dragged across a continent, or brought around the Horn, or built with their hands afterward, were gone. There was a steady hatred now of the savages, but there was no grumbling and no self-pity, and the hatred did their souls no harm. Indeed, the hatred spurred them on.

They were determined to set their homes on the bank of the Columbia and they would do it despite rains and winds and forests, despite even the depredations of savages. It is dangerous business to intimate to a white man that he cannot keep his home on his own little land. The savage, with few ties and always a roamer, never quite understood this; and, not understanding it, pressed too far, and in the end was defeated. He believed that he was fighting only men and muskets. He had weapons of his own. He did not lack courage, and he was far more reckless than his enemy. Further, he knew the country and how to wage war among its forests and hills. Possessing these advantages, he was deluded merely because he did not consider the enemy's fierce desire for a little land of their own.

The people of The Cascades were not much like the ones who were to come up the river later on. They were more like the traders and the mountain men who had been in the West since Lewis and Clark, and were in a way descendants of overland marchers who had been drifting south and west from New England since the middle 1700s. Some of the older ones had never been to school simply because that was the way of life at the time when they were young and in the region where they had lived. They had been handed a rifle when they were twelve and become men. And even those who had once lived in settled and civilized communities had reached the West by wagon train—and when a man has traveled the width of this country by wagon train he has already learned much of what a generation of pioneering would teach him.

Already most of them had had their training in self-reliance and self-preservation. They had become almost a peculiar race, with peculiar characteristics. They were brown and lean, and tremendously alert. They could not be surprised by nature. Their eyes were piercing, focused to a rough country in which anything might happen. Their hands and arms and limbs and heart and lungs were strong, for the weak had been taken early. And they possessed a stubborn endurance in the face of adversity.

So the little settlements at the Lower Cascades, and the Middle Cascades and around Bradford and Company's store, sprang up again within a year. New goods came into Bradford's from Portland. New portage roads were built, and the cars which the savages had destroyed were replaced. Profiting from experience, the settlers built larger and more substantial and convenient cabins than before. There was continually the sound of axes ringing in the woods above the settlement, and of men urging teams to greater effort. The exciting smell of newly split wood was over the bank of the river, and the green monotone was relieved by the splashes of bright unweathered cabins. Within two years it was almost as if no attack had occurred, except for the graves in the clearing beyond the store. But they were long years, filled with work and more work, with back-breaking toil that dimmed the memory of the tragedy.

As an orphan I received considerable attention, despite the tasks that faced every man and woman in the settlements. Mrs. Hunt offered to take me to Dalles City with her, and old Mrs. Leigh cut down some of her husband's clothes for me to wear. A number of the couples from the Middle settlement where, due to the protection of the blockhouse, the loss had been slightest, wanted to adopt me. But somehow I gravitated naturally into taking shelter with Lawrence Coe. In the rush of the days after the attack he needed help in the store, and I fell to helping him and sleeping right in the store. It was fascinating work for a young boy. The goods which came up from Portland on the steamers were of every description. Blankets and muskets, candles and lye. Shining tools, and bolts of cloth for ladies' dresses. Flour and bacon and beans. Beer and ale by the keg. And, sometimes, California cheeses and dried fruits. Some of it we placed on the shelves, and some we segregated for trans-shipment up to Dalles City. As we worked, Coe would tell me where the stuff came from. A widely traveled man, he could tell me something about each place he mentioned. It was a most excellent and painless education for a stripling.

Passenger traffic began to increase considerably, too, for the news that Wright was establishing safety in the interior, and had given the Indians a hemp lesson at The Cascades, encouraged more and more people to venture out of Portland. All who transferred from the *Belle* or the *Fashion* to the upriver steamboat stopped in at the store—soldiers and fine ladies and questionable nondescripts and, most awesome of all, Chinamen. I had never dreamed I was missing so much when my mother had forbidden me to go to the store when the boats were transferring cargo on the portage road.

The Cascades seemed to me to be the center of the whole world. When things were slack in the store I would wait on the wharf boat at the lower landing for the arrival of the *Belle* and the *Fashion.* When they landed I would watch until the last cargo was unloaded and then, if I were lucky, ride the mule-drawn portage car as far as the blockhouse. At that point I would be torn between a desire to have a visit with Mike, or accompany the portage car to the upper settlement where I could watch the cargo loaded aboard the *Mary* or the *Wasco,* bound for Dalles City. Sometimes I was unusually fortunate. That was when Mike climbed onto the car with me and together we'd watch the upper river boats. He was still derisive of my ambition to be a steamboat captain. But since the Indian attack my feeling for the boats was keener than ever. The massacre had been a horrible nightmare, but it is impossible to imagine what it might have been if the *Belle* had not brought Sheridan and the *Mary,* Wright.

I could not help but feel that it would have been more satisfying if Vicky Hunt had stayed. She would have been suitably impressed by my importance when she called to buy corn meal. There were not more than half a dozen boys in the upper settlement, and all of them were older than I—old enough to be working on the wharf boats or cutting wood, or going on hunting and fishing expeditions. I had long envied them, and now I had reason to believe that they envied me, although none would admit it. At least they never let me get to the point of explaining my duties and retailing to them some of Lawrence Coe's knowledge, such as that the axes came all the way from Buffalo which was in New York State. I was sure that Victoria would have been more satisfactory as an audience.

The women of the settlement did not let me go to Lawrence Coe without a conscientious struggle. They all had troubles enough, and none could really afford a ward, but they fretted about me sincerely. Once when I was out of sight in the rear of the store I heard

Mrs. Leigh lecturing to Coe. "It's too bad that his mother's gone, Mr. Coe, and you were wonderful for taking him in here. But I wouldn't be able to face Louisa Paige in Heaven if I didn't say this, Mr. Coe. A child ought really to have a home." When she had quite finished, Mr. Coe made a grumpy noise and inquired in mild good humor if she did not think that the store was a home and him a proper father and mother.

He convinced most of them, I think, for he was a flawless man and they knew it. The difficulty was that he could not quite convince himself, and after the first year he began to worry about me. Further, he did have his own responsibilities as manager for Putnam Bradford. It was not that he was sorry for his decision, or wanted to shirk his feeling of duty toward me. But he was, after all, an ambitious man, with plans in his head that did not include an adopted son. He tried his best not to let me see that I was a problem, but a child is quick to sense such things. It was for this reason that I was more ready than not to accept Mike Shea's startling proposal.

CHAPTER 5

Mike and I were sitting on the bank of the river, as we had used to do, and he had carved out a particularly successful boat from a thick pine bough. It was at least a foot long and had a cabin and a pilot house. When it was finished he did not put it in the stream, but sat holding it, pretending to sight along the hull to see if the lines were fair. I knew he had something on his mind, and waited.

"You know," he said finally, "I'm leaving the Army."

I sat up straight. I could not imagine such a thing as Mike leaving the Army. Although I had no idea how a man entered the service, I figured it must be an intricate and ticklish business. Once a man had got in, I thought, he stayed. Until that moment I hadn't realized a man could honorably leave the service except through meeting death at the hands of an enemy.

"You mean—you don't mean you're going to . . . to desert?"

He gave me a hurt look. "Of course not. My enlistment period's up and I'm thinking I won't sign in again."

"But what will you do?"

Mike did not answer for a moment. Then: "A man can't stay in the Army all his life, boy."

"Mike, you shouldn't leave. Pretty soon you'll be a Colonel and have a horse to ride."

The Irishman grunted. "Not Mike Shea. I never went to West Point." His tone grew bitter. "No sir, I learned my fightin' on the plains, and in California, and back in there where they're sendin' Steptoe. So I'm no good. I should've learned my fightin' in a school. So I'll always be a private, probably, if I stay in the Army."

"I'd rather be a private than any old Colonel," I said, swiftly contrite.

Mike clapped his beefy forearm around my shoulders. "Sure, kid. But I just figure I better get out of the Army. I had a brother who stayed in the Army and it wasn't very good for him."

"Why?"

"Well, it just wasn't, boy. So I think I'll be gettin' out and making something of myself. Maybe I'll go into business or something." He looked at me defensively. "I've a little saved up from my pay."

I felt pretty bad. "That'll mean you'll leave here, won't it?"

"Yeah. There isn't much chance to go into business around here. I figured I might go to Dalles City."

My heart was like lead, and then Mike said, "I thought maybe you'd go to Dalles City with me."

I considered this unbelievable prospect, but the influence of my parents was still strong. "I'd like to, Mike. But I—I couldn't."

"Why not, now?" Mike demanded. "What would be holding you back if I'm wanting you?"

"I don't know as Mr. Coe would like it," I said.

"And if he didn't like it, then to Hell with him," Mike said. "He hasn't ever adopted you. At least not legal. You been working there, so you've paid for the board and room he's given you. You can skin out any time you want."

"But I—" I had to stop. There were a lot of objections I couldn't voice. After two years, I knew that an orphan boy was a problem, and somehow I could not picture Mike with one to worry about.

"I could use a likely lad," Mike broke in. "I could use him in my business. I don't know yet just what I'm going into—but Dalles City is a lively town and I could use you. You're—how old are you now, Caleb?"

"Fourteen," I said, and was startled to realize it. It had been almost two years since my parents had been killed there on the bank of the Columbia. I felt quite old, and I said it again, this time in a firmer tone. "Fourteen."

"There, you see? First thing you know you'll be fifteen and ready to go into something. We can make a name for ourselves in Dalles City. It's going to grow to be a big place, boy. I know a lot of people there. What do you say?"

"I don't know," I admitted.

Mike took another squint along the hull of the pine vessel in his hand. Then, almost carelessly, he shoved it into the stream. It showed a perfect balance. The bow faced downstream resolutely and it rose and fell on the waves with the grace of a full-sized boat. "Look here," Mike said suddenly. "I'll have a talk with Lawrence Coe. Come along if you want."

I said that I would.

"The thing is, if we can't fix it up for you to be partners with me then I don't want to leave the Army." He got up from the bank and I followed suit. Together we trudged toward the store, neither of us saying a word all the way.

Coe was getting some sun, leaning against the store and smoking his pipe. I saw him watching us up the path, and as we drew nearer he smiled and waved at us. The thought that he liked Mike Shea was comforting at that moment.

Mike had been thinking hard about it, I could see. I imagine he rehearsed a dozen approaches. But when he stood in front of Lawrence Coe all the speeches fled his brain, and he blurted out, "Lawrence, I'm goin' to be leaving the Army next week. I'm goin' into business in Dalles City, and I'd like to take Caleb here along with me."

Lawrence Coe's smile vanished and his jaw dropped. I stood first on one foot and then on the other. It seemed to me minutes before Coe spoke up. "Well, Mike . . ." he said, then stopped.

"You've got your own lay-out here," Mike said. "You're busy as it is." Then he added, "And you ain't got any woman in the house, Lawrence."

Coe puffed at his pipe. "Then you figure on going into business and getting a woman in the house, all at the same time?"

Mike Shea grew even redder than usual. "Well—no. But what I mean is, you got a store here. I figure the kid and I will get a house in Dalles City and live in that. Another thing is, there ain't much here, Lawrence. But in Dalles City they got a school and all."

This was pure inspiration on Mike's part. I am sure it had never occurred to Mike Shea except at that moment.

"Tell me, Mike. What sort of business are you going into up there?"

"Maybe the printing business," Mike said. "I might even start a newspaper."

Coe's eyebrows raised. "You a printer?"

"My father was. I been in the Army myself ever since I was sixteen."

For a time Coe said nothing. He stood there looking at me as if he had never really seen me before. Finally his eyes raised to Mike's face. "I want Caleb to go to school," he said. "And there isn't anything here except what Mrs. Watkins can teach him."

"Then it's all right with you?"

Another puff at the pipe. "I don't know. But I'm telling you, Mike, I feel a little for Caleb."

"I know what you mean," Mike said. "But look, Lawrence, I've known Caleb a long time, too. I always had a sort of hankering for the kid."

Coe rubbed his shoulder blades against the rough logs of the store. "But here's the idea, Mike—I took him in. Right or wrong, that makes me responsible for what happens to him from now on. To tell you the truth, I'm not sure he ought to be kept around here. I think maybe he ought to go somewhere and get some schooling. But you're an Army man, Mike, and I never heard tell of an Army man taking a kid to raise. You got to let me think about it a while."

"Well," said Mike, embarrassed, "I'd be glad to have you come up to Dalles City any time and see how he's getting along. But," he added with magnanimity, "it's all right for you to think about it. And there's something Caleb wanted to say, only he wasn't sure he could get it into the right words. He wanted to say he wouldn't ever forget what you did for him after the vermin done away with his pa and ma that way."

I was grateful for Mike putting that in. I hadn't any idea of stating any such thing myself, but it was what I should have said—and if it hadn't been said I'd have regretted it afterward.

Coe met my abashed gaze. "I've been glad to have him," he said. "He's a real help. But I don't want to hold him back." He looked at Mike again. "If you left here, when would it be?"

"Kelly says he can fix it up so I could take next Thursday's boat."

"Well, I'll be thinking it over, Mike. I guess I can tell you something before then." With a sigh of relief, Mike turned and went up the path toward the blockhouse. Somehow I knew that the moment he got there he would have a long pull at the canteen—the one that was innocent of water.

I followed Lawrence Coe inside the store. He went behind the counter and began rearranging things on the shelves, things that did not need rearranging very much. Finally he said, without looking at me, "You've wanted to see Dalles City, haven't you?"

"Yes, but I could visit it some time. I don't have to live there."

"You could go to school there. A boy ought to go to school."

"I reckon he should," I agreed, not very enthusiastic.

"Mike seems to know the printing trade. That's a good trade to be apprenticed to. It's educational."

This time I said nothing. "There wouldn't be much notion in your staying around here," Coe went on. "You could work in the store, like you been doing. But there isn't much in that—and then maybe I won't be staying here, either. What is it you want to do when you grow up?"

"I'd like to be a steamboat captain."

The promptness of my reply must have startled Coe, for he turned around and looked at me. "A steamboat captain? Well, now a steamboat captain has to be smart. He ought to have some schooling—and you can't learn to be a steamboat captain in a store. I know that because I tried it once. I let the lines off before we got steam up—and I lost the boat, too. Some day I want to go into steamboating again, but when I do I'll get me a real captain."

He walked down behind the counter, stooped out of sight and brought up a rolled chamois skin. "Mike Shea is right, Caleb. You ought to be sent to Dalles City. I can come up once in a while and check up to see how things are." He began unrolling the chamois. "I want to give you a little present. You're too young to need it yet, but it'll make a nice mantel decoration."

Out of the chamois he brought a beautiful flint-lock pistol. It had the date 1842 carved on the handle, but it looked brand new. Coe handed it to me butt-first. "A good charge of powder, a ball, and maybe half a dozen buck shot," he said, "and you'd be all right. That is, if you pull the trigger soon enough."

I stared at him, amazed. The proposition was that I was going into a real town, not deeper into the forest. Coe saw my question. "You'll be in a fairly civilized community, Caleb, and a fairly civilized community is always dangerous. Here you had just two enemies, nature and the Indians. But you always know pretty well what to look out for in them. By and large, they can be figured out ahead of time. But a white man you can't ever figure out. That's something you want to remember in Dalles City."

I should have been overjoyed at such a gift. But something in Coe's manner restrained me. Quietly I held the revolver, then reached for the chamois and began rolling it around the weapon.

"I'll always keep it," I said—and then, at the thought of leaving The Cascades and Lawrence Coe, I burst into tears.

CHAPTER 6

Beside Mike Shea, I stood at the rail of the *Mary*. Down on the bank Lawrence Coe appeared through the mist that stood in my eyes. It was a mist that threatened to condense into tears at any moment and shame me before the only world I knew. I dared not look up toward the wooded hill which shielded my mother and father. So I stood very stiffly, not daring to move my head for fear of spilling what filled my eyes.

Suddenly the *Mary* let out three terrific blasts of her whistle, startling me into grasping the rail. I had no sooner regathered my composure than two more blasts sounded out. "There'll be another," Mike warned, putting a hand on my shoulder, "when they draw in the gangplank."

I knew it well enough. A long whistle followed by a short one. But when I had heard them before I was sitting on the bank. It was different, much different, when the whistle was directly over your head. I clutched at the rail more tightly and waited. At last the signal came. The gangplank was drawn in, and Coe started waving farewell.

"Come up and see us soon!" Mike yelled.

"I will. Take care of yourselves, you two."

For my own part, I could not speak. The difficulty of leaving my parents and, almost as sharp in my heart, Lawrence Coe, was fighting against the excitement at being aboard the *Mary* and bound for Dalles City. It helped a little when Coe did not stand on the bank, watching us around the bend, but turned and started along the shore path as if he had work to do.

Instantly Mike Shea became the center of a group on the boat. To me he looked odd without his uniform, but the strangers patently admired the big Irishman in his dark suit and black felt hat. There was something friendly and awkward and powerful about Mike Shea that drew people to him instantly. But he kept me close by, and when someone asked him if I were his boy he'd say, "That he is," and grip my arm in his big paw.

The little *Mary* swung out from the bank, pointed her nose upriver and began to churn the stream. I had thought I was prepared for the river, for I had crossed to Bradford's Island many times in a skiff. But now I knew that the river was big indeed. It was much bigger when you were smack in the middle of it. I could have felt no more helpless had I been upon the sea. Only the sight of the dripping paddles and the groans of the thrusting rods revealing that the *Mary* was alive and competent, comforted me.

I was filled with awe merely at our passage through the water. Movement I had known, on foot, and on the little portage car between the wharf boats at The Cascades. But that was movement not nearly so positive and majestic. When I peered down at the stream it seemed to me that the *Mary* was traveling at an incredible speed. Yet when I raised my eyes to the bank I was reminded that our progress was steady rather than spectacular. After a while I asked Mike when we would reach Dalles City and he told me it would be many hours more before we docked. I knew then that I was really getting over the earth and became impressed with my own worldliness.

We stopped frequently to take on fuel for the boilers. Easily the *Mary* would nose against the bank where stood a pile of cordwood, and in no time at all the crew covered the foredeck of the steamer with the pine chunks. When the *Mary* was under way again the men tossed it stick by stick down into the hold. "It takes a lot of steam to push her up to Dalles City," Mike explained. "But coming down you don't stop at all." He brushed his palms together with a swishing sound. "You come down just like that!"

It was not long before Mike Shea and his new friends were grouped in the cabin embroiled in a political discussion. Mike was a Republican, and so were the others, which was a little disappointing to Mike, for he would have enjoyed himself more had he been able to do some arguing. As it was he could only strengthen his own opinions.

There had been considerable politics in the air lately, and I had listened to some of the talk at Bradford's store. It fascinated me, not because I could understand it but because I felt that anything over which men could become so intense must be deep and strange and wonderful.

That very year the Territory of Oregon had voted to become a part of the Union. The issue which had brought Oregonians together and swung us toward the Union was slavery. The immediate cause was the Kansas-Nebraska bill which repealed the Missouri Compromise and literally threw the Territories open to slavery.

As nearly as I could ascertain from the talk in Bradford's store, the people of Oregon did not want slavery. They had no particular need for it; and, moreover, they preferred not to mix into the issue. But the passage of the Kansas-Nebraska bill made the problem unavoidable. And if they were going to have slavery, the Oregonians wanted to embrace it themselves and not have it foisted upon them by politicians at Washington.

One of Mike's new friends had read a piece in a Democrat paper which had called the Republicans "nigger-worshipers" and he took violent exception to the term. "I'd like," he said, "to lay my hands on the editor of that paper, that's all."

Mike nodded understandingly. "And so would I. The trouble with Democrats is, they believe all they're told by these Democrat newspapers. They won't ever read the *Argus* or the *Oregonian* to get a look at the other side. Now take yourself, sir, you say you're a Republican and yet you're broad-minded enough to read a Democrat paper. Take me, for instance, I'm not all one-sided, either. I don't want to see Oregon a slave state, but I don't want to see any free niggers comin' in here, either."

They all agreed to that. "Leave it clear alone," said another of the men. "The Democrats say that if we let Oregon accept slavery then a lot of rich Southerners would come out and bring their property and money. I say let them stay home where they belong.

We don't need anybody that's got to have a lot of niggers to wait on them. What we want is people that will work. And it's like you say, we don't want any free niggers, either. I don't believe in making slaves out of anybody, but niggers is niggers."

"They say," mentioned Mike, referring to the Democrats with an ambiguity meant to be insulting, "that any change in the slavery system is the same as talking disunion. What do we care? When we try to get into the Union I don't see none of them Southern senators helping any. They try to keep us out."

"Well, we're going to be a state now, anyhow, so we'll have something to say, too."

One of the men hooked his boot heels in the rungs of his chair and squinted menacingly at a cuspidor. "Who do you gents figure will make our next President?"

"It's kind of early," said Mike Shea. "But I like Edward Bates."

"He's from Missouri, ain't he?"

"Yeah. I been reading about him in the *Argus* and I think he'd make a good man."

"That's right," said another of the group. "I'm for Bates, all right, and I figure he'll be picked at the convention. Reckon the Democrats will choose Lane or Stephen Douglas?"

Mike snorted. "No tellin' what they'll do." He waved disgustedly into the air. "Look at them! Always fightin' and squabblin' among themselves."

"Well," said the man with the boots, "us Republicans ought to be getting together a little ourselves. You said you were reading in the *Argus* about Bates. I saw a copy of the *Argus* at Vancouver only last week and now it's talking about a fellow called Lincoln."

"Lincoln?"

"Lawyer from Illinois."

"Why do we have to have a lawyer from Illinois?" demanded Mike. "Why not somebody from Oregon?"

This brought guffaws, for everybody knew that Oregon was too young a state to furnish a President. "Instead of a lawyer from Illinois, an ex-soldier from Oregon, eh?"

Mike blushed. "I didn't mean that. But why shouldn't the West have a President? It's a big country and the President ought to know something about it. Look what happens to us. Things like sending old Johnnie Ellis Wool out here to fight Indians."

"One thing," said the man with the boots, "nobody could be much worse than Buchanan."

As we pushed up the river, the wind increased and became warmer with every mile. We were getting the breeze now from the broad flat lands where no cooling evergreens grew.

Mike looked down at me and grinned. "What say we unlimber the eats, boy? You must be getting hungry." From beneath his chair he drew his Army knapsack which I judged he had retained with some sentiment.

The river between The Cascades and our destination was deep and broad—scarcely ever less than a mile in width. Mike pointed out to me the sunken forests at the sides of the stream. From the deck of the *Mary* the submerged trunks were clearly visible. "It's an old forest, they say," Mike explained. "Slid down there years ago." He went no further than this, and I could see that it sufficed him.

He had less hesitancy in calling my attention to the more apparent phenomena—to the spires and castellations of basalt, alternating with the green slopes, that stood along the first fifty miles east of The Cascades. He knew their names expertly: Mitchell's Point, Shell Mountain, Wind Mountain—"that's where the *Mary's* boilers gave out as Wright was coming up the river when the vermin were after us." He pointed out Bald Mountain and Mount Defiance. I tried to remember the names, to affix in my mind a basaltic outline to go with each name. I dreamed of coming along these banks and pointing out the peaks and points by name to awed strangers.

Late in the afternoon, Mike took me to the rail. "We're coming to Memaloose Island," he said. "That's where the vermin hereabouts bury their dead—and the thicker that island is populated the better I'll like it."

I began to feel uncomfortable. For one thing, I was having difficulty in accustoming myself to the weird change that had taken place on the banks of the river. The country was growing barren. I missed the green trees so thick on the lower river, and now instead of pinnacles and spires there were walls of rock as regular as though the work of man. In the lengthening shadows the land seemed strange and forbidding, and I asked Mike, "Is it all this way?"

He laughed. "You'll get to like it, boy. You just wait. I'll bet that in a year or two, when you get down on the lower river, you'll feel shut in and cold."

I doubted this, but if I were going to cast my lot in Dalles City I certainly hoped that it was true. Suddenly Mike pointed out over the bow of the *Mary*. "There she is. Memaloose Island." I looked ahead. The island was directly in mid-channel. As we drew closer I could see that it was rock into whose clefts white sand had blown in great drifts like snow. And on it stood wooden platforms upon which were little heaps I did not at first make out. Then, on one of the platforms, I saw distinctly the forms of men swathed in cloth, and knew that these were Indian dead.

Mike looked at the scene with obvious satisfaction. "When the wind's right," he said, "it don't smell so good along here."

I shuddered. "How long have they been burying people there?"

He shrugged. "Hundreds of years, they say. They just hoist them up there and leave them. Pretty soon the old bones roll off the platforms and get covered up with the sand."

I was mighty glad when the *Mary* had safely maneuvered past the gruesome island, and grateful when Mike said that we were coming to the mouth of the Klickitat which wasn't very far from Dalles City.

"Those cliffs there look like a blockhouse, don't they?" he asked when we neared the mouth of the river. "They call them the Paha Cliffs. See that big half circle of a wall over there? The vermin say that once Speelyei built that."

I knew Speelyei well. He was the Indian coyote god and had done many things along the river. Speelyei was the one who had outwitted Wishpoosh, the giant beaver who ate trees and men with equal ease. Speelyei was like our God, for he had created all the Indian tribes—and he had done it by transforming the carcass of Wishpoosh.

First Speelyei had let himself be swallowed by Wishpoosh, and then he had drawn his knife and carved the insides of the giant beaver until he was dead. From the head he made the Nez Perce tribe. The Cayuses were made from the arms, and the Klickitats from the legs. From the belly he had made the Chinooks, the great eaters. And the indiscriminate mass of hair and blood that was left Speelyei threw far from him, into the east, and it sprang into the beginnings of the Snake River Indians.

So when Mike Shea said that Speelyei had built that wall of rock I was ready enough to believe him. "What did he do it for?" I asked. "Was it a fort?"

Mike shook his head with a grin. "Nope. Old Speelyei did something bad, they say, and he was going to build a wall around it so the report wouldn't get out. But while he was building the wall on the west, the report got out on the east. So he just figured it was no use and he quit building it."

I was sorry that it was growing dark, for I wanted to get my first glimpse of Dalles City by daylight. But this was not to be. Suddenly Mike pointed, and off the starboard bow of the *Mary* I saw what seemed to me to be hundreds of lights. The sight took my breath away.

"There she is," Mike said proudly, as if he owned the town. "We're there."

At my back the *Mary's* whistle blasted. My heart was beating fast. I had never seen a town. I had not dreamed there could be so many lights scattered along the bank of the river.

"How many people live in Dalles City, Mike?"

"About five hundred," Mike said, "not countin' the people that come through on the steamers, and the soldiers at the fort. And," he added, impressively, "it's got twenty-seven saloons."

I was overcome half by the enormity of the town and half by weariness. I leaned against Mike's big frame and felt his warm palm against my cheek. "Reckon you're tuckered, all right. We'll get ourselves a good bed and tomorrow I'll show you the town."

He was silent a moment as the blinking yellow lights grew nearer. Then he said, "Well, we're here, boy. Yes sir, we're here.

You and I."

I had never heard Mike's voice in just that shade. He seemed a little troubled and that worried me. Mike Shea had never been troubled, so far as I knew. Could it be that he was as afraid of Dalles City as I was? I dismissed that thought as nonsense. He had visited Dalles City often and had friends there. He had been a soldier, and a soldier was afraid of nothing.

CHAPTER 7

WE stayed at Ed Danby's boarding house on Front Street, an arrangement which Mike said was only temporary. "As soon as I get into something, we'll find ourselves a house up on the hill, near the Army post," he said.

Danby's boarding house had really been built as a store with living quarters above, but the restless owner had decided at the last moment that there was no future in Dalles City and he had better go up to Puget Sound to establish his business. So the Danbys, husband and wife, bought the place, partitioned the back into small, box-like rooms, and divided the rest of the first floor into a combination dining-and-sitting-room and a huge kitchen.

The place was much too large, in fact, for the Danbys' household furnishings, and the living quarters somehow gave the impression of a warehouse waiting for more goods. But the elderly couple did occasional business with those who could not afford to stay at the Umatilla House, Dalles City's finest hostelry, or preferred not to get into the midstream of the town's excitement.

The Danbys appeared to know Mike well from previous visits. In the morning at breakfast the weazened, white-thatched Ed Danby made several sly references to Mike's adventures in Dalles City, but I noticed that Mike was not responding in his usual jovial fashion. Finally, with an embarrassed glance at me, the old man discovered Mike's reticence. "Sure," he said hastily, "but you're all done with the didoes now that you're out of the Army and got your young friend here."

"That I am," Mike agreed.

"Are you going to work here in town, or go on inland?"

"Work?" enquired Mike largely. "I'm going into business, me and Caleb."

This impressed Danby. "You don't mean it!"

"You bet I do. I'm thinkin' of starting a newspaper."

"But we got a newspaper," Danby told him. *"The State Journal."*

"Well, you can have another one. Lots of towns have two newspapers."

Mrs. Danby sailed in from the kitchen with a plate of flapjacks and Danby's quizzing ended. Her appearance seemed to have a dampening effect on both men, and indeed she looked as if she would bear little nonsense. She was a tall woman, almost as tall as Mike Shea himself, and dwarfed entirely her husband. Even at that hour, and coming from the kitchen, she wore a formal-looking black dress with a lace throat-collar re-enforced by whalebone. I do not know whether it was this or her nature which kept her head so erect. But I know that I was glad to be away from her piercing gaze when breakfast was over.

As soon as we had put down the last of the flapjacks, Mike took me by the arm and announced that I had to see Dalles City. Ed Danby offered to accompany us but his wife quickly changed his course. "You've something to do, Ed Danby, besides going on any sightseeing tour with Michael Shea and the young one."

The business houses of Dalles City stood directly along the river bank, and its few modest homes were scattered without pattern back along the slope toward the Army post.

We went directly from Ed Danby's boarding house to the livery stable across the street, and there Mike was greeted enthusiastically by a skinny, sandy-haired individual who smelled of horsehide and fresh manure.

"Mike, you old son of a gun! Where in the Hell have you been?" He looked at me curiously. "Who's the sprout?"

Mike took the man's outstretched hand and wrung it vigorously.

"He's a partner of mine, Bert. Caleb, this here is Bert Patterson, the most worthless livery stable proprietor west of the Stony Mountains."

I nodded awkwardly, but Bert Patterson apparently did not notice for he made no acknowledgment of my gesture. He and Mike fell to guying each other in a quick, strange jargon that I could scarcely understand. It was well sprinkled with profanity and seemed to refer to a number of past escapades in which Mike had either failed to return livery equipment before leaving for his post, or had returned it in damaged condition. But Patterson seemed to be very good humored about it, and I gathered that Mike had been a good customer despite his eccentricities.

"All that kind of shenanigan is over now, Bert," he said. "I'm not a God damned trooper any more. Caleb and I are going to get into business."

"The hell you say!"

Mike assured him that it was a fact. "Right now we want to hire a couple of saddle mares so's we can look things over in style."

Patterson produced the horses, and gingerly I accepted Mike's assistance into the saddle. I had never ridden a horse in my life, but I was determined not to let Bert Patterson know it if I could help. Fortunately the mare I had was a gentle sort.

We rode along the bank east of town because Mike wanted to show me the Indian village. I think that he wanted me to feel comfortable and at home, and feared that if he showed me the town first I might long for The Cascades. I was astonished, in fact, that such a metropolis would endure an Indian village nearby.

"Sure," Mike said. "There's a village up at Celilo Falls. But don't let it worry you, Caleb. As long as the fort's up there on the hill these vermin ain't goin' to make trouble."

In front of the town itself the river flowed smoothly, with only a gentle whirl in its current. But a few miles east of Dalles City the stream was suddenly lashing itself into a fury greater than at The Cascades. I could see the mists of spray rising and hear the thundering waters long before we rode within sight of the disturbance.

At last we reached the top of the knoll and looked down on a beautiful and awesome sight. The river had literally turned on edge and was pouring through a channel that was certainly not more than two hundred feet wide. It widened out again below us and plunged down in a roaring cascade to a lower level. When I saw Celilo Falls I knew why no "fire-canoes," as the Indians called the steamboats, had ever gone beyond Dalles City.

Soon we came in sight of the village. It was larger than the one at The Cascades, but had much the same appearance, and the odors which drifted on the east wind were certainly familiar. Such is the strange formation of the middle Columbia country that it is difficult to discern human figures at any great distance. The basalt rocks, the patches of brown and green vegetation, and the shadows thrown by both, confuse the eye. However, as we watched, I discovered that the village was not entirely deserted. Down on the very edge of the river were perhaps a dozen savages. Some crouched on the wet and slippery rocks near shore, and these had lines around their waists with the ends made fast ashore. Each carried a spear whose handle was attached to the wrist by another line. Their movements were lightning and rarely did a spearhead, once it had disappeared beneath the raging surface, fail to emerge into the sunlight without a glistening salmon impaled.

Mike sensed that I cared to get no closer to the village, so we watched from where our horses stood munching the knots of prairie grass. If any of the Indians saw us they gave no sign of it. A few children and dogs played about, and half a dozen squaws in a single file carried fish from the river to a central hut.

"You see?" Mike said at last, helpfully, "It's not much different from The Cascades."

By noon we had reached the town again, and although I wouldn't admit it to Mike, I was saddle sore. Mrs. Danby's dinner made me forget my discomfort, and by the time I had tasted her hot apple pie I was ready to change my opinion of her. I did such an excellent job of the first piece that she insisted I have another. She seemed to like me well enough, but I was sure she disapproved of Mike as a guardian. She had obviously ignored his announcement that we were going into the printing business and kept plaguing me for my own opinion as to what I should like to do. At last I said, "I'd like to do whatever Mike says—only some day I want to be a river captain."

"Well, now!" she exclaimed with satisfaction. "Did you hear that, Ed? The lad wants to be a steamboat captain."

Ed Danby chuckled. "Good enough! When the missus and I got here in 'fifty—let's see, now—don't seem like it was eight year ago, but it was—there wasn't a steamboat on the river up this far. No sir, took us six months to get acrost the plains, and all we saw when we got here was Indian canoes and them Hudson Bay batties."

"You made a raft," Mrs. Danby reminded him, bitingly.

"Yes siree, I sure did. And she worked fine, too. I used to take her downriver a piece and load her with wood, and then wait for a wind that would bring her back against the current. I had a big square sail on her and she'd do all right in the windy seasons, say March to July. But one day I lost her, and had a mighty narrow squeak myself into the bargain. Then the missus wouldn't let me build another one."

"I certainly would not."

Ed Danby grinned. Later I began to understand that he was not really afraid of his wife. He simply let her be as she wanted to be; and in his way, I am sure he loved the tall, gaunt woman.

"The year after the missus and I got here," he went on imperturbably, "the old *Flint* was built to go downriver. Then there was the *Allen*, but she got busted up just a little while after she was built. There was a landlubber captain from down your way, and he had the lines let loose afore the boilers was warm."

"Was his name Coe?" I asked.

"Coe. That was it! Lawrence Coe. Then I guess it was 'fifty-four that they built the *Mary* and the *Wasco*. Now there's the *Hassalo*, too, so I guess the steamboat business is growin' slow-like, and maybe you got the right idea, son."

The seriousness with which Ed Danby met my ambition made me feel old and important. His casual acceptance of it made him unique among adults and I warmed to him. Even Mike Shea, as we went along together, never seemed to take seriously my notion of being a Columbia River steamboat captain.

After dinner we saw the town—which is to say that we walked up one side of Front Street and down the other. There were boards in front of the stores, laid edge to edge to walk on. Mike called this a "sidewalk," a word I had never heard. And the buildings themselves were equally amazing. The structures at The Cascades had been of rough-hewn logs, and those few which were planked used lumber turned out at the little mill, as shaggy as buffalo hide.

These buildings at Dalles City were built from lumber which, Mike explained to me, had been shipped up from Portland on the steamboats. It was "dressed" lumber and, moreover, some of it had been painted. The majority had a characteristic which seemed peculiar to me: the peak of the roof was hidden by a square face which jutted up from the eaves. On these false fronts were signs, some of them painted by an owner unskillful with the brush, but the letters were large and unmistakable. Mike read them off to me as proud as if he owned every establishment.

"There's Gate's Restaurant and Lodging House . . . and over there is Powell's Saddle Shop. That's Vic Trevitt's saloon across the street. He's a fine Southern gentleman, Vic Trevitt, and a good friend of mine. He's got another saloon down the block that he owns with a partner."

He showed me the office of Bradford and Company. I began to understand a little of what the world of commerce meant and it thrilled me to think that already I had had a part in it with Lawrence Coe. But it was the collection of stores which awed me most. Downriver we had only Bradford's to serve our needs, and what else we wanted was made with our own hands or taken from the river and the woods. Here at Dalles City was luxury—hotels, an apothecary's shop, a bakery, a grocery store, and a big general store.

"This is nothing, Caleb," Mike said, pleased that I was so impressed. "You just ought to see a place like 'Frisco. 'Frisco would have your eyes buggin' out of your head."

At the end of the street, near the boat landing, he showed me the Umatilla House, the largest of the three hotels in town. "You were too sleepy to get a good look at it when we landed. But there she is—and that's where we're going to live when we get into business."

"I thought we were going to live in a house," I said, gazing at the three-story structure dubiously.

"Oh, sure. We'll build a house when we get settled and all. But when we first get into business we'll spend some time livin' in the Umatilla. Business men like us ought to do it, so we can get acquainted."

I decided privately that I wouldn't want to live on the top floor. The idea of a house of our own appealed to me more; but I was willing to leave everything to the wisdom of Mike.

The signs most noticeable on Front Street were those which said, simply, SALOON. It was in front of these establishments that Mike was most often delayed, for there was a knot of men in front of every one and they all knew the ex-trooper. They would hail him heartily and slap him on the shoulders until the dust flew from his black suit. They all asked him inside for a drink; but each time he refused, explaining how he and I were going into business and were just looking around. I would stand beside him, trying not to appear self-conscious, looking off into space as if in search of a satisfactory site for our enterprise.

The grander buildings were near the wharf landing and from there east along the river the structures grew gradually less pretentious. At the east edge they degenerated into a row of sprawling shacks—with one exception, a two-story clapboard structure emblazoned with the orange and black legend THE GOLDEN RULE. A pair of saddle mares were hitched to the rack in front of the place and as Mike and I walked along two men came out of the place, unloosed the bridles from the rack, and mounted.

Two men more unlike I had never seen. One was big, bigger even than Mike. On his head was a hat that seemed nothing except a shapeless piece of black felt. His gray flannel shirt was crusted with dried mud, and over this hung an open waistcoat whose lining was yellow with age. His companion was a small, but well-built man dressed in what I assumed to be the height of fashion. His boots were spotless, his waistcoat buttoned impeccably. He held the reins carelessly in one hand; his other hand, loose at his side, was covered with a glove.

When they saw Mike and me they reined up. "Hello there, Shea," the smaller one greeted Mike. The big one only nodded his head, and watched his companion.

"Hello, Kirt," Mike said. "How's things?"

"Fair to middling. Where's your fancy suit?"

"I've quit the Army," Mike told him. "I'm goin' to stay in Dalles City now—me and the kid here."

The small, dark man surveyed me. Then his glance shifted back to Mike. "What do you figure to do to keep you busy?"

"I ain't decided yet, Kirt. I been looking around."

"I could use a man. I could use a man that's been in the Army."

Mike grinned. "That's right nice of you. But I think I'll have a look around."

While Mike talked to the dark man I saw a woman watching us from one of the three windows in the second story of The Golden Rule. She was pretty and red cheeked, and quite young, it seemed to me. She rested her bare elbows on the window ledge, her thin oval face between her palms.

"Well," said the man Mike had called Kirt, "I reckon you'd have a drink with me, wouldn't you?"

"Sure," Mike said. "I don't give a damn if I do."

The other nodded and whirled his horse. "See you at Trevitt's, then." The other fellow unhooked his leg from his saddle horn, stopped sucking his teeth, and followed Kirt.

I was surprised at Mike's acceptance of this invitation when he had refused all the others. He must have felt the need to explain himself, for he said to me as we started back toward Trevitt's saloon, "It ain't a bad idea to have a drink with Kirt Inge when he asks you. If a man don't want to have a drink with him he gets the idea that maybe you don't want to be friendly."

I was puzzled still. Why should Mike be showing such deference to this small dark man? But I said nothing, and went along with Mike. The two men were waiting for us in front of Trevitt's.

There were more than a dozen men inside, a few at the tables and the rest lined along the bar. When they saw the man called

Kirt they greeted him cordially enough, but it was different from their greeting of Mike. It was as if they did not quite like the small man but were afraid to show him their coolness.

He led the way to a table and Mike and the big fellow and I followed him. "What'll you have?" he asked Mike, sitting down. The three of them ordered rye whiskey, and when the bartender brought it they tossed it down with a facility which fascinated me.

"You don't know Pete Forrest here, do you, Mike?" The man called Kirt nodded toward the giant beside him.

"Mighty glad to know you, partner," Mike said, and reached his red hand across the table. Forrest took Mike's hand, but said nothing. He had not opened his mouth since he and Kirt had ridden up on their horses.

Kirt ordered two more rounds of drinks in quick succession, and suggested a fourth but Mike said that he and I had to be getting along. "Thanks for the forty-rod, Kirt. I'll be repayin' you in kind."

The dark man smiled. "Okay, Mike. Sorry you won't let me give you a good job. Forrest here has come with me and he's going to be a real help in my business." He looked half affectionately at his grizzled companion. "Pete's the most skookum individual in Dalles City at this writing."

Mike flashed a good-natured grin. "Don't forget I'm livin' here now."

The smaller man's eyes widened a little; his face flushed slightly. "Hell, Mike—you ain't in it with Pete. Why, the other day I saw him—"

"I always got ten dollars that says nobody can sit me on my butt in an Indian rassle." I looked up at Mike. His tone had been tinged with hurt pride, and now his face was serious.

"I'd want to make it at least fifty," Kirt smiled. "Because I'd want to split with Pete when he sets you down."

Nervously I looked at the big fellow opposite me. He hadn't let a flicker of interest cross his face, and he was still keeping his eyes on Kirt. He was like a big sheep dog waiting an order from a master.

"Fifty it is," said Mike, and stood up. He looked at Pete Forrest with the greatest of good nature. "Are you game, partner?"

There was a faintly perceptible nod of Kirt's head, and the big fellow got out of his chair and stood away from the table. Mike walked beside him, but facing in the other direction. They planted their right feet together and gripped each other's right hands.

Immediately everyone left the bar and the tables to form a circle around the two. Forrest towered above Mike; I had not realized how big he was. Mike himself was over six feet, with a chest like a barrel and great thick flesh-and-bone posts for legs. But Forrest dwarfed us all in that circle of men.

"The first man to go down or lift his left foot off the floor is the loser," I heard Kirt say. "Okay . . . start."

At first nothing seemed to be happening. I couldn't see Mike's face because it was turned away from me, but the cords in his neck began to stand out, and the muscles in his right shoulder smoothed out against his shirt. Forrest's face was screwed up as if in pain, and suddenly I was aware that the struggle was on. Their clasped hands were shaking, yet neither fist moved more than an inch.

There wasn't a word from the crowd. A man with his chin over my shoulder was breathing whiskey too close to my face, but I hardly noticed.

"By God," somebody said, "them two is pretty even, I'd say."

He had no sooner spoken than Pete Forrest's arm swung back and he struck the floor flat on his rump with a thud that could be heard all over the place. The crowd broke into laughter and profanity, while the big fellow sat there, surprised and dazed, his face a study in unbelief.

I looked at Kirt. Impassively he was reaching into a small leather pouch with a draw-string dangling from it. I saw him hand some gold pieces to Mike, and then he turned to the giant, still sitting on the floor, and said, "Get up. You look like a baboon."

The fellow raised himself awkwardly to his feet, and for the first time since I'd seen him he spoke. "I got off balance. That Injun rassle is no good. It's a trick."

Mike was grinning, his face red as fire from the exertion. Suddenly he whipped out a chair from one of the tables. Turning to the man nearest him he said, "Sit down there, will you, partner?" Enjoying himself hugely, a lanky fellow obeyed Mike. "Mind havin' a couple of buckos on your lap?"

"I reckon not, if they smell sweet."

Two more volunteers were easily obtained. One sat forward on the man's lap. The other sat astride them both, clinging to the back of the chair. I don't know what they must have weighed, but none of the three was undersized. I saw Mike bend down, grasp the rungs of the chair with one shoulder against the back to steady it. And then in what seemed to me to be a single movement of his arms and body he put the chair and three men atop the table at which we'd sat.

The crowd was delighted. And Mike, his face flushed with pride and exertion, obligingly lifted them down again. "There you are, Pete," he said.

Forrest, now sullenly angry at the jibes of the crowd, strode up and grabbed the rungs of the chair. He brought the load half way up to the table, but at that stage his whole frame began to tremble. His lips were open but his teeth were clenched tight, and his throat became so swollen that I thought it was going to burst. Suddenly he broke wind resoundingly, lost his balance, and spilled himself and the occupants of the chair onto the floor.

The crowd in the saloon went crazy with laughter. They gathered around Mike and slapped him on the back. One old fellow literally rolled on the floor, holding his stomach with laughter, unable to rid his mind of the picture of Forrest's swift humiliation.

"Come on, Caleb," Mike said. "We better be going." He strode through the crowd, smiling at the comments that were thrown after us. I walked beside him proudly, and when we were outside and the raucous laughter of the saloon was lost to our ears I said, "I guess you're about the strongest man in Dalles City."

"Well," ventured Mike modestly, "I ain't hardly ever disputed."

"I didn't know you could do that, Mike—lift three men on a chair that way."

Mike grinned down at me. "I don't show it off any, except on occasion when the matter comes up, like it did in there. I don't mind a little show of stren'th when it's all in spirit with no hard feelin's."

"Who is that man you called Kirt?"

"Kirt Inge? Oh, he's a bucko around here. He does some gamblin' now and then, and he owns The Golden Rule."

"I saw a lady in one of the windows of The Golden Rule, Mike. I didn't know ladies stayed at hotels."

"What?" Mike looked at me, startled. "Sure—sure they do. About this Kirt Inge, there's talk that he's a bad actor, but him and me have always got along all right. Did you notice how he only wears one glove all the time? That's a false hand. He's supposed to have got a hand cut off in an Indian fight, but there's other stories about it, too."

"What kind of a job did he have for you?"

"Well, I wouldn't know about that. He likes to have big fellows workin' around him. I reckon maybe that's because he's kind of runty and 's only got one hand. But I ain't wanting to be doing his kind of work on account of I don't figure it's respectable."

Next day we paid a visit to Mrs. Hunt, catching a ride up the hill with a man who was hauling feed to the Army post. "Mrs. Hunt will be mighty glad to set eyes on us, I'll bet," promised Mike.

I jostled among the feed bags while Mike sat on the seat with the driver of the wagon. The creaky vehicle meandered along a road that was not laid out evenly like Front Street, but there were houses along it. Most of these, too, were made from dressed lumber and painted, although there were a few log cabins like the ones at The Cascades. Unlike the stores, they showed their peaked roofs without shame. There was a church which I recognized by its spire and cross.

What impressed me most as I lolled comfortably on the feed bags was the prodigality of outhouses. Every home had one adjacent, and this seemed to me to be a luxury beyond all reason. I rather hoped that Mike and I would live in a house with its own little outbuilding in matching architecture.

As Mike had predicted, Mrs. Hunt was delighted to see us.

After she had introduced us to her widowed sister, Mrs. Cartwright, who owned the house, she did a good deal of crying. At length she got hold of herself and asked about people at The Cascades, and particularly of Lawrence Coe. She had been helping her share of the expenses by doing sewing. It had been only two years since I had seen her, but she had grown much older. Her face was thin, and before she spoke her lips would tremble a little.

"Vicky should be in from school any minute," she said, and then she looked out of the window anxiously.

"And how is she?" asked Mike. "Growin' like a bad weed?"

I thought that Mrs. Hunt looked uncomfortably at me. "Yes . . . she's growing." She turned her half bewildered gaze to Mike again. "It's hard, raising a girl here. Sometimes I wish I'd stayed in The Cascades."

"But sure you don't, Mrs. Hunt! There's a good school here and she can get educated."

"I never went to school," said Mrs. Hunt firmly. "But my mother had me cooking and sewing when I was as old as Victoria." She sighed. "I could run a house as good as my mother when I was Victoria's age."

"But things are different now," Mike pointed out. "You take me and Caleb. I could stay in the Army all my life, and Caleb could stay down at The Cascades working in the store."

Mrs. Hunt nodded bravely at this progressiveness. "With men and boys it's different. But Vicky—well, she's a strong-willed one, and with no father. I have trouble with her getting down on the street and listening to the talk of the men. . . ."

Her worried monotone was interrupted by the arrival of Vicky herself, and as she entered the room my mouth grew so dry I wondered if I would be able to speak.

Vicky was tall—taller than I, and this caused me excruciating embarrassment when her mother pointed out the fact to Mike. Victoria smiled at Mike and me, and shook our hands, but I could see that something had changed her. Perhaps it was living in a town, or perhaps it was going to school, but certainly she felt herself superior. Piqued, I said roughly, "I don't see how you can live in a country like this."

"What's wrong with it?"

"There aren't enough trees."

"At The Cascades that's all there is, trees," said Victoria Hunt. "I like living in a town. It's exciting."

That stopped me completely. Satisfied, Vicky flounced into a chair and, totally ignoring Mike and me, began thumbing through a book which she had brought home from school. Her dark hair was parted directly in the middle and brought down on each side to a pig-tail which terminated in a tiny tightly tied bow. Occasionally, and very absently, she would toss one of these pig-tails aside, but it would always fall back again precisely where it had been. The continued gesture annoyed me and I wanted to tell her that her hair made her look like an Indian. Only the fragile appearance of Mrs. Hunt restrained me.

Mike and I promised to visit them often when, as Mike said, we got settled. "We're staying at Ed Danby's boarding house right now," he told Mrs. Hunt. "But when I get settled I'm going to build a house."

We started down the dusty slope toward Front Street. When we were out of earshot of the Hunts I asked Mike whether we would have an outhouse on our new property.

"Sure," he said, "we'll be having as fine a one as there is in Dalles City."

But we stayed on in Danby's boarding house, and Mike had trouble getting settled in business. He soon decided against setting up a newspaper. It was not exactly because *The State Journal* was having meager going as it was. That simple fact would never have deterred Mike. He would have thought nothing of competing with another newspaper, even in a town so small. The difficulty, I began to realize, was that Mike actually knew nothing at all of the printing business, and less still about newspapers. It was true that his father had been a printer, but Mike Shea had left home long before he was old enough to learn what movable type really looked like.

I did not know these things until we had been in Dalles City a week or more. Mike's announcement that he was going to start a newspaper had been an inspiration as he talked with Lawrence Coe about taking me away. And when he had got to Dalles City and the Danbys asked him his plans, now that he was out of the Army, he had simply carried on the illusion. I do not believe that he did it to impress me. He had begun to believe a little of it himself.

There was something else I did not realize at the time. Mike hadn't enough capital to found a newspaper or, in fact, much of anything else. He had been in the service a long time, but on leave he had spent his wages wildly. The money he managed to take from the Army upon his discharge was barely enough to keep us for a month.

I did not blame Mike Shea for his bad planning. He was neither stupid nor devious, but simply an Irishman possessed of a boundless confidence in himself and a faith that things would come out to his advantage. The Army life had, of course, contributed to these characteristics in the man. He had quarreled with his father when he was twelve, and stolidly and stubbornly left the town of his birth to work on farms until he was sixteen. Then he joined the Army, and stayed with it until he was thirty-seven years old—too old, really, to think of leaving it. I do not believe he would ever have left the Army if it had not been for my being made an orphan.

In the Army he had been an alert young private, and he was smart as he grew older in the service. But at twenty-five he was already a veteran who had learned all the tricks of doing one's duty with the minimum of effort, and had lost all real ambition to gain a promotion. Gradually he had come to like being ordered about, and told what to do. On his leaves he could express himself and give orders to other people—and in his battles he could kill Indians. I can well imagine that the victor of a hundred brawls and a man who has escaped death in a score of Indian skirmishes begins to feel that he has something of the immortal in him.

But against the practical life of Dalles City he grew puzzled. At The Cascades I had never known him to be moody, but there were moments in Dalles City when I would catch him staring out of the Danby's window at the river, or looking blankly at the wall.

I grew to pretend that I had not seen him in one of these lapses, for whenever I did he would straighten his shoulders and put on such a blast of courageous, blustering talk that I felt ashamed for him.

He stopped taking me with him on his walks along Front Street, and when he returned I would smell whiskey. He would tell the Danbys and me how he had been looking things over. "I talked with Bert Patterson this afternoon. He wants me to buy into his livery business, and I don't know but what it's all right. But he wants a little too much for a half interest. I guess he thinks I'm a fool because I was in the Army."

In a month, though, he had stopped talking about buying into establishments, and there was a noticeable difference in the attitude of Mrs. Danby toward him. She had treated him as a paying guest who must be politely suffered. Now she began to sniff ostentatiously at the aroma of whiskey which hovered around Mike, making queer noises when he told tales of talking with Dalles City merchants. One night she said pointedly, "I should think you'd be taking any job until you decide what you want to be doing."

That stopped Mike for a moment, but at last he said, "It's not a job I want. It's my own business. Something I can bring up Caleb in."

Then one night, after I had gone to bed, I heard Ed Danby talking to Mike outside our door. "It's not that I'm worried," old Danby said. " 'He's always paid,' I told her, 'and I figure he always will.' But you know how she is, Mike, and she says you got to get a job and pay something or you'll have to leave. She says she'd have said it before except for the young one."

"You tell her to be doing her own worrying, and I'll do mine," the Irishman said. But when he came into the room he did not light the lamp, and his figure was slumped and old. I pretended I was asleep as I watched his huge bulk motionless in the rocker for at least an hour.

It hurt me to see him. I wished that we had never come to Dalles City, and I wondered what was to become of both of us. I began to hate Mrs. Danby with all my heart. But I knew that she had no money with which to be feeding a couple of eaters like Mike and me.

At last Mike had to give in. He took a job with Bert Patterson at the livery stable, which was no doubt what Bert had wanted him to do when Mike talked so grandly about buying a half interest. And he seemed happy enough at it, although he still talked of getting into a business I could learn and take over when he died. He spent a good deal of time at the Army post on the hill, yarning with cronies he had served with in other days.

That autumn I started to school. Vicky Hunt was ahead of me, but I did not mind this so much. Most of the boys of my age had made little more progress than I. None of them stressed intellectual achievements to any degree, and I quickly established a reputation by relating my experiences in the Indian fight at The Cascades. Heretofore Victoria Hunt had held this honor alone, and she dared not deny any of my slightly embroidered tales for fear I would give the lie to some of her own versions of what had happened there.

It was a two-room school in a slab-sided building set between the river bank and the Army post. There were about sixty pupils, divided not so much by age or aptitude as by their willingness to conform to regimentation. Both Vicky and I were in the conservative room, but I could not hope to attain her abilities at figures and reading. Mr. Harrington, the schoolmaster, was a worried looking wart of a man with an ungovernable temper and very little enthusiasm for his work. He would teach one room while the students in the other did sums or practiced their reading. But they, being the recalcitrants, frequently became noisy, disturbing us at our recitations. When this happened, Mr. Harrington would dodge into the other room, very quickly, so that his coat-tails whirled, and deliver a harsh lecture which quieted the rebels for a while and set up a tittering on our side of the partition. It was not a very excellent arrangement for either pupil or teacher.

Once or twice a week I would walk home with Vicky Hunt on my way to Danby's boarding house, and Mrs. Hunt would ask me into the kitchen for a piece of gingerbread. When the days grew longer, and I could loiter without getting home after dark—Mrs. Danby disapproved late hours—I would stay and play with Victoria. Like most girls, she was delighted when she could trap a boy into playing house with her. I do not say that I endured it. Rather I suspect that I enjoyed it. Most of the boys I knew at school lived on the hill, and while I was never made to feel it directly I suppose that their mothers were a little hesitant about having them invite home an orphan who lived with a bachelor ex-trooper from The Cascades.

Although her mother was nice to me, Vicky still held herself slightly superior, and the fact of my residence in Dalles City had not softened her on this point. She ordered me about ruthlessly, and half the time our "play acting" ended in a noisy row with me trudging down the hill, bitterly promising that I would never see her again. Once Mrs. Hunt got me off into a corner and explained that it was perfectly natural for little girls to want little boys to do things their way, and that little boys, if they were also little gentlemen, always did them without complaining. This theory seemed to me wholly unfair, and I resented what seemed to be a conspiracy between Vicky and her mother. But I was willing to conform to the world if I could, and thereafter I got along better with Victoria.

I must say that I was fascinated by her imagination. My own ingenuity did not stretch to great lengths. I could suggest that we pretend a dry goods case was a steamboat and that, standing inside it, we were captain and pilot, going up a dangerous stretch of the river. Or I might insist, mildly, that Victoria pretend she was a string of mules and I the skinner, carrying supplies from the river landing to the Army post. But Victoria regarded these fancies as insipid and vulgar and only when she was in a very good humor would she have anything to do with them.

She never said, as I did, "Let's *play* that we are such-and-such." "We are at the Army post," she would say, "and it is night. There is a big dance and you and I are dancing." She would think this over a moment, and add, "I am very beautiful."

I was willing to accept the fact of her beauty, but I could not pretend to dance. "Then we will just stand together and that will be dancing." Victoria would say. "Now—there is a soldier who wants to dance with me, and that makes you mad."

"That's crazy," I would say. "What if he does want to dance with you?"

"You get mad. His name is Lieutenant MacPherson and you and him have a fight."

It was hard going, but I went through with it. "You can't dance with this lady," I would say, and swing hard at my imaginary adversary. That part was fun. I would just get well into the battle when Victoria would interrupt coldly. "Now the Captain has you arrested. I am the Captain. We will have a military trial, like Colonel Wright had for the Indians at The Cascades, and you will have to be shot."

It was very difficult, following Victoria's changes from a lovely sought-after lady into a gruff and ruthless Captain, but with a little practice I began to get the hang of it. As I became more adept, I even enjoyed it. Sometimes, when she went into a male rôle and began abusing me I would get out of hand, and with good-natured energy take her down and sit on her, pretending to flail her wildly with my fists. This was always a mistake. She would grow cold and regal, or burst into tears—and either reaction spoiled the fun.

I don't know where she got her ideas for the scenes we played, but I think there was a good deal of gossip in the Hunt household about the goings-on at the Army dances and that Victoria overheard it. There were many young belles in Dalles City and between them and the officers there was naturally an attraction.

Victoria had one sure way to squelch me when I got out of hand. That was to remind me of a weakness in Mike. I think that whenever she got tired of playing with me, and wanted the thing to end, she would bring Mike into the conversation in a disparaging way. And one day she hit upon a spot that was particularly sore.

"I thought you and Mike were going into business," she remarked suddenly.

"We are. Mike wants to wait until I get finished with school, that's all."

"So he's brushing horses until you do!"

Mrs. Danby must have been talking to Vicky's mother. "What's wrong with brushing horses?"

"Well, then I suppose there's nothing wrong with spending all your spare time in a saloon, the way your old Mike Shea does."

That remark did not anger me. It puzzled me. I had never thought about there being anything wrong with spending spare time in a saloon. In fact, I assumed that this was the purpose of a saloon, to consume spare time. Certainly that was the attitude of Dalles City, and it had been the attitude of all the men I had known. I'd never heard a woman express an opinion on the subject —until now.

"I guess there's nothing wrong with a saloon," I said. "If there was, there wouldn't be so many of them in Dalles City, would there?"

"Well, your friend Mike spends all the rest of his time with Lottie Moore."

"Who is Lottie Moore?" I asked, and then wished I had slit my tongue. I wouldn't for the world have let Vicky know I wasn't acquainted with all Mike Shea's friends.

"Mother says she's a bad woman."

I explained to Victoria Hunt that Mike Shea didn't mind bad people. "He always says that none of us are as good as we think we are," I added very pointedly. "So I'll bet Lottie Moore isn't as bad as you think she is, either."

I do not say that Vicky accepted this, but it stopped her from further reference to Mike on that occasion.

I did not ask Mike about Lottie Moore, but Vicky's remark worried me considerably. I wondered if he planned to marry her, and whether, if he did, I would have to be like a son to her. I wanted very much to see her, but since I did not know where she lived, and dared not ask, this was impractical. Some time soon, I told myself, Mike would tell me all about it.

Yet the days went on, and Mike never mentioned anyone named Lottie Moore. In fact, I began to see less and less of Mike. He was on duty late at Patterson's Livery Stable, and sometimes he did not come back to the boarding house at all. When he did, he slept long after I had departed for school. But I always stopped in at Patterson's on my way home, and this was the part of the day I liked best of all. It reminded me of the days when I had visited Mike at the blockhouse down at The Cascades. He was always as glad to see me as ever, and would listen proudly while, after his quizzing, I would tell him what had been accomplished at school.

"And what did you find out up there today, boy?"

"Mr. Harrington told us about the cable they're laying clear across the Atlantic."

"And now what would that be for? To run the ships on?"

"No. It's on the bottom of the ocean. It's so they can telegraph from one country to the other, clear across the ocean."

"What will they be thinking of next, I wonder? And who would be doing all this?"

"A man named Cyrus W. Field, Mr. Harrington said. It's from Valencia, Ireland—"

"Sure, I knew the Irish would be in it!"

"And the other end is at Trinity Bay, Newfoundland."

"Newfoundland?" said Mike, "and where might that be?"

I didn't know. It was always like that. Mike would keep on asking questions until there was something Mr. Harrington hadn't told us. I began to be very dubious about the completeness of Mr. Harrington's knowledge. After all, Mike Shea was just an average person, not a teacher, and if he could ask questions which Mr. Harrington hadn't prepared me for, what kind of a teacher was Mr. Harrington?

I'd have to build up another defense with another piece of learning, however irrelevant. "Mr. Harrington says the cables may be landed by this time."

Mike would let me off then. "That's fine. It's a smart lad you're getting to be. When we go into business you'll be the one to run it. Me, I'll just sit back and wear fine clothes and talk to the customers while the money rolls in."

Mike's job at Patterson's was fair enough, and I suppose some money did roll in. But it rolled out again, too, from Mike's widespread fingers. We were forever behind with Mrs. Danby and she was increasingly grim about it. I began to lose my liking for her, despite the fact that she plied me with food and seemed to worry about me. I could not like her as long as she disapproved of Mike, and I did not care for the way she took everything out of Ed Danby's hands. I think my dislike began when I learned that she had made Ed Danby stop going out on the river in his bateau. It did not seem right to me that a man who had been on the river should be reduced to helping around a boarding house operated by a woman.

Sometimes after dinner, when Mrs. Danby was occupied with the dishes and there were no other boarders for Ed Danby to entertain, I would ask him to tell me again about the time his bateau had broken up. He enjoyed it as much as I, and it grew to be quite a tale, a little better each time.

One night when he had finished, I asked suddenly, "Ed, who is Lottie Moore?"

He looked at me queerly. "Where did you hear of her?" I noticed that he did not repeat the name, and glanced apprehensively toward the kitchen door.

"They were talking about her up at school."

"Up at school?" Ed seemed astonished.

"Yes," I insisted. "Who is she?"

"Oh, she's a—a woman who lives in town."

"Does Mike know her?"

Ed Danby looked uncomfortable. "I don't know as he does. What say we go out and set on the back stoop and watch the old river a while before you go to bed?"

CHAPTER

8

LAWRENCE COE came up to Dalles City on Christmas eve.

He brought a young fir with him on the *Mary*, and set it up in Mrs. Danby's parlor for a Christmas tree. He brought me a pair of Indian moccasins, and Mike a four-bladed jack-knife. And when he found that Mike and I had been with the Danbys ever since we arrived in town, he went out and bought gifts for them, too; a whole bolt of dress goods for Mrs. Danby and a flannel shirt for Ed.

Mike wasn't home when Lawrence Coe arrived. I was sure that he would have been if he had known Coe was coming, but Mrs. Danby was of a different opinion. "We haven't seen hide or hair of him for four days," she explained. "No doubt he began celebrating Christmas a little aforetime."

"Now, Martha," Ed remonstrated. "Mike will be along."

Lawrence Coe looked at me, but I couldn't meet his glance. I think he knew the moment he saw my face that it had been going on this way, and getting worse, and that there wasn't anything certain about Mike being there.

"Come on along," he said to me. "Get on your cap and jacket and we'll find Mike. I'll bet a dollar we'll find him loading himself with Christmas presents."

"I think Caleb ought to stay here," Mrs. Danby said. "No telling where you may have to go to find Mike—"

Coe cut her off with a jovial laugh. "Caleb and I have been through a lot together. We won't mind."

I rushed to get my wraps and soon we were out in the snow of Front Street. Every place of business was still lighted, and from down the street came the sound of celebrating. For a moment Coe did not start out, but stood there looking at me.

"Say, son—is everything all right?"

"Sure, Mr. Coe."

"You've been going to school?"

"Yes."

"Getting plenty to eat?"

"Yes."

"Like it all right at Danbys?"

I nodded.

"And you and Mike get along fine?"

"You bet."

"All right . . . let's see if we can find that wild Indian."

Coe had heard in The Cascades that Mike was working for Patterson, and we went there first. But Bert Patterson hadn't seen him for two days. "I don't mind," he told Coe. "It's Christmas week."

"Got any idea where he'd be?"

"He was in Delkin's saloon this morning. If he ain't there now you might see up at The Golden Rule. A bunch of the boys were going to put on a party for the girls."

Coe took hold of my arm. "Do you know which place is Delkin's?"

I was proud to show off my knowledge of the town. I took him directly to Delkin's. Mike had been there an hour before, purchased a stock of liquors, and left. We went out into the cold again.

"He's probably lost all track of time," Coe said. "But we'll remind him, won't we?"

I didn't much want to ferret Mike out, because I felt he might be embarrassed when he saw Lawrence Coe with me, and both of us searching for him. But there was nothing to do but go along. We plodded on down the board sidewalk. In front of each shop the snow was neatly scraped into banks. But before the empty places along the street our feet crunched along the ravines of well marked paths. Down to the end of Front Street we trudged, walking abreast before the shops and dropping into single file for the paths. Soon we stood in front of the two-story building where I had seen the pretty woman staring from an upstairs window.

From inside came the sound of a piano and many voices—and above everything I heard Mike's laugh booming from wall to wall. There were women's voices among them, and this was not the same kind of a noise I had heard often coming from the saloons late at night. This was gayer and more intimate, with an undercurrent of something I was beginning to understand at last.

"You wait here, Caleb," Lawrence Coe said.

I stood in the snow, hunching my chin down inside the collar of my jacket, and watched Coe disappear into The Golden Rule. Somehow I expected the piano to stop, but it did not. The singing and the laughing, too, continued. But as I listened I heard Mike's voice cut off suddenly.

Presently the door opened and Coe stepped into the snow with Mike Shea. Mike's face was very red, and his eyes looked queer. "Hello there, Caleb," he said. And then, haltingly, "M-merry Christmas."

"Merry Christmas, Mike."

"Never expected to see Larry Coe." Mike tried to get his voice to booming again, and slapped Coe on the back. Then the three of us went up the street, saying nothing. At first I thought Mike was a little angry at Coe, but possibly he was only drunk and very tired. Once he scraped some snow from a window ledge and rubbed his wet hand over his face. But by the time we reached the Danbys, he seemed something like his old self, and greeted the Danbys with a cheerful "Merry Christmas!"

"And where," asked Mrs. Danby, "did you find the man?"

"At Delkin's," said Coe shortly.

Mrs. Danby had prepared a fine dinner. There was baked salmon, roast chicken, roasted potatoes, and butter beans. She knew that it was a fine dinner—and was insulted to think that Mike was so drunk he wouldn't realize it was a fine dinner. Danby and Coe did most of the talking. I kept quiet, and Mike sat there as if he were stunned. Whenever I looked at him he was glancing at me guiltily, or his eyes were veering fearfully away from Martha Danby.

"That wine I brought," said Coe to her. "Have you forgotten it, Mrs. Danby?"

Mrs. Danby was loathe to bring the bottle to the table, but there was little else she could do. She not only objected to wine at her board, but she believed that Mike had had enough to drink. Reluctantly she brought in the bottle and glasses and Coe poured wine for everyone, even a little for me. Mike took half his at a gulp and perked up a little.

"And now," said Coe, beaming, "let us drink to a new enterprise."

We all looked at him. "I'm leaving The Cascades," he said. "I've a scheme that's either going to make or break me." Coe looked around the table, enjoying this moment before he sprung the news. "Well," he went on, drawling it provocatively, "I'm going in with a fellow named Thompson to build a steamboat to run from Deschutes to a little way below the old Hudson's Bay post."

If he had said he was planning to build a flying machine for the same purpose we would have been only a little more astonished. It was a long way from the Deschutes River mouth above town to the old fort, and if ever a stretch of water seemed unsuited to a steamboat, it was that one. Only a few bateaux and sailing craft, and Indian canoes, had made the trip, and never very satisfactorily. The only practical connection between there and Dalles City was along the river bank by way of the little toll bridge which Victor Trevitt had built across the Deschutes.

"You can't get a steamer up there, Mr. Coe," said Ed Danby flatly.

"We're going to try," Coe was all smiles, pleased pink with the consternation he had created. "Yes, sir—they've been up there in sail, and we figure that steam will go anywhere that sail will take a boat. And if that's not a fact, then steam and sail together ought to do it. So we're going to rig a squaresail on her and get the regular upriver trades along with our engine power."

Ed Danby wrinkled his forehead, trying to picture the possibilities. "I don't hardly see the point, even if you could get the darned boat up there. There ain't much freight between here and there."

"There's some," mentioned Coe imperturbably. "And those sailing barges are getting a hundred and fifty dollars a ton for taking it fifteen miles. We figure we could do it for eighty or ninety dollars—so that ought to encourage more of it. And there will be more. Steptoeville is getting to be quite a settlement, and the only way to that country is through here."

Danby was still not convinced. "There ain't a stick of wood bigger than your thumb east of here."

"I know that. But the boat will be built to carry all the fuel she'll need from here. We can pay up to ten dollars a cord, and come out on top."

Mike had been silent through all this. I knew what he was thinking: that he had planned to come to Dalles City and do big things —and now Coe was really going to do something big, as casually as though any man in the world could get such an idea and carry it through. I could see Mike fighting with his envy. "What are you going to call her?" he asked, at last.

"The *Colonel Wright*," Coe said. "I figure we ought to name her for the man who saved our lives at The Cascades."

I was so excited over Coe's news that I completely forgot the plum pudding. I threw a dozen questions at him, one after the other, until he protested that there were a lot of things I'd have to wait to see. "You can watch her building up on the Deschutes," he said.

"Look, Mike," I said, "there'll be a portage road at Dalles City, too, just like at The Cascades. We can ride on the cars."

Mike nodded dully. "Sure, boy. Ride on the portage cars."

"I still don't see—" began Ed Danby, and then stopped suddenly. Mike Shea had slid out of his chair and dropped heavily to the floor. Coe and Danby and I were beside him at once. Above us, Mrs. Danby cried, "Never under a roof of mine has it happened!"

Mike sat up almost as soon as he had fallen. He followed the carpet design with glazed eyes. "Got to get some sleep," he said.

"Yes," Coe agreed. He lifted the Irishman under the arms and walked him to our bedroom. As he closed the door we heard

Mike's solid body hit the springs.

"I declare, I never . . ." began Mrs. Danby. But she got no further, for Coe interrupted with talk of his steamer. I listened to him and Ed Danby until I had grown as vague and groggy as Mike and had to be sent to bed.

Softly I went into the room. Mike lay across the foot of the bed, snoring. I undressed quietly, put a blanket over Mike, and slid between the sheets. Fortunately my lack of stature allowed me to take a natural position in the bed without disturbing Mike.

It was some time after midnight when I was awakened. Mike had lifted my head and shoulders from the pillow and his arms were around me tightly. He was sobbing, sobbing so terribly that I was frightened.

"Mike! What's wrong, Mike?"

"Your Christmas present . . ." He could hardly talk. "I—I meant to get you one. I didn't forget it, even when we were coming back with Coe. But I didn't have any money and I didn't want to borrow any from Coe."

"I don't want any present, Mike. Anyhow, Lawrence Coe bought me a pair of moccasins."

He broke into uncontrolled paroxysms again. "But I didn't get you one. Me, who should have got you the finest present a boy ever had."

I didn't answer. I was too frightened and too sorry for poor Mike. "What was I doing?" he asked, torturing himself into new grief. "I was spending money in whoring and drinking and carousing. That's what I was doing."

"Look, Mike. It's all right. I didn't want you to get me anything. You brought me to Dalles City. You been taking care of me and sending me to school."

He searched my eyes in the half light, his face horribly distorted from loss of sleep, drinking, and grief. "I know," he said, "but that don't make it right. On Christmas . . ." He stopped. "On Christmas," he began again, and then heaved a great tired sigh. "Oh, God," he said, "I'm no good," and threw himself down on the bed again with his face in his hands.

I did not touch him. I wanted very much to try again to explain that I didn't care about his forgetting the present. But I didn't want to start that sobbing again. Carefully I slid down against my pillow, hoping that Mike would go back to sleep. At last his snores resumed, rhythmically.

I had never seen a grown man sobbing, and it was a terrible revelation. I did not know then that sometimes a man will cry when he is drunk. But this knowledge would not have helped me very much, because with it I would have known, too, that his tragedy is none the less deep because he is drunk.

CHAPTER 9

LAWRENCE COE did not stay on at Mrs. Danby's. As befitted one who had business, he transferred himself to the Umatilla House the day after Christmas, and he stayed in Dalles City all that spring to supervise the building of the *Colonel Wright* and the portage road from below The Dalles Rapids to the mouth of the Deschutes, above Celilo Falls. The portage road he began immediately, for it aided in the construction of the steamer by bringing materials from Dalles City much of which, in turn, had been brought from Portland.

The Deschutes is a turbulent and cranky little stream before it reaches the Columbia. But when it comes within sight of that great, majestic river it is ashamed for having made so much fuss. Quite suddenly it grows mannerly, broadens out to go quietly and be taken up by the Columbia. In flood seasons, its delta waters cover a comparatively wide area. Consequently there is a spot of pleasant meadow land at this point on the upper river.

It was here, on the west bank of the Deschutes, just a stone's throw from Trevitt's toll bridge, that Coe began the building of the *Colonel Wright*. I was there on the Saturday the keel was laid, and from then on I thought of little else than the steamer. The keel was a beautiful piece of Douglas fir, a hundred and ten feet long, which had been brought through the Strait of Juan de Fuca and down the rough coast and over the treacherous bar of the Columbia to Astoria. There it had been carefully transferred to a river boat and taken to The Cascades, trundled over the portage road to the upriver steamer and brought to Dalles City. No shipment of jewels had ever been watched more than that stick of rough fir, and I could hardly wait until I saw what manner of vessel would grow from it.

But to wait I was forced. The boat ways were too long a hike from town for me to go there after school and get back in time for Mrs. Danby's supper. During the first two months I had to confine my visits to Saturdays and Sundays. But when the portage road was completed, I was often able to get a ride on a load of lumber or nails and go in style to the site of the building of the *Colonel Wright*.

My attention to Mr. Harrington wavered so markedly that he put me into the room with the recalcitrants, believing I was rebelling in a new and effective way of my own. I no longer walked home with Victoria Hunt, for then I might miss the afternoon departure of the portage wagon which was sure to be loading some new and fascinating piece of equipment for the steamboat. I had calculated to a foot the shortest distance between the school house and a point along the river bank where I could watch the passing of the mule-drawn wagon.

Building a steamer on the bank of the upper river was not a sinecure. There were no marine supplies to be found nearer than Portland, and for a boat like the *Wright* most of them had to be ordered from San Francisco or brought around Cape Horn. Further, there were few men in Dalles City who were experienced in the building of water craft. The boilers and the engine had to be taken down at the iron works in 'Frisco and then set up again when they arrived at the Deschutes.

I was so fascinated with the creation of the steamboat that I wanted to share the experience with Victoria Hunt, and one Sunday afternoon I obtained the permission of her mother to take her to the bank of the Deschutes to see where the frame was rising. Mrs. Hunt prepared a packet of gingerbread and gave us a lard-pail filled with milk to carry. We started out gaily enough, striding down the slope toward the town, and east along the river bank past the falls and the Indian village. Then Vicky professed to grow tired.

"Let's don't go to see the old boat," she said. "Let's just sit here and eat our gingerbread."

"But you've got to see the boat, Victoria," I said. "You won't know how grand she is until you see her."

"An old boat," said Victoria. "Who wants to see an old boat?" Then she sat down on the prairie grass and refused to move. I had to agree we ought to eat the gingerbread then and there before she would move another inch. We ate all the gingerbread and drank some of the milk, and put the pail in the stream to cool it for our return. First I washed off some stones, to weigh the bucket down against the current, and put them into the pail. Then I nested it in the pebbles of the river, close to the bank.

"Now come on," I said to Victoria. "I'll show you the boat. Some day I'm going to be captain of her."

"Look," said Victoria, "you are an Indian chief and I am a beautiful girl. I am the wife of a Major in the Army and you are taking me to your village to make me the queen of your tribe."

"All right," I said, screwing my face into an expression which I hoped made me look like an Indian chief. "Get along there. I'm taking you as a prisoner. I want you to be the queen of my tribe."

That was the way I got Victoria to see the partially built steamboat. But when we were there she sniffed at the naked ribs of the *Wright*. "Think of it, Vick! That boat is going up the river—there's never been a steamboat up there." I was using both Lawrence Coe's words and tone, but I was fired by them and I hoped to excite Victoria.

I was not very successful, and her lack of interest made me angry. I thought of leaving her, as punishment for her contrariness, forcing her to make her way back to town alone. But I didn't. She looked at me with her dark, wide, defiant eyes—and I could feel nothing but admiration for her willfulness. I have observed since then that there are little girls who possess a power over men of all ages and who continue its use so much that it becomes a habit for which they cannot really be condemned. They have a power that has come to them naturally, and they use it naturally. They think no more of using that power than a bird thinks of using its wings to fly.

Soon I realized that the *Colonel Wright* was to make the *Mary* and the *Wasco* appear like Indian canoes by comparison. She was almost twice as long as the *Mary,* and twenty-four feet at the beam. She'd carry fifty tons of freight, beside her wood for fuel, and accommodate twelve passengers in a style never attempted on the *Mary.*

The *Colonel Wright,* in fact, was equipped with a dining room, and there would be a steward to see that the passengers were taken care of as to food and comfort. She was a side-wheeler, but as Coe had promised, she was fitted with a tall mast forward upon which could be run up a sizable squaresail.

When I was not getting into the way of the workmen, or plaguing Coe with questions, or tearing my shirt and breeches on unfinished joiner work, I sat in the shadow of the vessel and dreamed of what it would be like to be her master. I knew from the talk in town that it would be the captain, as well as the boat, who would make the Coe and Thompson venture a success or failure.

It was a great day for me when I first saw the man who would be at the wheel of the *Colonel Wright.* It was a Saturday and I had got to the Deschutes very soon after daybreak. But this was not too early for the workmen. On the hurricane deck Coe was talking with a tall blonde man who wore short-clipped chin whiskers. He was not more than thirty, yet he carried himself with the neat dignity of Coe, and from the proprietary way he surveyed the *Colonel Wright* I suspected at once that he must be her captain. In Dalles City they were saying that he would get a salary of five hundred dollars a month—if he didn't wreck the vessel on her maiden trip.

Coe looked down and saw me staring open mouthed. "Come on up, Caleb, if you want to meet a real river captain."

I climbed over the scaffolding to the bow, and hurried toward the hurricane deck. Coe towered above me, but this blonde giant dwarfed us both. His glance was friendly, and I liked him at once.

"Caleb, this is Captain Len White. He's going to be in command of the *Colonel Wright.*"

The great man held out his hand. "How are you, son?" I was speechless. Coe laughed. "Caleb wants to be a river pilot, Len, and I reckon he's overcome."

"Will you take me on her first trip?" I blurted out.

White considered this. Then: "We'll have to see about that." He smiled at Coe. "Maybe, Lawrence, the *second* trip would be better."

I followed White around most of that day. I knew all about him, from both friends and detractors in Dalles City. Len White was one of the first men in Oregon to devote himself to river navigation, and he had the thing that could never be taught—an ability to "feel" his way up an uncharted stream. The Willamette was where he had started, and when he took his first command, Albany was the head of navigation. Soon, apparently with little difficulty, White pushed it to Corvallis. Then, still not content, he had run the *Phenix* as far as Harrisburg.

For weeks now he had been traveling the Columbia from Deschutes north in an old Hudson's Bay bateau studying the river, trying this channel and that, taking soundings, making hourly calculations of the winds. I had heard that he could draw a perfect chart of that stretch of the river from memory, and when I looked at the broad, well-shaped head and keen eyes, I could believe it.

I saw him often, after that, as the *Colonel Wright* took on her finishing touches, and I grew aware that Len White had his eccentricities as well as his talents. He was, for one thing, a champion of the theory of phonetic spelling.

"You go to school at Dalles City, don't you?" he asked me one day.

I said that I did.

"How do they teach you to spell 'fight'?"

I spelled it for him, wondering what he was getting at. Instantly he made a sound of disgust. "Silliest damned thing I ever heard. F-i-t-e is the way it ought to be spelled. Things ought to be spelled the way they sound. That's called phonetic spelling, and by God they even got to spell 'phonetic' wrong—with a p-h instead of an f."

I agreed with him, even though I was disturbed by the recklessness of an adult who questioned the way words were printed in the spelling book.

"Do you know what? Some day I'm going to own a vessel of my own, and I'm going to call her *Cayuse*. And do you know how *Cayuse* ought to be spelled? It ought to be *Kyuse*, and that's how I'm going to spell it. Paint it on her bow in letters a foot high."

I never knew whether Len White's interest in phonetic spelling was sincere or whether it was to cover up a personal weakness in orthography. Along the river there were two schools of thought on the subject, and White took considerable jibing in complete serenity.

He did not mind being joshed, and indeed he may not have always realized that he was. His greatest tormentor was Vic Trevitt, the Dalles City saloon keeper and owner of the toll bridge; a tall, shrewd Southerner who had early seen money to be made from a structure across the Deschutes. A good many pack animals and wagons trailed along the river bank into the upper country, and fording the swift little stream was dangerous and damaging. So Trevitt had built his bridge and levied toll—and if the *Colonel Wright* was successful it meant the finish of his enterprise.

Trevitt was a gentleman, and good natured about the whole thing, but he did not hestitate to do his doubting orally. He would often stroll down to where the steamer was building and make deprecatory remarks about her appearance, and offer dire predictions as to what would happen to her when she reached the Umatilla Rapids. His quiet, insinuating talk nettled Lawrence Coe, but Captain White remained unruffled.

"You know, Len," Trevitt said one day, gazing at the mast the workmen were stepping into the *Colonel Wright*, "up there by the John Day the wind blows all ways at once. What'll you do then? The boat will just stand still, that's what she'll do. There'll be equal pressure on both sides of the sail, and your packet will just stand there."

"We'll give her more steam, Vic."

"But the current's funny in there. No matter how much steam you get up, the current'll do you one better. Yes sir, Len, she'll just stand still."

When nothing else seemed to take effect, Trevitt would offer to wager White the latter's first month's salary that the *Colonel Wright* couldn't make it to the Walla Walla river. White at last broke down under this, for his salary was a matter of particular pride to him. One day he turned to Trevitt and said, "Maybe you don't know what I'll be getting."

"I don't care what it is," Trevitt said. "I'll meet it. Shucks, Len, I'd bet a hundred on that, just as soon as not."

That was the spark to set the powder off, and Trevitt knew it. "A hundred!" said White, drawing up to his full height. "My salary is five hundred a month, and I'll bet you the first five hundred that she does make it."

"Very well," said Victor Trevitt. "It's a bet, sir."

But the day after the *Colonel Wright* finally departed, Victor Trevitt sold his toll bridge—even before he had heard the outcome of the trip.

CHAPTER 10

THERE were people in Dalles City who believed sincerely that Coe and Thompson were crazy. They admitted that the ocean steamers putting into Portland were doing an increasing business, and that it was desirable to have the river boats go further east than Dalles City. But they could not bring themselves to believe that it was possible. The vast lands spreading from the upper Columbia had been, to many of them, as inaccessible as the wilds of Africa—and now came two men who talked of taking passengers and freight from Steptoeville to Portland in hardly more than thirty hours!

To my surprise, Mike Shea joined the doubters. When I discovered this I began to realize what a change was coming over him. At The Cascades he had been a happy man, full of optimism and with as much enterprise as a private in the Army is allowed. In those days he had believed nothing impossible. It was wholly foreign to his old nature to doubt the success of the new boat. Too, Lawrence Coe was his friend of long standing. And Mike was wholly unqualified to give an opinion on whether a steamboat could navigate the upper river. Yet, hour after hour, he could be found in front of Patterson's livery stable with a group of scoffers—for by now the town's chief topic was the *Colonel Wright*.

He did not forbid me to visit the *Wright*, but I could see that he liked it less and less. Consequently I stopped talking about the boat, or Coe and Captain White, when I was with Mike. I disliked doing this, for Mike and I had always talked together about what interested us. I felt somehow disloyal to Mike, but the attraction of the steamboat was too strong to be denied.

Naturally Coe was aware of the destructive criticism in Dalles City, and when the time came to test the *Colonel Wright* he made no show about it. He invited two or three men from Portland, and half a dozen from The Cascades. The rest were from Dalles City. Captain White was not anxious to have many passengers, and Lawrence Coe did not invite more because he wanted no skeptics aboard.

I knew, of course, when the vessel was to leave, and I resolved I would somehow be aboard. Nothing could keep me from it—not school, and not even Mike Shea. I had dared not press my ambition further with Coe and Len White, for I feared that at the last moment they would tell me to wait. So I said nothing to anyone, and I prayed that Mike would not come home on the night before the sailing.

My prayers were answered, and at midnight I slipped out of bed and dressed. The Danbys were the soundest of sleepers and I anticipated no difficulty in getting out of the house. Nevertheless, just to make doubly sure of my success, I slipped out the window frame from the bedroom, and took the long drop from the ledge to the soft mud of the river bank, sinking over my ankles in the slime. Each step I took caused a high sucking sound that seemed to be loud enough to wake even Mrs. Danby. Slowly I made my way along the side of the house and up to Front Street. In the darkness I sat down and with a stick removed the heavy mud from my feet. Then I started hurriedly east, bound on the long trek to the mouth of the Deschutes.

There were workmen and part of the crew already there, busy around the boat by lantern light. But I knew that Coe and White, and the invited passengers were still asleep in town and would come out on the portage wagon. The sharp-eyed White was the only one I really feared might spoil my chances as a stowaway.

The *Colonel Wright* had been slipped into the water with no launching ceremony and stood now beside the landing. The men's chief work seemed to be loading freight from the wharf. My chances were good if I could get to the other side of the boat.

I could swim a little and I had no fear of the river, and only one course was open to me. Staying well beyond the light of the lanterns I slipped off my breeches and shirt, for I had no desire to lie in wet clothes aboard the *Wright*. Making a rough bundle of the clothes, with my shoes wrapped inside it, I stole down to the bank of the stream. Although the water was cold, and the April air far from soothing to my nakedness, I was too intent to care very much.

When I reached the edge of the landing wharf I made my way along it, feeling the round pebbles carefully at every step. The water came up over my knees, then struck my trembling belly. There I waited, my teeth chattering so hard I feared the men above would hear me. But their endless talk and the noise of their work went on, and I kept going out, holding my bundle of clothes above the surface.

The boat drew five and a half feet, and I knew I could not wade to her starboard side without holding to the wharf landing. Cautiously, clutching my clothes now in one hand, I slid the other over the edge of the wharf. It was not at all likely that the men would detect my fingers slipping along the shadows at the end of the landing, but that hand felt as large as my head. I went out a little further, and my feet left the bottom so that I had to tread water. Inch by inch I went along, beginning to be a little afraid. If I slipped beneath those dark waters there would be nothing to let it be known. I would be carried out of the mouth of the Deschutes and down the Columbia. I would be shot over the Celilo Falls and through The Dalles Rapids. My body might be carried clear to the sea and never found at all.

I do not know whether I was simply unnerved, or whether my fingers slipped on the boards of the landing. But suddenly I was clutching at the wharf with both hands, and my clothes, weighted down by the boots, were at the bottom of the Deschutes. Hastily I made my decision. It was a dead certainty that I could not walk into town wearing nothing but the dawn's reflection, and knock for admission at Mrs. Danby's door. I kept going, and soon clutched the guard rail. I followed this to the wheel, the cold making me reckless now, and skinned up by way of the wood fretwork which encased the paddles.

Not a soul was on deck and I headed at once for the pilot house on the theory that no one would violate this sanctum but Coe or Len White, and meanwhile I could think. I found it difficult to gather my wits because I was wet and shivering and my chattering teeth jarred the daylights out of my brain. But gradually I dried and thawed, and I began searching in the darkness for something with which to cover myself. The pilot house was barren of blankets or clothes, so I sat in a corner with knees hunched against my chin and my arms clasped over my legs, trying to get a little warmth.

I was scared of discovery, but worse was my embarrassment. I could only hope that Coe's astonishment would make him forget to be angry with me. My original plan had been, of course, to dress myself on board, hide until the *Wright* was well up the river, and then appear and take the consequences. Now here I was, naked as a singed turkey, unwanted and unexpected.

Then the unfortunate happened. I fell asleep. My early rising, the long hike from town, and my struggles in the cold water, were too much for me. My head dropped down on my knees, and in the gradual gathering warmth as night faded, I went dead to the world. The last thing I remembered were the spokes of the big wheel outlined against the glass of the pilot house. . . .

"My God Almighty, Coe! Look at this!"

It was the voice of Captain White. I could only sit there and stare back at them, not wanting to unfold my nakedness in its entirety.

"Caleb!" Lawrence Coe said. "Caleb, what the devil!"

"I lost my clothes, Mr. Coe."

"So I see. But how—what are you doing here, anyhow?"

"I—I wanted to go on the trip. I waded around the boat to get aboard and that was how I dropped my clothes."

To my immense relief, Captain White burst out laughing. He leaned against the pilot house wall and filled that little space with sound that was music to me. But Coe only stood staring. "I don't see anything funny about it," he remarked, more to himself than to White. "He might've drowned. He still can get consumption."

"No sir," I said. "I'm all right. I won't be any trouble. If I could get some clothes—"

"Let him come along, Lawrence," put in White. "My God, he deserves to come after all that trouble."

Coe still kept his eyes on me. "Does Mike know you're here?"

"No." I thought the time had come to lie a little, and so I added, "I was going to tell him, but he didn't come home last night."

"Let the boy come," White urged again. "You can fix it up with Shea when you get back. We'll tell Pete to let Mike know where he's gone." Pete drove the portage wagon mules and would be returning to town.

"I thought you didn't want any more passengers aboard than you could help?"

"Hell, he's no passenger! He's a stowaway. And we can't send him back in his birthday suit."

"He can't run around on the boat that way, either."

"I'll get one of the crew to lend him a pair of britches and a jacket. Shorty isn't much bigger than he is."

Lawrence Coe hesitated a moment. Then, resigned but exasperated, he turned onto the deck. "All right, Len. Get him Shorty's clothes. But he ought to have a hiding and be sent back on the portage wagon."

I was not as near to Shorty's size as Captain White had estimated. But I did not care. I was going to witness the maiden trip of the *Colonel Wright*. In trousers with four or five rolls at the bottoms and a jacket whose sleeves persisted in covering my hands, I lay flat on the hurricane deck with my chin over the edge, and watched the preparation for departure. They were swift and practiced. The freight and fuel had all been loaded before dawn. Although the *Colonel Wright* was a new vessel, going into waters strange to the steamboats, the crew had been brought up from the lower river.

Coe's passengers had come on the portage wagon with him and the captain. They stood on the forward deck pretending a study of the boat and her crew. But everyone was stealing anxious glances up the Columbia, wondering what was in store for us. On shore were a few men from town who had got wind of the *Wright's* departure. Most of them, I imagine, had come to jeer—but there was something about the brave little steamer which silenced their skepticism, and before the whistle blew I think they were frankly envious. At any rate, as the lines were cast off, and the cry "All clear!" came up from below, every last spectator cheered and waved.

She eased out into the Deschutes, then drifted down at a slight angle until we reached the broad Columbia. There she turned her nose upstream and we entered a deep and awesome rock gorge which tossed back to us the sound of the *Wright's* engine. I got up from the deck and went to the pilot house. Through the side window I saw Captain White, standing in shirt-sleeves, his hat tossed on the floor, his feet wide apart. He looked more grim than I had ever seen him, but there was a sort of a shine to his face, too. He saw me standing by the window and nodded for me to come inside.

"How do you like it?"

I looked ahead. "We're coming to a rapids already, aren't we?"

"Just a little one. This is still civilized water. We'll go through three like this. If it weren't any worse than this there'd have been boats up here long ago."

"Do you think we'll make it?"

"Sure, we'll make it. And when we've got her to Wallula and back, why then next time we'll take her up the Snake as far as we can."

"Maybe I'll go with you," I said. I didn't believe it—then. I was sure that Lawrence Coe would see to that. I didn't know I'd be going into the back country on the *Wright*. If I had known the circumstances which would lead to this, I wouldn't have been so happy in the pilot house with Captain White. I have heard people say they wished they could look into the future, that they would give anything to know what was going to happen; if only they knew this they would become rich or happy or famous. But I am sure that if we knew it we would destroy ourselves with dread. We would become weak in the anticipation of troubles which, as it is now, come suddenly and shock us into strength enough to meet them.

"Maybe you will," Captain White agreed, but his tone was not convincing. "Or maybe this trip will give you enough steamboating for a while."

I kept my face against the pilot house window, watching the white water. "We'll come back faster, won't we, Captain?"

"Well, I reckon we will, fast enough. But not as fast as we would on a certain stretch on the Willamette where I used to pilot." He looked at me out of the corner of an eye. "I was purser on a boat down there that was so fast downstream she was always ahead of her whistle. We'd whistle four miles from the landing and we wouldn't get the sound until we were all tied up at the wharf."

Lawrence Coe had come into the pilot house. "What're you spinning up here, Len? You're supposed to be taking this boat to Wallula."

"I'm taking her there," said White imperturbably. "I was telling Caleb here about the old *Connaught* that piled up down in the Willamette five years ago."

"*Connaught?* How'd you spell it?"

"K-o-n-o-t," said White, "is how *I* spell it, and I don't give a damn how anybody else spelled it. She was a fast one, all right. I was just telling him how she was always ahead of her whistle. Well, we got out to her just two hours after she'd piled up. There was only the house left, sticking on top of this rock, and everybody had washed overboard. Well sir, do you know, we heard the voice of the dead captain ordering his dinner from the dead steward. Of course the voices were from the live captain and the live steward, because the captain had ordered that dinner forty or fifty miles upstream. The voices had drifted down, 'way behind the boat. Another time—"

"I've had enough," Coe said, returning to the door. "You'd better forget about the *Connaught,* or they'll be hearing our voices down at Dalles City."

When Coe had gone, I asked White if that were true about the old *Connaught*.

"As true as a lot of things you've heard, Caleb, and as a lot of things you will be told." He looked out to starboard at the vari-colored rock cliff. "See that?" he said. "That's diabolical strata in those rocks. Yes sir, that's diabolical strata, if ever I've seen it."

Later I told this to the Reverend Condon, the preacher at Dalles City who got so intrigued with the country that he began to consider it from the viewpoint of geology. Thomas Condon was amused, but he said, "The man was right, Caleb. That's exactly what it is. Diabolical strata."

As we progressed upriver, Coe was in and out of the pilot house a dozen times an hour. But gradually, as we cut through the lesser rapids, his nervousness subsided. He had had an opportunity to see how the *Colonel Wright* carried herself. The other passengers, having accustomed themselves to the adventure, likewise were breathing easier, and began to visit the captain. One in particular seemed as interested in the boat as Lawrence Coe and his partner. He was a tall, slender fellow with sharp, dark eyes, a cool thin mouth, and coal black chin whiskers and sideburns. An old friend of Coe's, his name was Baker. He owned a store in Portland where he had amazed and angered the merchants by advertising a new method of doing business—allowing discounts at the end of the year according to the amount of goods purchased by a customer.

He asked White endless questions, and he seemed very familiar with the country. Presently, from the drift of his talk, I could see that he was interested in moving his business either to Dalles City or Steptoeville and the success or failure of the *Wright* might make the choice for him. He was one of the keenest and most alert men I had ever seen. There was something almost fearful in his concentration, the impact with which his mind met a fact. Doctor Baker made a profound impression upon me there in the pilot house of the *Wright*, but I did not dream that I was to see him again or that he would have any part in the river's destiny. He regarded me with enough interest not to hurt my feelings, but no more than that, for he was the sort who never makes a false or unnecessary move.

Captain White seemed not to mind company in the wheel house.

He had a way of talking about the most irrelevant matter while he was examining the river at his keenest; before long he was holding forth on the subject of phonetic spelling.

At dinner the rest repaired to the dining room. But I stayed by the side of White and shared sandwiches and warm milk with him. He ate absently, his hand on the wheel, eyes on the river. After a while he peered ahead, tense, and he hurried down his last sandwich with a swallow of milk. "We're coming to the Lower John Day."

I saw the white water ahead. And within ten minutes I had had my first taste of steamboating in a rapids. As the nose of the *Wright* struck the rapids I could feel her slowing perceptibly. Suddenly Len White swore. I looked up to see him spinning the big wheel around, clear around. He grabbed up the speaking tube and yelled, "Steering gear's busted—" He turned to me. "Go below and get Shorty up here." I ran out of the pilot house and down the companionway. My heart was racing as swiftly as my feet and I wondered if this was to be the end of our trip—perhaps the end of all of us.

I couldn't find Shorty at once, and when I did find him it was at the stern. He had already sensed the faltering of the *Colonel Wright* and was examining her rudder cables. Meanwhile, helpless if he stayed at the wheel, Captain White had come to the main deck and stood bellowing orders to the engine room below. It was steam and the paddles which had to guide the *Wright* now. Carefully, awkwardly, the vessel swung downstream, turning until she stood cross-wise in the channel. Len White kept his eyes on the bank until he saw a cove of quiet water near the bank, and when we were just a little above it he yelled below for more steam. The side-wheels churned, and soon we were safe with two anchors ahead.

Coe was white-faced and trembling, but White assured him that our predicament was not serious. "Have her fixed in no time at all, Lawrence."

"But look what we've got ahead. Can we make it with a repaired steering line?"

"Sure we can. I hadn't had the feel of her yet when I hit those rapids. I jerked her a little too quick. I know better now."

Coe had to be satisfied with that, and so did the rest of us. But we all wondered just how well Len White had learned his lesson. If there were greater rapids ahead, and the steering gear broke again, would we be so fortunate? Only time would tell, and we had to place ourselves in the hands of Len White with what confidence we could muster. Within half an hour we were steaming up the river and into the Lower John Day Rapids once more. I had taken my stand beside the captain, and when we had cleared the white water I let out an involuntary sigh. Len White laughed.

"Don't get relieved too soon, fellow. We're hitting the Middle John Day next. That's where the John Day river comes out and mixes it up with the rapids." White's voice was full of enthusiasm and anticipation. I could tell that he had been itching to pit himself and the *Colonel Wright* against that rapids.

Out from the mouth of the John Day there is a small island in the Columbia, and it does not add to a river pilot's security when he bucks the rapids. The water rushes down in short, sharp pitches, and when the west wind howls against the current the surface of the river is even more confusing. On that April day no man knew whether a steamboat the size of the *Wright* could pass on either side of the little island. But three men had thought she might: Coe, Thompson, and Captain White. The Captain had more reason to think so than the other two, for he had been studying the river. But even he erred, as it turned out, for he chose the right hand side of the island as the most logical channel for the *Wright*. We had not picked our way a boat length before there was an ominous scraping against the vessel's side.

"Slack her off!" bawled White into the speaking tube. "Slack her o-off, if you love me!"

We began to drift backwards, slowly. "I'll be damned!" said White, to himself. "I'll be double God damned." He paused a moment. "Well, if we can't make the other side of the island, we'll have to try this one again—and that won't be so funny."

But the other side of the island let us through. It was a curious little stretch of water that had fooled White when he had been making his calculations on the bateau. It looked more vicious than it was—much more vicious than the opposite channel. White's face was strained, for if this channel, too, had proved unworkable then the upriver jaunt of the *Wright* would have already finished.

As we passed the eastern end of the island and emerged into the wider stream a cheer came up from below. Len White smiled. "Listen to 'em!" he said. "They're feeling good because they figure we made it ourselves. But I'll tell you a secret. We couldn't make that in low water. And if we get back down it we'll be in luck. There's a rock down there that's got to be blasted."

"A rock?" I said. "I didn't see any rock."

"Neither did I," said White. "I felt it."

"You mean it struck the side of the boat?"

He shook his head. "Nope. I just felt it down there. And I'll bet you a silver dollar it's there, too."

After the Middle John Day Rapids came the Upper John Day, and the Indian Rapids, and Squally Hook. But none of these were as bad as the rapids which split themselves on the island. Coe was beside himself with delight. He ran back and forth between the pilot house and the guests below, until finally Len White checked his enthusiasm. "We're coming to Umatilla Rapids, Lawrence. It's almost nightfall, and I'm going to anchor below them."

Coe was as disappointed as a child who had been told he has to go to bed before the guests arrive. "It'll be forty-five minutes before sundown. Forty-five minutes at least. It would be fine if we could get to Wallula tonight."

"That Umatilla Rapids isn't child's play, and I won't try it before morning."

"Who owns this boat, you or me?"

"You own her, Lawrence. But *I'm* taking her up the river."

They were perfectly amiable, and Len White won the argument. We made fast to the shore below the rapids, and passengers, as well as the crew, were quite ready to turn in. The strain of the day had exhausted them as certainly as would physical effort.

"Caleb," said Coe, "you'll have to make yourself comfortable in the pilot house." He handed me a blanket. Meekly and obediently I repaired to the pilot house, and spread the blanket on the floor. I was about to stretch myself gratefully when the door opened and Len White walked in.

"Hey there, fellow, what's the idea?"

"Mr. Coe said I could sleep on the floor in here."

"Sleep in my wheel house? Not by a jug full you can't. A pilot house isn't to be slept in. It's—well, it's bad luck. I got a wide bunk, and you can sleep with me."

Soon, scarcely able to believe it, I lay beside the great tall river captain, almost afraid to breathe.

"Got enough room?"

"Yes, sir."

"If I snore, poke me on the shoulder."

That gave me courage and I asked a question which had been plaguing me. "Captain White, what's so bad about the Umatilla Rapids?"

"Well," came the Captain's voice out of the darkness, "maybe there isn't so much bad about them. Maybe we could have got through them like Coe wanted, and been at the depot tonight. But we were lucky today, and I don't think a man ought to crowd his luck. You don't get much of it in a lifetime, so you ought to make it last."

I could hear the rapids roaring above us, a strange and frightening sound. "They sound like they were swift," I said.

"Sure. Maybe some of the others would have sounded as bad if you'd been on the river bank with everything else quiet. Up there in the wheel house, with the engine throbbing, and the sound of the water against the hull and the wheels, you don't hear the rapids themselves."

Presently Len White went on. "It's not the current in the Umatilla that's so bad. I reckon the current isn't any worse than it was down there by the John Day, or at Squally Hook. But the channel is twisted. There's three reefs in there, one after the other, and they stretch clear across the river."

"How'll we get by them, then?"

"Oh, there's an opening in every one of them," said Len White. "Trouble is, the openings aren't in line with each other. And when we find those openings, if we do, the green water will be busting clear over the foredeck and getting some of those fine gentlemen wet."

I considered this for several minutes and then I said, "You'll find the openings all right."

Len White did not acknowledge the compliment. He was snoring gently. As I lay there, the snore increased appreciably in volume. But I did not poke him in the shoulder. He was a great river captain and he was taking this ship up a stretch where no other steamboat had ever gone before. He could snore if he wanted.

And soon I, too, was asleep.

"CHEERILY, heave ho-o!"

The sound outside the stateroom awakened me and I sat up in the berth excitedly. Captain White had gone. From the wall beyond I could hear the escape of steam. Somewhere dishes were rattling.

"Cheerily . . . heave ho! . . ." There was the thud of an anchor on deck. Then from the pilot house above I heard White yell, "All clear?"

"All clear, sir."

"Full a-head!"

I leaped out of bed and dressed—no great feat, inasmuch as my only costume consisted of Shorty's jacket and breeches. When I reached the rail, the *Wright* was already in the middle of the stream and headed for the whitecaps of the Umatilla Rapids. I hurried to the wheel house, where Len White greeted me with a grin.

"You certainly were tearing off some sleep when I got up this morning."

"I wish you'd waked me up, Captain."

"I knew you'd come awake when we hit the Umatilla."

He was right. Neither was there any lethargy on the part of the other passengers. I hadn't thought of breakfast; the others must have hurried through it, for one by one they came into the wheel house, ranging themselves behind Len White to watch him negotiate the last rapids between us and Wallula.

Peering through the pilot house window, I could see the first of the reefs White had mentioned. That is, I could not see the reef itself, but rather its effect. The whole rapids was a checker-board of white caps, but stretched across the stream I saw a line of white, broken in the center. Through this break the current plunged at us with such swiftness that there was an overfall. It was toward this that White directed the nose of the *Colonel Wright.*

As we struck it, the vessel trembled from stem to stern, seemed to stand still. Green water broke over the bow in great sheets, drenching two of the crew who had been standing at the rail watching the action of the current.

I stole a look at White. His eyes were narrowed, his mouth a thin line from which stuck a black, unlighted stogie. His hands were firm on the wheel, but his chest was pressed against it, too, as if he were pushing the *Wright* through by sheer physical force.

Suddenly she leaped forward like a salmon in the stream, and I knew that we were through. *"By God, Len, you made it!"* cried Lawrence Coe, but White silenced him with a shrug.

"The middle reef's worst," he said. "If we can get through there we'll make the last like nothing at all."

I soon saw the second reef. It looked no more hazardous than the first, but I did not for a moment doubt Captain White's opinion of it. The opening, I could see, was further to starboard than the break in the first one. The *Wright* started for it an an angle, and then, possibly two boat lengths below it, Len White turned sharply so that we would meet the onrushing water head on.

He reached for the speaking tube. "More steam!" he shouted down.

We stood tense there in the crowded house, for within a quarter of a minute we would know whether the *Colonel Wright* was a success. Or perhaps, in a quarter of a minute, we would know nothing at all. What if the current swept the vessel back, broke her rudders, sent us smashing against the rocks? I did not know the power of the rapids then as I do now, yet I could sense their strength, and a wholesome respect for them was written into every line of Len White's face.

Then the *Wright* struck so solidly that we were all lurched forward, and for a moment I believed that we must have hit the reef. But it was simply the pitch of the current that we met. Once again a great sheet of green water plunged over the prow, and below us I heard the sizzle as some of it swept below and lapped at the base of the boiler.

"More steam . . ." Len White bawled. "More steam, if you love me!"

I did not realize the size of the overfall, until I saw the nose of the vessel actually rising. I looked toward the shore. We seemed not to be moving at all! Then suddenly the *Wright* stood on a more even keel and I thought we were going through. But to my great astonishment, we slid back until we were again below the reef.

"I'll go below and tell them you've *got* to have more steam down there," Coe said, reaching for the knob of the pilot house door.

"Won't do any good, Lawrence," White said. "We got enough steam. The trouble is that when we get the nose over, there's such a fall that our wheels aren't catching deep enough."

I looked back at Coe and the passengers. Never was there a more helpless group. "We're stuck then," Coe muttered dismally. "We'll never make it."

"By mighty, Lawrence, we've got to!"

With this, White sent her up toward the reef opening again while we all waited for the shock. For full minutes we stood there against the current. The nose rose up again, and then Len White shoved the *Wright* bodily over that little fall. I know of no other way to explain it. It seemed to me that we were in precisely the same position as before. Certainly the current was as swift. It may have been, as one of the passengers opined afterward, that a little stronger wind got behind the squaresail and gave her the last ounce she needed. But I doubt that. Since that morning on the Columbia I have seen a lot of swift water flow past me. I have seen men build hulls a little differently from the ones already on the stream. I have watched dozens of steam engines turning paddle wheels. But I still can believe that it is the captain who, almost literally, pushes a river vessel through the bad spots.

White pulled the whistle cord and hung to it. The shriek echoed and re-echoed along the basalt cliffs, and we mixed our shouts with it there in the pilot house. The Captain had said that success on the middle reef meant we'd get through, and in another few minutes he proved he was right when the vessel sailed through the third reef with only a slightly perceptible slowing.

Excitedly the men crowded around him, voluble in praise of his skill. But Len White only grinned at the river ahead. "There wasn't a damned one of you thought we'd make it," he said. Then: "I wasn't sure of it myself!"

When we reached Wallula and I saw our destination it seemed indeed a desolate spot. As we had struggled with the river at the Umatilla Rapids we had been in the shadow of escarpments of rock seven or eight hundred feet high—then had come a stretch of quiet water which led us to sand heaps that seemed to roll clear to the horizon.

The only building in sight within all that lone land was a small adobe near the river's edge. It was the old Hudson's Bay fort, a relic of the days when the great company had ruled with an iron hand and a clever brain. Now the adobe was occupied by John Higgins, quartermaster for the Army, and used as a storehouse and depot.

Yet, as Thompson and Coe knew well, here was a key landing for a steamer. It was at the mouth of the Walla Walla River, and thirty-two miles east, along a faint but easy wagon road, was the town of Steptoeville, already a promising center for the interior. And a few miles up the Columbia was the entrance to the Snake River along which was the way to a vast interior.

At Wallula the incoming settlers stopped before taking on their packs again. Here reached, eventually, much of the Army supplies which came up from San Francisco, for at Steptoeville was an interior post and an Army fort. I was told that only twenty miles beyond, the sand hills ended in a beautiful and fertile valley. It was difficult to imagine in such a bleak and barren spot which the *Wright* was choosing for its landing.

On the bank stood Higgins, waiting, a solitary figure in all that desert. He had been aroused by the vessel's whistle as we made the rapids, and was waiting in frank astonishment, a round little man whose lonely job had made him suspicious and unfriendly. But he greeted us, and came aboard for an inspection of the boat. He told Coe that he had dispatched an Indian rider to bring ponies for any passengers who planned to ride into Steptoeville.

"You expected us?" asked Coe, amazed.

"Well, no, I never expected you at all," Higgins admitted. "I did hear about a month ago that somebody was building a boat at Deschutes and figurin' to bring her up as far as this. But I didn't take any stock in it. Not until I heard your tootin' down at the Umatilla riffle. Then I knew you'd made it, and sent after the ponies."

Baker and three of Coe's guests were going on to Steptoeville, hardly able to believe that they had left Dalles City only the morning before, and would be at their destination by nightfall, sleeping in beds.

The rest were anxious to return to Dalles City and break the good news. I think that Len White was most anxious of all. "Wait until I see Vic Trevitt," he said. "I'll take pleasure in collecting that five hundred!"

So, within an hour, we boarded the *Wright* and started downstream. The return trip was swift, exhilarating, and uneventful. We traveled with such speed that we were plowing the John Day Rapids before dusk, and we reached the wharf landing at Deschutes just as our steward was lighting the cabin lamps for supper.

"Never mind the supper," Coe told him. "We'll all go to the Umatilla House and have supper—with champagne!"

Pete was there with his portage wagon, waiting dubiously. He had expected us no more than had Higgins, and he had driven us almost to town before he was convinced that the *Wright* had actually reached the post. As we neared the lights of the town, Lawrence Coe turned to me, "Well, I reckon I'd better forgive you for stowing away, Caleb. You brought us luck. Want to come up to the hotel and join us at supper?"

My conscience troubled me. I felt I should get back to the Danbys' and tell Mike where I'd been and what had happened. But the invitation to supper at the Umatilla House was a great temptation. Too long I'd gazed wistfully through its lobby windows, or listened openmouthed to tales of its grandeur and hospitality and amazing dishes.

I told Mr. Coe I would go with the party.

CHAPTER 11

THE Umatilla House was to grow greater along with the river, but to me it never seemed more luxurious than on the night Lawrence Coe and his guests celebrated the voyage of the *Wright.*

It was an imposing structure, easily the largest in the town, a full three stories in height, painted a light gray, and with fine tall windows spaced in pairs on Front Street and singly on the other three sides. The rear rooms looked straight across the Columbia, while the east and west windows allowed sweeping views of the stream.

This friendly inn was easily the center of Dalles City, which is to say that it was the center of a vast area that stretched from Portland to far beyond Steptoeville, that went northwest to Puget Sound and south to California. Every week, in the columns of the newspaper, was an advertisement for Umatilla House:

A Fine Place for Study,
And to Spend Your Winter Evenings!

Where you can look at the "Bulletin," where you will find the "Statesman," the "Oregonian," "Herald," "Unionist" and the "Democrat" with "Gleason" and "Frank Leslie" and other literary characters, and where at a glance you can see the "Nation"—in fact, the whole "World"; and find representatives from every clime—English, French, Dutch, Scotch, Irish, California, Oregon, and others, including "Old Bourbon" himself; and can also enjoy the delightful company of the "Havanan." All this can be seen and done at the Umatilla Cellar, Dalles City, Oregon.

HANDLEY & SINNOTT, Proprietors

The Umatilla Cellar was the bar in the Umatilla House, and in truth it was the town's library as well as a rendezvous for informal meetings and a spot for the exchange of miscellaneous information gathered all along the river. The dining room of the hotel was the town's social hall, always requisitioned for important social festivities.

From the beginning of the enterprise, Nick Sinnott and Dan Handley made an invariable rule: no one was to be turned away from the Umatilla House. Lack of funds did not mean that you could not get a meal and a bed there, and the privilege was not abused. It was a boast of the proprietors that they were always paid—eventually. Sometimes a joking doubter would enquire of Dan Handley if he'd heard from a certain party, known to be a blackguard and a deadbeat, who had received free lodgings at the Umatilla House. "Not yet," Dan would say, "but we will."

"He got shot with an ace up his sleeve up in Steptoeville last month."

Handley never cracked an expression. "Yes? Well, either Nick or I will be seeing him later. All debts aren't paid on earth, me boy."

Sinnott and Handley were there when we arrived from the *Wright*, and they entered quickly into the spirit of the occasion. The hour was late, but they brought tapers for the chandeliers of the dining room and rousted from upstairs three sleepy-eyed waiters and a cook. Their hospitality was spontaneous, and characteristic; neither could have known that the success of the *Wright* was to make their hostelry inseparable with the inland traffic, make it known from San Francisco to Port Angeles, from Portland to St. Louis. The only well-known hotel in the whole Northwest—known, that is to say, from San Francisco north—was the New York Hotel in Portland. That was "the two-bit house" where tired men flopped for a night between the coast steamer and a river boat, before they made their fortunes. The Umatilla House was unusual from the moment its three stories were built on the river bank at Dalles City. And the difference lay in Nick Sinnott and Dan Handley. They were the Umatilla House. The big gray building, the sumptuous furnishings, were simply the medium through which their genius worked.

When the crowd from the *Wright,* led by Lawrence Coe and Captain White, filed into the bar, I lagged behind to examine the lobby. I was fascinated by the wonder of the great brass cuspidors, the low-backed chairs with the moulded seats, the round iron stove garlanded with leaves of bright metal. But what awed me most was the mahogany counter and the pigeon-holes behind it with dozens of key-tags hanging like spangles off a Christmas tree. The walls were covered with a red-flowered paper, and framed behind glass was a printed schedule for the downriver boats. On the face of the counter was tacked the notice of a dance at the Army post, and looming large on the wall was a steel engraving, surrounded by a gilt frame, of a shipwreck under glowering skies. A curious and exciting smell permeated the place—of cigars and tobacco juice and varnished wood and boot leather and wallpaper scorched a little by the fire in the stove. It was the smell of a room in which much has happened and it was new to me. It did not have the flat, dead smell of Mrs. Danby's rooming house where nothing had happened and where, I felt sure, nothing ever would.

While champagne corks popped in the bar, I strutted myself across the lobby and tried one of the low, round-backed chairs, wishing that Victoria Hunt or Mr. Harrington could see me. I imagined myself a steamboat captain, resting a while before taking my command back to The Cascades.

As I sat there it occurred to me in a breathless rush that I was beyond pretending. I was, practically, a man. I was one of a party which had gone upriver, and in the bar of the Umatilla House that voyage was being celebrated with overflowing glasses. I wondered if Mr. Harrington would let me tell the school about it. He had allowed Jeb Dutton to tell about what his uncle had seen at the New York Fair in the Crystal Palace, and he had let Mamie Duprue tell how her father had trapped a coyote by setting the trap in the carcass of a horse. But this was something more important than those things, and furthermore it was something I had done myself. It wasn't an uncle or a father who had done this. It was I.

I got up and strode through the lobby toward the Umatilla Cellar. But I stopped, dead still, in the entrance. It was not the noisy crowd centered around Coe and Thompson and White that made me pause. It was the splendor of the room itself. A massive mahogany bar refused to be inundated by the sweep of men against it, and behind it arose the largest mirror I had ever seen. I had supposed that all mirrors had to be made small, lest they break off at the edges. But this was a sheet of reflecting silver that covered almost an entire wall. And, as if this were not enough, at the far end of the room was a smaller but hardly less impressive mirror, framed in gold, which stretched from floor to ceiling. Reflected in it, looking small and disreputable in Shorty's jacket and breeches, I saw Caleb Paige.

Dismayed, I backed away, but before I could turn tail Dan Handley detached himself from the convivial crowd and came rolling toward me, an imposing figure in shirt-sleeves and red galluses.

"Hey there, me boy! I saw you comin' in with the crowd and clean forgot you."

"Yes, sir. My name is Caleb Paige. I'm a friend of Mr. Coe's."

"Good! I'm Dan Handley and any friend of Lawrence Coe's is a friend of mine. He's a guest here at Umatilla House and so are any and all of his friends."

He guided me through the lobby, and for a moment I feared that his greeting had been one of irony and that, not believing my story, he was going to lead me outside the hotel. But in the center of the lobby he wheeled toward an open doorway.

"I'll bet you're hungry," he said, pushing me toward a brilliantly lighted room filled with white-clothed tables flanked by plush chairs. The trio of waiters were dashing in and out of the room, bearing plates and silver from the kitchen. They had pushed four or five of the tables together to form a banquet board. Handley went forward to give them further orders and I could see that he was in his glory. When he had finished he turned again to me.

"I'll be here," he said, pointing to a chair, "and you can sit beside me. Suppose you be sitting there now and taking the edge off your hunger with a little bread. And I'll have you brought a glass o' buttermilk."

I was too flabbergasted at being served by one of the proprietors of the Umatilla House to tell him that I didn't care for buttermilk.

When it came I was amazed to find it palatable, made so, no doubt, by the lush surroundings of the dining room.

I had just finished a second slice of bread and was furtively brushing away the crumbs when the men came in from the bar. They were in high good spirits and there was considerable chafing as they tried to seat Coe and Thompson together at the head of the table. Both men refused, shoving Captain White into the place. He attempted to get up but was pushed down again and somebody called out that he'd be glad to forego his dinner and hold the Captain in his seat if necessary. Although the men were feeling the champagne, there was not the kind of noise I had heard come out of the saloons down the street. I remembered Ed Danby saying that nobody ever got drunk a second time in Umatilla House.

I felt wedged-in and out of place in the crowd. Occasionally somebody would remember that I was present and throw me a word or two, or crack a joke at my expense, they were for the most part too elated to think of making an awed fifteen-year-old feel comfortable. I had been a stowaway on the voyage, and despite Coe's invitation I began to feel like a stowaway at the banquet. I think if it had not been for Dan Handley's occasional nudge, and Captain White's broad winks I would have fled.

White looked weary. The champagne had raised his spirits some, but as the meal progressed his face became tired and lined. The strain of the trip was beginning to show itself, and he was no man for fuss, anyhow. I am sure he would have preferred to go upstairs to bed.

Perhaps I exaggerate the captain's emotions due to my own feelings at the time. In my head, at least, I had piloted the *Wright* along with Leonard White and was myself ready for sleep. I half dozed through several speeches, some impromptu and humorous, others weighty and dull which came with the California brandy and the coffee. Coe and Thompson had little to say, and White refused flatly to make any sort of speech. The others, who had had little to do with the actual enterprise, were not so reticent.

It was half way through one of the longer speeches that I looked up at a mirror on the wall to see Mike Shea walking across the dining room. Something in his manner startled me, and I half rose from my chair. Lawrence Coe signaled me to sit down. He himself got up and advanced to meet Shea.

"Well, Mike! Glad you're here. We're celebrating the success of the new boat."

Mike's eyes were narrow. What frightened me was that he was cold sober. It was almost midnight, and Mike, if out of bed, should have been as full of liquor as an oak keg.

"I've come after Caleb," he said. "That was a hell of a note—taking him up there and not telling anybody."

Dan Handley's voice boomed out. "Well, he's back all safe, Mike. Sit down and have a glass to the boat."

"To hell with the boat," Mike said. "Come on, Caleb. Get out of there."

I felt Dan Handley start to rise, and I put my hand on his leg and got up quickly to obey Mike. Coe stood there, not saying anything at all. I could feel the men at the table grow cold. Mike had insulted them and the thing they were celebrating and with one more word he could have got a fight out of any one of them.

But he said nothing more. As I came away from the table Mike took my arm and led me out of the room, out through the lobby of the Umatilla House and into the street. As we started towards Danby's I said, "It wasn't Lawrence Coe's fault, Mike. I sneaked into the boat and they didn't know I was on board until she was part way up the river."

"Don't be standin' up for him," Mike said. "And don't be tryin' to tell me what to think." A flame of resentment welled up inside me, the first I had ever felt toward Mike Shea. But even then I was not prepared for his next remark. "I'm going to give you a damned good whaling, Caleb. You deserve it plenty." He began unbuckling his belt. "I'm going to give it to you right here so's we won't wake up the Danbys."

I was aghast. Mike had never laid a hand on me, had hardly spoken a cross word to me. It was unbelievable. If he had been drunk I would have let him whale me as much as I could stand, but he was sober and I felt he should have been able to think straight. I hated his unfair judgment of Lawrence Coe, and his feeling about the *Wright* seemed to me to be wholly unreasonable.

He stood with the belt dangling from his wrist, apparently uncertain, and I think he would have given up the idea of a licking if I had kept silent. But I was angry.

"You haven't got any right to lick me," I said. It was a foolish thing to say. If anybody in the world had a right, it was Mike Shea. I meant that there was no *reason* for Mike to lick me. He misunderstood my meaning; his pent-up temper flooded into his face and he made a grab for me.

I swung upward with a clenched fist, determined that I would get no whipping there on Front Street simply because I couldn't keep away from a steamboat. I did not think what I was doing. I simply hit out at Mike as he bent over to grab me, and my fist struck him full in the face.

It could not have been a hard blow. Mike's broad red face had received a dozen to which this was only the settling of a fly. But his hand let go of me and he staggered back, the expression of his eyes cutting into my heart.

"Mike!" I cried. "Mike, I—I didn't mean it!"

He said nothing. He went on down Front Street, the belt still dangling from his wrist.

PART TWO

CHAPTER

1

For more than a year after Mike Shea took me home from the Umatilla House I did not go near the steamboats. Sometimes I watched them from the river bank, but a sense of loyalty to Mike and a vague understanding of his jealousy of Coe made me careful. Too, I had begun to recognize that Mike had mentally got himself into a devil of a back-eddy. I could not rid myself of the feeling that I was really responsible for it. And although neither of us mentioned it again, I could not forgive myself for striking him.

But whenever I was in the school house and a steamboat whistle blew, I always managed to find an excuse for going by the window; or, on occasions sufficiently separated so as not (I hoped) to raise the suspicions of Mr. Harrington, I would raise my hand for permission to leave the building. From the back schoolyard I could not see the *Wright,* for she moored and landed too far upriver. But through a wide crack in the outhouse door I could watch a boat from The Cascades. She would make her presence known first by an arrogant whistle which echoed and re-echoed along the banks; then by a trail of black smoke if the day was clear and the "woolies" were not beating it down. Finally she would steam in full view, cutting a beautiful white curl with her bow and leaving a proud flat wake, faintly rippled in the sunshine.

There came the day, however, when Mr. Harrington discovered the connection between these calls of nature and the whistle of a steamboat. One day, as I raised my hand and turned a worried look upon him, Mr. Harrington said, "When the steamboat has tied up out of sight, Caleb, you may leave—and not before." He accompanied this with a wide and ironic smile which did not add to his popularity with me.

Naturally I saw little of Lawrence Coe. Mike's attitude had completely alienated him and he visited the Danbys no more. As for White, he now was a busy man whose regular appearances in Dalles City were brief. The *Wright* had in a year grown to be a great financial success that was the talk of the river. That first summer she had made three round trips a week, with a full cargo furnished by shippers who were attracted by the rate of eighty dollars a ton. Receipts of two thousand dollars for passenger tickets alone was not unusual. The run became so strenuous and regular that Captain White was given a pilot, Captain Bill Baughman. Still not content with his record, Len White had taken the *Wright* on an experimental voyage fifty miles up the Snake River. Not even the bateaux had ventured so far into the interior. Only Indian canoes had nosed into Priest Rapids, and the report of the savages had always been *hias skookum chuck*—very swift waters. Len White was delighted with the accomplishment, and satisfied at least for a while. But thus far a run up the Snake was not profitable, so the dauntless captain was forced to be patient.

News of the *Wright* spread quickly, however, and there were many heated conversations among the river men on the lower Columbia and the Willamette, even down as far as Astoria. Some came to Dalles City to take passage on the *Wright* just to be certain that the tale was true. More than one tried to buy into the boat, but Lawrence Coe stood firm. Some threatened competition, but there wasn't enough travel yet for two boats on the upper river—and, when there was, he had plans to own the second.

However, it began to look a little as if even the building of one boat for the upper river was banking too strongly on the future. Talk of Secession had been drifting westward all that year, and uneasily men were beginning to wonder if there was going to be war. War could mean that troops would be withdrawn from the frontier posts, for the Indians appeared to be under control at last. And if the military activities lessened, certainly the *Wright* would fall into evil days.

Whereas the talk in Dalles City had so often been of the promise of upper river steamboating, or of immediate local problems attending the building up of a new community, it now began to focus on the larger issue. Democrats and Republicans alike were cursing Buchanan because he appeared stubborn and vacillating by turns and did not come to grips with his problem in the direct rough way of the West. The big question of the East began to shape the politics of Oregon which had never been noted for their mildness. The Democrats were divided on slavery, but the Republicans had held together. There was even talk of an alliance between the anti-slavery Democrats and the Republicans in Oregon, but it was more in the discussion than the reality. Ed Danby and Mike argued about it incessantly. Danby, who professed to be a Democrat, thought it might be a good thing. But not Mike.

"You talk like a damn fool, Ed. You can't get a Democrat and a Republican together on anything!"

"Well, I don't know," opined Danby. "Over in Linn County Delazon Smith and Judge Williams are going around the country speaking against each other on the same platform and sleeping in the same bed at night."

But Mike was not convinced. And he was considerably disturbed when the news came that the Republican Convention date had been moved up and the Oregon delegates would not be able to attend. The rumor that Horace Greeley, champion of the West, would act for Leander Holmes did not appease Mike. He was sure that Oregon was going to be the recipient of foul play and that Democratic connivance was behind it somewhere.

Ed tried his best to soothe him. "I read in the *Argus* where Frank Johnson of Oregon City is studying theology in New York and he'll go over to Chicago and represent you Republicans at the convention."

"What's theology?" asked Mike suspiciously.

"He's studying to be a preacher."

The ex-trooper snorted. "That's what I thought. I don't trust preachers!"

Dalles City waited impatiently for the arrival of newspapers or letters, or an oral report, that would bring the news of the convention. At last it came, and Mike's fears were proved groundless. Oregon was represented adequately. The delegates had started out for Bates, but on the third ballot, when Abraham Lincoln was within a few votes of the nomination, they had switched to the lawyer from Illinois.

We were all surprised, yet quickly accepted the nomination for a man about whom we had heard but vaguely. After all, we were a long way off, and the delegates had supported Bates only until they saw the convention's enthusiasm for Lincoln. And it was not long before in the Umatilla House, in Vic Trevitt's saloon, or in front of Bert Patterson's livery stable, Republicans were reading to each other in clear, approving tones editorials extolling the virtues of "Abe." All through the State the Republican newspapers hewed to the line for the candidate, and took great glee in the fact that Democratic organs were flailing at each other, Secessionists on the one side and Unionists on the other.

"Lincoln will be elected," Mike would tell Danby. "It's like they say. When thieves fall out, honest men get their dues."

He couldn't rile Ed Danby who took his politics easily. And he was no more exercised on that morning when the *Hassalo* brought the news that Abraham Lincoln was to be the sixteenth president of the United States.

It was a great day for Mike. He spent all that day helping to organize a torch-light parade, and by nightfall he was too drunk to join it.

But the political excitement in Dalles City was not over by any means. Almost as many had voted for Breckenridge, the Disunionist, as for Lincoln. And the town's vote for Douglas was close on the heels of Breckenridge. The disagreement reflected itself very directly in our school and grew so acute that Mr. Harrington seated the Democratic factions on separate sides of the room, with Republicans like myself down the middle. In the schoolyard there could be no such division. Fights were so numerous that timid parents kept their children home. This was a sad state of affairs, but despite the threats from the school board and Mr. Harrington, the fights continued.

At last Mr. Harrington reached a momentous conclusion. He decided upon an appeal to reason. One day at the close of school he announced that, on the following morning, he intended to make a speech, which, he hoped, would restore sanity. We were instructed to so inform our parents, and invite them to attend.

We went to school that morning without reluctance. The two small rooms were jammed to the windows. There were present several dozen parents whose curiosity had been aroused. I sat far at the rear, effectively hidden, contentedly munching an apple I had had the foresight to bring along. I could not see Mr. Harrington for the broad, adult and taffeta-covered back in front of me. But I could hear him nervously clearing his throat, and at last he began. In a moment I had forgotten the apple. I had never heard Mr. Harrington in such fine fettle.

"Ladies and—gentlemen—and pupils," said Mr. Harrington carefully. "These are troublous times, as we all know. There is bad blood here in Oregon as elsewhere in the nation, and it will be well for all concerned to keep quiet and cool. There has been some—disturbance in the school. Undoubtedly a—reflection of discussions in the home or on the streets before the pupils."

Mr. Harrington paused, possibly to let sink this inference that parents could do a great deal toward properly influencing the child in school. "I want it distinctly understood," said Mr. Harrington diplomatically, "that—politically I am entirely neutral. It is not the place of a teacher to relate his political views. But it has been my observation that most of our trouble here in the school is due not to a—difference in opinion between representatives of two opposing parties. It is a—"

The teacher coughed twice, then went bravely on. "It is, I think, due to differences within *one* party. I would like to say that there really should be no cause for dissension. There is really no way in which any state may resume the power it has relinquished to the Federal Government in the bond of Union. I think that all of us should resist any attempt against the laws of the Federal

Union, and I—"

Mr. Harrington got no further. All through his last words there had been a drawing of tension in the room. The broad taffeta-covered back in front of me stirred, and suddenly a man in the front of the room interrupted him. It was George Marshall's father, a Virginian.

"Mistuh Harrington, I beg leave to take issue with you, suh. If that is what you wanted me to come to hear, I am afraid I am wasting your time and mine. And if that is the kind of poison you have been instilling into my son's mind then I intend to make a formal, written complaint to the board of this here school." Whereupon the tall and stately Mr. Marshall reached down, took his son's hand, and worked his way from the room.

I peered around the taffeta to have a look at Mr. Harrington. His mouth was open and he was a faint pinkish tinge. "I'm afraid," he said, "that I'm being misunderstood. All I intended—"

"You ain't being misunderstood a damn' bit," yelled a deep male voice.

Mr. Harrington straightened. He became again the schoolmaster. "Please do not swear in the presence of the pupils, my dear sir."

The male voice refused to be intimidated. "I'm saying what I got to say. You're a black Republican, Mr. Harrington. You're a nigger lover, and I don't want any truck with you and I don't want my children should have any truck with you."

The broad taffeta back raised in front of me. It belonged to a big woman whose unruly hair straggled a little from beneath her tiny straw bonnet. "Please, *please!*" her voice was quiet and clear, the patient voice of a woman who handles unruly children in a small house. "This is no place for an argument. I think that Mr. Harrington is perfectly right. It is too bad when one can't send children to school without having them beaten by the children of parents who can't stand to have their candidate defeated by Abraham Lincoln."

Her opinion was not unanimous among the females present. Another woman told her to sit down. Under cover of the confusion, Davey Everetts threw an inkwell at the wall. Men began milling nervously and a little girl started to cry.

"Order!" cried Mr. Harrington. *"Order!"*

But his appeal fell upon deaf ears. Quickly he saw the impossibility of attaining his demand, and necessity forced inspiration upon him. "Attention. Attention, please! This meeting is adjourned—and school is dismissed for the day!"

At this pronouncement a joyous shout went up from the pupils and they began scattering for the door. The adults, left alone, were reminded of their rôles as parents. Sheepishly they filed out, leaving Mr. Harrington sad and disillusioned.

CHAPTER 2

LATE in April we got the news that Fort Sumter had been fired upon. It stunned us. True, we had fed upon the bickerings in the *Statesman* and the *Argus*. The town had been filled with that bitterness demonstrated so forcibly to Mr. Harrington at the school house. Mike and Ed Danby had argued as if neither intended to give an inch though he die to defend it.

Yet few people, deep in their hearts, had believed that the South would actually secede. And when she did secede, few believed that the North would want to fight to hold within the Union those states which wanted to be out of it. We were far away, and the problems of the North and the South had grown rather dim. Almost every man and woman had roots back in the East, but they were more concerned with the destiny of Oregon than with anything else. The mountains were a great barrier, as the majority of settlers knew full well; and a trip around the Horn took a sizable slice out of any man's time on earth.

These were the sons and daughters of people who had come to America to be free of wars and oppression, who had pressed on to the farther West because they wanted to be even more certain of a chance to shape their destinies. They mightily mistrusted diplomats and politicians in the guise of God. They did not care too much for distant political and economic pressures masquerading as Fate.

Behind the unmistakable boundary of the Stonies it had not been unusual to hear talk of a great Pacific Coast Republic composed of Oregon, California, and a State to be formed out of Washington Territory. The Pacific delegation in Congress had even gone so far as to hold a caucus favoring secession and the formation of three republics—in the North, in the South, and bordering the blue Pacific.

But such flights of fancy fled before reality. Now the Union was actually threatened and the South had set up its own government. We began to consider more carefully what the stars and stripes meant to us. When word came to Dalles City that Senator Lane had been talking Pacific Secession the feeling ran high along Front Street. He had made the mistake of writing to Southern friends, congratulating them upon their actions. The Southern friends issued the letters to their own newspapers, and they eventually found their way into the Oregon weeklies. One morning on my way to school I heard a violent shout from behind the doors of a saloon. *"Let's hang old man Lane when he gets home, and fire thirty-four balls at him for the Union!"*

So while emotion was thick in the town, things quieted in the school house on the hill. The Douglas Democrats were on the side of Lincoln now, and the Disunionists, badly outnumbered, could only fume and sweat when we cheered the flag as Mr. Harrington raised it every morning at the opening of school.

Mike was beside himself with excitement when War began. He would have returned to the Army at once and asked to be sent East if it had not been for me. So, far from the scenes of battle, he let off steam in the only way he could. He organized a Union Club, getting the idea from one formed over in Marion County by a band of German settlers. He set up headquarters in a vacant store building next to The Golden Rule, and plastered on it a huge sign which read, AGAINST ALL FOES FROM WITHOUT AND TRAITORS WITHIN!

Ed Danby objected feebly to Mike's activities and told him that such business was as bad as the Knights of the Golden Circle. "Don't call me no damned Copperhead," Mike flared. "What's wrong with wanting to protect the Union?"

One afternoon as I walked into the livery stable on my way home from school I heard Mike and Bert Patterson arguing violently. I stood there in the brown mat of damp smelling straw and listened.

"It's not that I care, Mike. But I've got a lot of good customers who came from the South and they don't like the idea of being called traitors. They got their notions, too."

"What are they if they ain't traitors?" Mike demanded hotly.

"I don't think they're traitors at all. I think they're just Democrats and the reason they don't like this Union Club is because they figure it's just a blowout for the Republican Party. You can't blame 'em for that."

"You're plain daffy, bucko. If you don't want me around here, just say the word."

"It ain't that, Mike. But I'm tryin' to do business."

"Well, I ain't sure at all that I want to be associatin' with anybody that puts a few dollars before his country—so maybe I'd better be sayin' goodbye to you and the nags."

Mike was keeping his temper under control, for he had always liked Bert Patterson and I think he had come to like the stable with its comfortable smell of leather and horsehide and fresh manure. He had enjoyed the good-natured chafing and the violent arguments that went on all day long in front of the place. I think he had come to love the mares, and old Benjamin, the stallion, and think of them as perhaps part of the few friends he had in Dalles City. For Mike's frustration had progressed as time passed, and he had lost more friends than he'd made since we had come up from The Cascades on the *Mary*.

I rather think that this was why, too, he fell with such fervor upon the job of organizing a Union Club in Dalles City. A cause cements friendships and Mike found it good to have people agreeing with him again, with back slapping and cursing and a drink over an oath to see all Southern sympathizers in Hell, by God!

One morning Mike went down and found the banner in front of the Union Club tattered to shreds and lying on the board sidewalk. Immediately he had another painted on canvas and nailed it up himself. "Let 'em take that down," he said, "and there'll be trouble."

It came down the next night, and lettered in red chalk on the front of the building was WE DONT WANT WAR FOR LINCOLN. WE DONT WANT HIS RUMP CONGRESS. WE DONT WANT A BANQUET OF BLOOD SERVED UP FOR NIGGERS.

I walked to the club with Mike that morning on my way to school. When he saw the chalked legends his face went white. He stood stock still, staring at the insults.

"I'll get another banner up today," he said, "and tonight I'll stay in the place. The first man that tries it again is going to feel lead in his belly, or I'm a Chinaman."

I didn't think much about it at the time. But when Mike didn't show up at Danbys' that night for supper I grew worried. Mrs. Danby sniffed at my uneasiness. "It's nothing for him not to be home for supper," she said.

But lately Mike had been pretty regular about coming home. There were meetings at the Union Club two or three times a week, and even when there were no meetings Mike went there right after supper to hand out literature and sign up new members. He might have a drink or two in Vic Trevitt's before supper, but afterward he was all business now. I had never seen Mike so interested in anything since he'd left the Army and stopped fighting Indians.

"They took the banner down again," I told Mrs. Danby. "Mike said he was going to stay there all night. Maybe I better go down."

"You certainly will not!" returned Martha Danby. "If Mike wants to get into trouble, let him. But there's no cause for you to get mixed up in it."

Old Danby agreed. "Martha's right, Caleb. There's a lot of talk in the town and something is liable to flare up. I wish," he added plaintively, "that Mike would keep his opinions to himself and let others have theirs."

"It says in the *Statesman,*" mentioned Mrs. Danby, "that the Republicans shouldn't be flaunting these Union Clubs in the face of Southerners, and I reckon that's right. It's men like Mike Shea that make trouble. It's probably men like him that's causin' all the trouble down East. I can't imagine people of one country fighting with each other. It's not right."

I pecked at my supper, while Ed Danby tried to console me.

"Don't you worry about Mike. He's all right. He can take care of himself."

But after supper I went into our room at the back of the house and saw that Mike's carbine was gone from the wall. I guessed he had sneaked into the place and made out the back with it. That was bad. It meant that Mike was going to make good his morning's threat if anybody molested the club quarters. And I was sure that there'd be another attempt to take the banner down again tonight. I went to the box I'd brought from the Cascades and got out the pistol Coe had given me. Then I came back into the front parlor and tried to listen while Ed read a newspaper aloud to his wife. Everything he read seemed to have something to do with the War and made me think of Mike down at the club waiting for trouble. Finally I couldn't stand it any longer.

"I'm going down to see Mike," I said.

Martha Danby jumped so hard that her spectacles almost fell off. "You're not going to stir out of the house!"

"I've got to go," I said, starting toward the door. I was ready to break into a run if she tried to stop me.

"Caleb Paige, you heard what I said!"

Ed Danby looked at me over the newspaper. "I wouldn't do it, boy. Mike's all right."

"Well, I just want to walk down and see."

"Caleb, if you go out that door . . ." I did not hear the rest of Martha Danby's threat. It was to be a long time before I heard her voice again, and if I had known this I might have tried to convince her that I was right instead of walking out into the night while she was still talking. I did not know then that at every leave taking, however casual, it is not pointless to think that perhaps you may not hear that voice or see that face again ever.

I hurried down the street in the direction of the Union Club. The lights of the saloons were ablaze, and voices, louder and more determined than usual, drifted against each other. Down at the end of First Street The Golden Rule loomed large, dwarfing the little frame shack that was the headquarters of the Union Club. To my immense relief, I saw a knot of men standing in front of it, talking quietly. The light from the window streamed over their shoulders, throwing shadows into the dust at the side of the board walk.

Knowing that Mike would be annoyed if I showed up at that hour, I slipped into the shadows between Gate's Restaurant and the saddle shop. There were no windows on the side of either building, and the ground dipped sharply down toward the river bank so that my shoulders were on a level with the sidewalk. I was quite effectively hidden.

It was queer standing there in the darkness, being so close to the life of the town and yet so apart from it. Voices and other sounds took on a strange new quality. Far up the street I could hear a pair of boots pounding on the boards of the walk. They grew closer. As the man passed the opening between the saddle shop and the restaurant he turned and spat a thin brown stream from out his heavy black beard. It missed me by an inch and I moved farther down the bank so as to avoid further citizens whose neatness might cause them to hold their fire until they came abreast of a gap in the building fronts.

A buggy outfit came down the street slowly, one of the wheels squeaking with every revolution. A man sang loudly in one of the saloons and another was asking him even more loudly to stop. From beyond the saddle shop I could hear the piano in The Golden Rule. It reminded me of that Christmas night when Lawrence Coe and I had gone there to get Mike. I wondered about Lottie Moore and if Mike still liked her. I wondered if Victoria Hunt was asleep by now, and what she would think if she knew that I was down on the river bank, listening to the town at night. She was almost sixteen now and talked of quitting school. Her mother was always worried because Vicky liked the soldiers at the Army post. I decided she wouldn't care where I was tonight.

When there were no other noises up on the street I could hear the river, running along toward the sea. When the wind shifted a little I could hear it very plainly as I could sometimes when I was in bed at Danbys'. It made me drowsy, so that I had to concentrate on the noises of the street in order to keep awake.

A horseman came into town from the north. I could hear the hooves a long way off as the horse clattered along the river road.

Then I saw the rider flash by, and a little way up the street the horse stopped and I guessed it was at the hitching post in front of Trevitt's. I heard the rider yell out Dan Handley's name, and although I did not catch the reply I could picture Dan standing in his shirt sleeves and red galluses in front of the Umatilla House.

Two men walked up from the direction of the Union Club. One of them was talking about Mike, and I held myself close against the wall of the restaurant and listened. "If they try any funny business tonight they'd better watch out. Shea means business."

The other man laughed. "I wouldn't mind seeing it, but I don't like to get mixed up in that kind of shenanigan. Havin' a horse thief for breakfast is one thing, but putting a ball into a pro-slave man is another."

They were alongside of me now. "I guess maybe Mike sort of misses shootin' Indians."

When they had gone I stuck my head over the sidewalk and looked down the street. There was no one in front of the club building, so I started toward it. When I got to the window I peered inside. Mike was alone, writing at a table with a lamp at his elbow. His broad-brimmed hat was shoved back from his forehead, and his shirt was open, leaving the curly red hair of his chest peeping above his flannels. He wrote laboriously and furiously, with much scratching out and starting over again.

At last he looked up, his expression vague in the throes of composition. "Hello, Mike," I said.

"Well! . . . What you doing here?"

"I couldn't sleep. I thought I'd take a walk."

"A walk, is it? Does Martha know you're out?"

I nodded. "Yes. She didn't want me to come."

For a scant second Mike seemed amused, then he grew dutifully stern. "You ought to mind what Martha tells you. Let's have a bit of the truth now. What you doing here?"

"I remembered what you said this morning—about the banner. And I saw your carbine was gone."

Mike looked at me oddly. "Well?"

"You going to stay here all night, like you said?"

"I am, indeed. I'll show those yellow-bellied slavery buckos what I'm made of." He poked the pen at the paper in front of him. "I'm writin' a letter to the paper, too, tellin' what I think of them tearing our banner down in the cover of night like sheep stealin'."

"Mike, if you stay here I want to stay with you."

Mike grinned. "What good would you be doing yourself or me?"

I hesitated a moment, then decided to go through with it. From my hind pocket I took out the revolver Lawrence Coe had given me. "I guess I could help."

Mike looked at me unbelievingly. Then he reared back in his chair and laughed until I thought his temples would burst. Although his laughter hurt my feelings a little I was glad to hear it, for it meant that Mike was in good humor and might let me remain. Suddenly he stopped, brushed the tears from his eyes, and held out one of his beefy arms. "Come here, boy," he said.

I went over to him and he encircled my shoulders hard. "Yes, I guess it's a man you are now, all right. You've already given me a piece of your knuckle—and now you come with a revolver to help me teach these dough-faces the proper respect." He paused a moment, looking deep into my eyes. "But I'm thinkin' you'd better be home in bed, boy. I'll be all right."

"Why can't I stay, Mike? I'm sixteen. You were in the Army when you were sixteen. You told me so yourself."

"So I was, but times have changed, Caleb. And anyhow I don't want to be mixin' you up in trouble. Now go on with you before I have to tell you again in a different way." He doubled his big fist and brushed it against my cheek. He got up from the table, took me by the arm and led me to the open doorway.

We were about to step from the building when there was a resounding crash and one of the panes of the window shattered to the floor. There went bouncing along the floor a stone half the size of my fist. Mike and I peered into the shadows of the street, but we could see nothing.

Without a word, he drew me inside the room again and shut the door. Then he blew out the lamp on the table, plunging us into darkness. I could hear him fumbling against the wall for the carbine. "Keep away from the window, Caleb. They might try that again."

I drew out my pistol, my hand trembling a little. I held it close to my side to steady it, but with the barrel leveled and a finger on the trigger. Gradually my eyes became accustomed to the darkness and the street in front of us grew clearer. Four men were moving across the street abreast of one another.

"Look, Mike!"

His hand went over my mouth, and he nudged me away from the window. We stood back and watched them as they came on, very casually. Their audacity amazed me. I felt sure they did not know very much about Mike Shea to believe that they had intimidated him with a stone hurled through a window.

Suddenly Mike stepped forward, kicked open the door, and shouted: "What do you want out there?"

The four stopped where Mike's question struck their ears. "We come to take down that sign, sir. We're makin' a little collection of signs like that." One of them snickered.

"You better get back across the street," Mike warned, "or you'll be makin' a collection of lead. You might keep on goin' until you get where you can join your Army and shoot white men legal and above board."

One of the men started on toward us, the other three following a little way behind. As they drew nearer the lights of The Golden Rule fell on their faces. They were young fellows. The one in front could not have been twenty, the others not much older. It was plain that this time they intended to take down that sign once and for all, and beat up Mike and me into the bargain.

Their raw insolence angered me, and I heard Mike's breath draw in sharply. He could have broken the backs of the four of them in a fair encounter. But their arrogance, their firearms, and perhaps the nature of their enterprise, led them to think that Mike wouldn't attempt any violence. There was the chance, of course, that these were not the same men who had torn down the banners before, and chalked on the building front. But this never occurred to Mike and me then. And it is also possible that they were filled with Dutch courage.

The man in front was quite close to the sidewalk now. "If you step on them boards," Mike said, "I'll let you have it. Get back."

I saw the dusty boot raise in another step, and I saw the hand drop down from the lapel it had been holding. And in almost the same instant a shot exploded from out the trio who stood behind the leader. Involuntarily I let go toward the shadows with Coe's pistol.

It all happened so quickly that I could not be sure, but the three who stood in the street seemed to disappear into thin air at the sound of the shots. I saw the leader staggering back, almost to the middle of the street, then drop to his hands and knees in the dust.

For a long time Mike and I said nothing. We stood there just looking at the man in the middle of the road. Then I heard Mike whisper hoarsely, "The crazy God damn fools shot their own man in the back. It sure looks good for the Union if them bastards can't do no better than that!"

It might look good for the Union, but it didn't look good for us. And as we stood there with our brains whirling, we both knew it. If my shot had gone wild, and I was pretty sure that it had, the three survivors of the party would be convinced that either Mike or I had shot their friend. In any event, they wouldn't be admitting they'd shot their own man—and they wouldn't miss a chance to point out that pro-slavery advocates were being shot in the back by Union Club fanatics.

"Say, kid," Mike said, "this don't look so good, God damn it."

He had no sooner said it than there was a faint yet unmistakable and ominous sound far up the street. I guessed that the three men were already spreading the news in the saloons. In some of the lighted windows and doorways I could see the outlines of men peering curiously. They had heard the shots, but could not distinguish Mike and me in the darkness. One by one the silhouettes dropped away and I knew that they were joining men who were coming after us. In a moment I could see a slowly moving bulk. Each time it passed a lighted window or doorway the faces would flicker like white discs in the night, then disappear again as they slipped into the shadows.

I could not believe they were coming for us. Mike Shea had friends, and I boarded with the Danbys who had friends. The faces of the four young men who had come at us so insolently I had never seen before in Dalles City. But as that mob came up the street it gathered strength in numbers and so in fearsomeness, and I knew they were not coming just to see the man lying in the street.

Probably not more than half a dozen were active. These were in the front, waving and talking loudly. I suppose the rest were hardly more than stragglers, gathered from the shops and houses and curbs along the way. I suppose the most of them were only curious, but those noisy ones in front gave the whole mob a vigor that chilled me through. I remembered Ed Danby saying that the towns around were organizing Vigilantes to take care of those who let their political quarreling cause deaths.

Mike whirled. "Come on, Caleb!" At the corner of the shack he jumped down onto the river bank next to The Golden Rule. Blindly I followed Mike.

Like all the structures along that side of Front Street, The Golden Rule was built on stilts. But, unlike most of them, there was a rear entrance on the river side. Lengths of two-by-fours were nailed onto one of the pilings, like the rungs of a ladder, and these led to a door which stood staring out high above the muddy ground.

Mike half lifted me against them. "Climb up," he whispered. "The door's unlocked." My own impulse had been to run pell-mell down the river bank, but I obeyed Mike and started up the splintery rungs. I could hear Mike panting hard below me, his bulky shoulders pushing against the back of my legs. At the top I reached and turned the knob of the door. It was rough and crusted from the river dampness but it turned easily and the door swung into a dimly lighted hallway down which ran a strip of red carpet. Mike pushed me headlong and quickly shut us inside.

The place was quiet except for a dull droning that seemed to come from somewhere above us. It was perhaps a full minute before I realized that this droning was the sound of women talking together somewhere upstairs. There was one voice which could be heard above the rest, but the others kept on, too, and occasionally there would be a high, mirthless laugh from the voice that could be heard over all the rest.

Mike tip-toed down the hallway and stopped before a closed door. He leaned toward it and listened, then rapped at it softly with his knuckles. I heard a woman's voice from the other side.

"It's Mike. I got to see you a minute, Lottie."

A key turned in the lock, the door opened half way, and out stepped a woman. At last I was seeing Lottie Moore, and could understand how Mike could fall in love with such a creature. She seemed to me to be the most beautiful woman a man could find anywhere in the world. Her jet black hair was brushed high off her ears and away from the back of her neck. Her throat was a round white column unmarred by whalebone stays or lace collar, decorated only by a narrow black band caught together with a tiny clasp. She wore a brilliantly colored pelisse. I wondered why all women did not dress this way instead of encasing themselves from the waist down in skirts padded with horsehair or flared out with steel wire frames. Lottie Moore's skirt followed only the curve of her hips, then swept down in a line that made her tall and straight like the pictures of Greek goddesses I had seen in one of Mr. Harrington's history books.

"Lottie, I'm in a fix."

She turned her face down the hall, as if fearing that Mike's pursuers were already there, and her glance fell upon me. "Is he—the kid?"

Mike nodded. "There's a gang coming down the street. They'll probably go away again when they find we're not at the club. Give us a room, and if the bell rings you'd better answer it before Boozy does."

"Boozy's drunk and telling stories. You'll be better off if you stay here. It's all right." She pushed open the door. "It's only Kirt and Pete."

As I recalled what had happened in the saloon, Kirt Inge and Pete Forrest were the last two men on earth I wanted to see at that moment. But without hesitating, Mike followed Lottie into the room.

It was a large room, but almost every three or four square feet of it was occupied by some article of furniture or decoration.

There were two tall windows, their green shades drawn tight, and there was something about the room which made me sure that the shades were never lifted. There was a sweet odor in it, as of saccharine alum, but beneath this scent was a dampness, as if the sun had never streamed in.

The furniture was heavy green plush, and there was fringe around the seats of the chairs. Against one wall was a great mahogany bed, and over it a gray woolen blanket in strange contrast to the elegance of the rest of the room.

I did not see Inge and Forrest until I was in the middle of the room. Forrest stood in the corner, his battered felt miraculously hanging to the back of his head. When he saw Mike he reddened, and his dull eyes fastened at once on Inge with that waiting, hangdog expression. Then I made out Kirt Inge in the thin lamplight. He was seated by a little marble-topped table, and his gloved hand rested on it heavily. The fingers were set stiffly in one position, neither open nor quite closed. Tonight he was more fancily dressed than when I had seen him before. He wore his boots inside his trousers, like Mr. Harrington. Beneath his coat was a plaid double-breasted waistcoat with a gold watch chain across it. His face was dark and thin, and the skin seemed stretched a little too tightly on his high cheek bones.

With his ungloved hand, Kirt Inge reached into his pocket. Mike had his carbine, but with my heart in my throat I reached for my pistol. Inge grinned at me. "Take easy, kid." His eyes narrowed at Mike. "What you been tellin' our young friend about me, Mike?" The ungloved hand came out of his pocket with (to my complete mortification) a cigar. This he handed to Mike with a flourish that was for my benefit. "What's up?"

"Mike's in trouble," Lottie said quickly.

Inge nodded. "I heard the shots outside. Damn it, Mike, a soldier shouldn't get mixed up in politics. A soldier's supposed to leave politics to the politicians. All he's got to do is go out and take part in the shooting when the politicians tell him to."

"A Hell of a lot you know about it," Mike said. "Anyhow, I ain't in the Army now."

Lottie Moore was at one of the windows, listening. "Be quiet," she said. We could hear a crowd threshing around inside the Union Club. "Nobody here," somebody shouted. "Let's divide up and take the river bank."

Inge looked at Mike Shea. "Sounds like they was really interested, Mike." I did not like the way his eyes shifted without any movement of his head.

Through the thin walls of The Golden Rule we could hear another shout, "We better have a look next door."

"Hell, he wouldn't run in there after killing a man!"

"Won't do no harm to make sure. You and Mac have a look."

Lottie turned from the window, her face pale. "Mike, they're coming!"

Inge got to his feet. "Why don't you and the kid step into that wardrobe there? Pete and I can handle them."

Mike looked hard at Inge. Out in the hall I heard the tinkle of the front door bell, then a knocking. A man yelled out, "Open up there, Boozy! An' there's a guard at the back door, so don't try nothing!"

I was keeping my eye on Pete Forrest, my heart pounding hard. He had taken his glance off Inge and was watching Mike with those dull eyes. Mike must have had the same thoughts as I, for suddenly his carbine came up and he said, "You got to forgive me, Kirt, for bein' just a little nervous. . . . Caleb, Mr. Inge is goin' to get in the wardrobe with us, and I'll thank you to keep that pistol of yours right close to him."

"Yes, sir." I brought out the Coe pistol, hoping that Inge would not see the tremor of my hand. The ball was gone, and I had not reloaded. But I cocked back the hammer and waited.

"Pete," the Irishman went on quickly, "I'll be keepin' you in line with this carbine—so just keep your big mouth shut and let Lottie do the talkin'."

He began backing toward the wardrobe and stepped up into it. Then he motioned for me to follow him. "Come on, Kirt," he said in a low voice. "And when you're standin' beside Caleb remember he's nervous with a gun on account of he ain't very used to 'em."

When we got into the wardrobe and pulled the gingham curtain across the front it was a fairly tight squeeze. My weapon was against Inge's side. Mike held the barrel of the carbine up and watched the tall shadow of Forrest through the thin cloth. The lamplight on the other side revealed the whole room to us through a fog.

Lottie opened the door of her room and called out, "Hold on, Boozy. I'll answer it."

I heard her greet someone in the hallway and for an awful moment I had the fear that she was going to betray Mike. Hadn't Mike said that Inge owned The Golden Rule, and wasn't Lottie a part of it?

"The place is yours, boys," I heard Lottie say. "Do you mind lookin' in my room first?"

Through the gingham covering I recognized a lanky fellow as one of the men Mike had lifted in the chair down at the saloon. He walked half way into the room and saw Forrest. Then he stopped short. "Hello, Pete. Beggin' your pardon—and Lottie's, too. I'm lookin' for Mike Shea." He laughed. "But I don't reckon I'd find the both of you in one lady's room!"

"I haven't seen Mike," Lottie said. "Maybe he's upstairs, though."

The lanky man laughed again. "I don't reckon he'd be anywhere but here if he was in The Golden Rule."

"If I see him I'll tell him you were looking for him, Mac."

"You won't be seein' him for a while, Lottie, is my guess. He ventilated a party in the back tonight. Funny you didn't hear the shots next door."

Lottie gave a little cry of disbelief. Cramped behind the wardrobe, I listened in admiration. I suppose that in her business she had to be a good actress, and I have heard it claimed that the more innocent a woman the less histrionic ability she possesses. "I heard some shots. But Mike wouldn't shoot anybody in the back."

"Don't seem right to me, neither. But it sure looks like it. . . . Well, sorry to be causin' you trouble."

The presence of Forrest there in Lottie's room had drawn all his suspicion. It was impossible for him to believe that Lottie could be shielding Mike with Pete Forrest alive and breathing in the same room. I heard him from the hallway, "Come on down from up there, Jim. He ain't in here."

We stayed in the wardrobe for some moments after we heard the big front door close. When Lottie had shut her own door and turned the key, Mike slid back the curtain and stepped out. We were dripping with sweat, and as we stepped down to the floor Kirt smiled at me. "Would it be all right if I got out my handkerchief?" Without waiting for my permission he pulled a white square from his breast pocket and mopped his face. If the man was angry, he did not show it.

"I hated like Hell to do that," Mike said. "I really ain't sure I had any cause. But you been in tight squeezes, Kirt. You know a man can't take chances with his own grandmother."

"Forget it," Inge said. He turned his glance to Lottie, smiled slowly and without humor. "That was a nice piece of work, Lottie."

Mike went to the window and peered through a crack in the shade. "They've gone," he said, and turned to Lottie. "As soon as the other bunch gets back from downriver we'll leave."

We had not long to wait, for soon we heard them down on the river bank. Apparently they had gone only a little way, realizing the futility of a search for two men in the black of night. It was not much fun stumbling through the mud; unsure of their quarry, they preferred to get back to their cards or their drinking or their wives and forget all about it until they saw Mike again.

As their voices died out Mike said, "We'd better get going, Caleb."

Lottie put her hands on the lapels of his coat and stood looking into his eyes. Her face was quite close to his, but they did not kiss. "Write me where you are, won't you, Mike? And take it easy." Her voice was friendly and gay instead of sad, and I thought it a queer way to be saying goodbye.

"I'll tell you where I light," Mike said. "And you be telling me when things quiet down. Or maybe I'll send for you, Lottie. If I find something good, I'll send for you."

"Sure," Lottie said. "Just say the word, Mike, and I'll be coming."

Mike turned to Kirt and said shortly, "You were all right, Inge."

Inge waved his ungloved hand slowly toward us. "Don't mention it, Shea. Glad to be of service. Maybe you can do the same for me some time."

Mike and Lottie and I left the two men in the room, and she closed the door against them. As Lottie turned down the wick of the hall lamp she gave me a warm smile that made me tingle inside.

"If Kirt makes trouble for you—on account of this—" Mike said.

"He won't. Kirt's all right, Mike."

"Be seein' you, Lottie. . . ."

He opened the door through which we had fled into The Golden Rule. Upstairs there was still that heavy drone of women talking, and the high voice that nobody paid any attention to. Mike let himself down on the rungs nailed to the piling, and I followed into the darkness after him.

CHAPTER

3

WE struck out in the darkness, down toward the river. At the bank Mike turned east. Now as I watched Mike's broad back hurrying on, saw him skulking along the river's edge like a hunted dog, I understood that we were face to face with something bigger than he was. It was embodied in that mob I had seen coming along Front Street; it was given voice in the strained, eager, nervous tone the lanky man had used when he asked for Mike. I knew now what it was to run afoul of society, to be wanted in order that you could be punished, and it was not pleasant.

I hated seeing Mike run through the night, afraid. I realized more than ever that he should have stayed in the Army where his Irish impulses could be guided, or dissipated in routine, where the enemy his nature demanded could be staked out and declared fair game.

There was a light in the Danbys' bedroom as we hurried by, and I wondered if they had heard what had happened to us. I remembered now what Martha Danby had said, and while she had been right I was not sorry I had disobeyed her. There was always with me the feeling that Mike wouldn't be what he was if it had not been for me. That man had fallen in the street up there because I had been foolish enough to let Mike bring me to Dalles City to try to educate me.

He was saying nothing, but I could hear him breathing hard from the exertion of making his way hurriedly along the rough stones and the stretches of green-smelling mud. Every few hundred yards he would turn around to see if I was making it all right. When we got well past the town he said we'd better take the portage road, because it would be deserted at that hour and would be easier going.

We scrambled up the bank, scratching ourselves in the brush, and when we got to the road Mike said, "Let's rest a while." He looked all around him, a long time in every direction, and then he dropped down on his haunches, like a man in front of a fire.

"What are we going to do?" I said.

He didn't answer for a moment. Then: "I'm damned sorry I got you into this, Caleb. But there's nothing for it now. If you stayed in town, and I wasn't there, they'd hang it on you, maybe. And God damn it, *I* don't want to go back there and be hanged for shootin' a Southern sympathizer."

"Would they really hang us?"

Mike considered this. "You can't tell about a mob," he said. "I saw a mob once in Portland, handling a little fellow that wasn't half as big as you are. They kept walkin' along with him, and every once in a while he'd show up from somewhere inside the mob and every time you got a glimpse of him he was a little less like a human being. I remember the way his head was—just a ball of blood shinin' in the sun."

"They wouldn't do that to you," I said.

"You can't tell. There's some mighty high-up people in that town that wouldn't mind seein' a Unionist swing. Of course, they'd say I murdered him in cold blood. You might get put in prison as an accomplice." Mike dropped back on his rump and stretched his long legs out in front of him. "I haven't done much but make trouble for you, Caleb."

I told him that wasn't true. "We got to get away from town for a while, though," I said. "Maybe if we stay away a while it'll all be forgotten about when we come back."

"I'd like to go to Steptoeville," Mike said.

A sudden thought struck me. "Look, Mike. If we go up to the landing before dawn we can get aboard the *Wright*. Captain White will take us up to the Wallula landing."

"On Coe's boat?" Mike said. "I wouldn't be caught dead on his boat."

"We'll have to, Mike. We haven't got anything to eat and if we start overland we're liable to be seen before we can get far." I was as patient with him as if he were half my own age. He was a seasoned trooper and he knew perfectly well what the trip on foot to Steptoeville would be. But he was trying to blind himself to it because he didn't like Lawrence Coe.

He didn't say any more for a while, and I kept silent, too. Finally he turned and said, "Leastwise Coe ain't on the boat. He went down to Portland yesterday. Is this Captain White all right? Is he a Union man?"

"I don't know whether he is or not, but he'd let us stay on the boat somewhere. I know he would."

"Would he make us pay fare?" Mike asked. "I only got forty-three dollars, and we'll need that, most likely, when we get to Steptoeville."

"I don't think he would. Anyway, he'd let us pay him back when we got some money."

Mike considered the thing again. "You know, that might be all right, Caleb. I mean if you're sure this Captain White is good stuff. Because it ain't likely at all that they'd figure we'd try to take the boat upriver. But the whole thing depends on White. I wish you knew whether he was a Union man or not. Suppose we got on the boat, and one of the passengers told him what had happened in Dalles City and he decided to snake us out and give us over to 'em?"

"He wouldn't do that. I know he wouldn't. You let me talk to him first."

"All right," said Mike, getting up. "I guess that's what we got to do."

Refreshed a little from our rest, we started along the portage road. It was easier walking than on the stones of the river bank and we made good time. While we swung along I planned what I would say to Len White. I hoped that he hadn't decided to stay tonight at the Umatilla House instead of on the boat. But he wasn't one for sociability and most times he remained in his cabin on the *Wright* until it was time for her to start upriver again. If this was one of the rare occasions when he'd gone into town then it didn't look good for us. He would be riding in with passengers on the portage wagon. It would be difficult to get him alone before the boat sailed, and he might already have his mind made up about what we deserved.

When we got near the wharf boat on the bank of the Deschutes I told Mike he'd better stay in the bushes until I went aboard and had a talk with the captain.

"I'll kind of see how it is," I said, "and if it don't look all right I'll come back without telling him you're around."

Mike nodded. He was pretty embarrassed at having to depend on me, and he still didn't like the idea of using Coe's boat. But he promised to wait and not show himself.

There wasn't a light aboard anywhere, and, as far as I could see, nobody was on deck. This was not unusual, for whoever was aboard would be asleep and there was no watchman when the *Wright* was tied up between trips.

I tiptoed onto the wharf boat, grateful for the cranky sound of the Deschutes pouring into the Columbia. Nobody would be likely to hear my footfalls above the sound of the two rivers. I walked alongside the *Wright* until I was near Len White's cabin, then I skinned up over the rail and knocked softly at his door.

There was no answer and my heart went to the deck. I tried again, and from the other side of the door there issued a welcome sound—the well remembered, sonorous snore of Captain Leonard White. I did not knock again, but turned the latch and pushed open the door.

"Captain White?"

A snore cut off midway in its length, and the Captain sat bolt upright on his bed. "Stay where you are!" he roared. "I've got a gun!"

There was the scratch of a sulphur match, and the flame swung out to a thick yellow candle by the side of the bunk. White's hands were innocent of any weapon.

"What you doing here? You scared the Hell out of me."

"I got to talk to you, Captain."

He looked at me closely, sitting tall in his bunk, his woolen underwear all unbuttoned down the front, his hair standing skyward. "You in trouble, son?"

"Well, not exactly. Did you hear about the shooting in town?" I didn't see how he could have heard, but I wanted to be certain.

"No. You mixed up in a shooting?"

"Kind of. There was a man killed. He was trying to break up the Union Club."

White's eyes snapped wider. "So the blasted Copperheads are in the open?"

I could have leaped to the cabin ceiling for joy, but caution demanded that I restrain the impulse. "I was there when it happened," I said. "I saw it all. They've been tearing down banners every night, and writing on the building with chalk. There were four of them going to do it again, and this man got killed."

White had been watching me closely all through this narrative. "I see," he said slowly. "Then what?"

"Well, then, Mike Shea and I were there. But we didn't shoot him. His own men shot him accidental, trying to kill Mike and me."

Len White nodded. "Why are you up here to tell me about it?"

"I'm sort of mixed up in it, because I was right there—and I thought maybe I ought to go up to Steptoeville a little while. They'll say Mike and I did it. I haven't got any money and I wondered if I could pay you back when I got some money. You know, the way Mr. Handley and Mr. Sinnott do at the Umatilla House."

"Look here," he said. "Where's Mike?"

I tried to evade the question for the moment. "Would you let me stow away somewhere, Captain White, away from the other passengers?"

"How do I know," he said, looking at me hard, "that you didn't shoot that fellow yourself?"

"Well—I guess you'd have to take my word for it."

Suddenly Len White leaned back against the bunk and roared. "Listen son, I'd take you to Wallula even if you shot him. I'm gettin' sick and tired of this talk against the Union. We bellyached until we got into the Union, and now half of us ain't sure whether we want to be there or not."

"You mean—even if I'd done the shooting, you'd take me up the river?"

"Sure."

"Then, will you take Mike up, too?"

Len White's jaw dropped a little.

"Please," I said. "It's the only chance we've got to get there in a hurry. Chances are there'll be some mounted men after us tomorrow, and we're not outfitted to camp and we haven't got any food."

He interrupted me. "Shea is out there somewhere, isn't he?" He nodded toward the shore.

"Yes," I said.

"I'd have no business helping Shea. I don't like the way he acts, and I don't have any idea that Lawrence Coe would be hankering to help him any. Why don't you leave that fellow, Caleb? He's going to get you into a lot of trouble. Even more than he has now."

"I can't," I said. "He's been good to me."

White shrugged. "All right. Let me get some sleep. Get that good-for-nothing Irisher aboard before dawn."

CHAPTER 4

THIS trip was to be far different from my first voyage aboard the *Colonel Wright*. Mike and I lay in the brush until just before dawn, then stole aboard to take Captain White's cabin. He was already up and dressed, and with hardly a word he stepped out onto the deck and locked the door against us. The blinds of the single window were down, and Mike and I sat in the dark, not daring to light lamp or candle, and waited for daylight to filter in through the blind-slats and give us a little cheer.

For a long time we exchanged no word, but as the dawn began to show rosily we began to converse in low tones. Captain White had given us no instructions, left no word of caution, but simply said that his cabin would be the safest place for us since no one would attempt to enter it but the master of the vessel.

"This is going to be fine," I said to Mike, trying to get my spirits up.

"We aren't off the boat yet," Mike said. "But once we're in Steptoeville we'll be all right. Nobody will bother us in Steptoeville."

I knew that was true. Every town took care of its own bad men and once the criminals had escaped, citizens didn't worry any more about them. If the man had cheated at cards, or worked a gyp game, the editor of the newspaper might write to some of the editors around the country and these letters would be printed as warnings. But other criminals were forgotten when they were hanged or chased out of town or escaped as Mike and I had done.

After that it was the problem of the town they chose next. We had bad men from Steptoeville in Dalles City, and they were let alone until it developed that they were going to be bad men in Dalles City, too.

"Mike," I asked, "what'll we do when we get to Steptoeville?"

"Let's wait until we get to Steptoeville and see," Mike said.

That question and the answer were typical of the difference between Mike and me. I was a worrier, but Mike crossed his bridges when he came to them. I knew that we had forty-three dollars between us, and that with prices so high it would not go very far, and I wondered what we could do to earn some more money with which to live. My parents must have been great ones to worry, for there was nothing in my own life to make me uneasy, and certainly I inherited this tendency to be pessimistic about the future. It was to fade before the dazzling promise of a new country.

Mike and I listened without fear to the sounds aboard the boat; but when the day broke full and the portage wagon drew alongside the wharf we were nervous as witches.

Earlier we had heard the rattle of pots and pans from the galley, and the engineer had arrived before dawn in a buckboard wagon. Through the slats in the cabin window I saw him swagger aboard, no doubt from some romantic rendezvous for he was whistling softly and happily. Almost at once we heard him throwing wood into the boiler below.

The crew came along with the passengers on the portage wagon, and it was then that Mike and I began to sweat. We knew that everyone on the portage wagon must know by now of the shooting in front of the Union Club.

I tried to watch the passengers through the blind-slats, but it made Mike nervous. "Get down from there, Caleb. They'll see those big eyes of yours peekin' out and then we'll be in for it." After that I sat there, straining my ears until I thought they must be growing as big as an elephant's, trying to overhear some mention of what had happened in town. But I heard nothing; they all found places on the upper deck because it was such a fair day.

At last the whistles blew and the lines went loose. The rumble of the engine vibrated through the cabin floor. We could feel her start downstream, stern first, on the surface of the Deschutes. Inside the wall the creaking of the rudder cable was plain to our ears.

She backed into the Columbia, was caught a moment in the downsweep of the current. Then came the ahead bell from the pilot house and she swung so sharply that I veered against Mike as we sat together on the captain's bunk. Down below, the steam plant began to labor, and we heard the swishing of the buckets. We were on our way to Wallula!

"Well," said Mike. He looked around the cabin. "I wonder if White's got any whiskey?"

He began searching systematically, into the cabinet beneath the basin stand, then on the shelves above the bunk, and under the bunk itself. Finally he had exhausted every possibility except one cabinet nailed high against the wall. Across the wood panel was painted the word MEDICINES. Mike pulled open the door and revealed four shelves which might have been taken bodily from the shop of a particularly neat apothecary. From the bottom one Mike took a squat dark bottle.

"Never been opened!" announced Mike as his thick thumbnail worked at the seal.

"Look, Mike," I said. "That's for the passengers in case they get sick. Do you think you ought to take it?"

Mike winked broadly. "I'm a passenger," he said. "And I don't feel so good." My question must have reached his conscience, however, for he drew out two silver dollars and set them on the shelf where the bottle had been. "There we are," he said. "Now the captain can get a new bottle for his sick passengers."

Mike had the open bottle halfway to his lips, then he brought it down and looked at me. "Sometimes you remind me of Mrs. Danby," he said. "Maybe you been living with the Danbys too long. Maybe it's a good idea for you to be getting out of there." He brought the bottle up and took a long swig. Then he set it on the little table by the side of Captain White's bunk.

I said nothing. I was getting hungry and I wondered if Len

White would bring us something to eat. I decided that maybe he wouldn't take the risks and I tried to think of other things than the fact that I hadn't had breakfast. I wondered what Mr. Harrington would think when he heard what happened. I suspected he would tell himself that he had always known something like that would happen. He might make an object of me before the school, and this prospect was rather entrancing. I could imagine what talk there would be in the schoolyard during recess. "Caleb Paige," they would say, "he and Mike Shea shot a man, and a mob was after them, and nobody knows where they are now."

But I found that even this prospect did not appease my hunger.

About eleven o'clock I heard the key turning in the lock. Mike was asleep on the captain's bunk. I backed into a corner so as to be behind the door when it opened, and put my hand on my revolver.

But it was Len White, and to my great joy he had a pail of food with him. He shut the door quickly and set the burden on the table. Glancing from the whiskey bottle to the dozing Mike, he said, "Looks like your friend has had all the nourishment he needs, but you might be getting hungry. There was a lot of talk in the dining room about your little fracas." He began bringing out plates from the bucket, each one covered around with a napkin. "Here," he said, "light into this before it gets cold. I'll have to relieve Baughman now." He looked disgustedly at Mike.

"Mike paid you for the whiskey," I said. "The money's on the shelf there."

White went to the cabinet, held out one palm and scooped the silver dollars into it with the other hand. He turned back my coat and slid the money into my shirt pocket. "The company buys the medical supplies," he said. "And there's no call for me to be taking the money. You keep it, son. You may need it."

"The people in the dining room—were they pretty mad?"

"I don't think they're particularly mad. But it wouldn't be a good idea for you and Mike to be seen on our boat."

"I wish there was a place I could hide where I could watch

the river."

Len White grinned. "You'd better stay where you are, Caleb. And eat your breakfast. Now I'll have to take a turn around with the passengers." His hand on the door knob, he added: "Better see that Mike doesn't hit that bottle any more. He might get noisy and the jig would be up."

He listened for anyone who might be coming along the deck, then slid softly out and locked the door again. I tried to rouse Mike, but he only grunted and rolled over with his face to the wall. I wasted no time lighting into the grub. It was a typical steamboat breakfast: ham and two eggs, a slice of sirloin steak, some fried potatoes, a chip of venison, four big hot-cakes and a jar of coffee. I readily consumed my portion and stowed Mike's away in the bucket in case he changed his mind about wanting to eat.

After that heavy meal I was drowsy myself, and I slid beside Mike on the bunk. As I stretched out I realized for the first time how tired I was, and the soft feather ticking was soothing to my aching muscles. I tried to sleep; I knew that it was going to be a long and dull trip with nothing to look at but the four walls of the cabin. But I could only half-doze. Some of the passengers were getting restless and taking turns around the deck. Each time one of them passed it would startle me and I would try to make out the profile behind the blind-slats to see if it might be someone who knew us.

I was sick with impatience at not being able to watch the *Wright* run through the rapids. From the feel of the boat and the sound I tried to determine where we were, and though I was probably woefully inaccurate, it gave me a sense of power and knowledge, and made me feel very superior to Mike who—even if he'd been soberly awake—wouldn't have known our position. At last from boredom and weariness I slept and when I awakened it was by the blast of the *Wright's* whistle. As I opened my eyes the sound was bouncing along rock crags and I knew we were at Wallula.

Mike was no longer beside me, and I peered over the edge of the bunk to see him sitting on the floor, his feet pulled in and his arms hanging limply over his knees. "Have a good sleep, Caleb?"

I got off the bunk. "The captain brought you something to eat. It's in the bucket there."

"It ain't now," Mike grinned. "It's in here." He patted his stomach. "What's all the noise about?"

"We're at Wallula," I said. "I can tell by the way the whistle sounds. There're some high rocks on the other side of the river."

It was shadowy in the cabin now, and when I peered from the blind-slats I could barely make out the high bulwarks on the far side of the river. The captain's cabin was on the port side, and the landing was being made to starboard. There was shouting outside, and above us we could hear the shuffling of feet as the passengers milled about, getting their belongings together in preparation for the landing. Below us engine room bells were tinkling; the swish of the paddles had slowed. At last I heard the thud of the long poles from shore to keep the vessel off, and the placing of the gangplank. There was considerable talk and shouting as the passengers filed off, and on shore I could hear the driver of the stage scolding a fractious horse.

But Mike and I sat unbidden in the darkening cabin, and presently the sounds were gone and we wondered when Captain White was going to let us out. We stayed there at least an hour after the landing, and finally Mike could stand it no longer.

"He's going to keep us here until he gets a sheriff, that's what he's going to do!" He took hold of the knob of the door and started to shake it.

"Don't, Mike! Maybe there's somebody still on board that the captain is afraid will see us." I couldn't believe that White would betray us, yet I knew he was a strait-laced man with convictions and as we sat there waiting I began to suffer the gnawings of doubt.

At last we heard White's familiar step on the deck outside. He was alone. He unlocked the door and stepped into the cabin with a lighted lamp. "I thought I'd better give the others a little start. There's an Indian on shore with two extra horses. He's a Nez Perce and all right. He brings horses down to the landing sometimes to take passengers when the stage is overloaded."

Mike was still half suspicious, but he held out his hand toward White. "You're all right, Captain. If ever I saw a man who was all right, it's you. And I'm sayin' that we'll pay you back some day in good measure."

"I'd rather you'd forget it," Len White said. "I'm glad to do it, but I shouldn't do it—so the best thing for us all to do is forget it." He grasped Mike's hand. "Good luck, and if I were you I'd try to keep out of trouble. I've noticed that when a man starts heading for trouble he usually goes the whole way."

Mike took the advice with surprising grace, hanging his head like a chided youngster and he was grateful to slip out into the night. We walked ahead in the light from White's lamp, our shadows long and grotesque on the deck. As we passed down the gangplank I saw the Indian. He sat astride a white, long-legged pony and beside him were two darker horses, saddled.

White held up the lamp, full on the features of the Indian. "This is Cut-Mouth John," he said to us. The pitiless rays revealed the reason for the queer name. The poor fellow had got a bad wound and there was a scar intersecting his mouth from nose to chin and where it crossed his lips they were twisted and gnarled. It gave him an evil appearance which I did not relish, and I could well imagine Mike's feelings. Nevertheless there was something about the savage that commanded respect. Without the unfortunate wound he would have been handsome, and his bearing was full of dignity. Captain White had said he was a Nez Perce; I had always been told that the tribe was far superior to the river Indians, was more civilized in its family life and, until pressed too far, had been friendly to the whites.

"These are two very good friends of mine," Captain White told the savage. "They want to go to Steptoeville."

"I take 'em," said Cut-Mouth John in surprising English. He nodded toward the two saddled horses.

A little dubiously, Mike and I got on the horses, and the Indian handed us the reins he had been holding. Then he wheeled his own horse and started out briskly. We waved goodbye to Len White, still standing on the bank with his lamp.

"So long," he said. "Take care of yourselves."

When I looked back the lamp was bobbing up the gangplank, lighting the white cabin walls of the *Wright*. I saw it swing along the deck, cross the foredeck and disappear on the port side as Len White went to take possession of the Captain's cabin again. Ahead of us there was only blackness. The ground was level as a floor, but we were following some sort of a road thick with white dust. I did not relish the idea of leaving the river and the steamboat, following Cut-Mouth John into that unknown blackness ahead.

Mike rode alongside of me. "How do you like the look of that vermin?" he said. "He's a cut-throat if ever I saw one."

"He must be all right," I said. "Captain White said he knew him."

Mike didn't answer at once. "You set a lot of store by anybody from a steamboat, don't you?" In his voice I could detect the old resentment.

"This must be the stage road he's taking," I said.

"Stage road or not," Mike answered, "I don't like the idea of him riding ahead that way. I'm thinking that we'd better be riding one on each side of him. It's more sociable, and then maybe we can see what he's heading for." With that, Mike urged his horse ahead and I followed suit—or rather my horse did, for I was discovering that an Indian pony and a horse from Bert Patterson's livery stable had very little in common.

Cut-Mouth John did not seem to mind when we flanked him. "Just thought we'd keep you company," Mike said.

"Yes," said the Nez Perce. The monosyllable was precise.

"I notice you talk a pretty good white man's lingo," Mike went on. "Where would you be learnin' it?"

"Many years ago at Waiilatpu—at the mission of Doctor Whitman."

I heard Mike grunt. "Yeah. He got killed by the ver—by the Indians, didn't he? He figured if he treated 'em Christian-like he'd be treated Christian back."

I wished that Mike would be less frank when we were so much in the hands of Cut-Mouth John. But if the savage took offense he did not show it. "Doctor Whitman was killed by bad Indians," said the Nez Perce. "Their leader was an Indian with white blood in him."

Cut-Mouth John made the remark in his even tone, without apparent rancor. I thought perhaps that it would hold Mike a while, but it didn't. "Yes, sir," Mike went on blithely. "You get a little Injun blood into a white man and he's a bad one."

"I liked the Whitmans," said Cut-Mouth. "Mrs. Whitman gave me the white man's language. She gave me the story of the God. When the fight came at the mission I tried to help. I was a boy, and that was when I got this wound and began to be called Cut-Mouth."

I realized that the Nez Perce was proud of both his wound and his name. He was proud, too, of his use of English, and I guessed that he liked to rent horses at the steamer landing because it allowed him to display this ability. Indians are great show-offs, and Cut-Mouth was hardly an exception. Because he could talk good English he was, for an Indian, almost voluble. As a rule, the savages were not very talkative around whites, although among themselves they were full of words and gestures and expressions.

"They are having a big noise in the town," said Cut-Mouth after a bit.

"Celebratin', eh?" asked Mike, interested at once. "What they got to celebrate?"

Obviously *to celebrate* was a verb omitted in Mrs. Whitman's sober book of grammar. "I mean," said Mike, "why are they having a big time in the town?"

"They are giving the town a new name," said Cut-Mouth.

"You mean they ain't going to call it Steptoeville any more?"

"It is a name they do not like," said Cut-Mouth. "The name they are giving the town is Walla Walla."

"Walla Walla?" repeated Mike. "What are they callin' it that for? The Walla Walla tribe ain't anywheres near the town and never was."

"They are calling it Walla Walla because the valley has many waters," said Cut-Mouth John with the patient simplicity of a primary grade schoolmaster.

"Well," said Mike, "they been hangin' some mighty queer handles on things out here, and I guess Walla Walla ain't any funnier than some of the rest." Mike leaned over the pommel of his saddle and addressed me. "They'll think a man is stutterin', saying a name like that. Wonder why they don't call it Walla and let it go at that?" Mike roared with laughter, and Cut-Mouth John joined him without the slightest notion as to what the joke was.

"I sure don't be blamin' them for not wanting to call it Steptoeville," said Mike. "Now there was an officer to give a man the gripes! Steptoe blowin' that bugle at The Cascades was what let the Yakimas go free. But that wasn't near as bad as his march to Fort Colville. He just calmly leaves without hardly any ammunition at all, and he knew he was going through Indian country. So when he gets half way to Fort Colville the Palouse tribe orders him out. And he gets out, too. Only they follow him and worry the Hell out of his rear. He left wounded all the way back to the fort, and they weren't given nothin' to kill themselves with, either."

Mike's voice was getting higher and higher, for Steptoe was not one of his heroes. "No, sir, I don't blame 'em for not wanting to call a town after the name of that Steptoe. He was a good 'Johnnie Ellis' man, he was. They sure did somethin' when they put General Clark in as Commander of the Pacific Division. And this man Wright—there's a soldier."

"He is a great warrior," said Cut-Mouth John.

"That he is," agreed Mike heartily. "He showed the vermin what for. He let 'em know that you can't monkey with the U.S. Army."

"He is my friend," said Cut-Mouth John proudly.

Mike answered this with a skeptical silence. But privately I was vastly amused by Mike's conversation with the Nez Perce. Mike had been talking to Cut-Mouth almost as if he were a white man, a great concession for the ex-trooper. I think that after a while he realized this, for he fell snobbishly silent and we rode considerable distance with no more words.

It grew very warm a few miles from the river. The white dust sifted into my nostrils and settled like powder on the fuzz of my cheeks. I veered my mount a little so as to get off the stage road and this was more comfortable because there was no wind and the dust from the other two ponies did not bother me. By riding off the trail I could smell the rye grass and the sage, and that was comforting, too. It gave me an idea of the country whereas before I had had an eerie feeling of riding nowhere, of being somehow suspended in the night. With the smell of the grass and the sage I could imagine that the country was much like that north of the Deschutes.

But as we rode on I could sense that the land was changing. Time after time we topped a slight rise, rode down again, to a road flattened out like a floor. Occasionally I could see the outlines of cottonwoods or poplars marching along a little stream.

How long we rode before we reached the town I do not know, for in the darkness I lost track of time—and it did not seem long. When you ride in daylight you see a landmark in the distance and it is long before you reach it, but at night when there is nothing you cannot gauge your progress. I did not grow weary, for I had rested well aboard the *Colonel Wright,* but I was getting saddle-sore for I was not used to riding and the Nez Perce pony persisted in a running walk.

Mike grew impatient before I did. "It's glad I'll be when we get to Steptoeville or Walla Walla or whatever it's callin' itself. My head is as big as a beer keg and my eyes are poppin' from starin' into the black. Look here, Cut-Mouth, the minute we get into town I want you to make a bee-line for a saloon. I could be taking a drink with no harm at all." Growing mellower at the prospect, Mike added: "And I'll buy you one, too, Cut-Mouth."

"I will not have any," said the Indian with dignity. "I know the story of the God. It is not good to take whiskey."

"Well, now," answered Mike, considerably abashed, "I know the story of the God, too, and Mrs. Whitman—peace be on her soul—Mrs. Whitman and I don't just agree on all points. I don't say that spirits do a man any good, Cut-Mouth, but I don't say they do him any harm, either."

Soon after this little tilt on morals between Mike and Cut-Mouth John, I discerned lights ahead of us. "That is the town," the Nez Perce said, in answer to my exclamation.

"Look, Mike!" I cried, delighted to be near the end of our journey. "It seems pretty big."

"It ain't as bright as Dalles City," said Mike, "but it'll do."

Drawn by the lights, we urged our ponies to increased speed and it was not long before we were near enough to hear a considerable noise which bore out Cut-Mouth's statement that they were having a big time. There was shouting, and periodic volleys, and as we got nearer we could see a huge bonfire in the middle of the single street.

My heart sank when my eyes determined the boundaries of that street. The place was nothing more than a village. We crossed a low swale, flanked by willows, and before I realized it we were there. The first building was a long low structure of split timber covered with clapboards. Its sign, illuminated by the bonfire, said SETTLERS' AND INDIANS' SUPPLIES. On each side of the street there was a stream of men milling in twos and threes, men marching up one side of the street and down the other. For the most part they paid scant attention to us, although a few noticed our arrival and, lifting bottles high in the air, shouted greetings which were apparently friendly. One man, hatless and wearing only a pair of breeches and moccasins, ran out to us and shouted, "Welcome, strangers! Welcome, by God, to the little city of Walla Walla!" Drunken and meaningless though it was, the greeting made me feel better. After our experience in Dalles City I would not have been surprised to have been confronted with quite a different reception.

Cut-Mouth drew rein before a two-story building of whip-sawed lumber with the words BALDWIN BROTHERS painted across the front. "Here is where travelers go," he said.

But Mike's eagle eye had spotted a more interesting structure on the opposite side of the street. It was only a small shack, but on the window there was the name "James Galbreath" and beside it the outline of a whiskey bottle. Mike slid off his horse. "You get us a room," he said to me. He reached into his jeans, pulled out two dollars and handed them to Cut-Mouth. "There you are, Cut-Mouth, and many thanks to you. Caleb and I will be seein' you around." It did me good to see Mike his old self. "Go ahead," he ordered. "Get us a room! I'm going into Galbreath's here, and if you ain't sleepy you can come on over." I dismounted, bade good-bye to the Nez Perce, and started across the street. Two men, their breaths heavy with liquor, closed in on me. "Well, well, young'un! Where you from?"

They seemed friendly, but I was careful. "I—I come from down-river," I stammered.

They looked at each other and burst into guffaws. "He ain't tellin' just where he's from!" said one. "Well, that's all right, young'un. Where you're from ain't important. What's important is that you're in Walla Walla now. Not Steptoeville—but *Walla Walla*. This town is getting rebirthed tonight."

"I want to get a room for my friend and I."

Together they lifted me to the sidewalk. "That can be taken care of," the taller one said. "If you and your friend calculate to stay here, that's all right with us. We can use population, can't we, Pete?" Into the two-story building we went, with my new friend shouting, "Hey, Baldy, dust off that there best room. We got a customer!"

We were in what appeared to be a general store, and a pudgy little man with spectacles peered at me from behind the counter. "Got one room left," he announced. "The stage just came in from the boat and we're kind of full up." He looked at me more closely and, somewhat taken aback by my youth, he added, "Hope you don't figure to do any sleeping for a time. The boys are whoopin' it up somewhat. We voted to get a new name for the town today."

"I don't want to sleep yet," I said, trying to sound worldly. "I just want to get a room."

My two new friends, apparently feeling their duty done, left me as quickly as they had come, reeling out to the street in search of new enterprises. My pudgy little host led me upstairs and to the very end of a hall where he shoved open an unlocked door to reveal a narrow cubicle containing an iron bed, a stand with a basin and pitcher, and a rocking chair, all set atop a well worn rag carpet.

"There you are," he said. "Two dollars a night."

"Do I pay now?"

"Pay now? Hell no! Pay when you leave—only be sure you do." He slammed the door on me. A little bewildered and stricken suddenly with nervous nausea, I went to the window and raised it. From here I could get a fair view of the town. Galbreath's whiskey shop was directly across. I saw that the building in which I stood, the whiskey shop, and the store for settlers and Indian supplies were the only three buildings of consequence. The rest of the street was made up of shacks set up with poles on end and roofed with split boards. At the end of the street I made out a small creek with a foot bridge across it, and beyond this I could see, in the reflection from the bonfire, several log buildings, built square and hip-roofed and thatched with rye straw.

I left the window and went back into the room. It seemed bare and strange and unfriendly. I blew out the candle which Baldy had carried up for me, and went to join Mike.

Galbreath's was jammed with men—I had not yet seen a woman—but from the back of the place Mike's voice was booming loud and sure. Presently I saw his red thatch and broad shoulders at a table. Facing me and him were a group of men, already fascinated. A feeling of pride came over me and I walked boldly to the table and said, "I got our room, Mike."

He turned to me. "Fine, my boy!" His great red hands swung out toward the others. "Meet these friends of mine, Caleb. Yes, sir, Caleb here was in that little mess at The Cascades. Lost his mother and father—and he and I been partners ever since. Of course he was only a lad, then. But it's like I say, I been in the Army and I know, you can't trust one of those vermin any farther than you can smell 'em—"

"That's pretty damned far," put in one of his audience, and shook appreciatively.

"I ain't jokin' at all, at all," Mike said. "You may think Wright's got 'em whipped, and I ain't saying he didn't do a good job of it. But you put 'em on a reservation, like the government done, and they'll just get their stren'th up and try to raise trouble again."

Somebody shoved a chair behind me and I sat down. But I was

plenty worried. Mike had had a couple of whiskies and he was on one of his favorite subjects. I didn't know at what moment he would get into the question of the North and South, and I feared his listeners might be Secessionists.

I was particularly distrustful of one heavy-set individual about forty-five who sat directly across the table from Mike. He kept regarding Mike through thick spectacles whose nose-piece had been broken and was bound together with string. I had never seen any man quite like him; he was in marked contrast to the rough fellows in the whiskey shop. He looked gentle, like Mr. Harrington and Lawrence Coe, yet there was a readiness about him, too. He smoked a great curved meerschaum, yellow with age. His drink was beer and the more than a dozen rings in the glass showed how slowly he was nursing it.

When Mike had run down, he spoke. "Yah, perhaps what you say is true. But I think we should stop thinking of fighting the Indians and do some farming. That is what this country is for."

The man beside him slapped him on the shoulder. "Don't start that again, Heinie. Suppose you do farm—where the Hell you going to sell the stuff?"

"If I do not sell it I can eat it," said the German imperturbably.

"Well, we're eatin' regular as it is," said the other man. "This country is good for cattle and nothin' else. You can raise cattle and Hell, and that's the size of it."

The bespectacled, heavy-set man nodded. His two fat chins went up and down, but it was a nod of negation nevertheless. Stubbornly he said, "Heinrich Kiessling farmed in Ohio, and Heinrich Kiessling is going to farm here, you bet. The land is good."

"You can't farm, Heinie. You got four daughters, not four sons."

"Yah. Four daughters I have. They will work." His eyes twinkled behind the spectacles, but there was iron in his tone. I was taken with him, without knowing just why. Among these men he seemed solid and secure. To them he was a joke, but I got the feeling that to him they, too, were a joke and that he would have the last laugh.

The other turned to Mike. "Heinie here came out with an emigrant train under Medorem Crawford. Eighty of them—all farmers, by God."

"All poor as church mice yet," explained Heinrich Kiessling. "Most of them went on, but I like the looks of this valley. I have taken my hundred and sixty acres from the government for homesteading. Baldwin Brothers across the street are giving me flour and sugar and coffee for a year. Kiessling will be all right, you will see."

"The cattle will eat your corn, and your daughters will marry Injuns," the other man said good-humoredly.

"Yah. Maybe." Kiessling went on puffing at his pipe.

Impatient at all this attention to the German, Mike slapped the table with his big fist. "I was born on a farm—and I got away from there as soon as I could walk. I'm buying a drink around." He raised his voice. "Drinks around at this table. And add one for my friend, Caleb Paige."

He slapped me on the shoulder. "Caleb, my boy, we're going to like this town. We've got good friends here already. We'll start into business here. It's going to be a prosperous place, Caleb!"

Befuddled and embarrassed at so much big talk, and at being taken into the table as a grown-up able to hold a drink, I could only blush and fidget. I wondered how this village could ever be any more prosperous than it was, away from the sound of the steamboat whistles and the roar of the great river.

NT PAGE

WAYNE BUCHANAN / U.S ARMY CORPS OF ENGINEERS/AP, FILE

Native Americans fish from platforms over Celilo Falls on the Columbia River in 1956. The platforms were washed away after the gates of The Dalles Dam were closed in March 1957, raising the water level above the falls.

ST

Patient-related calls to police alleging assault at Seattle health care facilities

People seeking help at Seattle's hospitals for mental-health issues are being arrested for assault, according to a new report by Disability Rights Washington. The report is based on assault-related calls to police that reference patients at seven facilities between July 31, 2018, and June 30, 2019.

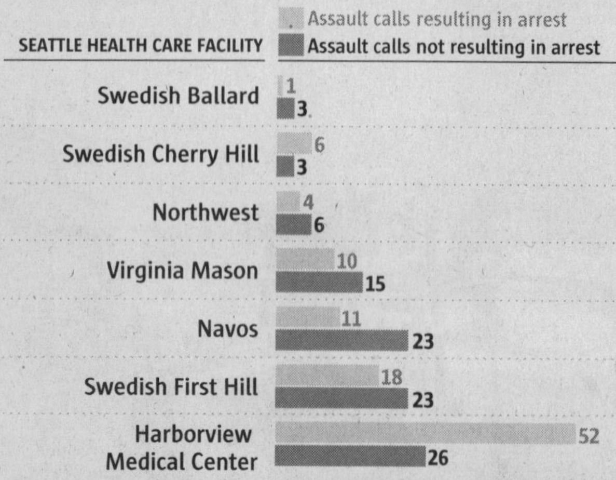

Source: Disability Rights Washington

MARK NOWLIN / THE SEATTLE TIMES

Swedish medical system — did not offer an immediate response to the report.

"Despite our prevention and intervention efforts, there are situations where the safety of Navos patients and employees is in jeopardy," according to a statement from MultiCare. "In these circumstances, each staff member or patient that is assaulted has a right to notify police and file a report. We do not influence that decision for the individual."

And, "In several situations of severe assault, Navos staff

Medical Center result in a staff member's call to the Seattle Police Department due to an assault by a patient," according to spokeswoman Susan Gregg. "In reviewing the circumstances around these calls, a majority of the calls have been because of significant bodily harm to the employee."

Virginia Mason has worked hard to create a safe environment for patients, visitors and staffers, wrote hospital spokesman Gale Robinette in an email, but "Threats and aggressive behavior, includ-

health care facilities in Spokane and Tacoma — and is seeing a similar pattern with assault-related arrests.

DRW reviewed 275 calls to the Seattle Police Department coded as assaults coming from the seven hospitals between July 1, 2018, and June 30, 2019. It determined 201 of those calls were alleged assaults by patients against hospital staffers or other patients.

Of those, 102 calls resulted in arrests, according to the report. Those arrests included some people who had been involuntarily committed by a civil judge to a psychiatric setting for treatment, according to Mosolf.

DRW then reviewed case information on those incidents from the King County Prosecuting Attorney's Office (KCPAO) and the Seattle City Attorney's Office.

The prosecutor's office handles some of the cases, because state law defines an assault against a health care staffer as a felony. The report contends that 22 of the 101 arrests were referred to that office, which ultimately filed charges in 20 cases.

In five cases, charges were dismissed, according to the report, and people in seven other cases pleaded guilty to lesser charges.

"Many of the KCPAO cases

the defendant w aware of at the tin referral, spokesman McNerthney wrote.

McNerthney also cite example of a psychiatrist Virginia Mason who was attacked by a patient while trying to perform an exam.

"The defendant was there just weeks after assaulting a security guard at Harborview Medical Center," McNerthney wrote. "In this context, it is the responsibility of the criminal justice system to … reduce the exposure of others to the individual's violent behavior."

Meanwhile, Seattle police referred 77 arrests from that one-year period to the Seattle City Attorney's Office. The office declined to file charges in 13 of those cases, or 17%, which the report contends is a lower rate than for assault charges citywide.

In the 2018 calendar year, the City Attorney's Office declined to file charges for nearly half of all misdemeanor assault referrals the office received, according to the report.

The office takes "assaults against our healthcare professionals seriously, and the aim in filing a charge is to holistically address a person's underlying behavioral health issues to ensure an assault never happens again,"

CHAPTER

5

WALLA WALLA had been settled because of Colonel Wright and no other man. More than a decade past, Marcus Whitman and his wife Narcissa had started their mission at Waiilatpu, near where the town now stood. The doctor had seen the vision—he wanted the valley for the United States. But of Indians he knew nothing, and he would learn only from the Bible. They killed him and his helpers, and the massacre was not encouraging to settlers.

Much later, Colonel Steptoe began the erection of barracks. But the luck of the Army with the Indians was so bad that still no serious settlers dared come into the country. Wright had changed all that. His defeat of the red man was so positive that General Clark announced formally that the country in that part of the Territory of Washington was open for settlement. The news had spread fast. In the spring of 1859 they began to filter in, eager to take up fertile land or to live upon those who did.

A part of the great trail of the Nez Perces formed the main street of Walla Walla. It was this trail we had followed from the Columbia with Cut-Mouth John. It stretched north and east across the Touchet and the Tucannon, along the Pataha and the Alpowa to the Snake and the Clearwater.

It was not entirely the opportunities of the Homestead Act which led men like Heinrich Kiessling to desert their wagon trains at that point. The bottom lands and the lush, green valleys were attractions, true, but sharp emigrants like Kiessling saw that the fort at Walla Walla would afford more than protection. It would be a market for produce. The town drew on a vast territory and Kiessling believed that the government would maintain a big force there at all times.

Next morning when I awakened in the "hotel" that the Baldwin brothers operated in connection with their store, I got a new and favorable impression of the valley. From the window, the village itself looked more disreputable than it had by the light of the bonfire which was now a circle of black and gray ashes in the middle of the dusty street. But beyond the poor structures there stretched a country whose beauty no one could deny. Mile after mile it rolled in gentle knolls until it reached the mountains blue in the haze of early morning. I learned afterward that they were called "the Blues" and no better name could have been found.

It was prairie country, but not the kind of which I had heard from the wagon train men who struck Dalles City. Bright wild flowers grew in profligate profusion over the rolling hills. There was the orange-pink of Indian Paint-Brush, the deep blue-purple of a tall bell-like flower, and the splashing yellow of mountain daisies. They were everywhere, set in color against the prairie grass which now was gray-brown after a long hot summer.

I turned into the room again and pulled at Mike's legs beneath the covers. "Mike, come and look, will you?"

Mike rolled over and sat up, his eyes bleary and unseeing. "What's the matter, bucko?"

"Come and look out of the window."

He stared at me long enough to determine that his trip to the window was imperative. Then he yawned prodigiously. "Look out of the window, is it? And what might be out of the window?"

"Look at the hills," I said.

Mike nodded. "I know. Them wild flowers are pretty, ain't they? I've seen 'em. They been there all the time. They were here when we marched acrost on the way to The Cascades once—but there wasn't any town then."

So as not to throw cold water on my enthusiasm, he yanked back the covers and stood up, a great gray figure in his woolens. Then he padded in his bare feet to the window and looked out.

"Yes, sir," he said. "It's a great place and that's a fact." He went over to the rocker, sifted his clothes from mine, and drew on his breeches. "I'm hungry," he said. "Let's see what they got for breakfast."

As soon as Mike and I had eaten breakfast I told him I wanted to go down and have a look at the settlers' store. I wanted to buy Victoria Hunt a present.

"You go ahead, boy. I think I'll smoke a cigar and then maybe walk up to the barracks. I'll see you here at noon-time for dinner?"

When I walked into the store dedicated to "settlers and Indian supplies" I was dismayed. There appeared to be little in it that would appeal to a young lady. From the rafters hung steel traps and tin canteens and rawhide quirts. On two great tables was piled hard-woven clothing. Broad-brimmed hats were stacked by sizes underneath the tables. The shelves were a conglomeration of staple groceries, wool underwear, heavy blankets, and a few bolts of bright cloth. I saw at once that my hope lay in a case of "Indian goods." Here, thoughtfully separated by glass from the inquisitive fingers of the natives, were odds and ends of trinkets calculated to appeal to the red man's interest.

In one corner I saw what I wanted. It was a colored toy book, and although the price printed on it was six cents I was informed by the proprietor that due to the great distance we were from New York City it would cost me one dollar. It seemed well worth the price. It was a picture book called "Mary Goodchild" about a girl of Victoria's age. Each page carried a colored picture of Mary Goodchild at some activity. Beneath the picture was a verse, and beneath the verse a comment by the author. One of the pages showed Mary walking along a street with a parasol over her head, and the verse was:

Drest out so trim and very neat
See Mary shopping in Broadway;
A sweeter girl you scarce can meet,
If you should search a livelong day.

Underneath this the author had written, *"Going shopping is a very favorite pastime for young Misses, and is often apt to learn them to be too fond of dress."* It seemed to me that this was an ideal gift, combining as it did entertainment with good sense. I asked the man if he would wrap it up for me so that I could send it by stage to the steamboat and thence to Dalles City.

"You bet I can," he said. He was quite pleased with my purchase. "It's good to see somebody buy one of them books besides an Indian. They tear out the pages and paste them up in their shacks. I guess you're the first white man I've sold one to. Those're good books for young people, too. Published by McLoughlin Brothers back in New York and they don't put out anything that ain't all right for a young lady."

Carefully he rolled the yellow-covered book in paper, turned in the edges and wrapped it around with string. "Want me to address it for you?" he asked solicitously.

"No," I said. "I'll do it."

"There's a stage going out at six tomorrow morning."

I thanked the man, paid him one of the dollars Len White had given me, and returned to Baldwin's. There I laid out another fifty cents for the transportation of the paper book from Walla Walla to Dalles City. I put no identifying mark on the package, as I was sure Victoria would know who had sent it. And I hoped, too, that she would be gratified to know I had thought to send her so elevating a gift.

The book delivered into the hands of Baldwin Brothers, and tossed into the box which would be carried to the river by the stage, I was at loose ends until noon-day when I was to meet Mike for dinner. I resolved to see what I could for myself. The street was almost deserted except for the shop keepers who leaned sleepily on their doorways, and I guessed that most of the population must be sleeping off the celebration. From beyond the town drifted clearly the sound of an officer's commands in drill, and I wondered how it seemed to Mike to be watching the proceedings instead of marching in uniform. I rather wished that he had taken me with him, for I would have liked to see Colonel Wright again but I judged I would have plenty of time for visits to the barracks.

Mike seemed to like the town, and while I could not quite bring myself to feeling content away from the river, I supposed I would have to make the most of it. I little dreamed that Mike and I and Cut-Mouth John were to be the ones to make Walla Walla a town far different from what it was on that sleepy, hazy mid-morning. My thoughts were back in Dalles City, and it was strange to be thinking of what I would be doing at this hour if I were there instead of in Walla Walla. I wondered what Martha Danby was saying about Mike and me, and I could imagine Ed Danby defending us, telling his wife that there was a reason behind everything and that she mustn't jump to conclusions. I wondered if anybody would run the Union Club now that Mike had gone, and if Kirt Inge was in Lottie Moore's room with his black-gloved hand resting on that little table with the marble top.

Suddenly my dreaming was interrupted by what, as I already knew, was an unusual sight in Walla Walla. I saw a woman—a girl crossing the dusty street toward a buckboard wagon, her arms piled so high with bundles that her face was hidden.

CHAPTER 6

OFTEN I have thought how strange it was that I met Mary Kiessling that morning because I had gone to the settlers' store to buy a colored book for Victoria Hunt. A book that turned out to be about a girl named Mary. It is stupid and futile to try to trace back and determine the turning points of one's life. I could say that if the young Southerner in Dalles City had not reached for his gun I would never have met Mary Kiessling at all. I could go back still further and say that if Mike Shea had not left the farm and joined the Army I would probably have stayed at The Cascades after the massacre. Such speculations are idle, and yet it has always seemed to me to be curious that I met Mary as I did. It may be that this is the purpose of my writing now—very humanly, to justify my actions and to correct, if I can, some of the stories which have been told in Dalles City. I have never resented these stories, and I have never condemned in my mind those who told them. Still, I believe that no one has a right to tell what a man did with any part of his life unless the teller really knows what was in the man's mind and heart when he did it.

There was every reason, I suppose, why I should have noticed Mary Kiessling that morning. Already I have spoken of the fact that she was the first woman I had seen since our arrival in Walla Walla. Perhaps the warm lush climate of the valley stirred whatever there was in me of my Italian grandfather's blood. It may be that at that moment, at that precise second there on the dusty street, I stopped being a boy. Or perhaps this had occurred a little time before—say in the damp, green plush surroundings in which Lottie Moore looked so tragically and yet so gaily into Mike Shea's eyes.

At any rate, I stood dead still at the sight of the girl with the bundles. I stared, unwittingly but nonetheless frankly, at her full figure. Ordinarily I would have been amused at the way her feet lifted out of the deep, white dust, like the paws of a cat caught in the rain. Ordinarily I would have delighted, in the superiority of boyhood, at her plight as she struggled with bundles that were too much for her. But now I did not. Now I stared, strangely entranced, at her Garibaldi blouse, at her full crinoline, her hair gathered in the chenille net.

She had come from one of those little shops with the clapboard roofs and the owner, apparently unused to lady customers, had made no effort to assist her across the street to where the buckboard was standing in front of James Galbreath's liquor store. And my own courtesy, so little used, did not come to the rescue. She continued her way across the street as best she could, and she would have made it without mishap except for an errant gust of wind which blew a piece of paper from the bundles. It swept down, directly across the eyes of the team hitched to the rail in front of Galbreath's. One of the mares took it without blinking, but the other reared her head so fiercely that the reins snapped like string.

The girl gave a little cry, dropped the bundles voluntarily, and grabbed at the harness of the nearest mare. She was, however, no match for the chore and I could see that she stood a chance of being hurt. I had been around Bert Patterson's livery stable just often enough to know what course to pursue. I ran to the heads of the team, grabbed their bridles and hung on with all my weight. I would have had less difficulty with them if Mary Kiessling had stopped screaming.

There was quick help, however, from Galbreath's in the shape of the white-aproned barman together with Heinrich Kiessling, whom I had met the night before. The latter quickly took charge of his team while I went belatedly to help the girl load the bundles onto the buckboard behind the trembling spring-seat. She did not look at me as we piled the bundles, but this was not from shyness. When we had got all the bundles transferred from the street to the wagon, she turned to me and said precisely, "I am so grateful to you yet, and for saving the horses and the wagon papa should thank you also."

The first time Mike Shea saw Mary Kiessling he said that she was "Dutcher than sauerkraut." Mary Kiessling was unmistakably German; but, unlike her father, she did not much care to be thought of as German. When she talked, on that first day that I met her, you could see that she struggled a little to try to keep the German out of her speech. But her blue eyes, the round cast of her face, her maize-colored hair, and the solid squareness of shoulders and hips, would have betrayed her without a word spoken.

Mary Kiessling was pretty. She was not beautiful, like Lottie Moore. But she was prettier than Victoria Hunt by far. Victoria had a face that was almost like the face of a boy. The eyes were brilliant and knowing, the nose finely chiseled, the mouth straight and firm. But Mary Kiessling's face was open and feminine, the lips were full and questioning. There was no steel in her eyes, yet they were eyes that could be stubbornly faithful to whatever she believed.

I turned from her, reluctantly, to Heinrich Kiessling. "That was a fine boy, yes. This is my daughter Mary. Where is your joyful friend who was a soldier? Your name last night I did not get."

"I'm Caleb Paige."

The blue eyes, so much like Mary Kiessling's, twinkled at me behind the thick lenses. "A team I would have lost and maybe a wagon busted while I was drinking beer and letting Mary carry bundles."

"It wasn't anything, Mr. Kiessling."

"Maybe you would like to come out on the wagon and see the farm we are getting. It is four miles back to town but that is no walk for a boy like you. Come on, Caleb, and we will get some of Else's apple cake."

"Apple cake is not on Tuesdays," said Mary Kiessling.

"No?" He seemed surprised. "Then maybe Caleb would like

to come anyhow."

From what he had said at the table last night and his tone now I knew that Heinrich Kiessling was tremendously proud of his farm and that he wanted me to see it. And somehow I was not averse to climbing onto the buckboard wagon beside pretty Mary Kiessling.

"I'd like to go," I said. "I'll look at the farm and then I'd better start back, because I'm supposed to meet Mike for dinner."

"That red-headed loafer!" said Heinrich Kiessling good-naturedly. "He wants to fight Indians all the time." The German winked at me broadly, then added, "Mary, this young fellow is an Indian fighter. Since he was in the cradle almost he has been fighting them."

I could see that she was impressed, although she tried to take on some of the good-humored contempt of her father. "So?" she said; and then, embarrassed: "Is that so, Mr. Paige?"

I gulped, speechless. I had never been called "Mr. Paige" in my life, and to be called that by a young woman was almost too much. I stood letting Heinrich Kiessling help his daughter onto the wagon seat, and when I followed I was so flustered that my foot slipped on the rim of the wheel and the German's great paw had to keep me from falling.

"I guess I'm not used to wagons," I said, red to the ears. "I'm from Dalles City."

This apparently meant nothing to Mary Kiessling, and if it did to her father he did not help me out. "Don't they have wagons there?"

"Oh, sure," I said. "But they have steamboats, mostly. They sail up from Portland, you know. Mike Shea and I came on the steamboat to Wallula."

"On a Sunday once papa and I took the wagon to the Wallula landing to bring home a plow that was carried on the steamboat," said Mary Kiessling. "It was all right on a Sunday," she added "because the plow was to turn up the ground for the sowing."

The piousness of this remark unsettled me so much that I rode along in silence. With the sway of the wagon seat, Heinrich Kiessling lapsed into a pleasant coma in the warm air. In less than a hundred wheel turns we had passed the last hip-roofed cabin and were out of the town, traveling over a thinly marked road which was nothing more than parallel trails with a ridge of prairie grass between. I could tell by the nature of the "road" that it was used more by horsemen than by wagons, and there were stretches where it disappeared altogether so that the Kiessling team made its way across the prairie grass with no visible guidance.

"You are going to the social?" asked Mary Kiessling at last.

"The social?"

"Yes," she said. "In Simon Harmon's new barn it is going to be."

Heinrich Kiessling stirred out of his doze. "A fine barn that is, my boy, and one like it I am going to have before it gets to be summer again."

"Can we have a social in it when it is built?" asked Mary Kiessling.

Her father grunted good-humoredly. "So a barn I should build for a social? A barn is for horses and cows and I am going to have one with split timber sides and shakes on the roof, like Simon's. Only his roof is not steep enough, I have told him."

I was still grappling with Mary Kiessling's question. "I don't know," I said. "I've never been to a social."

"Don't they have them in Dalles City?"

"I guess so. Seems to me I used to hear about them, but I never went to any."

Heinrich Kiessling chuckled. "What Mary is trying to find out is if you will go to this one."

"Papa! I was not! I should be caring—" She stopped. I turned and looked at her. Her eyes were straight ahead, her face flaming. The right wheels of the wagon went over a jutting rock and she swayed quite close, so close that I caught the sweet warm scent of her skin.

"The young men at the socials," Heinrich Kiessling was going on, imperturbably, "are not so much the kind that Mary likes. But music she likes and talking, and—" he stopped to laugh at his own joke, "eating from her own basket she likes."

"The boys here are not like the boys at home," said Mary

Kiessling firmly. "They are not boys at all, even."

"That is foolishness," said her father. "They are just the same. They have to change a little in a country that is so big and so full of Indians and sharpers. I think that maybe Caleb here is not so much of a boy as he would be back where he came from."

"I've always been West," I reminded him. "I was born at The Cascades downriver."

Mary looked at me with interest. "So? I did not think that anybody had been born here except Indians."

"You think maybe," said Heinrich, "that Mrs. Harmon's baby is an Indian?"

"You know what I mean, papa. I mean anybody grown up." Then she added, "You will come to the social next Saturday night then, Mr. Paige. Everybody is invited. I thought I had better tell you because you are new here and you might not have heard about it."

"I hadn't," I said. "I'll—I'll come, and thanks for telling me." I turned to Kiessling. "I suppose you and Mrs. Kiessling will be there, too?"

"I will come with my daughters. I have no wife now. She—she died on the way across." Heinrich Kiessling's voice grew so low that I could scarcely hear. "In a way I think it is what it should be. Mama did not like leaving. I think it was that she could not leave. I think she would not have liked it here so far off from her preserve cellar in the orchard."

I stole a glance at Mary. Tears were stemming in her eyes. I could have flung myself from the wagon for my stupidity in asking about Mrs. Kiessling.

"It could not be helped that we had to leave. I thought it was better yet that we start all over again and I thought I had convinced mama."

"She did not know," said Mary Kiessling. "She did not know until we got into that terrible plain with nothing around us anywhere."

Kiessling nodded. "And she would not say that we should go back."

"You mustn't keep blaming yourself, papa. You know that

mama was not well. You thought that maybe out here she would be better, and that at home she would not be."

Heinrich Kiessling drew a deep breath and slapped me on the knee. "Well, we did not bring you along to tell our troubles, did we?" He pointed ahead, between the mares. "At that clump of alders is where the creek turns and we turn there also, and then only down a little way is our place."

The road had petered out of existence a little while before we reached the bend in the creek. I could see where the Kiessling wagon had pressed down the grass but not traveled often enough to wear it off. The wagon slid crabwise down a little knoll and we began riding in the cool shadows of alders and cottonwoods that flanked the creek. It was not a very lively stream, but its deep banks and the heavy broken saplings bent downward along it told me that in the spring it showed a braver spirit. After riding over so much prairie grass, with the sun beating down on my back, I was relieved to see the rippling water.

"Simon Harmon's farm is not with a creek," said Mary proudly. "Papa likes a creek near the house."

"I would, too," I agreed fervently. "I don't think I could stand living where there wasn't some water running along. I'd feel shut in. I'd feel like nothing could ever happen."

Mary Kiessling laughed. "I like creeks, but not that way. I don't see why being away from a stream would make you feel like that. It's the sky and the land that makes you feel like things can happen."

"What is it you are talking about skies and creeks?" Heinrich Kiessling wanted to know indulgently. "Look sharp now, Caleb, and there will be the place."

So far I could see no sign of it. We seemed to be on fairly level ground, yet there was only the double line of cottonwoods and poplars, flanking the creek. But the rolling hills and the haze of the Walla Walla valley are deceptive. They make you think that you are gazing along a level plain, when suddenly your horses dip down and you see laid out before you one of the thousands of little valleys that are within the big one bordered by the Blue Mountains on the one side and the sage hills of the Columbia far to the west.

We let ourselves into one of those smaller valleys now, and there I saw the Kiessling place. As it came into view I hardly knew what to say. Certainly the sight did not seem to justify Heinrich Kiessling's enthusiasm, and I wondered if perhaps he and Mary had been joshing me.

"There it is, the house and yard," Kiessling said. "And a hundred and sixty acres also of the best land in the country anywhere. More of it I am going to have."

I could not now mistake the feeling in that voice. To Heinrich Kiessling what I saw down there was part of his heart, his religion, his life. But all I could see was a sweep of land ahead, a square of it stripped of prairie grass. There was a staggered rail fence and within the enclosure a house so small that I could not believe that Heinrich Kiessling and his four daughters could possibly live there. It was built of whip-sawed lumber, whitewashed, and the roof was overlapping pine boards. The covered porch was twice as big as the house itself and its strong underpinning made me suspect that the careful Heinrich planned that this would be the next addition to the living quarters. Completely surrounding the house was a square of poplars, newly transplanted and no higher than a dog's back.

Two heifers nuzzled hay in a corral near the house, and half a dozen great hogs were bogged down contentedly in a black-and-brown heap in the shadow of the heifers.

"On the other side of the house is a smoke house that you cannot see from here," said Heinrich Kiessling, "and a shed where I kept the two cows when they were calves." He handed the lines across my knees to Mary, jumped out and went to the fence. There he pulled back two rails and Mary drove the team through. "Yah," he said, coming back to the wagon and helping Mary down, "it is not so fine a place as we had back home—but the ground is better and on it we will make a finer place."

We had no sooner arrived than three girls came rushing from the house, greeting Kiessling as if they had been separated from him for years. I stood in confusion by the wagon wheel wishing

I hadn't come.

"My other three girls I want you should know," said Heinrich. "This is Caleb Paige who is new in Walla Walla." He pointed with a red, stubby forefinger at each of the girls in turn as he named her. "Sidonie, Else and Hulda. Else is the oldest, and then Hulda, Sidonie and Mary."

"No, papa," said Else. "It is Sidonie and *then* Hulda."

Heinrich waved helplessly. "Always I am getting it mixed, they came so fast. There is not enough difference between them to make a fuss about. All I know is that Else is the—the mother. And Mary is the baby. Mary is the one who is ashamed of being German."

"Papa, that isn't so!"

"It is yet," said Sidonie. "You wouldn't be called Magda and you kept it up until papa let you call yourself Mary. But it's Magda written in mama's Bible."

I didn't know what to make of all this. They argued as if I were not there. I had never been around a sizable family, and if they were all as noisy and confusing, and as irreverent of strangers as this one, I didn't know as I wanted to be around any more.

"Here, here, *here!*" said Heinrich Kiessling, waving his arms up and down. "Stop the foolishness and take the bundles into the house while Caleb and I unhitch the horses." Instantly the girls obeyed, falling into silence and taking the packages out of the wagon. The three at home were dressed alike, in gray figured calico padded only a little, and when Mary came back to the wagon for a second load of bundles she had changed to a dress like her sisters wore. She did not much resemble the others, and I imagined that they took after their mother. Mary had the round features of Heinrich Kiessling, while her sisters' faces were oval, their eyes darker and more narrow. And they were thinner. It seemed to me that Mary was easily the beauty of the four.

I helped Heinrich unhitch the team and he turned them into the corral with the heifers and the pigs, but the latter promptly disbanded and scraped beneath the bottom rail grunting their disgust. From a wooden box at the side of the corral Kiessling scraped out two small buckets of oats and poured them into the feed trough. Then he persisted in showing me around the yard, explaining the smoke house, and showing me, across the fence, where he was going to erect the new barn.

When he had completed the tour he asked me to stay for dinner but I reminded him that I had to get back to town to meet Mike at Baldwin's store. "Well, then, a mug of cider you got coming at least," he said, and pulled me into the house.

The interior of the Kiessling place was simple. The porch led directly into the kitchen which took up most of the structure. Beyond this was a large room in which were set four beds with headboards against the wall. Another door led to a much smaller room and in this I saw a log-frame bunk and a chair—Heinrich Kiessling's room.

"Back home," said Mary, ladling the cider into thick mugs, "we had a grand parlor, but here it is the kitchen only."

"A parlor," said Heinrich, winking at me, "comes after the kitchen."

I thought the kitchen a lovely room, but I did not quite know how to say so. The floor was of wide pine boards scrubbed to a soft white. In the center was a big table with turned legs and drawers beneath. The cook stove was huge, the largest I had ever seen, and I could imagine Mama Kiessling insisting that, weighty as it was, it be taken with them on the trip across the plains. Poor Mama Kiessling, being so insistent about the stove, and then not getting to cook a meal on it where it sat now so shining and black. It was probably she who had packed away the glistening pots which hung in neat rows, no doubt in the same order as back home, on the walls.

The room was redolent with cooking smells—warm bread, and simmering apples, and spices spilled a little in some corner of the cupboard. The cider was sweet and warm; willingly I drank three full mugs before I decided I had better be starting for town.

"I sure have enjoyed myself," I told Heinrich, and suddenly realized how true it was. Embarrassed as I had been at the presence of the four Kiessling girls, I was at home in that kitchen, and I had begun to feel a sympathy with Heinrich's love for what he was doing on the new land he had got from the government. The tiny poplars, planted so carefully and in such straight rows, and with so many years to go before they would furnish either shade from the sun or shield from the wind, were mute evidence that Heinrich Kiessling planned to stay and work hard. I knew now what he had meant to say there in Galbreath's whiskey shop, among the careless, unseeing men who had drifted into Walla Walla and would drift out again when they were restless.

Mary and Kiessling came out onto the porch with me while the other girls began to ready up the cider mugs we had used. "You come again any time," Kiessling said.

I thanked them. "I'll see you at the social," I said to Mary Kiessling.

When I got back to town it was far past the dinner hour. The moment I saw Mike pacing back and forth in front of Baldwin's I knew that something was up. At first I thought he had word from Dalles City that they were coming after us.

When he saw me trudging up the street he started toward me. "Caleb, where in Hell have you been?" He was not so much angry as excited.

"I rode out to Heinrich Kiessling's place with him."

"That crazy Dutchman! Listen, Caleb . . ." Mike lowered his voice. "Caleb, you and I are goin' to make a fortune. I can feel it this time. It's goin' to work." He looked over his shoulder, then urged me along the street toward Baldwin's. "Come on up to the room where I can tell you about it."

Puzzled, I followed him to our quarters over the store. He shut the door carefully, and bolted it behind him. "Look, Caleb, we can't talk too loud. These damned walls are like paper. But you and I and Cut-Mouth John are goin' out of town on a little march."

I would have been no more astonished if he had said we were going to the moon with the King of England. Mike's voice fell almost to a whisper. "To get a diamond that's bigger than your head."

"Diamond?" I said, and Mike put his hand over my mouth.

"Caleb, you've got to keep quiet! If anybody finds out about this, they'll follow us sure as shootin'."

I nodded fearfully. "Does Cut-Mouth John know where it is?"

"Yes—but he don't know *what* it is. If he'd knowd he'd never told me."

But how do *you* know, Mike?"

"It couldn't be anything else," Mike said. "It just couldn't be. And then I got a hunch. I knew damned well it was time for my luck to turn, and now it has."

Little by little I got it out of the excited Irishman. He had been coming back from the barracks and run into Cut-Mouth John between the fort and the town. The Indian, still proud of his English, had intrigued Mike into conversation and they had fallen to recalling the Nez Perce country in the hills east of the Snake.

"Then he told me about this 'big eye in the mountain' he called it. It shined so bright that none of the vermin would go near it on account of they figured it was the eye of their manitou. But Cut-Mouth and a couple of others who'd been to mission school and didn't believe in that stuff any more, they got close."

The thing, Cut-Mouth told Mike, was bigger around than two fists together and shined in the sun in great brilliance. It was imbedded in a rock and would not be pried out.

"But hasn't Cut-Mouth ever told anybody else about it?"

Mike shook his head. "I quizzed him upside down and backwards, and I'm dead sure he never has. It just never's occurred to him, because he don't know what a diamond is. And it happened a long time ago, when he was goin' to school at that Whitman mission, and he just sort of forgot it until he got to talkin' to me about that country up there."

"What about the other Indians who saw it?"

"God damn it, Caleb, you're just like a Philadelphia lawyer with all your quizzin'. You're skeptical, like Martha Danby. I tell you this is big, Caleb! Think what a stone like that would be worth. Millions, that's what! We'd chip off a chunk now and then and polish it up and sell it for a few thousand whenever we wanted cash. A stone like that would wreck the diamond market if you sprang it all at once."

I stood there trying to grasp what Mike was saying, but he

gave me small chance to absorb it. "We're slippin' out of here with Cut-Mouth before dawn. I'll get the grub here at Baldwin's, but I want you to get the rest of the stuff at the settlers' store. I don't want anybody knowin' we're lightin' out for a long hike."

"How far is it, Mike?"

"About a hundred and fifty miles, I reckon. We go through the Palouse country to the north fork of the Clearwater, then through the Lolo cut. We'll take Cut-Mouth's nags." Mike looked at me eagerly. "Of course, you don't have to go if you don't want. But I want you to be in on this. I got to let Cut-Mouth have some of it, naturally, and I sure wouldn't feel right about splittin' with him and leavin' you out of it."

"I'll go," I told Mike.

"That's the talk! We can get another carbine from a friend of mine at the barracks. He's goin' to cache it in the grass and we'll pick it up on the way out tomorrow mornin'." Mike hauled off and slapped me on the back joyously. "We're goin' to be rich, bucko!"

CHAPTER 7

When I rode along with the Kiesslings I did not expect to be traversing the same thin road after dusk of the same day. But I found myself doing it, without quite knowing why, without being able to give myself any reason for it except that I did not want to leave at dawn without telling Mary Kiessling. It was a strange, new feeling that possessed me, and I struggled to understand it. Time after time I stopped in the prairie grass, telling myself that I should return to town and go to bed.

"You've got to be up before dawn tomorrow and there's a long journey," I said to myself.

"But Mike is going on the journey, too, and he's not in bed. He's at Galbreath's whiskey shop and he won't be home until after midnight."

Then I told myself that Mike was a man, that it didn't make any difference how late he stayed up at night.

"But you're a man. You're seventeen. Mary Kiessling called you 'Mr. Paige.' "

Mary Kiessling! I stood thinking of the soft roundness of her breasts beneath the Garibaldi blouse, of the scent of her milk-white skin when she was near me on the wagon seat. I saw her round blue eyes, brimming with tears as Heinrich Kiessling told about her mother. And I could hear her voice asking me if I would be at the Saturday social. I could hear it plainly, above the chirp of the crickets there in the tall grass.

I knew I could not leave at dawn without telling her why. She expected me to be at the social. I would not let Mike take me away, as if I were a small boy with no control over his own movements. I would have to tell her. "Mike and I are going up the Nez Perce trail," I would say. "It's a special mission. A secret mission. I'll tell you all about it when I get back."

As I drew nearer the Kiessling farm I stopped arguing with myself. Something exciting and warm in my veins was driving me, a feeling I had known once or twice while playing with Victoria Hunt. But now it was sustained, carrying me along, frightening me, daring me as well.

Quickly, as rapidly as had Kiessling's team, I made the place where the road turned with the creek. The cottonwoods and poplars shown in black outline against a gray, starlit sky. I could hear the little creek bounding along and it occurred to me that maybe, since I was leaving for an unknown country on the morrow, I had better take a bath. It might be that I wouldn't be near any creeks for a long time.

I slid down the bank among the cottonwoods, peeled off my clothes, and waded in. It was not very deep, only half way to my knees. So I lay in the water, feet to the head of the stream, and let the water rush over me. Cushioned with the buoyancy of the water, the pebbly bottom felt almost soft. I lay there and looked at the stars, over the tops of the cottonwoods swaying gently in the wind. I began to feel clean and cool and hated to think of putting on my dusty clothes again.

After a while I stood up in the stream and waded nearer shore. There I brushed the water from me with the flats of my hands, pushing it down, flinging it off the ends of my fingers. I stood there naked by the creek, letting myself dry, looking at myself, proud of my husky legs and flat stomach, hoping that my chest was beginning to barrel out, like Mike's. My arms, I thought, were too skinny. But they seemed strong, and my shoulders, when I felt them, were round and hard.

Reluctantly, I went to my clothes. They smelled of dust and horsehide. Struck with a sudden inspiration, I broke off a branch from one of the cottonwoods, hung up my breeches and coat on a branch, and flailed them good. As I wielded the cottonwood I resolved that as soon as I got back from the Nez Perce country I would buy a new pair of breeches and a new coat and keep them to wear for Sundays or whenever I wanted to be presentable. That would be if we found the diamond that Mike was talking about. But even if we didn't, I told myself, I'd get work and buy the new clothes with the first money I earned. I wanted to look like Captain Len White, who always dressed very neatly when he was at the wheel of his steamboat. The river captains on the Mississippi, he said, had uniforms, but that was a lot of show. Why should a man put on a uniform to run a steamboat any more than to run a bank?

Maybe, I thought, I could get Mike to buy a new outfit, too. For the first time it occurred to me that Mike usually looked pretty disreputable. He never thought much about his clothes, and I hadn't, either. We just put them on in the morning, to cover our nakedness; and then we took them off at night to get into bed.

I wondered, as I dressed there on the bank of the creek, if it would cost very much to buy a waistcoat like Kirt Inge had worn, of double breasted plaid wool. I'd have to send to San Francisco for it, of that there was no doubt.

Dressed, and feeling much better, I climbed up to the road bank and renewed my trek to the Kiessling place. I was relieved to recall I had seen no Kiessling dogs. But as I got nearer I began to wish that there would be a few protesting barks. I had not the slightest notion how I would announce myself. It was not earlier than eight-thirty and the Kiesslings might all be in bed. Should I knock on the door and, when Heinrich answered, tell him I wanted to see Mary? Or should I knock at the window of the girls' bedroom? The latter possibility I rejected hastily. I would be singularly fortunate if Mary awakened first, instead of Else or Hulda or Sidonie. And they all might become frightened and begin to scream.

I wanted to talk to Mary alone. I knew how audacious, how utterly fantastic, this wish was—and yet I swung onward, believing in it. And somehow, as I walked along, I knew that it would happen. I knew that Mary and I would see each other alone that night, because that was what I wanted.

So I was not surprised when I saw the shadow of a girl walking up from the Kiessling place. Down at the house there was still a dim light in the side window. "Mary?" I called softly, not wanting to frighten her by coming suddenly into her vision. She stopped, and I added, "It's me. Caleb Paige."

"Oh . . . out of my wits you almost startled me." She too spoke softly as if she did not want the others down at the house to hear. But there was no astonishment in her voice.

"Did you expect me to be coming again tonight?" I said. My words were tight in my throat."

"No," said Mary Kiessling. "Why is it I should expect you?"

"You don't seem surprised to see me."

"I was thinking about you, coming up the road," she answered simply. "I was thinking about you and so when you were there it did not seem strange even."

"Why are you out like this?"

"Often I take a little walk before I go to bed. Most of the times Else goes with me, but not always. Sidonie and Hulda, they do not like to take walks before bed."

I touched her arm, forced myself to hold my fingers against it. "I came out to tell you something, Mary. I came out to tell you that I can't be at that social."

"So? Why not?"

"Mike and I are going into the upper country tomorrow."

Her voice came to me out of the faint white blur of her face in the darkness, came quick and breathless in a way that made my heart pound. "Oh, Caleb! You are not going to stay in Walla Walla?"

"No," I said. "But we will be coming back real soon and I'll be going to a social. We—we'll go together."

I put my arm through hers and we started walking away from the house, down toward the creek. We had not gone far when Mary stopped. "Let us not go beyond here. Papa may call me and I want to be able to hear him." She put her hands behind her, swept her dress up under her knees and sat down. "You must tell me what you are going to do in the upper country."

"I can't tell you," I said. "It's a secret mission."

But it was not long before I had told her, swearing her to secrecy. I told her because my heart was bursting to confide in her, to own a secret with her against the world. I told her about the diamond, and how rich I would be. I grew as fired as Mike Shea.

She listened, rapt. At first she was unbelieving; and then, as the thing grew in her mind, she believed in it. With a great sigh she lay back on the grass, her arms behind her head. "Oh, Caleb, it would be a grand thing to find a giant diamond on a mountain."

Suddenly, unaccountably, I stooped and kissed her. I kissed her full on the lips and held my face to hers. She wrenched her head away and sat up, beating the sides of my head with her small fists.

"A thing like that you should not do—you—you clumsy *dumkopf!*"

I grew angry. Angry at what she had called me, but more angry still because I knew that she was lying—lying to me and to herself. For she had cried out in a whisper when she might have screamed to Heinrich Kiessling.

"I shouldn't?" I retorted hotly. "Run home, then. Or yell for your father."

She stared at me, her clenched fists in front of her.

"Go on," I said. "Yell—or run home. I don't give a damn which."

"Oh! . . ." It was a little cry. "You cannot swear at me." She burst into tears.

"Mary! Mary, please don't do that." I reached out and took her by the shoulders. She jerked away. I tried it again, and she jerked from me a second time. "Mary, listen to me—don't do that. I kissed you because I like you. You don't figure I'd come all the way out here again to tell you goodbye if I didn't like you?" Awkwardly, on my knees in the grass, I held her head against my breast. For a long time she did not move. Then: "Oh, Caleb. Your heart is beating so fast." She searched my face. "I am sorry

I called you a *dumkopf*."

Suddenly from far out of the darkness came the sound of Heinrich Kiessling's voice. "Mary? . . . Magda? . . . It is time you are coming in now."

She stood up quickly, and I with her. "Yes, papa!"

"I'd better not go with you," I said, holding her close again.

"No, Caleb—but you will be coming back soon. You must promise it. Sometimes I am afraid out here in such a strange country and with mama gone. It does not seem right to me. I want it that you should come back soon."

"I promise it," I said, and this time when I kissed her she made no objection. Heinrich Kiessling called to her again.

"I must go, Caleb," she said. "Papa will be coming to the road."

She ran into the darkness, leaving me strangely weak and breathless. I heard her answer Heinrich Kiessling once again. I stood there until I heard the closing of the door.

The feel of her soft lips was still on mine as I turned my face toward the town. Word by word I reviewed in my mind what had happened; step by step I went over it, my heart singing in my breast, my feet with wings. I felt strong and alive and reckless. The edge of gloom that had hovered over me since that awful day on the bank at The Cascades seemed to lift. I felt the urge to do something—anything, so long as I was doing. I would help Mike and Cut-Mouth find the diamond. And when we had found it I would buy a great river boat with my share. I would make more money with it than Lawrence Coe had ever made with the *Wright*.

There was nothing I could not do. As I took great strides through the prairie grass, bound for the town, I thought I knew at last what moved men and the world. I could still feel the petal-like softness of Mary Kiessling's lips upon my own, and I wondered if Mike's ebullience, his great roaring vigor when he was in fine fettle, came from the memory of Lottie Moore's touch.

It was an amazing discovery to come upon: that possibly the love of a woman or the scorn of a woman could drive a man into action that would shape his life. Suddenly I found caught up within myself all of Mike's enthusiasm about that diamond, the great shining light in the mountain of the Nez Perce country.

I stopped in the prairie grass, there in the night of the rolling plain, struck still with the wonder of what had happened to me.

CHAPTER 8

It was hard to figure why Mike wanted to be so secretive about the buying of the supplies for our journey, for they seemed to me to be so light that they would arouse no suspicion. We bought a little flour, a chunk of bacon, a small bag of salt, some saleratus, a medium-sized iron skillet, and an axe. Nevertheless, Mike split the purchases, sending me to the settlers' store for the bacon and the salt. "If they ask you where you're goin'," he warned, "tell them you're up from Portland to do a little surveying for the troops." That sounded pretty important and I hoped the man at the settlers' store would ask me a question. But he set out the bacon and the salt with never a sign of curiosity.

When I rejoined Mike in front of Baldwin's he had purchased the flour, the saleratus, and the skillet; and in addition he had six bottles of whiskey, three each packed in grass in canvas bags tied together at the ends. "We're all set," he said. "All we got to do is pick up the gun and a canteen. Cut-Mouth is going to meet us by the creek."

"Do you think we got enough to eat for such a long trip?" I asked dubiously.

Mike laughed. "There's grub along the way, Caleb, if we hustle for it. An' Cut-Mouth will have a sack of dry powdered fish that won't go bad if the hunting don't show."

We started out in the cool, hazy dawn, Mike with his carbine, his whiskey bags, and the flour, I walking beside him with the rest of our stuff. As soon as we had crossed the little foot-bridge we bore along the creek. About an eighth of a mile from town, near a clump of willows, Mike stopped and brought up from the tall grass a carbine and a canteen. He grinned back at me. "Old Ben Guiness didn't fail us, bucko."

Half a mile further up the creek, the Indian was waiting. We saw the horses first, heads down to graze, and as Mike and I trudged along the bank Cut-Mouth rose up out of the grass like a bright flame. He wore a crimson shirt of Hudson's Bay flannel, and as we got closer I could see that it had some fancy glass bead-work on the front.

"Dressed within an inch of life," Mike muttered. "On account of he's goin' into his home country. I reckon he wants to let the boys back there know how well he's makin' out down the river. I'll bet an educated Injun is an awful pain in the butt to the old bucks!"

Obviously Cut-Mouth was impressed with the glory of his shirt; and I was amused to see, hanging from the saddle of his horse, four or five other bright overshirts. With them was something which worried me a little, a strip of hide to which was sewed with sinews two strips of porcupine hair. One strip was long and natural-colored, the other short and dyed a brilliant yellow. I had seen such a head-dress when the Indians attacked Bradford's store at The Cascades. The savages wore them fore and aft on their shaved pates, the porcupine hairs sticking straight into the air.

A little later on, when Cut-Mouth was riding ahead, I mentioned the porcupine head-piece to Mike. To my surprise he passed it off as of no significance. "He just brought it along to show his people he's well equipped all around. Don't worry, he ain't goin' to cause trouble. He's too all-fired proud of his education to get caught in dirty work against the whites."

Certainly Cut-Mouth's greeting was friendly enough when he rose up out of the grass beside the three horses. He hurried forward to relieve us of a part of our load, and he set to work immediately getting it fastened to the saddles.

"By God," said Mike enthusiastically as he swung his whiskey bags behind the saddle, "we're gettin' a good early start. That's half of any march."

Cut-Mouth nodded soberly. "It will be good for us to go fast," he said meaningfully.

Mike turned and looked at him. "What do you mean by that?"

"I have heard that other white men have started into the hills."

I thought Mike was going to have a stroke of apoplexy. He glared at the Indian, speechless. Finally he burst out, "What the Hell do you mean, Cut-Mouth? Did you tell anybody else about this?"

Cut-Mouth shook his head imperturbably. "Two days ago they went. I did not know until now."

"Do you think they're after the same thing we are?"

"I do not know," said the Nez Perce.

"Well, by God, I can't figure what they'd be goin' back there for. It's been set up as an Indian reservation, ain't it? Nobody's got any damned business back there." Mike was very indignant at the idea. With a flourish he set his foot in the stirrup and lifted himself into the saddle. "Come on, you two," he growled. "We got to get movin'."

Mike and I were glad to get astride the horses. The trek from town with the grub had fairly winded us. It had been a long time now since Mike was in shape for the trail, and although I was young I wasn't accustomed to marching with any kind of a load. It was surprising how heavy the burden became by the time we reached Cut-Mouth and the horses.

I soon found I was hardly more adapted to riding, but that morning I was in high spirits—and even Cut-Mouth's news that another party had gone into the hills failed to dampen me. I did not see how we could fail. It seemed to me that this was the great adventure, and when we left the creek and bore to the northeast and I saw the long, rolling, green-and-yellow hills before us I felt a kinship with the earth I had never before experienced.

I have felt that kinship many times since, and I think it is a part of the things which go to make a river man. A farmer has it, but he is not a river man because he has no love for the swift water and the white whirls among the rocks. A deep water man has a feeling for the river, but none for the land, and to me that is an unnatural thing. I know there is a real affinity, set off from somewhere within man, for the sea. Yet if it is there without a feeling for the land, it is not a natural thing, for man is of the earth.

Breasting a river, a man sees the hills and the cliffs move slowly past. Standing in the high pilot house there is around him everything there should be—the air, the waters that run to the sea, the ancient earth. I am sure that on that journey with Cut-Mouth and Mike I received for the first time something of what I had to have to be a river man. I think that the journey, after my upbringing on the bank of the river, would have made me a river man even if fate had not gone against us and forced me to bring a frightened Nez Perce and a pain-racked Mike Shea down the Clearwater and the Snake on a rickety bateau.

The Indian set us an easy pace which foretold the long journey ahead. Mike said that we were heading for the junction of the Snake with the Clearwater, and that alone was a distance of over a hundred miles up hill and down, only the beginning of the journey. Cut-Mouth had been vague about the location of the bright mass in the mountain, but as nearly as Mike could figure it was in the vicinity of one of the three branches of the Nez Perce trail, high up from the south fork of the Clearwater. It would be a journey of four or five days to where the Clearwater emptied into the Snake. Beyond that Mike would not venture a guess as to the length of time it would take us to reach the diamond. From there the country grew rougher, the hills steeper and more craggy; and there, even in June, there would be snow in the gullies.

By the afternoon of that first day I was not viewing the journey with the same lofty spirit of the morning. My groin was raw from the saddle and my ankles ached from the drudgery of the hours when I thought to relieve myself by walking ahead of my pony. By mid-afternoon the long sweeping views as we reached the top of each new prominence were no longer filling me with delight and wonder. I wanted nothing more than to lie down. Mike had let me borrow horses from the stable, and I had thought I knew how to ride—but I was mistaken. For a while I held out against making my weariness and pain known to Mike and Cut-Mouth John, but when the sun grew low and weak and our shadows streaked long on the prairie grass I had to give vent to my feelings. Lying in the creek by Kiessling's farm, awed by the wonder of my naked body, I had thought myself a man. Now I felt once again a raw and untried boy, too poor in build and callow in spirit for the ventures of men.

"Mike," I said, "I got to stop. My legs are so sore I can't sit on the saddle any more."

"You got to stick it out, son. Don't forget that party that's ahead of us. By the third day you'll be all right." He spat over the horse's mane, probably to hide his feeling for my plight. "The thing is, Caleb, we got to keep going as long as the sun's up. It's a Hell of a long way we got to go, and when you're on the march you got to be on the march."

I nodded, trying to keep back the tears of pain. The country was big—bigger than I had dreamed of there at The Cascades and at Dalles City. I thought of Heinrich Kiessling, driving across it with the wagon train. I thought of Else, and Sidonie and Hulda—and above all of Mary, coming with him, clear from the East, and was ashamed of myself.

But at last we stopped. Not when the sun went down, not even at dusk, but an hour afterward, when it was black as pitch and we could ride no longer because we had got into a gulch packed with pines and could not see our way. I dropped from my horse, unloosened the cinch, and let the saddle fall to the ground. Then I too dropped and lay motionless while Cut-Mouth hobbled the ponies and Mike went to work with the skillet and the bacon and a quail he had knocked over that afternoon with his carbine.

After a while I took off my breeches, gingerly and painfully, and examined myself in the firelight. The insides of my legs were crimson from the knee to the crotch. There were rolls of skin torn back from blood-red areas. I was in such agony that I wasn't hungry, and Mike suggested that I try to get some sleep at once. It seemed impossible until Mike made a mud pack for me. By smearing this cooling mess over my afflictions I managed to lose consciousness.

An hour before dawn Mike awakened me. I sat up and rubbed the sleep out of my eyes, moving my legs tentatively.

"I yanked your stirrups a little higher," Mike grinned. "When you get tired of sittin' down today, you can stand up a while."

The three horses were already saddled, their bridles hanging loose. There was a small fire, and bacon was sizzling in the skillet.

"Where's Cut-Mouth?" I asked.

"He's gone up on the ridge to have a look around."

It was still fairly dark and I wondered what Cut-Mouth expected to see from the ridge. I soon found out, for a moment later the Nez Perce returned with excitement in his eyes. He had seen a campfire. A white man's campfire, he was certain; and he thought that it was at least a day away from us.

Mike swore. "You sure it ain't Indians?"

Cut-Mouth shook his head. "No Indians would build a fire where this is. Those men are fools to build such a fire on a mountain where it can be seen."

"Well," said Mike, "I hope those Nez Perce brothers of yours do catch 'em poachin'." The Irishman looked across our own small blaze. "I don't like the idea of them bein' around, Caleb. It ain't only that they might find the diamond—but too many white men around here won't be good for us, either. When too many white men get to foolin' around in Injun country the vermin ain't likely to be partial to any of 'em."

"But we've got Cut-Mouth with us," I said.

Mike laughed. "Sure—but we don't know what kind of a reception *he* might get, either."

We rushed through our meager breakfast and were on our way the moment the horses could distinguish a shadow from a rock. Surely enough, as we topped the ridge I could see the faraway glow of what must have been a sizable campfire. "Must be cold over there," Mike muttered. "I'd say there's six or eight in the party with a blaze like that. They're sure damn fools, or else they don't value their scalps."

This second day was not as bad for me as Mike had predicted. I don't know whether it was the readjustment of the stirrups; hardening on my part; or whether it was the delightful variety of the country that opened out to us. Each new hilltop revealed something new, a sweep of folded hills, or an alien gray rock flung down in precarious balance with glacier scars still deep along its sides.

The descent into the gullies was more difficult than the climbing; a hundred times a day my staunch little pony would stumble to its knees, then struggle to pick its way more carefully. It was nothing for Mike or me to be pitched headlong, and soon such tumbles brought forth no comment except (whenever it was Mike) a string of profanity addressed to nobody in particular. Only Cut-Mouth kept his seat, although he would sometimes slip to the ground voluntarily when the horse was in danger of falling. As we progressed further into the interior and the descents became more precipitous, we would dismount and walk down the slope, a procedure easier on both man and beast. Too much could not be said for these Indian ponies, of which our three were excellent examples. Although the savages let them run wild and took no care in making a selection for breeding, they were almost always alert and fleet, and possessed of an amazing stamina. Mine was a dark-brown bay, with white feet and a white star on his forehead. I grew to be quite attached to him before that fatal day, to come in such a little while, I had to give him up.

The hills began to take greater folds, so that we would descend a thousand feet, then climb to a height of fifteen hundred or two thousand. From the higher altitudes were visible the great canyons of the Snake River, and once when we reached a high point we looked back to see the great high cliffs of the gateway at Wallula, where Mike and I had landed on the *Colonel Wright*. It was bathed in a shaft of sunlight streaming down from lowering clouds. It seemed incredible that we had covered as much distance as we had already managed; and when I looked at the hundreds upon hundreds of folded hills ahead I wondered how far such a wild and profligate nature would allow us to proceed in search of the great diamond.

From peak after peak my awed gaze took in a vast land that was at once beautiful and terrifying. Thousands of years beyond the memory of man the great Columbia had been dammed up by ice and, flooding over its old walls, rushed off to tear out another channel—the Grand Coulee, the voyageurs had named it, a great shadowy chasm deserted after the melting of the ancient ice. It stood high about the older gorge to which the river had returned, and out from it swept a basin of thousands upon thousands of acres.

It was difficult to believe in the reality of such wide reaches of land so filled with paradoxes. An empty gorge as wide as five miles in places, stretching for a distance ten times that. A flat barren land with no sign of life except the slow-growing clumps of sage. Forests, and lush valleys, hills and granite mountains, rivers and streams so intricately woven that they seemed all of a pattern. The land was everywhere and in an infinite variety that could not be missed even by a raw boy who had spent most of his life in the green shadows of The Cascades far to the west. Yet it had not failed to awe men of greatness whose experiences had been wide and worldly. It was not so much the headwaters of the Missouri that had given Captains Lewis and Clark the thrill of discovery as it was the sight of that magnificent slope toward the blustery Pacific, their dawning realization that beyond the Stony Mountains was a whole new world so vast and so distant that, despite its promise, it would be long years before its newest conquerors could make the most of it.

Had we been traveling that flat country that bordered on the Grand Coulee we could have made faster progress. But Cut-Mouth's guidance bore us far to the northeast where, he said, we would eventually find the junction of the Snake and the Clearwater. On the evening of the third day we camped on the bank of the Tucannon, and Mike was impatient and worried. In mid-afternoon, as we topped a rise, we had seen a thin trail of smoke which he feared was the fire of our possible rivals.

Yet from Walla Walla to the Tucannon we had seen not a living soul and by the law of average that fire should belong to Indians. The trail we had traveled was plentiful with their signs, with markings on rocks and trees. Whenever the forest was thick in our way we could see how the bark was worn smooth from the rubbing of many a pony's flank. I knew that the Nez Perce trails were as old as the tribe, yet this evidence of their presence, and the knowledge that we were in forbidden territory, was not comforting.

Continually I marveled at the meadow-like quality of the ground beneath these forests. I was accustomed to the thick underbrush of the Columbia at The Cascades—the stunted alder, the honeysuckle, the seven-bark and green brier, the fern. But here the floor of the forests was often covered with only the brown carpet of dried pine needles. It was eerily as if the hand of man had cleared beneath the towering pines; and yet there were no men, and no evidence of the clearing.

It was vastly different from the crowded firs and cedars of the lower Columbia. Here pine abounded, in five or six different kinds, and there was alder with a pale blue berry. Occasionally we encountered a woods much like the maples in Dalles City, and once or twice we crossed a thin belt of well-shaped oaks.

Whenever we built a fire, the burning qualities of the pine fascinated me. It left no charred residue, but only a little fine ash, a gray powder that could have been contained in the palm of the hand. When the fire was out, Mike was fond of drawing maps in the white powder, tracing our journey for the day. I suppose he got that from his Army days when every long march had been in the nature of a maneuver.

That night on the bank of the Tucannon he scraped some of the ash out of the dying fire, smoothed it with a round stick and began his tracing. When he had marked the spot where we were he looked up at Cut-Mouth. "Now suppose you just point out about where we're headin' for, Cut-Mouth?" He indicated the warm ashes. "Where's that damned manitou from here?"

"It has been a long time past since I saw it," the Nez Perce said.

His words fell like lead on Mike and me, for it was the first time there had been any doubt shed on the proposition that Cut-Mouth knew its exact whereabouts.

For a moment Mike said nothing. Then he laughed, more, it seemed to me, to buoy his own spirits. "You can find it all right.

An Injun never forgets where he's been."

"I was very small," said Cut-Mouth. "I was younger than this boy."

"You'll find it," Mike said. "When you get to the country it'll come back to you." I saw Mike's eyes suddenly narrow across the campfire. "Look here, Cut-Mouth, don't try any shenanigans. You said you knew where it was. I suppose now you'll be wanting something to go on and really find it. Is that it? Do you want money now to find it? Or have you already sold out to that party ahead of us?"

The shoulders of the Nez Perce squared. His pride had been touched. "I said I would try to find it. I keep my promise like a white man."

Much to my relief, Mike's attitude changed instantly. I did not fancy going on into the wilderness with any feelings between Cut-Mouth and us and somehow I believed in him. "Good," Mike said. "I knew I could count on you, Cut-Mouth. No hard feelings. No hard feelings at all. I just wanted to be sure. I been in the United States Army and in the Army we don't trust an Injun until we're mighty sure."

"You can trust a Kinapoo," said Cut-Mouth.

"Well, now, maybe I'll just believe that. Leastwise until it's proved wrong. It sure was Nez Perces that saved old Steptoe that time and no mistake."

After this we lapsed into a pessimistic silence. It began to rain, softly at first, then in great large drops that fell through the pine boughs and hissed at the fire. Carefully Cut-Mouth shoved the coals beneath a tree that had thicker foliage, and built the fire up again. The rain increased and lightning played in the sky. The storm was far to the east, but the rumble of thunder echoed and reechoed along the hundreds of hills. It seemed to me that the lightning always streaked in the same quarter of the sky and I remarked on this.

"It is the magic mountain," Cut-Mouth told me. "The fire from the sky always goes to the mountain."

"It's full of magnetic iron," said Mike practically. I think he relished getting one ahead of Cut-Mouth at last. Here, anyhow, was something Mrs. Whitman hadn't taught Cut-Mouth! "That's the reason it attracts lightnin'. That there magnetic iron makes it just like a big lightnin' rod." Cut-Mouth never said a word, but I could see him storing the information away. Mike took his silence for doubt. "It's a fact, because I was talkin' to a man in Galbreath's and he told me the lightnin' damn near got him when he was trappin' up there once. It did get his partner. Knocked him into a burnt crisp, by God!"

I watched the sky through the trees. The lightning continued to play always near the one place. My skin tingled, and the hairs at the back of my neck felt stiff. There was a burning odor in the air. That magic mountain was far away; but I hoped fervently that there was no magnetic iron in the hills which flanked the Tucannon.

By next day I was much more accustomed to the rigors of the trail. We had traveled through several distinct types of terrain. There had been the fertile valley land beyond Walla Walla which had petered into flat sage country dotted with an occasional basalt butte. Then we had meandered through a fairly heavy timber belt which was thickest in the gullies of rolling hills. Out of this we had come now into a stretch of land that was arid, where the only vegetation was stunted bunchgrass or a thin yellow rye grass.

My original feeling that our provisions were light for so long a journey was proved groundless every hour of the day. The open country abounded with large-eyed jackrabbits that sometimes took prodigious leaps to escape us, but more often stood frozen as we passed. There were prairie chickens almost the size of turkeys, and occasionally we sighted a ruffed grouse.

In the timbered areas I witnessed, each for the first time, a wolf and a civet cat, and while neither were probably very palatable they would have done in a pinch. Mike assured me that there were plenty of deer, although we did not encounter any. Whenever we passed through one of the meadow forests we were sure to frighten robins, black woodpeckers, or turtle doves, and magpies would follow us for miles to scold our presence.

I had been in the woods enough to know that what we actually saw was only an infinitesimal part of the game that was aware of us as we went along the trail of the Nez Perces. And Mike assured me that this was true. If we wanted to hunt, he told me, we could scare up a wild bird and animal population that would make my eyes pop. But we weren't hunting; and Mike was steadily increasing our pace, so fearful was he that others were seeking the diamond in the mountain. Consequently we depended less and less on food from his carbine, and more and more on the dried fish that Cut-Mouth had brought along. It was pretty tasteless, but once you got it mixed with saliva—not without considerable difficulty—the stuff was filling and, as far as I could tell, nourishing. Mike had the advantage of Cut-Mouth and me because he washed it down with whiskey. From the faces he made while he did it I judged that the advantage was a doubtful one.

However, we did have prairie chickens, and a ground squirrel; and toward the end of the following day we encountered a wild dog which had evidently lost its senses and strayed from an Indian camp. It was as vicious as a cornered polecat and would have attacked us if Mike hadn't brought it down with his carbine. Cut-Mouth was ahead, and the dog went after him first, but the Indian was unable to get his weapon unlimbered in time. Cut-Mouth's firearm was a musketoon whose barrel was two feet long, a smooth bore muzzle loader with the ramrod fastened to the barrel by swivels. The Nez Perce carried ammunition in a little hide bag, wads with three buckshot and a ball in each. I don't know how good a shot Cut-Mouth was, after his mission education, but the musketoon couldn't have been accurate for more than forty yards anyhow.

Because Mike killed the dog, and was so determined not to lose time with hunting sizable game, we had roast canine that night. I was shocked, but the powdered fish had palled on me. Mike was an old hand at dog eating; troops had often picked them up from the Indians when supplies were late and hunting bad.

"It's like this," Mike said. "I like dog better than bird, because there ain't a damned thing *to* a bird. I like deer better than dog, all right, but I'll add that I'd rather have a good young

Injun dog than a lot of beef I've bit into. And if you don't like dog you ought to try a horse ham from an old cavalry nag that's had a hard life and gone through its last sickness." Mike licked his fingers and rubbed them carefully on his breeches. "Yes, sir, a man will eat 'most anything when he has to. We've run across wagon trains where one of their party was disposed of thataway. They always claimed the party died a natural death, and maybe so. But once or twice I've doubted it. I think maybe I'd draw the line at that, but then I ain't ever been really *hungry*." He reached for another chunk of the roast dog and looked at it thoughtfully. "Hell," he said, as if to bring an adequate finale to his discussion, "they say these God damned Frenchmen eat worms, even when they got something else to eat!"

Busy with his own eating, Cut-Mouth had listened to Mike in silence. Occasionally he nodded his head as if in agreement. When he had finished with the meat he went to one of the smaller pines, cut a strip from the bark and began picking out the inner fibers with the point of his knife. When he had five or six strips on the end of his knife he transferred them to his mouth and began to chew diligently.

"You see," Mike said to me, "there's no accounting for tastes."

I felt there was some judgment in the Indian's selection of a dessert. My stomach was queasy after so much of one meat and I could have stood something of a vegetable nature. However, I did not follow the Nez Perce's example, partly in fear of Mike's scorn, and partly because I wasn't sure I would relish the pine fibers.

Nevertheless, I lay down that night with a comfortable sense of well being. The trees were protective, the creeks in convenient abundance, the food plentiful, and there was the companionship of Mike and Cut-Mouth John. I had lost some of my awe at the vastness of the terrain, of the endless rolling hills dotted with pines. I began to wonder if perhaps the tales I had heard of the emigrants and the trappers and the explorers had not been exaggerated.

If I had known how wrong I was in attributing pity to nature I wouldn't have slept so soundly that night. Yet even on the next day, as we pressed farther inland, there was little to disturb us, except the fear that we were too late for our reward. Once a cougar crossed our path, stood crouched for three or four irresolute seconds, then sped from sight as if to resign his kingdom to us. Occasionally a rattlesnake slithered through the yellowing grass, making the horses shy off, but none coiled to strike.

We were bearing now almost directly east, and to our left I began to discern through the blue haze a line of hills which Mike said was the canyon of the Snake where it made its big curve back toward the Columbia. These hills were brown and puckered, like a rumpled bed quilt drawn with thread from the under side. They seemed more gentle than the walls of the Columbia, and I mentioned this to Mike.

"You can call the Snake invitin' if you want, but don't depend on it too much. A river's just like a human, bucko. What's in a human depends on who his relatives are—and right close to here the Salmon River gets into the old Snake. So does the Clearwater and the Palouse."

"Palouse? Is that a river named after the Palouse Indians?"

Mike shrugged as we rode along. "You got me there, son. Old Cap Lewis and Cap Clark kind of buggered up the names around these parts, and the trappers and the missionaries didn't help none. They didn't savvy the sign language too much, and anyhow I reckon nobody can spell an Indian name. You take Cut-Mouth's outfit now. Nez Perce means 'Pierced Nose' in French, but none of them's got more than two holes in their noses and never did have more as far as anybody knows. And when you ask a Snake Indian the name of his tribe in sign language he wiggles his hand like a salmon—but Cap Lewis figured it was a snake, so he called 'em Snakes. Most ways, the names the Indians figured out for themselves are better, probably. Like Cut-Mouth's outfit call themselves Kinapoos."

"What does that mean?"

"They say it means 'the real people.' They don't think much of themselves now, do they? But nowadays when they're talkin' to white people they usually use the same name we do. They figure it's smart, I reckon, like Cut-Mouth there."

CHAPTER 9

On the fifth day out of Walla Walla we reached the place that Cut-Mouth John called "Tsceminicum," which he said meant the joining of waters, where the Clearwater poured into the Snake. We had struck the latter stream on a low, flat, sandy bank and followed its flow northward for perhaps five or six miles. Suddenly it seemed as if the river ran into the base of the brown puckered hills and disappeared. In reality, at that point, it took the Clearwater and, as if with the added impetus, turned sharply west to charge through a two thousand foot canyon toward the Columbia.

Across the river, and between us and the mouth of the Clearwater, there was a flat sandy expanse whose south limits were flanked by a high bluff. It was there that we decided to camp, so we retraced our trail upstream a way, then swam our horses across. The force of the current took us diagonally, making the fording a long and uncomfortable one. But at last our spent mounts brought us, dripping from waist to feet, on the opposite bank. And none too soon, either, for Cut-Mouth had calculated the current pretty finely. Another two hundred yards and, instead of striking the bank, the horses would have found themselves caught in the flow from the Clearwater's mouth. We could easily have been swept down the torrent before the combined forces of the two streams.

As exhausted as the horses, we dismounted and stretched on the white sand to dry and rest. It was indeed a beautiful spot for a camp. The ground on which we lay was as flat and soft as a carpet, and we were shaded by clumps of cool green young trees irrigated from beneath by the rivers. To the south was the high bluff which made it appear as if the Clearwater had once been a much greater stream. Across the Clearwater were the high brown hills we had seen at such a distance from the spot. They marched west, marking unmistakably the course of the Snake.

It had grown tremendously warm since morning. Cut-Mouth had tossed pride to the winds and his red flannel shirt across the horn of the saddle. Mike and I had rolled our coats and stuffed them into our blanket rolls behind the saddles. It seemed to me that we had come to a definite goal, and I was ready enough to stay there a while and watch the two rivers joining. But we had lain there in the sand less than half an hour when Mike rolled over on his stomach and looked at our guide.

"Which way is it now?" he asked. "We got to get goin'."

The Indian motioned up the Clearwater with a brown arm. "We follow the stream for a day, then we cross where it becomes smaller. Then into the mountains—toward the big stone mountains for two days. It should be there."

"It better be there!" said Mike, getting to his feet. "Come on, Caleb. And listen, Cut-Mouth, you keep a sharp look-out for those brothers of yours. I don't want 'em wingin' at us before you get a chance to explain things."

It had struck me as curious, the shunting of the Indians away from their land, and promising to keep inviolate what the government had decided the settlers would not want for yet a while. Since the death of my mother and father at The Cascades I had harbored a hatred for the savage. It had seemed to me that no end could be too vile for them. But the great rich country through which we had passed had made me wonder how I would feel if I had lived there always, and my people before me, and was ordered away because another race coveted it. Too, I think Cut-Mouth John's quiet dignity, his obvious pride in his Kinapoo blood, his trusting acceptance of the white man's language and religion, as nearly as the Indian could manage it, had affected me in favor of the red man.

During that journey toward the Stony Mountains I had opportunity to discover how Cut-Mouth really felt about it. He told me about the laws of the Kinapoos and they struck me as so good that I wondered why he had wanted to substitute the white man's for them. A Kinapoo was never to break a bargain. He was never to lie. He was never to take from another man his wife or property without paying for them. He was taught that the Great Spirit hears and sees everything and that He never forgets, and that in the hereafter He would give every Kinapoo his spirit-home according to how the man had lived his life on earth.

"But that's just about like our religion," I exclaimed when Cut-Mouth told me. "What did you want to change for?"

"There is only one God," the Nez Perce explained patiently. "He is the white man's God."

I asked Cut-Mouth when his people had first known about the white men. "My father has told me how the white men came first to trade for furs and skins, but there were not many then. My father was a friend of Captain Lewis and Captain Clark. The Kinapoos promised to let them pass through the land and not make war upon them. The trappers told some good things and some bad things. When Doctor Spalding and Doctor Whitman came they told only good things. But they did not tell us that white people would want to come here to make homes and hunt forever."

"Does it worry you, Cut-Mouth?" I asked. "I mean because there are white people building towns and coming to live?"

The Nez Perce shook his head. "Why should it make me unhappy? We live now in peace. There is plenty of room for all—the whites and the Indians." He stretched an arm out toward the horizon. "Once a white officer came to sign treaties so that the white man would have one part of the land, and the Indian another part of the land. But my father would not sign a treaty because he said no man owned the land and there was plenty for all to live together. I believe that also."

I felt sorry for Cut-Mouth as I rode along beside him, and I could not tell why. It must have been because he was so trusting, and because I was a white man and knew in my heart that we can be greedy and grasping and cruel. But then I remembered those awful days at The Cascades, and how childish and tricky and temperamentally vicious an Indian could be. That helped me some not to be sorry for Cut-Mouth, yet somehow I wished he had never gone to the mission school.

A few miles up the Clearwater we came to a small meadow near where a lively creek joined the river, and to my astonishment there was what at first glance appeared to be a settlement. There was a large hewn log dwelling with several fireplaces of stone, and grouped around it were smaller outbuildings. It was, Cut-Mouth said, the Spalding mission farm—but now it was unoccupied because the Spaldings had left after the massacre of the Whitman party at their mission near Walla Walla. The work had later been taken up by two spinster sisters, but now they too had gone, leaving the grass growing high around the log buildings, and the windows staring blindly at the brown hills. Through the tall grass were spots of blue—the camas flower which we had first seen near the Snake. I wished I had seen the place when the Spaldings were there, for I could imagine how neatly it would be kept by an orderly missionary and his wife and their loyal Indian helpers. Now there was something sad and foreboding in the sight, as though here something good had submitted to a powerful evil. I did not like the way the grass was growing tall around the blue camas. Then it occurred to me that if the Spaldings had not tilled that soil then the prairie grass would never have choked the camas. It would have stayed short and carpet-like, with the camas growing straight and beautiful from the bulbs beneath the soil.

Beyond the deserted Spalding buildings the country grew sharply rougher. As we followed the Clearwater, the trail climbed steadily with every foot, and there were points where, when I looked out at the river, the swift water seemed to sweep upward. The white sand-drifts by the side of the stream grew fewer and the trail more rocky. Some of the rocks along the bank were light brown, others a beautiful pale green. They were in sharp contrast with the deep gray-brown of the crags which bordered the upper Columbia, and the brown-red rocks of the country through which we had passed. They were sharper, more granite-like, with flecks of bright in them. Where the valley of the Columbia was full of dignity, the valley of the Walla Walla full of gentleness, the narrow canyon of the Clearwater was wild and reckless. We ourselves were quieter, and this was due neither to the noise of the rushing waters beside us nor our weariness after long days of riding over ever-changing ground. The deep hollow of the Clearwater's channel, its borders of multi-colored rock, and the thickly forested hills that hemmed us in, bade Mike and Cut-Mouth and I be silent. We had been under no such compulsion in the rye grass of the Walla Walla valley or the meadows of Rose Springs. The soft haze of the Blue Mountains, now behind us, had been comforting. Those were lands somehow hospitable to man despite their loneliness. But this was far different.

The delta of the Clearwater had warmed us with sunlight reflected from its sands. Now in the shadows of the canyon we were chilled. Cut-Mouth resumed his red flannel shirt, and Mike and I pulled our coats from the blanket rolls and put them on. This was long before night overtook us, and we had to halt much earlier than usual because the sun did not tarry in that deep place.

"By God," said Mike, after a pull at one of his bottles, "this damned place gives me the willies. I'd a damn sight rather be on the Tucannon any day."

Cut-Mouth, piling up small boughs for a fire, assured him that tomorrow we would leave the gorge and take the mountain trail to the northeast. Up there, he said, the sun would reach us again. Involuntarily I shivered. Already I had seen a thin streak of last winter's snow, still white and glittering in a dark gulley, and all around us were icy freshets tumbling into the gorge.

"How far is it now?" Mike growled at the Nez Perce. "Seems to me we ought to be gettin' to a place where you could tell us something." He added glumly, "I expect when we get there we'll find nothin' but a hole where those polecats ahead of us have worked a crow-bar on the diamond."

"We should be there in one day and one camp," Cut-Mouth said, but again I detected that quality of doubt which had earlier dampened Mike's enthusiasm. I realized with a sickening feeling that the poor Indian was not really sure, now, where he had seen the bright eye in the mountain of his youth.

However, Mike said nothing more. I knew that he suspected Cut-Mouth of playing for time. The Irishman was going to be lenient only a short while longer, for his patience was wearing thin. Due to the delay at the fording of the Snake we had taken no game, so the ex-trooper made biscuits with flour and water and the saleratus. These we ate with the last of our bacon which Mike scorched nervously in the pan.

"On the way back home," he said, "we'll try for some real grub—maybe a deer, eh? We'll be rich by that time and not in such a hell of a hurry." Mike was trying to stir himself into good humor, the way he always did when the dark mood was on him. But, as usual, it wasn't any good; and after supper he took three or four long drinks and rolled up in his blanket to try to escape the doubt that was gnawing his vitals.

A night's sleep in the canyon, however, did Mike a world of good. I was aroused at daybreak by his roaring voice. "Up and at 'em, Caleb!"

I sat up sleepily and looked around.

"Where's Cut-Mouth?"

"Down at the river filling the canteen. You know," Mike lowered his voice, "I got a hunch about that educated vermin. I was thinkin', maybe he's just pretendin' he don't remember exactly where that rock is. He's smart enough to figure we must be makin' this trip for an awful big reason, and I think he'd ditch us and spot the diamond himself. At first he was just Indian enough to think maybe we wanted to see it because it was good medicine. But, gradual-like, that missionary education got to workin' on him." Mike stopped abruptly, for Cut-Mouth was coming up the bank with the dripping canteen. The Irishman turned to him with rough joviality. "Come on, Cut-Mouth. Let's tie into this grub and get after that manitou. Caleb and I want to have a look at it —and if it's worth anything we'll cut you in and then get back to civilization where we can have some turkey legs and coffee and a bottle of wine."

The Indian smiled, pleased at Mike's change of humor. "Today we try hard. But it will be slow travel."

The Nez Perce was not overly pessimistic about that. It was painfully slow, up a trail so steep that we had to lead the ponies. We had struggled for more than two hours after swimming the mounts across the stream, and when I looked back I was astonished to see how near the river still was. Our way had been a zigzag trail filled with loose stones. We were on our knees almost as much as we were on our feet.

We did not reach the hog-back until long past mid-day. There the trail grew better. But still we could not ride, so closely packed were the mountain pines and so low the boughs that it was impractical to stay astride a horse for more than a short distance at a time.

"We ought to be hittin' a glade pretty soon," Mike hoped breathlessly, "and then we can climb these nags and get somewhere."

Cut-Mouth nodded agreement—but it was almost nightfall before we reached an open glade where the trees were sparse and the ground matted with pine needles. There were patches of snow everywhere now, and I dreaded to think how slow would be our progress if we were forced to go much further into the hills. Quite plainly now we could see Rocky Ridge and Sherman Peak and, a little farther on, the top of Bald Mountain, the forbidding sentinels of the Lolo Trail. And far beyond were the jagged white-capped peaks of the Bitter Roots.

From the Clearwater there were the South Fork, the Middle Fork, and the North Fork—and it was the latter that we followed, as nearly as the wild terrain would let us. We skirted in the deep shadows Huckleberry Butte and Hemlock Ridge and Lookout Peak, and were weary and breathing hard every foot of the way. We were so worn that night that all feeling and emotion were gone even though our progress had been heartbreakingly small. We did not even pause for the nourishment of dried fish, but simply rolled into our blankets and forgot the inhospitable country and the shining goal somewhere beyond.

An hour's ride took us out of the meadow land, found us following a roaring creek which seemed to defy our reaching its head.

I could hardly believe that other human feet had ever violated this strange wild place of green rocks and greener foliage and tempestuous streams. Yet beneath us was a trail as well marked as the tough mountain earth and the imbedded stones would allow. Thousands of moccasins over hundreds of years must have traveled it to mark it at all, this trail of the Kinapoos.

We had struggled perhaps three-quarters of that day, yanking the horses behind us, stumbling and cursing, when we ran into snow. We struck into its thin gray edges and trekked on until it was above our ankles.

Suddenly Cut-Mouth stopped and looked out toward the east, standing dead still until Mike could bear it no longer. "What the hell's up, Cut-Mouth?"

The Nez Perce turned. "Here the trail divides. I am trying to remember which way it was that I saw the manitou. It has been a long time."

I saw Mike's face change instantly. He was standing by his horse, half leaning against its flank in his exhaustion. Before I realized the meaning of his movement he had drawn his carbine from the saddle holster and thrust its barrel at the Indian.

"God damn you, Cut-Mouth, if you don't stop that play-actin' and take us where we're goin' I'll put you where you won't remember nothing!"

The Nez Perce did not move. "I am telling the truth. I do not want to take the wrong trail, for then you will want to kill me there."

Mike stood baffled. All his training, all his inherent suspicion of the Indian, told him that Cut-Mouth John remembered the manitou's location clearly. And yet the simplicity of the Kinapoo's statement was irrefutable. Slowly the carbine lowered. The butt dropped to the snow, and Mike glanced at me sheepishly. His eyes were wild and a little haggard.

I stood there in the snow, miserable and weary, wanting to return to the easy valley and yet not wanting to. If I went back now it would be empty-handed, as much of a nobody as when I had left. I thought of Mary Kiessling, lying in the grass with her hands behind her head, saying, "It would be a grand thing to find a diamond in a mountain, Caleb."

Cut-Mouth went on a few hundred yards, and Mike and I followed him, half hopeful and half afraid. Then he stopped again and turned to us.

"I see the smoke of a fire a day's distance. It may be some of my people. I will join them and some will remember what I saw."

CHAPTER 10

MIKE had no intention of allowing Cut-Mouth to get very far away from us. We followed him to that trail of smoke, fearful every minute of the way that when we got there it would be a ghost camp and that the party, Indian or white, would have moved on. Despite the obvious fact that Cut-Mouth was either lost or lying, Mike had no great desire to meet up with a party of Nez Perces in that region. Every step of the way he was hoping fervently that the builders of that fire were the men who had left Walla Walla ahead of us. If worst came to worst, he said, we could share the prize with them by pretending we knew its whereabouts. And there was the chance that we knew as much about its location as they.

By now the ponies were as stiff and weary as we were. Their backs had become frightfully sore, and the sharp rocks of the trail bruised and cut their feet mercilessly. Mike's horse, which had suffered most due to his great weight, was in bad shape and frequently, as Mike led him along, he would slip off an uncertain ledge and gash sides and rump into ribbons. It was cruel going, but we were giving neither the ponies nor ourselves any thought. Our only aim was to reach the spot from which that smoke lifted lazily into the clear blue sky.

It was not, we were to find, the sign from an Indian campfire. The men we saw in that clearing were more strange and weird than could have been any party of Nez Perces. At first, our eyes weakened and blurred by so much effort, we were not sure that they were human. I know that I, for one, in that first awful instant, thought that the wild mountains had revealed to us a huddle of pale savages, perhaps the vestiges of prehistoric man. Their coverings were so ragged and tattered as to be shapeless and without vintage. Their matted beards had crawled close to their stark eyes. Their arms and wrists were swollen and bruised so that they appeared out of all proportion to the rest of their bodies.

In our anxiety to reach the camp we did not shout ahead. This proved an almost fatal mistake, for at the first sound of our approach one of the men leaped to his feet, seized a rifle and sent a bullet through the boughs in our direction.

"What the Hell!" Mike shouted hoarsely. "We're friends." But his own weapon, I noticed, was clutched and ready. We had announced ourselves as friends; if we were not taken at our word we would soon be dead enemies, there was no doubt of that.

There were six of them, standing shoulder to shoulder, staring through the brush at us. The man who had fired the shot lowered his rifle a little, and that reluctantly, and not one of the six opened his mouth.

"Look here," Mike said. "We're lost, see? We're not after anybody and nobody's after us."

After a full minute one of the men said, "All right, then. Come on—but no funny business."

We advanced into the clearing. At another time and place there would have been something almost comical about the attitude of those half dozen men. They still stood shoulder to shoulder, in a half-circle around the fire, much like small boys who have been caught at something bad. It was as if they were not sure how much we knew, and were waiting for us to make the first move.

Mike dropped to his hams and looked at the coffee pot blackening on the coals. "A cup of coffee wouldn't go bad," he said. "It wouldn't now, and that's a fact. We didn't bring coffee, and for the last couple of days we been hurrying a little so all we ate was dried fish and some bacon hunks."

"Where you from?" said the man who had spoken first. He was not the one who had fired the shot, but obviously he was the leader. The soles of his boots had come adrift at the bow and as he stood there rocking slightly you could see his toes, black and scarred. What puzzled me was that, although these men had obviously been out much longer than we, had undoubtedly suffered hardships which we had not yet encountered, they showed almost no exhaustion. It was not simply that they were hardier. It was something beyond the physical. They seemed buoyed up by an inner spirit. They were either fanatics, I thought, or full of whiskey.

"From?" said Mike slowly. "I'm late of the United States Army. Michael Shea, and these are my friends, Caleb Paige and Cut-Mouth John. We started out from Walla Walla."

"Walla Walla? You mean the fort?" I thought that they all stood straighter and their eyes popped wider. "You here from the Indian agent—or for the Army?"

Mike cackled, feeling his way. He shot a glance around the group and answered, "No, I'm here in my capacity as a private citizen, and so is my young friend. Cut-Mouth is our guide." He paused a moment, then slapped his knee with a great guffaw. "I *see*. You thought I mean the *fort*." Mike roared again. "Listen, my fine buckos, I'll bet you all came from a town called Steptoeville, didn't you?"

"Yes," said the man with the scarred toes.

"Well, now, there *ain't* any town called Steptoeville. Yes, sir, we got some news for you, and as a matter of fact we ought to charge you for it. The name of Steptoeville has been changed to Walla Walla." Mike turned to me. "Ain't that right, Caleb?"

"Yes, sir."

The man turned to one of the others. "Joe, pour these men some coffee." He looked at Mike again. "A minute ago you said you weren't after nobody and nobody was after you."

"That's a fact," said Mike, taking the tin cup with a hand that shook.

"Well, then," said the other, "if you ain't up here for nobody you're up here for *something*. What is it?"

I saw Mike's eyes narrow. "It ain't quite fair for you to ask all the questions, partner, is it? You speakin' as a private citizen, like me?"

The man nodded.

"Well, then," said Mike, "I reckon what we're up here for ain't any more your business than what you're up here for is any of ours. This is a free country, except that maybe the Army might not like it much if they knew we were runnin' around up here, on account of we told the Injuns they could have it."

The man with the gun took a step forward. "Let's get 'em on their way," he said, looking at Mike sourly.

The leader shook his head. "Take it easy, Sam." He sat down on his haunches, across from Mike. "My name's Pierce. I guess you know what we're here for, and I guess we know what you're here for. What the Hell I'd like to know is how'd you figure it? You a mining man?"

I felt as if someone had struck me a blow across the heart. I could not look at Mike's face. I just stood there, numbly, waiting for his voice. It was a long time in coming.

"You got it, then?"

The man tapped his middle. "Sure," he said. A sudden elation sprang into his voice. He waved his hand widely. "There ain't a bar along the criks that you can't pan gold off of, and I'll bet a scalp on it."

Mike dropped the tin cup into the coals. I heard the spilled coffee sizzle, and the bubbling liquid smelled good.

"I was in California in 'forty-eight," the man named Pierce went on, "and I was on the Fraser up north. This is bigger than any of them."

"For Christ's sake, shut up," said the man with the rifle. "What do you want to have everybody know it for?"

Pierce hardly turned his head, but his eyes went cold. "They're up here, ain't they, same as we? Well, then, they'd found it, anyhow. Ain't we been seein' the smoke of a fire for a week everywhere we look? If you think you can keep gold a secret you're loco. We got to have this weighed, and the minute it gets to Portland these hills will be lousy with prospectors. I know. I been in California and on the Fraser. I seen it happen. You think nobody knows it, but they do."

Mike had retrieved the cup and was wiping it off with trembling fingers. He looked up shyly at Pierce. "How'd you figure gold was here?"

"From what the Indians said about the country. Sounded like gold country to me, and I was right." He patted his stomach again. "We're takin' in what I figure is about eight hundred dollars worth. There's silver in it, so she won't go more than ten to sixteen dollars an ounce, maybe. But there's plenty of it."

"You goin' back to Walla Walla now?" Mike asked.

Pierce nodded. "We got to outfit—and get this assayed. We're comin' back and work through the winter. You better get your claim staked out and do the same."

We left the Pierce party next morning, and Mike was so excited that he gave them three bottles of his whiskey and drank almost half of one himself for breakfast.

"Holy Mary, can you imagine what's happened to us, bucko?"

"Aren't we going to find the diamond?" I asked.

"Diamond be damned! I think this black-hearted Cut-Mouth was lyin' to us anyhow!" He slapped the Nez Perce on the back so vigorously that Cut-Mouth stumbled ahead. "But I had the right hunch, all right, all right—and we're goin' to ride in a carriage. We're goin' back to Dalles City and buy the whole God damned town! They won't dare touch us, boy, no matter what that Southern son of a bitch says we did. That's somethin' you'll find out, Caleb, when you're rich. They won't dare touch you. You can do any damn thing you want to and they'll just bow and scrape and say, 'Yes, Mr. Caleb Paige, that's fine and dandy.' They'll laugh at your jokes until their bellies are sore. An' wait until you see what the ladies will do!"

CHAPTER 11

Cut-Mouth followed back the trail of the Pierce party. Our going was difficult enough, but theirs had been worse. Pierce told us how they had been threatened by Indians when they reached the bank of the Snake, and had pretended to return to the Walla Walla valley. They had doubled back across the uplands, bearing north, skirting the Thatunas. At last they had forded the swollen north fork of the Clearwater and followed creek after creek, guided by Pierce's eyes, practiced in the lay of a gold region.

They had returned by a shorter way, and it was this return trail that Cut-Mouth followed, although not with speed enough to suit Mike. In a fever he drove the Indian as he would a plow horse, and dragged me after him as he would a mule. But we were as willing as Mike. The Irishman's words had fired me, for who does not want to be rich and powerful? I suppose that as the years roll on and one finds himself neither rich nor powerful he develops a philosophy to justify it, saying that money is not everything, and power is dangerous. But it seems to me that it is never the rich or the powerful who have such a philosophy. It is always someone who is relatively poor and who has no power at all.

I suppose that it was greed, and nothing more, which got into our blood there on the craggy hills. Whatever it was, it generated something within us. My legs had more drive, my heart more strength, my lungs more capacity for the thinning air. The journey from the bank of the Clearwater, not half so difficult, had taken much out of us. Then we had been sustained only by a hope. But now we *knew* that there was gold to be had for the taking, and we traveled at a speed which would have broken us under other circumstances.

Half a day from the Pierce encampment my pony shattered its leg in a stony ravine. Mike held his carbine to the animal's forehead and sent a ball crashing into its brain. Then Cut-Mouth carved a ham from the still warm flesh so that we might have meat without wasting time in hunting for it.

As we bore on, farther and farther east, the two remaining horses became more of a problem. We could no longer ride them with any practical success, and our outfit was so light that we did not need them for packing. At last we abandoned them, probably to be picked up as rich prizes by some wandering young savages before the winter came. Normally we would have struggled along with them, knowing that when we reached the lower country again they would be invaluable. But now our only thought was to reach the claims of the Pierce party. It was as if we believed the staking of a claim would give us wings.

We found the Pierce claims on the third day after leaving their party. They were well marked with heaps of stones and when we examined beneath one of them we found a piece of bark on which was carved the name of Samuel B. Reed. We did not examine the rest, but followed the heaps at intervals along the creek until they ran out. A hundred yards beyond this, Mike set up another pile of stones, and slipped beneath it a square of bark on which he'd carved *M. Shea—C. Paige.*

"I ain't puttin' your name on it," he explained to Cut-Mouth, "because I ain't sure an Indian can own a gold claim. It might make it illegal if we put your name on it. But I promise that Caleb and me will take care of you."

He set half a dozen markers, before he had hardly examined the ground along the creek, as if he were afraid that someone would appear from beyond the trees and claim the whole area. This done, he took the frying pan, broke off the handle, and began scraping away sand from along the water's edge.

"This looks about like the place where Pierce and his party was diggin'. And from what he says, we can't miss."

Mike admitted he wasn't very good with a gold pan, but from his years in the Army of the frontier he had a general notion how it ought to be done. When he had scraped away an area of white sand about ten feet square he began scooping up the bed rock, whirling the pan in his big hands. He was pretty awkward at it, and for the first hour was so impatient that he got nothing.

"What we need is a rocker," Mike said, wiping his brow. "We got to get back to Walla Walla and get ourselves a rocker and a real outfit—but I want to be sure we've hit it."

As inexpert as Mike was, so rich was the strike that his panning was finally successful. We squatted on the creek bank, our feet in the water, the wet lapping unfelt at the seats of our breeches, watching the swirl of water in the frying pan. Mike got better as he practiced. At first there was nothing, because he was too eager and impatient. But at last something was left settled in the bottom of the pan—a fleck of yellow no larger than a pin-head.

"There she is, by God!" Mike stood up, his face flaming with excitement. He gripped me by the shoulder and shook me as a cat shakes a rat. "We've got it, boy! We've got it!"

We were a happy lot that night, Mike Shea, the Nez Perce and I. We had horse steak and Mike made "dough gods" with the last of our flour. He cooked them in the same pan he'd used for the gold washing, burning his fingers considerable because the handle was gone. After supper he polished off the last bottle of whiskey and sent Cut-Mouth and me to sleep with grand tales of what we would do when we got to town. Of course, Mike said, we'd have to do some work to get the gold out. We'd have to get an outfit, and maybe a Chinaman to do the work. "Hell," Mike said, "I don't want to be stayin' up here in the snows of a winter. We got to get somebody to work the claim for us and we can supervise it. . . ." I fell asleep, happily as Mike entertained the Nez Perce.

We were up at the crack of dawn, and Mike constructed a rude rocker of two pieces of bark which Cut-Mouth held together in his hands. First we dug up material from the edge of the creek and put it in the rocker. Then slowly I ladled in water while the Nez Perce rocked. All that morning we struggled with the rude equipment, and when the sun was at its highest we poured the residue into the frying pan and Mike began carefully to wash it out. He found a quiet pool in a bend of the creek, and began whirling the pan, back and forth, occasionally dipping in a little water. After what seemed hours, we saw a little pile of black sand and yellow flecks.

"Now we're doing it!" Mike said. "There's three ounces there, or I'm a wall-eyed Chinaman! What was it Pierce said—sixteen dollars an ounce. That's—what?—forty-eight dollars." Mike squinted off across the creek. The amount did not seem to stagger him in relation to the work he'd done. Then he brightened. "Hell, that ain't bad for a beginning. When we got the equipment and I know the hang of this, it's more than a hundred dollars a day we'll be takin' out of the ground!"

He straightened up from the creek, holding his aching sides with his red hands. "Well, let's get started back, buckos!"

He said it as if we were going half a mile down the road. Everything had become tremendously simplified for Mike now that he had struck it rich. We were at least a hundred and fifty miles inland from Walla Walla, and yet to Mike the distance and the hardship of the way, had become as nothing. He had started out to find a diamond and found gold. You couldn't beat the luck of the Irish, his gleaming eyes were telling Cut-Mouth and me.

"Come on! Don't be standin' there, you two. We got to get to town!"

He poured the gold and sand into his palm, then sifted it carefully into the pocket of his shirt.

CHAPTER 12

We made fair progress to a point from which we could see the Clearwater far below us. Descending, and unhampered by the horses, with only our blankets and weapons, and the hand axe, we had come comparatively easy into moonlit nights which allowed us to march after sundown. We never would have stopped at all if it had not been for weariness, or the necessity of eating. Time after time Cut-Mouth warned Mike that we were traveling faster than was prudent. The Nez Perce knew that a man in a hurry cannot see his enemy, that he makes an unwise amount of noise, and that he lays himself open to the trickery of the inanimate trail. But Mike would have none of the Indian's caution. He was no longer the cautious Army man. He was Michael Shea, and he was wealthy.

"The Hell with it!" he'd reply to Cut-Mouth's warnings. "You sound like an old woman. I want to get to Walla Walla where I can get damn good and drunk and celebrate this thing!"

I will never forget the sight of the Clearwater, winding westward, the avenue into a great wide land to which I wanted to return as fast as my legs would carry me. It shone in the moonlight like the underside of a poplar leaf, disappearing behind a craggy point to reappear again half a mile in the distance. Its waters, rushing out to the world of men and women and towns and steamboats, drew Mike even at a greater pace.

How insanely heedless he had been, how right Cut-Mouth was, Mike did not realize until too late. The moon had suddenly disappeared behind a thick cloud, plunging the whole rocky hillside into blackness and blotting out the river below us. Immediately the Nez Perce halted.

"Come along, Cut-Mouth," Mike said. "We can make the bank of the river and then we'll camp. I'm damned if I'm goin' to sit on these rocks all night waitin' for the moon to show."

He had not taken two steps into the black when he went headlong, flinging his carbine over my head and rolling over and over to bring up with a sharp crack at the foot of a pine. He was clean out of his senses when Cut-Mouth and I finally found him in the darkness. There was a wide gash over his eyes where he had struck the tree. We poured the contents of the canteen over his face and revived him with difficulty. But when he opened his eyes his face went ashen.

"It's my leg," he whispered weakly. When I tried to raise his knee he let out a yell that echoed all down the mountainside. "Sweet Jesus!" he gasped, grinning sheepishly. "I've busted a leg sure as Hell."

He'd done more than that. He'd twisted a knee so badly that it was already swelled to twice its normal size, and at the same time a piece of sharp rock had cut into the twisted tendons.

"I guess we won't make any more ground tonight," he said, struggling to get his back against the trees.

"We'll have to keep on, Mike," I told him. "It'll be days before we can get to Walla Walla as it is, and you got to have a doctor for that leg."

"It'll be all right if I can rest it."

"It won't, though." It seemed to me that it was swelling before my very eyes. "You've cut it bad and we can't stay up here with it." I looked at Cut-Mouth. "Do you know what to do for it, Cut-Mouth?"

Mike started to speak, gasped, and tried again. "I don't want no Injun doctorin' on my leg."

When Cut-Mouth and I lifted him, the movement was so agonizing that sweat poured from his white face, and he cursed like a mad man. He could not bear to touch the injured leg to the ground, and it was equally agonizing for him to try to keep his foot lifted.

But something told me that we dare not linger, and by daybreak, when inch by inch we had gained the bank of the river, I knew it for certain. Mike's knee had swollen even more and had turned a sickening purplish color near the rock wound. I dug a hole in the sand, filled it with water from the river, then heated stones the way I had seen the Indian women do at The Cascades. When they were red-hot I poked them into the water-hole.

"Cut-Mouth," I said, "you'll have to give up one of your shirts. I want to try hot water on Mike's leg."

Not without some reluctance, for I think he had no faith in my treatment, Cut-Mouth sacrificed his fancy shirt and watched me with stricken eyes while I tore it into strips and immersed it in the boiling water. For an hour I packed Mike's knee with the steaming hot flannel until he was swearing at the pain and me alternately and impartially. But at last it began to help.

"God damn it, I wish I hadn't drunk all that whiskey. A shot of forty-rod once in a while and I could walk on the damn thing." He put his big hand on my shoulder. "Good boy, Caleb. I know you were tryin' to help me even if you were scalding me to death."

I sat there beside him, staring at the ripples of sunlight on the river, thinking how long it had taken us to come down the mountainside with Mike and trying to apply it to the distance to Walla Walla. It would take three weeks of painful going to bring Mike along that stretch, assuming that Cut-Mouth and I could manage it at all.

"Look here," Mike said, out of the silence, "why don't you and Cut-Mouth go on ahead and send back some help for me? Leave me a bird or two and a rifle and I'll be all right."

At this obvious lie, the tears welled in my eyes. Mike knew well what would happen if we left him there. He had been in the open too much of his life not to know what happens to the weak in the hills where the snow-swollen rivers rush through.

"There ain't a damned bit of use in all of us gettin' into a mess," Mike went on in a tight voice of pain. "Suppose you did get me to the Snake? How in hell would you get me across without horses?"

"We could make a raft," I said, looking at the river. And then it came to me—the way to get Mike out of there. The way to get us all out of there more quickly than we could ever make it on foot or by riding. Excitedly I jumped to my feet. "Mike!" I cried. "Mike, how far is it from the mouth of the Snake to the boat landing?"

Mike rolled his head and looked at me. "About twenty miles, I reckon. Why?"

"How far would it be from Walla Walla? Probably forty miles or so, then, wouldn't it?"

"I guess so. What you gettin' at?"

"It's good open country. If we could get to the Columbia with a raft, Cut-Mouth and I would have a chance to bring some help. And on a raft we'd make good time."

The Irishman grunted hopelessly. "We'd make good time while we lasted."

"Just the same, we're going to do it."

Mike tried to sit up, then sank down on his blanket with a groan. "You're talkin' like a damn fool, Caleb. You better take Cut-Mouth and get on your way. You'll run into some Nez Perces with horses and then you can come back and get me."

But I wasn't going to let Mike stay there with his gold dust in his shirt pocket and his dreams dying along with him. I shut my ears to his objections and turned to the Nez Perce. "What do you think about it, Cut-Mouth?"

"The Clearwater is very swift. When it joins with the Snake it is too swift."

"Then it'll get us there all the faster," I said, rising to my feet. "Come on, Cut-Mouth, build up the fire bigger. We've got to cut some trees."

All next day, and then by light of the fire on the white sand, the Nez Perce and I took turns with the hand axe. Sometimes poor Mike cursed our foolishness from the shadows, sometimes he lay moaning with pain. But Cut-Mouth and I worked on, and at last we had, lying side by side on the sand, ten rough pine poles, with the bark still on them, each about thirty feet long. Across these we laid five smaller poles to which to bind the longitudinals. We laid them in notches cut into the firm, straight-grained pine, but the problem of fastening them was more difficult.

I first cut strips from the blankets, and then from every item of clothing I felt we dared spare against the cold. With these strips I bound the cross-pole on what I planned to be the forward end of the raft, winding it again and again around the cross-pole and between the heavier lengthwise members. With that the strips of cloth were exhausted, and the remainder of the fastening was up to the ingenuity of the Nez Perce.

Cut-Mouth was equal to the occasion, and began collecting Kamo, or what the settlers called "Indian hemp." For years without end his ancestors had made rope and fishing line from the leaves and stems—for so many years, in fact, that *Kamo* had come to mean "rope," and *Kamiop* a place where the plant was made into useful articles. Although he grumbled that it should have been dryer, Cut-Mouth fell to work making line that was surprisingly strong and pliant, laying it out beside him in strips ten or twelve feet long. As he rolled and braided the stuff he worked tiny twigs and pieces of bark into it with brown fingers that fairly flew.

While the Indian worked with the rope, I took up the hand axe on a couple of young pines with plenty of top bush. At the lower ends I dug a hole clear through with Mike's jack-knife. Then I cut a thole pin for each and set a pole at bow and stern, with the brush ends sticking out fore and aft. How well the young trees would work as sweeps at bow and stern I had no idea, but my hope was that the thick bush would slow our progress in the faster currents. It was in our favor that the river had fallen from its spring high, and as the Clearwater seemed to be a relatively shallow stream I prayed that in the rockier stretches Cut-Mouth and I could stand on the bottom and keep the raft from dashing itself to pieces.

We worked furiously, not thinking of food. Mike had long since lapsed into a stupor and I was frantic to get him to medical help. Yet that raft had to be as staunch as we could make it. My body cried out for rest and I had to bite my lips to keep from dozing. But every strand of Kamo was important. If the raft broke up, we were done for. On a long chance, the Indian and I might save ourselves—but Mike would be helpless in the rush of the stream.

Again and again I went over the bindings and the cross-poles. I untied knots and tied them again, sometimes changing their positions. My one fear was that the raft would spread. If only we could hold the raft together, I felt, we'd have a fighting chance to ride her down. I'd have given an arm for a bucketful of spikes.

That night the Nez Perce caught a trout by the light of a flare, and the two of us sat on the bank and ate it raw. At intervals throughout the night I woke up to see how Mike was making out. His eyes were glazed and his face was drawn with pain that no longer brought any sound from his dry lips. Whenever I came into view he would nod his head stupidly. Around the clotted gash in his knee the skin had turned greenish and the wound stank horribly. I was afraid that the poison was working through his whole body. But there was nothing for it but to wait until daylight to embark on our journey. Cut-Mouth and I had worked on the raft two nights and a day, and during them Mike had eaten nothing and was out of his head most of the time.

At dawn Cut-Mouth and I slid the raft into the water and wedged it solid against a clump of cottonwoods. Then we carried Mike down to the river bank. He was half unconscious when we picked him up, and his knee had swollen out of his torn breeches like a discolored balloon. When we got him to the river bank he roused himself and remembered what I was going to do. He made a terrible fuss, flailing out at us and when we let him go to protect ourselves from his big fists his leg buckled like paper and he crashed down with a yell of pain that cut clear through me.

Even after that I couldn't argue with him. His words were crazy, but I could make it out that he wanted the Nez Perce and me to go on by land and not risk our lives on the raft. The more he talked the more he went out of his head, and he began pleading. "Look, Caleb, you were always wantin' to get on the river—but it'll kill you. You can't take that thing out there. It's the fault of that God damned Lawrence Coe and Leonard White, you always wantin' to get on the river. You're rich now, Caleb. You got a gold mine and you don't have to be foolin' with the river." There was a gasp after every word and he could hardly get them out.

I shot a glance at Cut-Mouth, and we tried to lift the Irishman. Mike began swearing at us and twisting around like a mad man. I clenched my fist down by my side where Mike couldn't see it. I watched his thick red jaw, and when it turned a little I let him have it as hard as I could. A great shock of pain went up my arm as my fist hit him, but his head dropped over to one shoulder and Cut-Mouth and I carried him the rest of the way to the raft.

We put him on his stomach so that when the water came over it would run out of his mouth and nose, and propped his head up on one of the cross-poles. We tied him fast with the grass-rope in a spot where Cut-Mouth could kneel astride of him as he worked the stern sweep. I wanted the Indian to handle the stern sweep because I figured that would be more familiar to him; it would be more like the handling of a canoe. I wasn't sure, yet, how the forward sweep would act. If it didn't work, I planned to put it out astern, along with Cut-Mouth's. But I hoped it would work because I wanted something out in front to take the shock if we struck.

When Mike was tied fast and the Nez Perce was in position, I waded out into the stream, shoving the raft with me, and then I clambered aboard just as she caught and started downstream. My heart was in my mouth and my stomach was trembling. We edged along the bank at first, and then slowly the eddy swung us out. I tried controlling the raft a little with my sweep, and I could feel Cut-Mouth helping me on the stern end. There was a great black rock jutting in a peak from the middle of the stream and I waved toward it for Cut-Mouth's benefit. The main current went straight for it, and did not swerve until it was in its shadow. The raft began to swing crab-wise. Quickly I let her have her head until we were almost on the rock. Then I swung the sweep wide, so wide that the tree curved and the bark split along it. But it kept our nose in the current and we got past the rock, only grazing it.

I shouted as loud as I could. I couldn't help it. It came out of my throat like an animal cry. My heart was still pounding and my stomach was still tight, but no longer from uncertainty. I was glad to be on the river, heading West at a free speed instead of laboring overland. The contest with the black rock had let me know that I had some control over the raft, that I could, in a measure, be master of our fate.

Beneath my knees the logs began working a little, but the fastenings were holding tight enough and I figured that it was better to have some "give" in our rough craft. I began to be proud of her, the way she lifted and fell, the way she hugged the falls and the whirls.

Suddenly we struck a spot so shallow that the bottom grazed and she stuck fast, pitching me forward. With a cry at Cut-Mouth I leaped into the stream and he followed suit. We held her there a moment, examining all the fastenings, and then we shoved her off and leaped aboard.

The sun began to beat into the canyon, warm on my back. The new wet logs gave out the pleasant odor of pine, and in my ears the rushing water was a steady music that made my pulses race along with the raft. On the shore the deep-green rocks and the greener trees sped past confusingly, and each time I raised my eyes from the river and looked ahead there would be a crag-hidden bend promising something new beyond it.

After a while Mike roused himself and lay there groaning. I did not know if he realized what was happening to him, that he was actually on the raft. His eyes were bright and feverish, his face a deep red, and he must have believed he was in a delirium. He was drenched from shoulders to feet with the water that splashed up between the logs. I was glad that the sun was getting stronger in the deep gulch.

Sometimes we made a terrific speed when the river fell deep in a gorge, and at other times we drifted at a pace no faster than a man's walk. After an hour I was feeling more confident. I had risen from my knees to man the sweep, and began to enjoy the sound of the river and the changing sights of craggy bluffs on either side of us. I grew over-confident, and once when the raft gave a terrific lurch I let go of the sweep momentarily. The craft swung into the edge of a big eddy that flung us suddenly sidewise across the river.

I grabbed at the sweep again and began pulling with all my

strength, but it was too late. We were twisting in a great circle, just grazing the main stream at every revolution. Cut-Mouth worked frantically at the stern sweep, but we were helpless in the swirl. Time after time we were swept around, the raft turning its own circle within the larger one, and time after time as we neared the main current we tried to maneuver into it. It began to look as if we would circle there forever, until the raft disintegrated or we died of starvation. But at last, after what seemed to me to be a full hour, some freak in the current broke the rhythm and we swung awkwardly into the main stream.

I was sweating from every pore in my body, and my arms trembled so that I could scarcely hold fast to the sweep. But I kept to my knees thereafter; I had learned that one cannot relax for a single second on the waters of a swift river.

As the sun rose higher I noticed that the stream was opening out a little. There was less current and fewer riffles. I judged that we must be nearing the entrance to the Snake. Shortly I began to experience that strange feeling that comes to a man when a river takes him to its mouth. It makes no difference whether the mouth is pouring into a greater river, or whether it is pouring into the sea. The land flattens with the water—but the sky seems to open up, too. I have noticed this phenomenon many times since that day I piloted Mike and Cut-Mouth on our rude raft. I am not certain whether it is something that happens actually in the sky, or whether it happens within the man who witnesses it. But it is like looking through a dim haze into the future. Nothing is clear there. It is only a great reflected light, and the curtains are not quite pulled back. But the sense of coming into the beyond is inescapable.

It hit me there as our raft went down into the mouth of the Clearwater toward the Snake. But I had little time to contemplate it, for we were nearing speedily the spot where we had paused for a moment's rest on the upstream journey. The broad sand dune, and the bluff beyond it, were to the left. And ahead were the folded brown hills flung together in a twisting furrow, the tortuous bed of the Snake. There blew in at us a great warm wave of air from the prairie lands beyond.

We swung out swiftly on the bosom of the Snake. I saw it bearing down on us from the south and as we shot out of the Clearwater the current bore us hard against the puckered hills that lined the course of the Snake clear to the Columbia.

I felt easier as we rode along on the Snake, because it reminded me of those broad stretches of the Columbia above Dalles City. The brown hills were home to me. But it was a queer feeling to be borne down the river and know that now we could not stop when we wanted, that we would have to take it as it was given to us. There was no slack water after we left the Clearwater. We bounced over one rapid after another, sometimes twisting and turning, but I no longer had any fear for the raft.

There were miles where the raft would rush us along a stretch at a speed that stopped the breath in our throats. Whenever we struck one of these I would steal a look at Cut-Mouth. His smile of approval was a reward that I cherished. I thought of dragging Mike inch by inch up and down the steep and treacherous gullies, along the twisting trails of the divides. Then I hunched there on my knees, holding tight to the sweep, feeling the rushing waters, reading the rapids with every ounce of mind, and I felt like a god.

In spite of our speed, I grew impatient to reach the broad valley that would herald the presence of the Columbia. The sun was burning our foreheads and parching our lips, and I let Mike's head down against the logs so that the upthrusting water would cool his mouth. He made no protest. He was too weak to move, and his groans were hardly more than scratching whispers now.

We started down a canyon whose walls towered two thousand feet above us. Short, choppy little rapids began to pull at the nose of the raft and send us sweeping by gyrating pits that were treacherous green saucers. Sometimes, in a clear stretch, I could see black rocks nosing up at us like eyeless fish out of a great deep.

Bend after bend went by, and still we did not come into the flat land. Our speed seemed so free that I felt we should have arrived long before. I began to wonder if perhaps we had somehow got into the wrong river. I had been sure that the brown puckered hills were the same we had seen on our journey inland, and Cut-

Mouth insisted that this was the Snake. But suppose we had mistaken another stream for the Clearwater?

But at last we shot around a bend and into the broad land I expected. Far to the west and south I could see the towering table of rock that marked the gateway of the Columbia into the country of the Grand Coulee. We were only a day's journey from help for Mike Shea—and still the sun was high in the heavens!

I saw the sky opening out to the westward, the sun filtering in yellow through a dusty haze. The Columbia was ahead, but I had no desire to be shot into that river and be carried down far beyond our destination. I turned and yelled at Cut-Mouth, "We'll stop her at the next chance and you can go overland to Walla Walla. I'll stay with Mike."

The Nez Perce nodded, and stretched an arm out to the south to show me that the town lay there. I tried to work the raft in toward the left bank, but the Snake would have its own way. I watched the water foot by foot, but it was difficult to anticipate it, so great was our speed. I would spot an eddy swirling toward the shore, and before I could get our sweeps into action we were far beyond it. The wild thought came to me that we would be whirled down the Columbia and piled on the rocks below the Deschutes, an ironic ending to my brave plan.

I could judge our distance from the Columbia by the position of the great table rock, and we still had a chance. It came when I had about given up. The river brought up sharp against a ledge of scab rock and the current went staggering back at right angles across the stream. The action on the raft was so swift that I almost missed the opportunity. But as we whipped back across the stream I yelled at Cut-Mouth and instantly he saw what was up. As we veered toward the bank he drew his knife, cut the ropes that bound Mike to the raft and rolled overside with him. I dived headlong toward them, on my belly, praying the water was as shallow as it appeared. With all my strength I kicked downward. Then Mike and Cut-Mouth swung against me with a solid impact and the three of us slid along the bank, the Indian and I fighting like mad men for our footing. The dead weight of Mike between us was a help. The lack of buoyancy in his giant frame made him an anchor which kept the Nez Perce and me from being thrown out again into the stream. In one last effort we flung ourselves against the bank and crawled up laboriously, dragging Mike.

There we lay exhausted, Mike muttering insane curses and obscenity at the steel blue sky. I rolled over and looked into the blazing sun. I saw the raft, bobbing and flashing without its cargo, diving into spray and throwing it clear, for all the world like a wild horse rid of its rider.

CHAPTER 13

It was thirty miles to Walla Walla from the point at which we'd abandoned the raft. But as I sped Cut-Mouth on toward the town, heading at a dog trot for the Touchet country that lay between us and help, I had hopes that he would be able to soon return. This near the settlement, he was likely to run into horsemen; and even if he did not, his way was comparatively easy across the flat land. The only obstacles would be the fording at the Touchet, and the rolling hills of the Waiilatpu country.

I stayed on the bank of the Snake, keeping a lonely vigil with Mike, not knowing whether to be glad or fearful because he had lapsed into unconsciousness again. There was not a tree within sight, but I dug out a small indentation in the bank, enough to give him a little protection from the blazing sun. And periodically I cupped up water in my hands and bathed his feverish face.

My stomach was growling with hunger, and I tried to kill rabbits with stones. But though they sometimes froze in their tracks my aim was too shaky, so that I was denied even the doubtful comfort of warm raw rabbit meat.

Fortunately Cut-Mouth returned the middle of that night. He had not, of course, reached the town—better than that, he had encountered an Indian with his squaw, and the squaw had been trailing a travois behind her pony. Onto this we loaded Mike, winding a piece of rawhide beneath his arms and tying it to the poles of the sloping travois so that he would not slide off. Then I lifted myself on the squaw's pony, Cut-Mouth took his place behind the brave, and our strange procession started into the night.

It was slow going, but fairly comfortable except for the crossing of the Touchet where we had to transfer Mike to one of the horses until the stream was forded. The greatest difficulty was with Mike's wound, for the rough jarring of the travois would sometimes set the gash to bleeding. Every half hour or so I would examine the wound to be sure it had not reopened.

We got to Walla Walla before noon of the next day and headed directly for the Army post. I will never forget that parade up the main street of the town. I, haggard and half-naked because most of my clothes had gone to make strands for the raft, sitting at the rear of an evil-smelling squaw. The proud Cut-Mouth, riding second fiddle with a shabby brave who had never been to mission school. And poor Mike, tossing on the travois in a high and ranting fever, screaming of nothing but gold. Quickly every man and boy in the town was following us up the dusty street toward the fort; and when we reached the parade ground, soldiers off duty crowded around us. Mike they took immediately into the sick ward where the gruff old Army surgeon, his white walrus mustaches dripping perspiration, rolled up his sleeves and bawled for an orderly.

The soldiers would not let me stay inside with the doctor and Mike, but took me out of the building to where Cut-Mouth was standing quietly, with all the dignity he could muster now. His face had taken on that impassiveness which the Indian reserves for white strangers. It was not now mobile and friendly as it had been in the wilderness with Mike and me.

The soldiers elbowed through the crowd of townspeople and stood staring at us. One of them was a big, unpleasant-looking fellow with campaign hat shoved back from his burned forehead and whose blue shirt was sweat darkened under the arms. He shoved his hands flat down inside his belt and spat a thin stream of tobacco juice toward Cut-Mouth. "What the hell you been up to?" he demanded.

Cut-Mouth and I had agreed not to mention the gold discovery, and I had transferred the evidence of it from Mike's shirt pocket to my own person. "Mike was hurt," I said to the soldier. I was stupidly weary, and wanted only to be let alone.

"So I see," said the soldier with sarcasm. "You three been up in the Nez Percé country, ain't you?"

I nodded.

"What were you doin' up there?"

"Just—just exploring," I said.

The big soldier turned to the others and laughed. Then he swung back, his face mean. "Exploring, was it? Well, you'll get hell. Nobody's supposed to be up in there, you know."

Cut-Mouth stepped nearer to me. "I was with them. It was all right."

The big fellow's eyes narrowed. "Who the hell bought your chips, buck? It's the order of the U.S. Army that nobody's supposed to be in there, and since when are you sayin' it's all right to disobey the U.S. Army?"

"Leave 'em alone, Sid," one of the others said. "The kid's all in. It's no skin off us if they went up there."

"That's okay," said Sid. "I just don't want no Mr. Lo tellin' me where to head in." He glared at the Nez Perce. "You're due for a damned good military trial, and don't mistake it."

In a little while they let us alone, and sauntered down toward the town. I went back into the fort and looked at the door to the sick ward. It was still closed, and I couldn't hear anything. Maybe, I though in sudden panic, maybe Mike had died and the surgeon didn't want to tell me. I stood still in the shadows and prayed. "Please God don't let Mike die. If you've already let him die make him live again." I said it half aloud, over and over, wanting to believe in it, and afraid that my half-belief would spoil everything. Then I went out into the sun again and waited, and after a long time the surgeon came out, turning down the sleeves of his shirt that stuck wet to his fat middle.

"Will he be all right?" I asked.

"Can't tell yet," he said. "Maybe we got it off in time."

The words meant nothing to me then. All I wanted to know was whether I could see Mike. "Take a look at him if you want, but he won't be out of it for a while and we'll have to dope him. Better come back in the morning."

But I couldn't wait. I had to see Mike. I had to listen to him breathe. I went into the dingy little room where he lay white as paper on one of the two wood beds. But he was breathing. I could hear him, faintly, and I could see the rise and fall of his barrel chest beneath the blanket.

And then I saw something else. Below the worn Army blanket only one leg showed. The words rushed back to me: *Maybe we got it off in time.*

I stood there with my fists clenched, wanting to kill that Army surgeon. I heard his step behind me, felt his big hand on my shoulder. Angrily I whirled away from him. "I had to do it, son. He's got a chance to pull through this way, and a man on a peg leg is better than no man at all."

I couldn't answer. I thought of Lottie Moore, tall and handsome in the hallway of The Golden Rule. I saw Mike standing before her—with one of his breeches legs strapped up behind, standing on a peg leg.

The Pierce party reached town that night, and Walla Walla went wild. The thing happened as suddenly as an explosion. I was sitting in Galbreath's with Cut-Mouth, having a drink. It was going through me, down inside, making me feel a little better about Mike. I had already had one whiskey and I was having another, and I said to the Indian: "It won't be so bad. I've heard they can make a wood leg that don't look anything like these peg legs."

There were a few men in the whiskey shop, but they knew what had happened to Mike and realized how I felt and did not plague me with questions as the soldiers had. They were ranged along the line of high board tables which served as the bar in Galbreath's. Hunched over their drinks, they looked oddly shapeless in the yellow light of the two lamps which hung from ridgepole nails. Cut-Mouth and I sat in one corner, almost in darkness, and I was grateful for the solitude, letting the whiskey worm its way falsely, trying to forget about Mike's leg, planning how tomorrow I would get some new clothes and ride to the Kiessling ranch to see Mary.

A man stuck his head through the doorway and shouted, "Pierce found gold up by the Salmon River country somewheres!" He was so excited that he was almost unintelligible, and he dodged out again at once but everybody in Galbreath's heard the word *gold*. They rushed outside, then down the street, searching for the man to get more information from him. We began to hear shouting. Then the news of Pierce's discovery seemed to hit the town everywhere at once, and in hardly more than five minutes everybody was on the street except Cut-Mouth and me.

Cut-Mouth looked guiltily at me, and I could not help but grin at the expression on his brown face. I knew what he was thinking. The Pierce crowd would see us, and our own discovery would be out. But, unlike the Nez Perce, and affected by the drinks, I was set to enjoy the situation. I couldn't help but be pleased at having got to Walla Walla first by means of my pole raft.

Outside we could hear the crowd roaring up and down the street, kicking white dust into the air, following Pierce and his companions wherever they went, into the traders' store and then into Baldwin's—and finally through the doorway of Galbreath's. The excited mob jammed the place to the walls. Everybody was shouting or singing or just rattling off words in sheer nervous excitement. Through the maze of bobbing heads and moving shoulders I saw Pierce being shoved toward the bar. Suddenly a little man who'd lost his hat and torn his shirt in the melee leaped up on the bar and began yelling and holding up his hands.

"Listen here, men!" he shouted above the racket. "We all want to hear about this first-hand. Let's hear from Cap'n Pierce. Quiet now, everybody, let's hear from the Cap'n."

The babel subsided to a drone and the little man looked down and said, "Go ahead, Cap'n Pierce."

"Well," said Pierce, "we got gold, all right." His voice sounded tired, and a little bewildered. "I figured it'd be there when I heard the Indians talk. It's along a dozen creeks that run into the Salmon and Clearwater. I don't know what our stuff will do, but I reckon we got eight hundred dollars worth."

At the mention of eight hundred dollars a great roar went up, and the little hatless man had a time quieting them down again.

"That's about all there is to tell," Pierce said. "We got our claims staked, and we're goin' to send this stuff down to Portland on the steamboat and have it assayed. But I'm satisfied it's all right. The thing is," Pierce stopped and drew a great, tired sigh. "The thing is, when this stuff gets to Portland all Hell will break loose. My advice is to get up there quick before the rush from outside starts. And it'll come. In a month you won't know this town. I seen it happen in California and I seen it happen up in Canada. Fact is, we run into a party already—fellow named Shea with a kid named Paige, and an Indian."

"They're back. Shea's at the fort with a rotten leg, but they never said anything about gold."

I heard Pierce's voice, unbelieving. "They couldn't have got back," he said. "They were on their way in when we were coming out. Must be some other party."

"It's the same party," somebody shouted. "The kid and the Indian were sittin' in here not more'n five minutes ago."

Cut-Mouth and I were in for it. That sea of faces washed toward the corner where we sat. Pierce pushed forward and looked at us. "Well, I'll be a blasted hyena if they ain't the ones! How'd you get here before us? Didn't you stake a claim?"

I said we had, and told him about the raft. Pierce turned to the crowd. "By God, why didn't *we* do that?" He looked at me again. "Why didn't you say anything about the gold, boy? You can't keep a thing like that to yourself."

"I wasn't trying to keep it to myself. But Mike got hurt and I figured if anybody should tell about it, it ought to be Mike. Anyhow, you were the one who discovered it."

"Did you get anything out?"

"A little," I said. "We weren't good at panning and we didn't have any equipment." I took out a piece of cloth in which I'd wrapped up the gold and sand and spread it out on the table. The whole crowd crushed in to have a look. Somewhere a chair cracked into a dozen pieces.

"Gentlemen, gentlemen!" old man Galbreath shouted. "Mind the furniture, please! Let's everybody quiet down."

"To hell with the furniture!" came a yell from the front of the shop. "You'll be furnishing this place with new gold chairs before long!"

At last they had to let Pierce and his partners go over to Baldwin's and get some rest. After that they turned their attention to Cut-Mouth and me. Over and over I told about the meeting with the Pierce party, and about the raft, and how Mike injured his leg. I drew a map on the table, showing about where the claims were.

"Well, by God," somebody exclaimed, "if I didn't ride right by there once and didn't see nothing!"

A gale of laughter greeted this remark. "It don't bite out at you, Jack. You got to dig and pan for it!"

All that night bonfires burned in the street, and men argued and shouted each other down, and drank prodigious quantities of liquor. Toward sunrise those who had stayed more sober in the excitement were in the settlers' store and Baldwin's, trying to get outfitted. Attracted by the excitement, a party of Indians had drifted down from the Walla Walla River and were bartering horses along every foot of the street. Soldiers jumped the fort and came down to join the celebration, and after a few drinks talked darkly of deserting and getting into the hills with the rest. A few citizens, probably more drunk than prudent, stumbled off into the darkness on foot with nothing more than their carbines. The few storekeepers were in a quandary as to whether they should join the trek or stay to get the business that would develop from it.

There wasn't a pessimist in all the wild mob. Not one man gave vent to the idea that possibly the Pierce strike would run out, or that he might be planning some scheme. There was gold in the hills, and while it was *oro fino*—not coarse like the gold of California—it was nevertheless gold, and it could be had out of the ground for the taking. Nobody wanted to know anything else. Nobody wanted to believe anything else.

By daybreak the town was practically deserted. Aside from the shopkeepers, the Indians gloating over the possessions for which they'd traded horses, the soldiers at the fort, and Cut-Mouth and I, there were not a dozen men left in Walla Walla that morning. And six of those were the Pierce party, asleep over Baldwin's store.

But this was to change. It was to change because at seven o'clock that morning Pierce came out of Baldwin's and handed a heavy locked pouch to the stage driver. "Have Captain White keep that in his own cabin," he instructed. "And I want it handled that way on the boats below the Deschutes portage, too."

It was to change because Pierce was sending that pouch down the river and into the world beyond where men still remembered the rush to California in 'forty-eight. Many an early Oregon settler had deserted his cabin after the discovery at Sutter's Mill, and while most had come back broke and disappointed, everybody remembered only those who struck it rich. The word would drift with the *Colonel Wright* down to Dalles City, and on the little *Mary* down to The Cascades, and on the *Belle* down to Portland. It would sail to San Francisco on the *Brother Jonathan,* and up to Puget Sound on the *Mongoose.* It would spread swiftly from camp to camp and post to post in the interior, and the Indians, not realizing what woes they were bringing upon themselves, would tell the stories of white men scarring the creek beds and gulches for yellow metal.

Even when I saw Pierce hand the locked pouch to the stage driver, and heard the stage rattle off toward the landing on the Columbia I did not realize what had been set in motion. I was bewildered and exhausted and anxious for Mike, and I wanted to tell Mary Kiessling that I had found something far better than a diamond in a mountain. I didn't know, really, what we had made happen to the country. When I did know, I was glad because of what it did for the steamboats. But for another reason I was a little sorry, too. Somehow I never got over a gnawing sense of guilt because Mike and Cut-Mouth and I had gone into the Nez Perce country to make ourselves rich.

CHAPTER

14

THAT morning when I staggered up the hill to the fort to see how Mike was getting along, the Army surgeon took one look at me and sent me to bed. "You can't talk to Mike," he growled. "Mike is still under opiates—and if you don't get some rest you'll be as bad off as he is."

I protested that I had to get back to town, that I had to buy some clothes and get out to the Kiessling ranch. To my protestations the old man gave answer by shoving me into a room with a bed and shutting the door. The suggestion of that bed was too much for me; I fell upon it and slept for fourteen hours without waking. I might have slept even longer if the old Army surgeon had not roused me to give me a bowl of warm but watery mush.

"How's Mike?" I demanded, sitting up.

The old man nodded. "I think he's going to make it. God knows how. I'd never have believed it."

"Can I see him now?"

"Not yet. When you've eaten this you're going to sleep some more. Next time you wake up you can have a real breakfast."

To my surprise, after I had eaten the gruel I was ready to sleep again.

When I was allowed next day to see Mike I resolved not to mention his lost leg unless he did. I resolved to be cheerful and pretend that I thought it was nothing at all. But when I walked into the room and saw him half propped up, his great broad face the color of a lemon, his mouth still twisted with pain, and that awful flatness under the blanket, I could not hide what I really felt.

"Well, bucko," he said, his voice ragged with the agony he had endured, "what do you think of your one-legged friend, God damn it!"

"I—I'm sorry, Mike," I blurted out. "I wish . . ." I couldn't go on.

"What the Hell!" Mike said. "I'm lucky to be here at all. The doc' said so. And by God, I wouldn't be here if it wasn't for you, Caleb."

A great wave of relief swept over me. Despite his pain, there had been something of the old Mike in that tone. I believed that he wasn't going to care about his lost leg. I should have known better than that. I should have known that big Mike would want two good legs to stand on. But now I somehow managed to believe that he was grateful enough to be alive.

Even in those first hours out of the opiates he was impatient to get something from our claim, and I was not surprised when, next day, he told me of an arrangement he wanted to make with Ben Guiness and Tom Ludden, two of his soldier friends at the fort. Their enlistment period was up and they were straining to get into the hills; but Mike had quite evidently persuaded them that our claim was better than any they might subsequently find. He had drawn up an agreement with them and one morning when I visited the ward he presented it to me, diffidently, for my signature.

"You see," Mike said, "I won't be so good with a wood leg for a while. And the way I got it written here, with Ben and Tom, it makes you and me the business end of it."

I read the agreement, in Mike's scrawl:

"Know all men by these presence that there exists a certain claim approximately sixty miles east of north fork of the Clearwater over the old Nez Perce trail and said claim is staked in the names of Michael Shea and Caleb Paige. It is hereby agreed by all parties that Ben Guiness and Tom Ludden are to receive each twenty-five percent of all proceeds from this claim, and Caleb

Paige and Michael Shea are to receive each twenty-five percent of all proceeds from it. It is agreed that Ben Guiness and Tom Ludden are to work the said claim in return for their share, whereas Michael Shea and Caleb Paige are to furnish all grub and equipment."

It was written on two sides of a ruled sheet and at the bottom of the reverse side were already the signatures of Guiness, Ludden, and Mike.

"It sounds pretty good, don't it?" Mike enquired proudly. "You see, we're entitled to an equal share with them because we were the ones that discovered it—and the grub and equipment won't amount to much. We'll come out fine and we won't have to work at all." Mike's eyes were shining. He'd almost forgotten his lost leg. At last he had his business, a grand kind of a business, in which he would do no work; and it was all there on paper and bound with signatures.

"Do you know Guiness and Ludden pretty well?" I asked.

"Do you mean do I know if they're honest? Sure, they're good honest buckos, them two. And anyhow we can check up on them once in a while to see if they're holding out anything or not."

"What about Cut-Mouth John?"

"You and I will have to give him some of our proceeds. We can't be signin' no agreement with an Injun. Besides, Tom and Ben wouldn't stand for that."

I asked Mike what he figured we ought to give Cut-Mouth, and he replied airily that it would depend on what we took out of the mine. "It don't do an Injun any good to give him too much money."

I read the paper again. It seemed all right to me. Certainly I had no great desire to go back into those hills and grub for gold. I was near the river again, and I intended to stay there. I wanted to stay there even if I did not grow rich, and if Mike's plan worked out it looked as if I could be rich and stay on the river, too. So I added my name to the other three.

I was satisfied that Mike was getting along all right, and a great load was lifted from my mind. I began to be able to enjoy a little my new position in the town. There had naturally been considerable talk about our adventure on the Clearwater and the Snake, and by now everybody knew that I was a quarter owner of a bona fide gold claim. When I walked down the street men spoke to me with a genial respect, just as Mike had prophesied. And although I had no actual cash, I found that I could walk into the settlers' store and buy a whole new outfit on credit. Promptly I adorned myself with new coat and breeches, new shirt, new boots, and a gray hat with a round brim and a leather band. Determined to return to Mary Kiessling in style, I even borrowed a saddle mare from Galbreath.

As if all this were not enough, more good fortune awaited me that very hour. I had mounted Galbreath's pony and started for the Kiessling ranch, riding proudly up the main street, when I heard my name shouted behind me. I turned in the saddle to see Len White, and with him a tall, distinguished man who kept up easily with Captain White's long stride.

Delighted to see my old friend of the *Colonel Wright,* I wheeled the horse and met them. "How are you, Captain?"

"Fine as silk. Tie up that nag and come into Galbreath's a minute. I want to talk to you."

I dismounted and made the bridle reins fast to the rack. Len White grabbed my hand in his two big fists and shook it hard. "Congratulations on that raft voyage of yours, I want you to meet a friend of mine. Captain Ainsworth, this is Caleb Paige, the young fellow I was telling you about."

I looked into clear gray eyes. The man's face was long, the nose aquiline, the mouth thin and straight. "How are you, Paige? Captain White's been telling me about you."

Swelling at my new importance, I went into Galbreath's with the two river captains, and sat down with them at a table near the front window. White ordered three whiskeys, slapped the table with his palms, and turned suddenly to me, "Caleb, we're going to see if we can get the *Wright* up the Snake to the Clearwater—and on up the Clearwater as far as she can go. I want you to go with me on the first trip."

At first I didn't get the import of his invitation. "Of course I'll go," I said eagerly.

"The idea is," said Captain Ainsworth, "you ought to be able to give us a good bit of information on the river, now that you've rafted it." He smiled slowly. "I reckon it was a fast trip, by and large, but you ought to remember some of it."

"I do," I said. "I tried to remember where the bad parts were —that is, I did after I was sure the raft was holding together and I wasn't so scared."

Len White laughed loudly and slapped me on the back. "What'd I tell you, Captain? The boy's a natural river man!" He turned to where I sat flushed with pride at the compliment. "You see, Ainsworth here is interested in a new company that's being rigged up. Lawrence Coe has turned over the *Wright* in exchange for stock, and he's building a new boat that'll go into the fleet."

Ainsworth cleared his throat. "This gold discovery ought to mean a lot of business for the steamboats," he said. "Our job will be to get the miners and their equipment as far into the interior as we can. That's why we want to try the *Wright* on the Snake and the Clearwater."

"I'll be glad to go on the trip," I told them.

"The Company will pay you well," Ainsworth said. "We don't expect to get anything for nothing."

"He lies like Hell," White put in good-naturedly. "He wants to cut me from five hundred a month to three hundred for the run up here."

"It's like this," Ainsworth said, not smiling. "The Company will have to expand in a hurry to take care of the trade and hold the river to itself. We'll have to be reasonably careful about expenses."

"Well," said Captain White, "as for me, I'll take the *Wright* up the Snake, and up the damned Clearwater to the head waters if she'll crawl there. But I ain't piloting on these upper stretches for a cent less than five hundred." He was perfectly amiable about it.

Ainsworth shrugged. "We'll have to see about it, Len." He looked at me again. "It's worth a hundred and fifty dollars to the Company to have you go with us on the *Wright*. We want to try it tomorrow."

I retained my composure as best I could. "I think she'll get to the Clearwater without any trouble, but I'm not sure about the Clearwater itself."

"We'll try," Len White said. "We may have to line her over the rough spots."

Ainsworth held his hand across the table. "It's a deal, then Paige?"

I nodded, grasping his smooth, narrow hand. I wondered at the quiet force of this gaunt man. There was an impression of steel behind his soft voice. There had been something strange and awe-inspiring whenever he referred to "the Company," something that made me respect it even when I hardly knew as yet what it was. And when he had said that "the Company" must build more boats and hold the river to itself I had never believed anything as implicitly as I believed that "the Company" would do both.

It was dusk when I finally reached the Kiessling ranch, but the hour did not matter. I was too filled with news to care. If it had been midnight I would have gone, and routed Mary Kiessling out of bed into the bargain.

Heinrich Kiessling was trudging across the farmyard with his full milk pails when I rode in. He halloed dubiously, set the pails down, and walked forward. Then he recognized me. "So—it is young Mr. Paige!"

I slid down from the horse and shook his hand. "How are you, Mr. Kiessling?"

"I am fine," Heinrich Kiessling said. "There is nothing wrong with me. But in town everybody is crazy."

I laughed and glanced toward the house. "Is Mary around?"

"They have all gone to bed, I think. But maybe they have not gone to sleep."

"I'd like to see Mary," I said. "I promised I would tell her about the trip to the back country, and I'm going up the river tomorrow on the *Wright*."

Heinrich Kiessling peered at me in the darkness. "Always you are coming or going. Why is it that you do not think of settling down? All this talk of gold is foolishness. It brings trouble."

I laughed, wondering what Heinrich Kiessling would think if I told him that I owned a quarter interest in a gold claim, and that I was being hired by the new navigation company. But I did not want to tell Heinrich Kiessling. I wanted to tell Mary.

She had heard us talking in the farmyard, and before we reached the porch I heard her call out from the window. "Is that Caleb Paige, papa? I am getting dressed."

Heinrich chuckled. "With four daughters I suppose this is what I am going to have to expect. Only I hope that for Else and Sidonie and Hulda there are three young men who call before it is time to go to bed."

He told me to wait on the porch, and carried the milk into the kitchen. I could hear him rattling the pan and dipper, getting ready to separate the milk from the cream. As he worked there with the tools of his dead wife he sang a song in German, low and fondly, and I suspected that it must be a song which Mary's mother had sung at her kitchen chores.

I did not hear Mary come to the door. I knew that she was there. I stood up swiftly and turned, trying to see her face as she stood outlined in the light from the kitchen lamp. Neither of us spoke. I reached out swiftly and took her hand, drawing her into the shadows of the porch. There I took her into my arms, feeling the soft roundness of her breasts against my chest, growing warm at the touch, feeling a tightness in my throat. Her lips were like wet petals, and above them there was a sweet salt moisture from the hot night. I felt as if we were swaying, together, through space.

"Caleb," she whispered. "It was that I thought you were not coming. You were in town. I heard it. And you did not come."

"Mike got hurt," I said. "I couldn't come right away."

Inside the kitchen Heinrich's singing stopped. "Mary? Magda, are you out there with Caleb Paige?"

She drew her breath sharply, but her voice was strained when she answered. I hoped that Heinrich Kiessling would not notice how strained it was. For myself I was not sure I could speak aloud. "Yes, papa. Do you care if we walk into the yard a way and talk, so that we will not wake the girls?"

Heinrich Kiessling laughed. "The girls are probably awake and listening yet. So you had better walk into the yard."

We went into the darkness, wordless, out of the yard and into the field above the little house that Heinrich Kiessling had built in a valley so strange to him and his daughters. We sat down in the wheat, pressing it down around us, until we had a place that was like a tiny room with the wheat stalks for walls and the sky for a roof.

"I heard it that you found gold in the hills, Caleb," Mary said. "You said that you were going to look for a diamond in the mountain."

"That is what we went to look for. But we couldn't find that. Gold is better. I'm going to be rich, Mary. I'm rich already. And today Len White introduced me to a man who has started a new steamboat company. They own almost all the boats on the river—from here down to Portland. They want me to go with them tomorrow up the Snake River and maybe up the Clearwater, too."

Mary was silent a moment. Then: "Caleb, will you always be going somewhere?" It was so like her father's question that I laughed. "I like the river," I said. "I want to work on the river." I searched Mary's face in the half-light. "You wouldn't like that, would you, Mary?"

Slowly: "I would not care, if you came back to me often. If you were with me more than you were away."

"That's the way it would be. And sometimes you could take trips with me on the boats."

I touched her arm. She was trembling. She was trembling because there was something in my voice that had nothing to do with the words I was saying. There was something in my eyes that I could not hide and did not want to hide now that we were alone. "Caleb . . ." I took her in my arms. I could feel her heart pounding. When my lips touched her temple I could feel the throbbing of her blood.

"Mary," I whispered. "Mary, it doesn't matter. It doesn't matter because you are going to be my wife. As soon as I get back from the steamboat."

"Suppose you would not come back?"

"I will, though. Nothing could keep me from it."

Her sigh was bewildered, frightened. "I want to please you, Caleb. I love you so much—that is what I found out when you were gone, after the night you came up the road."

"I found out the same thing, Mary."

"You would not leave me then? I have heard it about men who did not come back afterward."

Slowly we walked out of the wheat and down toward the Kiessling house, its windows dark now. Beside me, Mary seemed small and precious. I could not believe what had happened there in our tiny room with the roof sky and the walls of wheat.

"Sorry?"

For a long time she did not answer. Then she said: "Not if you love me, Caleb. Not if you will come back." She raised her face to mine, and I took it between my hands and kissed her, not like the other times, and found her lips still soft and sweet.

"I'll come back," I said. "You'll be the wife of the finest captain on the river, Mary Kiessling, and we'll have a big white house in Dalles City."

CHAPTER 15

It was strange to be standing again in the wheel house of the *Colonel Wright*—not, this time, as a raw boy who had stowed away and had to be suffered by the owner and the captain, but as a pilot.

"A pilot!" When I got aboard the *Wright* and took my place beside the wheel I said it over and over again to myself. The Oregon Steam Navigation Company was paying me a hundred and fifty dollars for the assistance I could give Captain Leonard White. The discovery of gold on that rugged creek bank faded into insignificance beside this fact. Even the thought of sweet Mary Kiessling fled from my mind.

And as we swept into the mouth of the Snake River, a few miles above the Wallula landing, Len White turned to me and said, "I'm at the wheel, Caleb, but she's all yours. I'll read it as well as I can, but when you think I'm wrong, sing out—and don't make it too late."

In that first hour I did considerable sweating. Fortunately we struck the Snake in the afternoon so that the sun was at our stern. There was little question but what the *Wright* could handle the current of the Snake. Any steamboat which could buck the Umatilla Rapids would be able to force its way in comparative ease to the mouth of the Clearwater. But following the channel was a different matter. As we pressed into the brown gorge and I glimpsed white water ahead I wished I had accepted Captain Ainsworth's offer less blithely. He stood behind me now, a seasoned captain in his own right on the lower river but saying never a word. I had navigated this stream, if only on a raft, and he had not. Neither had Len White. I began to feel the responsibility of my position, and I stood there, straining every nerve, every muscle, every part of my brain, trying to remember the waters we had encountered on the pole raft.

It was necessary, of course, to reverse the course in my mind. It had seemed a simple thing to do—merely to reverse my memory of the bad water as Cut-Mouth and I had encountered it. But in the *Wright's* wheel house, with the engine steaming up below me, and a hull carrying more than a hundred passengers, it was far from comfortably simple.

There were a hundred and twenty-six passengers crowded aboard the *Wright* to make the trip into the Snake. They had been told that it was an experimental voyage, yet not one had hesitated to come up the gangplank. When I boarded the boat at the Wallula landing I was astonished to see its rail lined with men; it had not occurred to me that the gold rush Pierce had predicted could already be on.

Our passenger list represented the first newcomers from Portland, those who had got away the instant the news filtered through the growing town on the Willamette. There were a few adventurers from Dalles City, too, who had thrown aside their interests to head inland for riches. Three-fourths were prospectors, or would-be prospectors, and the rest were those who expected to profit from the miners.

It was amazing how quickly this latter class had assembled themselves and their goods. On board was Seth Slater, a resident of San Francisco who, with the luck of his kind, had been in Portland on business when the news broke. He was a squat little man of tremendous enterprise and unqualified gall, and he had paid Ainsworth not only for his passage but for a large amount of freight as well. The freight he designated as "miners' supplies" and consisted mostly of strong whiskey. But, also, he had brought along all the shovels, picks and pans he had been able to buy up in Portland. He had cornered them before the news of the strike was generally known, had bought them cheaply, and now intended to sell them at fabulous prices in the interior.

There was a Jew named Fleichner who had subscribed to all the principal newspapers, and to *Harper's Weekly,* and he planned to set up a business of reading newspapers and articles aloud. Not more than one customer would be allowed to listen for a single fee—and the charges would be ten dollars for reading a complete newspaper; five dollars for an article in *Harper's.*

There was a man who had hurriedly written and printed three thousand pamphlets entitled "The Art of Placer Mining" and was carrying them up on the *Wright* to sell at twenty dollars per copy. I learned later that he sold the whole three thousand in four weeks. He had a right to be pleased at his success, for he knew nothing at all about placer mining. Aboard, too, was a fellow who called himself Dr. Bartholomew. His freight comprised five hundred empty bottles into which he would place a brew of his own concoction to sell for any ailment of which a hard-working prospector could conceivably complain. All these men had been through "booms" in the past. Many were veterans of the California rush. They knew exactly what to do in order to make money easily and quickly. It was only a question of geography and timing—and these fortunates aboard the *Wright* would be the first. The legitimate purveyors, the merchants of dry goods and supplies would lag behind those who catered to greed, and drunkenness, and lust, and, most pitiful of all, hope.

Kirt Inge was aboard—his goods consisted of three young women and a great rolled-up tent, a combination which was to comprise the first house of prostitution beyond Dalles City. I saw him but once during the trip, for I was in the pilot house continually. We exchanged only a word or two of greeting on the hurricane deck. If he recalled what had happened in Lottie Moore's room at The Golden Rule he gave no sign of it. Several times I glimpsed on the foredeck below the pilot house the three young women Inge was bringing with him. It was difficult for me to believe their calling. On board the boat they paid not the slightest attention to the men, and usually they were at the rail, squealing with delight when the boat plowed into a rapids. They might have been Else and Sidonie and Hulda Kiessling, I thought, on their first boat trip. Not once did I see Inge join them on the foredeck, and I suspected that he was engaged in a quiet game in the men's room.

There were hundreds of eccentrics following the rush. Just what attracted them nobody knew. I think we had one of the queerest aboard the *Wright* on that maiden voyage to the Clearwater. As far as anyone knew he was nameless. He wore an overcoat and hat made entirely from the feathers of birds. His partiality to clothes of feathers was as puzzling as the rest of him. Not a soul on board knew where he came from, what he intended to do in the interior, or what he had done in the past. He volunteered no shred of information, and when some of the passengers made light of him he demanded to be put ashore. At first Len White refused, but the fellow became such a nuisance that finally the captain nosed the *Wright* into a quiet bend—and let the man of the bird feathers leap ashore amid the cheers of the passengers. The boat backed into the main channel and steamed on up the Snake. The queer fellow trudged over a knoll and out of sight without even a knotted kerchief for baggage. I never knew what became of him, and never met anyone who professed to have encountered him thereafter.

The Snake to the Clearwater was a course to the *Wright's* liking, with plenty of water, however swift. Whenever I was able to recall, from the topography on the embankment, what was ahead, Len White would say, "Good going, lad."

Once I gave him a wrong course, to the starboard of a nest of rocks just below the surface. He started to follow it, then suddenly yelled below, "Hard astern, if you love me!" The *Wright* shuddered. The paddle-wheels stopped momentarily, groaned into reverse—but we had already slid back from danger with the force of the current. I quaked in my boots until Len White signaled for full ahead. This time he went to port, not speaking until we were well beyond the dark shadows below the surface. "You dang near did it that time, son. But better pilots than you have made mistakes like that."

"But how were you sure the starboard side wouldn't be right?"

He winked at me. "I just *felt* it wasn't."

Helplessly I turned to Ainsworth. His narrow face was impassive, though his eyes were still kindly. "I think Len was right, Caleb. But don't worry about it now. If you'd been on a steamboat, instead of a raft, when you came downstream, you'd have got the same feeling. You're doing mighty well. Don't let one mistake throw you."

I knew that one mistake was enough to rip the bottom out of the *Wright,* and took small comfort from Ainsworth's words. Len White continued to ask me questions about the course, and although I knew he was only trying to restore my confidence, it helped. When at last we reached the flat where the Clearwater emptied into the Snake, it was decided to anchor and attempt to ascend the Clearwater as far as possible.

I was not nearly as certain about the Clearwater as I had been about the larger river. On the raft, once I had accustomed myself to the rude craft, I had consciously tried to remember the Snake. But those first moments on the rushing Clearwater had been busy ones, so that my memory was confused.

We anchored near the sandy flat where Mike and Cut-Mouth and I had rested on the way to the upper country. Once again I shared Len White's bed, but this time his snoring failed to disturb me. I was dead tired from the strain and went instantly to sleep. Once or twice during the night I awakened to hear the passengers noisily celebrating somewhere below.

Next morning I told White that I believed there wasn't enough water in the Clearwater for the *Wright*.

"Well, we'll take her as far as she'll go without wagon wheels," Len said. "Ainsworth can't ask more than that."

We did not start immediately at daybreak because we had run low on wood, and the engineer suggested pointedly that the passengers get busy on some of the cottonwoods flanking the mouth of the river. Axes were broken out, and fifty or sixty enthusiastic passengers went ashore and fell to with a will. Inside an hour the foredeck was piled with wood fuel, and Len White jangled the bell for the start.

The broad mouth of the Clearwater was negotiated with no

difficulty, but as the stream narrowed and we struck the steep pitches so characteristic of the river, the boat slowed considerably. The green wood we were using for fuel wasn't as efficient as the dry pine we had been using on the Columbia and the Snake.

Around a sudden bend in the river we encountered a band of Indians on horseback. They must have seen steamboats on the Columbia, for although their ponies reared at sight of the *Wright*, belching black smoke, the savages showed no fright. They cantered along the river bank, abreast of us, to test the boat's speed. But soon they could keep up merely by walking their horses—and then, as the current grew swifter against us, they dismounted and led their mounts.

"Look at them damned aborigines!" Len White said disgustedly.

I turned to watch the Indians a moment. They were having a great deal of sport with our slow progress, laughing at white idiots who would try to ride a river at a speed no faster than a walk. Presently, after a few obscene gestures in our direction, they leaped to their horses again and rode far ahead and out of sight, screaming their derision.

I looked at Len White. His face was crimson; he was so angry that he couldn't speak. Presently Ainsworth saw the Captain's mood and burst into laughter. "Don't worry, Len! Next time we'll bring dry fuel—and show those playful rapscallions."

Another half mile up the river and we forgot the Indians, for we encountered, to our amazement, a cable ferry! An enterprising individual had rigged a line across the stream, and built a log raft ferry. What was more, he had customers. There were half a dozen men crossing the stream on the raft, their packs huddled in a pile in the center of the logs.

"What in blazes do you know about that?" exclaimed Len White. "He's getting an overland trade from Walla Walla! Looks like you got somebody to buy out, Ainsworth!"

White signaled for half speed, just enough to hold the *Wright* steady against the current. When the crude ferry had landed its cargo on the bank of the river, he yanked the whistle cord, then stuck his head out of the wheel house. "Hey, there! Will you un-hook that cable 'til we get by?"

The owner of the ferry, a tall settler the buckles of whose galluses glistened defiantly in the sun, shouted something which we could not hear. He then touched his thumb to his nose in a signal which Captain White could not mistake. The men he had transported across the river were delighted at his defiance.

Len shouted again. "We're coming through! Give you ten minutes to lower that cable."

For answer, the ferry operator sat indolently on the bank.

White turned to Ainsworth. "Guess there's no use waiting."

"Give him the ten minutes," Ainsworth said.

But when Len White impatiently returned his watch to his pocket and yanked the whistle cord in two long blasts, the ferry operator was still sitting on the bank. At sound of our whistle he repeated his nose-thumbing and was joined in the gesture by the prospectors.

"Full ahead!" Len yelled into the speaking tube.

The engine began throbbing, and we started ahead. The ten minute delay had helped our power. "We'll snap it like string," Len announced with satisfaction.

As the nose of the *Wright* neared the cable, the ferry operator saw that we were going to carry out our threat, and leaped to his feet. I saw him try to grab a carbine carried by one of the prospectors, but the latter wisely held it firmly in his grasp.

White leaned from the wheel house window and bawled out, *"Watch your heads below!"* In the pilot house we ducked beneath the windows. I heard the cable snap, then the whine of the ends as they ripped through the air. Cautiously we raised our heads and looked out. The only damage was to the cable and the feelings of the ferry boat operator.

Our triumph over the ferry was not to help us, for farther on it was as I had feared. The Clearwater would have none of the *Colonel Wright*. Just beyond the second big eddy we had to line her over a rapids, tying a long hawser to a pine and attaching the other end to the steam capstan on the foredeck. No sooner was the line made fast ashore than it parted.

White insisted upon attempting it again. We made some progress, but very slowly, and after a hundred feet the hawser snapped a second time. Len White let the boat drift back, maneuvering the stern toward shore. Suddenly he put the wheel hard over and demanded half speed. In another moment we were heading downstream. He had said nothing to Ainsworth, and the older captain made no comment on the maneuver.

We had no sooner changed our direction before the wheel house door flew open and Seth Slater burst inside. "What you turning back for?" he demanded.

Ainsworth fixed him with a cool glance. "Because the boat won't go up further. The terminus will be at the mouth of the Clearwater—where you saw the sandy flat between the river and the bluff."

Slater looked fretful. "You sure that's where you'll be landing after this? I got to know, because I got to set up my stuff where the boat landing will be."

"Don't worry. That's where the town will be," Ainsworth said.

Slater grinned at us. "Sure! A town. It'll be a pee-cutter, too, and no mistake!" His face lighted. "Say, I had the idea first of setting up business up here—it ought to be named after me, shouldn't it? Slaterville. Slaterville, by God!" He rushed out, evidently to reveal his inspiration to the other passengers.

The *Wright* slid back down the river, and Len White had to suffer the jeers of the ferry boat operator as we passed. Even though there would be a boat landing at the junction of the Clearwater and the Snake, the ferry man could set up business again—because men would have to cross the Clearwater to get to the gold creeks—and he was properly jubilant.

When we made the *Wright* fast at the sandy flat, passengers and cargo literally dumped themselves over the side. I had never seen such frenzied activity, had never until now realized the hysteria which the dream of gold creates in men. Few prospectors lingered in the spot. Almost everyone took up his pack and started at once along the river bank, heading for the interior. Within ten minutes there was a long, single-file of men trudging over the trail which Mike and Cut-Mouth and I had followed hardly a month before.

Those who stayed to set up business, like Slater and Inge and the Jew, Fleichner, knew that those men would return—many of them rich. And they knew that others would be coming up from below, hurried and frantic, ill-equipped to proceed into the wild, rugged country of the Salmon and the north fork of the Clearwater.

As I stood at the rail of the *Wright* a town sprang up before my very eyes. Seth Slater was already driving stakes for his tent, his cases of whiskey and shovels piled high beside him. Poor fellow, his dream of immortality was to be short-lived; only a few weeks were to pass before the town's name would honor, not Slater, but a man who had been there long before the enterprising merchant. After the tents began to have side-walls, but before the first all-wood shack was erected, they christened the town Lewiston—for Captain Meriwether Lewis.

Inge and two hulking fellows he must have recruited from the boat were unrolling the big tent which Inge had brought with him. I searched the shore for a glimpse of the women he had brought. They were far up toward the high bluff beyond the sand flat, picking camas and ferns, wholly oblivious to the labors of Inge and his henchmen. I was fascinated by Inge as he worked there, meticulous in his fancy clothes, helping the two men to get the tent up. Although I had nothing but contempt for his enterprise I could not help but admire the alert ingenuity which had brought him to that wilderness before the rest of his kind. And I noticed that when the three girls returned to the sandy flat, their arms loaded with greenery, they treated him with marked deference. Their attitude toward Inge, and toward the life he was staking out for them, was beyond me. I could not hope to understand it—and yet I could not resist a sneaking admiration for the small, perfectly featured man with the black gloved hand. He represented something which I could never be. He seemed to be wholly without emotion, always balanced to jump at every opportunity. I was certain that he made mistakes; but I was equally certain that no one but himself ever knew for sure that he made them.

He was already a part of this new town, just as he had become a part of Dalles City. When I returned again it would have changed from a tent town into a muslin town—a town of frames covered with white cloth, windowless, and the streets would be lighted by these transparent shelters, by the candles and lamps within them. When I returned, Kirt Inge's place would be, not a tent, but a frame structure covered with muslin, the beds protected from stray bullets with sacks of flour.

CHAPTER 16

MARY and I were married at the Kiessling house almost a year to the day after I had left Walla Walla to seek the diamond in the mountain. As soon as the *Colonel Wright* returned to Wallula we made the plans. I was all for marrying at once, but Heinrich Kiessling—aided, I think, by Sidonie—thought that it would be best to wait. I think that he half expected me to pick up stakes and leave for another adventure. But I had no such intention. I worked in Baldwin Brothers' store until I had saved a little money, and then, with almost a year gone, I sent word downriver to Thomas Condon that I was going to be married and wanted him to perform the ceremony.

It was the first real wedding celebration in the valley. True, men had taken squaws in the sight of God—and sometimes there was even a brief ceremony. There had been a few marriages with both parties white, but always in the office of the justice of the peace, and with scant trimmings.

Ours was a real wedding, with the preacher up from Dalles City. It was a real wedding, taking place in the bride's home, with her father and sisters looking on, and dancing afterward. Mary was very proud of all the commotion, and I confess I was not far behind her.

Else, Sidonie and Hulda had decorated the Kiessling place with sweet-smelling pine and cedar boughs, and garlanded the doorways with strips of colored ribbon. Heinrich built a special table of rough boards, a long wide table which Else covered with a white cloth that dropped clear to the floor. It sagged with cold meats—beef and sausages and venison on great brown-streaked platters; and there was rye bread and little pats of soft butter.

There were two kegs of beer with spigots, and at least enough champagne for the majority to toast the bride. But most of the male guests had brought their own enforcements which they kept discreetly in hip pockets until after Thomas Condon had pronounced Mary and me man and wife.

I think that almost everyone in Walla Walla was there, for Heinrich Kiessling in his meanderings up and down the main street had missed few. There were all the business men, and soldiers from the fort, and even a sprinkling of transient miners who, stopping on their way to the interior, had heard that there was "something going on" out at Kiessling's place.

Cut-Mouth John was there, and Len White came upriver with Condon. I had the devil's own time getting Mike to come, for the post surgeon had only a short time before strapped on his peg leg. It hurt him pretty badly yet, and he was awkward with it.

"You go along and get married," Mike said. "I don't need to be there."

"Look here, I couldn't get married unless you were there."

We argued back and forth, with Mike never really saying why he didn't want to come. At last he burst out, "I can't go anywhere with this damned wood leg!" He got up and started across the room. "Look! I hump up and down like a seal out of water."

"You just imagine it, Mike. You walk all right."

His eyes filmed with moisture. "I'll never walk all right, Caleb." He pulled up his trousers leg so that the oak peg showed. I turned my eyes away involuntarily. "You see! You don't like to look at it, do you? Neither does anybody else."

"Naturally I don't like to think of you losing a leg," I said. "But people won't notice it."

"The Hell they won't. What about Kirt Inge? He's got a false hand, and he wears a glove on it—and everybody notices that. And this—" Mike choked a little. "This is worse."

I knew he was thinking of Lottie Moore, and I ached for him—big blustering Mike who'd got too anxious up there on the mountain side above the Clearwater. Mike Shea who'd planned to burst into Dalles City on two good legs, and make them all bend to a rich man. I wondered what Lottie would say when she saw Mike now. I wondered how she'd treat him.

I tried to tell him he was making something out of nothing. I pointed out that there were at least four or five men in town with peg legs and that nobody thought anything about it, which was true. But Mike wouldn't listen.

"I don't want to go to your weddin', anyhow," he finally said. "The fact is, Caleb, I think you're makin' a big mistake gettin' hooked up. Not that Mary ain't a nice girl and all that, and pretty enough, too. But, Hell, Caleb, you ain't had any fun. You got part of a gold claim and you're all set to have some fun, like I told you."

The only way I managed to get Mike to the wedding was to rig it up with Ben Guiness and Tom Ludden to shanghai him. They had a way of their own. They took Mike into town and got him drunk enough to forget about his leg. Then they told him that a gang of hoodlums who didn't like me were planning to be there and break up the wedding celebration.

"The Hell you say!" remarked Mike, and got up from the table. The astonishing thing was that while he was drunk Mike could manage the wooden leg fairly well. But just to make things easier, Guiness and Ludden had a buckboard wagon waiting outside the liquor store. The three piled in, and so Mike Shea arrived just before the ceremony started.

Mary wore her mother's wedding dress, and I had never seen a woman look so sweet and lovely. I actually trembled with pride as I stood with her in front of the Reverend Thomas Condon. It seemed to me that this could not be true. I had done nothing to deserve such fortune.

The swiftness of the ceremony surprised me. Before I knew it, Thomas Condon was smiling at me, whispering, "Go ahead, Caleb . . . kiss your bride!" It was unbelievable that something so sacred and so lasting could be accomplished so simply. I groped toward Mary. My face got tangled in her veil, and the crowd began to laugh and cheer. Mary reached up and pulled the veil away, and it was she who directed our lips together. A moment later I was shoved aside as laughing and shouting men crushed Mary into a corner, demanding to kiss the bride.

Mike hobbled up, reeking of whiskey. Tears were streaming down his broad good-natured face. "It sure was all right, Caleb. I'm sorry for what I said about it bein' a mistake."

"Forget it, Mike. Aren't you going to kiss the bride?"

He brushed the tears away with the back of a hand. "That I am. I've had a bit to drink. D'you think she'll smell it?"

"Of course not, Mike."

He seemed relieved, and began pushing toward Mary. Then suddenly he turned again. "What's this about you goin' to work for that steamboat company?"

"I guess it's true," I said.

"What do you want to do that for? You don't need to be runnin' one of them damned boats."

"I want to do it, though."

For a moment he said nothing, just looked at me as if he were trying to understand. Then he broke into a broad grin, and resumed his search for Mary.

It was a long time before I saw Mary again. The crowd began attacking the food and the beer. Mary was toasted with the champagne, the beer, and the private bottles. The sparse Kiessling furniture was pushed back, and a fiddle and an accordion began playing. There were ten times as many men as women, and the ladies got plenty of attention. Once I glimpsed Sidonie Kiessling, perspiration at her temples, a curl plastered wet against her forehead, in the arms of a soldier whose waltzing was determined. But she was smiling happily.

The men without partners went out onto the porch and into the farmyard and sat listening to the music, or gossiping, or frankly getting themselves drunk in honor of the occasion. As I went through the door for a breath of air, a black bearded man held out a bottle toward me. "Here, son! I'll trade you a shot of my tanglefoot for a shot of yours."

"I'm afraid I haven't any."

"Well, then, damn it, take a shot of mine anyhow." He peered at me in the half light. "You're the groom, ain't you?"

I admitted it, proudly.

"Well, then, damn it, this is the stuff you'll need tonight. It'll make you do your business in fair and handsome shape." He broke into a roar at his jest.

"Thanks," I said, taking the bottle and tipping it. A fiery serpent slid down my throat and shot a forked tongue at my heart.

"There now, damn it, that stuff takes hold, don't it?"

I couldn't find the breath to agree. "I laid in a case o' that at Portland," the whiskered fellow went on. "Figured it might come in handy in the up country."

"You heading for the Salmon River country?"

"Bet your boots. I don't know a damned soul here, but I was in town addin' to my outfit and I heard there was a shindig out here. I figured nobody'd mind a stranger."

"We're glad to have you," I told him, and shook his hand. Inside I had got a glimpse of Mary. She had changed from her wedding dress and was dancing with her father. When she saw me in the doorway, she kissed Heinrich, stopped her waltzing, and brought him over to me.

"Did you think I'd deserted you?"

"I'd begun to be afraid." I looked closer. "Mary! What's happened to your cheeks? They're all bruised."

She laughed. "I should think so! Some of these men should shave before they kiss the bride."

"The idiots!" I said angrily.

"It doesn't matter," Mary said. "They're all our friends, and they wish us well."

She must have been, that night, unutterably happy—for I was to find that she was usually reticent to the point of coldness before strangers. Tonight I was delighted at her acceptance of our guests' wild enthusiasms.

I took her hands. "We'll have to be careful getting away. If this mob starts to follow us there's no telling what they'll do."

Heinrich Kiessling chuckled. "That I have got fixed up," he said. "The wagon Tom Ludden and Ben Guiness brought Mike in—it will be up the road, all ready for you, with the horses tied to a tree. I have talked to Captain White, and you are to go right to the boat."

Mary and I mixed with the crowd for another hour or so, sometimes dancing together, more often sitting on the side benches to watch. Most of the crowd had long since forgotten the original purpose of the celebration. The Kiessling house was echoing and re-echoing to the sounds of the fiddle and the accordion, the shouts and laughter of the dancers. The farmyard and the field beyond the house were dotted with the prostrate shadows of celebrants who had temporarily given up the ghost.

I saw Heinrich Kiessling looking toward us from the doorway. "It's time to leave," I whispered.

In the doorway we confronted Heinrich. I saw Mary's hand on his arm. She dared not kiss him now for fear of letting the others know we were leaving. "Papa, you must come and see us soon!"

"I will, I will," said Heinrich. "The wagon is up the road, Magda."

"I haven't said goodbye to Else and Sidonie and Hulda."

The old German patted her hand. "I will tell them, Magda."

We ran through the darkness, sidestepping unconscious figures. Mary was sobbing softly, and every so often she would say, "Caleb . . . oh, Caleb!" as if we were doing something we should not.

I found the wagon and the mares as Heinrich Kiessling had said. Quickly I unleashed the lines and helped Mary into the wagon. Up from the house floated the sounds of the music, the rhythmic scraping of dancing feet, and an occasional meaningless shout. I slapped at the mares' rumps with the ends of the leather and we jerked away, the cottonwoods flying past, the wheels protesting at every turn over the rock-bottomed ruts.

I drove like a mad man, but Mary said nothing until we reached the town. As we turned into the white dust of the street she said, "Caleb, why do you have to drive so fast?"

"It's a long way to the boat, Mary. And don't think they won't be trying to find us!"

I was dog tired, as I hadn't realized until now. The nervous drain of the wedding ceremony was beginning to get at me. As I urged the mares along the road to the boat landing I wished that I had taken a little more of the prescription of the black-bearded stranger. I could not bear the thought of having that mob at Kiessling's, half of them strangers, thrusting into this night. I kept feeling that we were pursued—as certainly we would have been if they had known we were escaping—and I pressed the team unmercifully.

It must have been three in the morning when we reached the river bank and saw the outline of the *Colonel Wright*. There was a light in Len White's cabin, and even in the night I could see the thin trail of smoke wafting from the stack, indicating a banked fire in her boiler.

I stopped the team, and lifted Mary off the buckboard. She was as limp as a rag after the wild ride. As we went up the gangplank I saw the gaunt silhouette of White.

"Well, well! On board at last, are you?"

"Captain White! I wondered what that light was doing in your cabin."

"I've been here an hour, Caleb. We're all set to sail."

I thought I hadn't heard him aright. "To sail?"

"Sure. The engineer's aboard—but that's all. Just me and the engineer. Thought we might go upriver a way—just in case the boys decided you ought to have a shivaree."

I was embarrassed at Len White's solicitousness, but I said nothing. "I'll show you your cabin," he said; and Mary and I followed him, like two sheepish children.

Len White led us to the best cabin on the *Wright*, on the main deck, about midships. There were two bunks, one above the other; a settee; and a wash stand with a basin and pitcher. There was a mirror, too, which was something I hadn't seen in any of the other cabins, not even the Captain's.

"Here you are," White said. "Make yourselves at home. Jake and I figured to take the boat upriver a way—just far enough so they won't find us. We'll drift down again in the morning."

He searched in his coat for a sulphur match and lighted the lamp on the stand. I glanced at Mary. "I'll watch her get away," I said nervously. "You don't mind if I go up in the pilot house with Captain White, do you, Mary?"

Len White laughed. "You'd better get used to him being in a pilot house, Mrs. Paige," he said.

It was the first time I had heard anyone call her Mrs. Paige and my heart did funny things inside my breast. As if from a distance I heard Mary tell Captain White that she didn't mind. Awkwardly I shut the door and followed the skipper along the deck. Together we unshipped the long poles that held the *Wright* out from shore against a rise or fall in the Columbia. Then White went aft and shouted down to the engineer.

"All set, Jake?"

A good humored drawl drifted up. "A-all set, sir."

I went with Len White into the wheel house and looked down at the river, over the nose of the *Wright*. "Full ahead," he called into the speaking tube, and I felt the vessel tremble as the buckets took hold. The nose of the boat shifted toward the center of the stream.

"You're going to a lot of trouble just so Mary and I won't be bothered," I said at last.

"A man only gets married once," Len White answered. "And God knows you don't want that crazy bunch of galoots hollering and beating pans at you all night. I know I don't, anyhow. Jake and I want to get some sleep. If we stayed at the landing the whole pack, like as not, would be aboard."

For the space of half an hour Len White nosed the *Wright* up the river. Then he began turning the wheel slowly. I recognized the berth he was heading for. It was behind a slight promontory that arrested the current of the Columbia above the mouth of the Walla Walla, and as the shore loomed close he turned the wheel over to me.

"Hold her nose ashore," he said. "Jake and I will make her fast." He ordered a dead engine through the speaking tube, and left me with the wheel. I stood there with arms stretched wide to encompass the big wheel, heading her for the cup-like indentation in the shore. Slowly we drifted and grounded, and I went below to join the engineer and Len White.

As I reached the lower deck Jake was clambering overside from shore. "She's all snug, sir," he said to White. He looked at me and yawned prodigiously. "I'm ready to turn in. The minute I hit that pillow I'll be dead."

"Here, too," Len White answered.

"Good night, Captain," I said, and the next thing I knew I was alone on the deck. I heard Jake's heavy footfalls on the companionway that led to the engineer's quarters below. Then, above me, Len White's cabin door slammed very deliberately. After that there was no sound save the lapping of the water against the sides of the *Wright* and the gentle stir of the current out beyond in the main channel.

Our cabin was dark when I reached it. Softly I turned the latch and opened the door, calling Mary's name.

"Yes, Caleb." Her whisper came across to me and I knelt down beside the bunk and held her close.

"I thought you would never be coming," she said. Then: "Until after tonight it will not seem right about that other time."

CHAPTER 17

As we went downriver the next day I began to realize that Mary was afraid of leaving the quiet little valley she had come to think of as home. Only a little while before, the Kiesslings had torn themselves from a soil they must have loved, and now, just as Mary had begun to think of the new ranch as home, I appeared to snatch her into something that was strange and which I think, despite her feeling for me, she never trusted.

So I tried to make her forget the valley and the fussy little creek and the tall cottonwoods and Heinrich's wheat yellowing in the sun. As we sat on the deck of the *Wright* I pictured Dalles City as gay and friendly and cosmopolitan. I told her about the Umatilla House, and how the town spread back over the slope toward the Army post. I told her about Mill Creek that ran through the town and I am afraid I tried to make Mill Creek much like the creek on the Kiessling place. I described the variety of shops along the main street, and was careful to include the board sidewalks that flanked them. And when I had exhausted myself with describing the town that I remembered, I embroidered the truth a little. I felt fairly safe in this, because I was sure that in Mary's eyes Dalles City would look grand enough in comparison with Walla Walla.

To my surprise, some of my exaggerations turned out to be realities. I had been away less than a year and had not dreamed that gold and the river could change the town so much. It was no longer simply a town by the side of a river. It was a river town; and there is a real difference.

I had heard the talk of Ainsworth and White about "the company" and their plans for it. I had gone upriver with a mad lot of optimistic passengers. I had stood at the rail of the *Wright* to watch a town created within a few hours. I had seen the cable ferry transporting men who were on their way to a country that had been an unknown land. Yet still I had not grasped the significance of the Pierce discovery, or fully realized what was happening to the Columbia, until I returned to Dalles City with Mary.

The reduction of freight rates from a hundred dollars a ton on the old bateaux to eighty dollars on the *Wright* had been impetus enough to give Coe and Thompson business and make Dalles City a point of commerce. But when the news of gold had come downstream, and Coe's new *Idaho* and the *Wright* were pooled with Ainsworth's boats on the lower river, the town really began its boom. The *Wright* herself was touching the portage landing three times a week, and passengers had to pause in Dalles City to transfer to another boat. What they did not invest in soberer outfitting they spent for various forms of unhealthy recreation.

I got my first taste of the boom conditions when I tried to register for a room for Mary and me at the Umatilla House. Dan Handley told me regretfully that there wasn't a square foot of space available in the place.

"Sure, it's a sorry note, Caleb," he said. "It's a sorry note that I can't put up a man and his new bride—especially," and here Dan gave Mary the look of his Irish eyes, "especially when she's as pretty as this one. But do you know how many people there are in Dalles City now? Twenty-five hundred, at least! We're always jammed with transients. You know how it is. They miss their boats —an' if they miss one boat they're liable to miss a dozen! I'll tell you what you do, Caleb. You go down to Ed Danby's for the night —an' the minute somebody checks out I'll let you know."

I thanked Dan, but told him it wouldn't be necessary to notify us. "We'll be looking for a house to rent."

"I wish you luck," replied Handley dubiously.

The truth was I had hoped to avoid seeing Martha Danby for a while. I remembered too well how I had walked out of her house against her orders. Furthermore, I had a clear idea of what she would think of my escapade with Mike. I had no hesitation in facing Dan Handley, for I knew that as long as Mary was with me he would never mention the trouble Mike and I had with the Southern sympathizer. But I was less certain about other citizens, and most especially Martha Danby.

It was the presence of Mary who saved me, although when Martha opened the door in response to my knock her reaction was immediate and as I feared. "So you're back?" she said. "Of all the nerve, Caleb Paige!"

"This is my wife, Mrs. Danby," I put in swiftly.

"Wife?" said Martha, looking at Mary.

"We were married yesterday in Walla Walla. Can you put us up until we find a house?"

Not moving from the doorway, Martha folded her hands beneath her apron and took another look at Mary. Then, apparently satisfied, she said, "I reckon we can. We're the only place in town that has vacancies. I'm particular about who I take in."

Old Danby came stomping forward, peering over his spectacles. When he saw me he let out a yell of delight. "Well, if it ain't Caleb Paige!"

"With a wife," mentioned Martha, as if it were not quite proper. "This is my husband, Mrs. Paige."

"How d'you do?" said Ed, bowing low. Then he got his back to the window and looked at me near-sightedly. "You've changed, Caleb. Yes, sir, things been happening to you." He turned to Mary. "This rapscallion walked out of this room one night against our advice—and he was nothin' but a stripling with a hard head. Now here he comes back lookin' like a man."

"I must say," sniffed Martha Danby, "that he's come back to town in much better company than he left with."

With that remark I knew that Martha had let down the bars against Mary. As for Mary, she seemed to take instantly to Mrs. Danby despite the seeming lack of warmth in our reception. I think that in Ed Danby's wife she recognized something familiar, something to tie to in a raw and strange town. Almost as soon as our carpet sacks were unpacked, the pair were in the kitchen comparing cooking recipes and I had a chance to corner Ed.

"I wouldn't know the town," I told him.

He nodded enthusiastically. "Goin' to be the biggest danged town you ever saw. Wouldn't be surprised if it got to be as big as New York. What's to stop it?"

"I don't know," I laughed. "I've been hearing a lot about this Oregon Steam Navigation Company."

Danby beamed as proudly as though he'd started the company himself. "Well, sir, there's a layout! Slickest thing you ever saw. You got The Cascades Rapids and you got the rapids here, both of 'em brass-bound obstructions to navigation. Likewise, you had three sets of boats operatin', and our friend Coe was sittin' nicer than any of them because his line was the one that went from here practically to the gold criks. But he wasn't the one who figured out the deal. That was Ainsworth." He looked at me sharply. "I hear you're goin' to work for him."

"I hope I am."

"But what about the gold mine you and Mike found?"

"Well, it's still there. Mike's pretty disgusted with me because I don't take much interest in it."

"But ain't you going to work it?" asked Danby in amazement.

"Sure. We've divided it into shares, Mike and I with a fourth apiece and the rest to a couple of fellows who're going to work the mine."

Danby's eyes grew sober. "Yeah. I heard about Mike's accident. I guess he wouldn't be much good workin' a mine."

"Not for a while."

"Is he comin' back to Dalles City?"

I told Ed how Mike felt about his leg. "But he says he'll come down, maybe in the spring. There isn't any more talk about what happened, is there?"

Danby shook his head in disgust. "Nobody's thought about the War since gold was discovered. Anyhow, you two hadn't been gone three months before it came out how that fellow got shot. One of the bucks got drunk and spilled the beans. But everybody that knew Mike knew he wasn't shootin' anybody in the back. We did figure at first that maybe you got nervous and did it accidental and that Mike got you out of town."

As Handley had predicted, Mary and I had a difficult time finding a house to rent. A room at one of the other hotels would have given us more privacy than we enjoyed at the Danbys', but I hesitated to take Mary anywhere but to the Umatilla House. The town was full of all manner of people and I didn't want to expose Mary too quickly to the life of a river town. So for two days I searched for any sort of dwelling that would serve temporarily as a home of our own. I had just about given up when another's misfortune came to my rescue.

I was tramping a dusty path back to town when from the doorway of a small ramshackle clapboard house I saw six men carrying a coffin. They brought their burden to a flat-bed wagon, shoved it carelessly aboard, and hoisted themselves beside it with their feet hanging over. Then the rugged funereal vehicle was yanked creaking toward the cemetery on the hill.

There was something about that cortege which made me certain that in the coffin was the body of someone who had been the sole occupant of the house. I went back to town and asked Ed Danby about it.

"Must have been Nick Barstow's place. He got into a little argument with a drunk soldier down in front of Tim Baldwin's saloon. They both shot at the same time and killed one another deader than mackerels. The soldier expired right off, but Nick ran up to his house and hid to die. It happened four or five days ago, but they just discovered Nick yesterday in the tall grass in back of his house. They figured he'd skipped town."

"I've got to get that house," I told Ed. "It's the only vacant place in town. Don't say anything to Mary about Barstow, will you?"

"Nope. But you better not tell her until I get a chance to post Martha not to mention it neither."

At Ed's suggestion I hurried down to see John Beck, the baker, who owned the house. He told me that I could rent the place for thirty dollars a month. That was steep toll for a roof over our heads, but I would willingly have paid a hundred.

It was as poor a dwelling as might be found in all Dalles City, but to Mary and me it was a castle. Constructed of rough, unpainted lumber, it was no more than a box with a peaked roof and one window in each of its four sides. The interior was dirty and odorous for Barstow had been old and tough and had evidently gone through his later years without caring how he lived. Between the rail fence and the house the grass grew tall and rank with thistle and tumbleweed.

Mary was not dismayed in the slightest. No sooner had we made our examination than she turned to me and said, "You go down to the store and buy a broom and scythe. I'll start to work inside and you mow the weeds."

"I'll find somebody to help you," I said.

She would not hear of it. "Don't you think I want to make our first home ready, Caleb, without help from somebody else?"

So I went down the slope to town and bought the broom and the scythe. When I returned, Mary had pinned up her skirts and had a towel around her hair. Everything that could be moved without a broom was piled in the center of the floor. "You stay outside," Mary ordered, "and mow the weeds."

"But I want to help."

"It's no help you'd be. Now get along."

I grabbed her and kissed her, and then made her dampen the corner of her apron with her tongue so that I could wipe the smudges off her nose. "All right," I said, "I'll cut the weeds. Then I think I'll run down and ask Lawrence Coe if he's heard from Ainsworth about what I'm to do. But I'll be back at six o'clock and I want you all ready to go to supper with me at the Umatilla House."

"Now that we have our own house, that would be foolish, Caleb."

"Just the same, Mrs. Paige, we'll have supper at the Umatilla House. You'll have done enough without trying to make that rusty old stove cook supper."

Outside, I peeled off my coat and started to work on the weeds and grass. I felt foolish, standing knee-deep in the grass in my shirtsleeves, swinging the scythe. I was awkward with it, and hoped that nobody would pass by and see me. After knocking around Dalles City with Mike, rafting it down the Snake, and piloting for Len White, this seemed to me to be infantile business. As quickly as I could I worked around to the back of the house.

CHAPTER 18

As I sat in the dining room at the Umatilla House with Mary I began to realize why Ed Danby had been so casual about my year-old escapade with Mike Shea in front of the Union Club. The people of Dalles City were too occupied with the Oregon Steam Navigation Company to be thinking about the War now. Danby was not the only one who took delight in the Ainsworth coup. Around our table the talk of Ainsworth and "the company" was on every tongue. It was of a piece with the bursting, egotistic optimism that was all over the town. It had grown to be a matter of local pride.

Ainsworth had already interested himself in steamers running from the Portland landing to The Cascades—but, I gathered from the talk around us, there had been difficulties at The Cascades. Better than anyone in that crowded room I understood why. I remembered that even when Putnam Bradford owned a portage road and operated the *Mary,* there had been a portage on the other side of the river—a tandem mule cart owned by Colonel Joe Ruckel, with two boats. Unlike Lawrence Coe and Bradford, Ruckel had a line straight through from Portland to Dalles City.

Apparently it had been Ainsworth who had engineered a coalition. Slowly, carefully, he had formed "the company," completely in control from Portland to the Deschutes, and then invited Coe into the group in order to get through to Lewiston. He had recognized Coe's advantages. The *Wright* and the *Idaho* were the links that joined Dalles City with the gold fields and the interior military posts. So Lawrence Coe got a big share of the stock in "the company" and, as well, a good job as agent at Dalles City. But it had been Ainsworth who had brought the fighting tom cats all to one saucer of cream. And it was the name of this tall, spare man which was on of the lips of everyone in the Umatilla House dining room that night.

What had happened to Mike and me a year ago could never happen now. If Mike returned and tried to foment another Union Club nobody would object; nobody would care one way or the other. To the Northwest, the War was largely Mr. Lincoln's. The newspapers were still dutifully editorializing upon it. The politicians, as stupidly baffled as always about the thoughts of their constituents, were steadily orating on the subject. But along the Columbia and the Snake to the Clearwater, the War was only a vague struggle which must one day end. Dalles City had come to believe that however it ended it could have no great effect upon us. War means bloodshed, and Dalles City had no bloodshed except for occasional fatalities accruing out of a disagreement in a saloon. War means pestilence, and there was none in the clean, windswept gorges of the Columbia. War means immorality, and even Irish Moll's place was too gay and casual to smack of that. War means poverty, and we were rich. War means hopelessness among the people, and we were envisioning an empire that would set us free forever.

I do not mean that we were without sympathy for the dead. We did not like to read in the *Statesman* or the *Oregonian* about the awful loss of life. But by the time the news of a battle reached us, the dead were buried, the last rites said, the mothers comforted.

Remote and occupied, we had never believed that the North and South would fight. And when they actually began the struggle, we regarded them as strange people who had little connection with what we were trying to build for ourselves across the Stony Mountains. In the beginning there had been a few hot heads, like Mike, who went wild on one side or the other. But even they cooled when gold was found in the mountains above the Clearwater. After that, there were more tangible problems to consider. After that there were cattle wanted for food. There was liquor wanted for rasping throats. There were women wanted for men aching with loneliness. All material wants, and the filling of them materialistic; and yet I would not say that the supplying of those needs is less honorable than murder with powder and ball for the impossible ideal that no man shall enslave another.

I was disappointed at the effect of the exciting buzz in the Umatilla House upon Mary. I had expected her to be awed and delighted with the surroundings and inhabitants of the finest hostelry on the river. It may have been that she was tired from her strenuous afternoon cleaning up the mess old Nick Barstow had left behind him. It may have been that, with the natural protective instinct of a woman, she wanted to give no sign that she was impressed. In either event, she appeared only bored and weary and I began to wish I hadn't insisted that we have supper at the Umatilla House.

"Tomorrow," I promised her, "you must sleep most of the day. Then we'll have a little supper in the house and I'll help you get it."

Mary smiled. "I would like to see you in the kitchen!"

"You'd be surprised," I said. "I know some very tasty dishes I learned when Mike and the Indian and I were up in the Salmon River country. For instance, dried fish, and dog steak—"

"Caleb!" Mary shuddered. "Caleb, that is not funny."

I felt uncomfortable under her scandalized gaze, and experienced a fleeting wish that I were back on the mouth of the Clearwater with Mike and Cut-Mouth instead of at white cloth and gleaming silver with a wife I did not yet understand. I must have looked quite lost and stricken, for Mary laughed and added quickly, "I'm sorry, Caleb. But really you should not talk so in a place like this where the supper is so good. It isn't nice."

I was about to apologize when I saw Kirt Inge walk into the dining room, and with him was a young woman. She seemed somehow tall, and yet her tilted hat reached only to Inge's shoulder so that its tiny stuffed bird, as she nodded to acquaintances in the room, appeared to peck grain from his coat. I realized that she was not so much tall as unbelievably slender—yet there was a soft curve to her hips, and a solidity about the way she walked that made me think involuntarily, "her legs are strong."

At that moment she turned from Kirt Inge and looked full at me. A silver-thin streak ran through my chest and caught my breath away. The girl was Victoria Hunt.

She was Victoria Hunt and more beautiful than I had dreamed she could ever have grown to be. I say dreamed, because I knew then, in that instant, that I really had dreamed of her—often. It did no good to tell myself now that she meant nothing, that, since she was the only girl I had ever known except Mary, I had merely wondered about her. I knew now that she had been inextricably woven with my dreams of the river.

Her dark, haunting eyes were the same—the eyes of the Vicky Hunt I had known, sultry and half mocking. They had always been the eyes of a knowing woman; now her body had grown up to them. Her face was thinner, the cheek bones high, her mouth soft and smiling. Beneath her hat, her blue-black hair was drawn smooth. Every strand set and perfect, it glistened under the lamps of the dining room; as she looked at me her hand went to the white net which held it at the back. On her wrist was a black band with a mosaic clasp.

"Caleb. . . ." Mary's whisper came to me out of the distance. "That girl looking this way. She has hardly any crinoline under her skirt!"

I did not answer. There had been the faintest flicker of recognition across Vicky's eyes, the ghost of a smile—and then she had turned again to Inge and sat down in the chair he had drawn out for her. Inge was talking now, and she was listening, still smiling, her dark eyes not wavering from his.

"Caleb . . ." Mary said.

"Yes," I said. "Her hoops are small, aren't they? That's why she seemed so slender."

"Do you know who she is, Caleb?"

I nodded. "Her name is Victoria Hunt. Good Lord, how she's changed!"

Vicky's voice came back: *I am a beautiful lady and you are in love with me. And you are angry because all the officers want to dance with me.*

PART THREE

CHAPTER

1

I HAD never seen the Mississippi and her boats, but I have heard men talk of them around a table in Umatilla House. It is possible, as these Missourians insisted, that the steamers of the Mississippi are a little grander than those of the Columbia—but they could not be very much grander than the *Daisy Ainsworth* or the *Wide West*. Even to hear the Missourians tell it, I never got very excited about steamboating on that stream. There were the sharpers and the show boat actors, true. There were the niggers on the levees. But those steamboats merely reflected the graceful life of the ports they made, while the steamboats from the Columbia always brought something from outside. They have always been anachronisms on the ancient stream. The suave skippers come ashore to rub shoulders with the men of a frontier still raw. The ladies who hold their skirts high in descending the gangplank must walk with prostitutes and Chinese on the streets of Dalles City and Walla Walla and Lewiston.

The Columbia's steamboats brought something beside their cargo. On their decks and in their cabins was a tight little civilization. But when the vessel reached an upper river port this civilization disintegrated and dissolved into the frontier.

Somehow I believe those Missourians realized the magnificence of the Columbia when they got West and that they talked just to reassure themselves. It is impossible for me to think that they could miss the wonderful, weird enchantment of such a rousing stream, or that it had so quickly sprung from a hunting ground for the savages to a mighty river bearing the vanguard of a new empire. If I understood those Missourians rightly, the Mississippi is a flat, broad, sluggish stream which seems to suffer a steamboat as a corpulent and lazy mistress suffers the blandishments of a lover. But the Columbia is as capricious as she is beautiful. She is wise as well as vigorous; she combines the virtues of age with those of youth. I have seen men escape from other rivers, like those Missourians in the Umatilla House—but I have never known a man to escape the Columbia for long.

It is difficult for me to say which part of the river I love best; and I mean, of course, which of the parts I know. For the Columbia is one of the great rivers of the world and of all time, and no one man has ever become familiar with all its vast flow. It consumes the Snake and the Clark Fork and the Kootenai, and countless lesser streams and creeks. And when it rushes past Dalles City it has become almost as large as the St. Lawrence or the Danube. Even before it has swallowed the Snake it is greater than the Nile.

Men raised on the upper Columbia often speak of it and the Snake in the same breath. The Snake, too, is a great river and much of the Columbia's wilfulness in the lower reaches comes from it. I have seen the Snake tear through a gorge deeper than the Grand Canyon of the Colorado. I have seen a falls in the Snake that is higher and fiercer than Niagara.

Of what the Columbia is like far up toward the boundary of Canada and beyond I have had to depend, regretfully, upon old Charlefoux. He was old when I knew him, but he could remember his days with McLoughlin as a voyageur, and could still sing in a cracked voice

Rouli, roulant, ma boule rolant
En roulant, ma boule rolant . . .

In a small boat he had traveled almost all of the fourteen hundred miles of the Columbia from its origin in the heart of the Canadian Stonies. He told me how, between the headwaters and Lake Windermere, the Columbia is a gentle river, running in bayous through low flats. But a little later, after she has swung beyond the Grand Coulee and begins to make the Big Bend, she grows to be the river I have known best. Charlefoux even ran Death Rapids, up in the cradle of the Columbia. "Only great fools do that," he said, "and most are drowned. But not Charlefoux."

It was this old voyageur who told me of the "region of the lakes" through which the river runs, long and narrow lakes set north and south, and always deep and clear and cold. Until Charlefoux reached Kettle Falls he would find the river quiet and unbroken, then: a three hundred mile stretch like a pool of melted snow. He would smile as he told me of this and his eyes would take on a faraway look, and I knew that he was seeing again those primitive purple forests at the water's edge, and listening for his song to come back to him from the rock walls to mingle with the sound of the paddle splash.

I will not forget the first time I saw where the Columbia sweeps into its widest valley, cutting hundreds of feet below the surrounding terrain. But where it enters its basaltic canyons and becomes more turbulent, there it begins to thrill the hearts of river men. I am quite sure that this is like nothing on this earth—the gigantic stream pounding its way to the sea, and on each side the great blocks of basalt, broken and strewn. That river pounding on the one side a cliff three thousand feet high, and on the other gently lapping a fertile benchland. And, in the next mile, split in half by eerie pinnacles of rock.

Now begin the obstructions that test the hand and head of a river man—the rapids at Umatilla where the reefs bound channels at right angles to the current. The Devil's Bend, the Owhyee, the Four O'clock, and the Rock Creek—bad rapids all, but not the end before Dalles City is raised ahead. There is still Squally Hook, the Indian, the John Day, Preacher's Eddy, Biggs Rapid, and Hell's Gate. And none is quite the same from one day to the next. There is the mild riffle of the spring, and the rock-toothed rapid of late summer. There is the white-topped rapid that blinds you in the sunlight, and hides, gray and treacherous, behind the first flurry of winter snow.

Dalles City will be reached at last, and there will be the respite of a portage past The Dalles, past "the trough in the flat rocks" as old Charlefoux translated it for me. But between there and The Cascades are a hundred smaller rapids with all the force of the upper river behind them.

Great uplifted mountains, steaming waters, quiet lake pools, desolate wastes among rocks older than Christ is old—that is the Columbia. And when you have seen this you are still not prepared for what is to come before the river reaches the sea. For now the Cascade Range flings itself across the stream and fails to stop it and here, a hundred and sixty miles yet to the Pacific, a river boat trembles to the faint pulse of the tides.

That November after I had returned to Dalles City I met the Reverend Condon on the wharf landing. It was turning into a bitter winter, one of the worst that men remembered along the river. Scores of roofs, optimistically built for a climate that promised mildness, were caved beneath wet packed snow. The fronts of stores were hidden with piles of white, shoveled up from street and walks. The drift in front of the Umatilla House was so high that one could have stepped from it to the fancy new balcony which Dan Handley and Nick Sinnott had built around the second story.

The river was iced over; all the boats were stuck fast to the landings. I had been down to the company office gossiping with Lawrence Coe. I had fought through drifts to get there and I was surprised to see the round, solid figure of Thomas Condon on the landing. We had not met since the wedding at the Kiessling ranch and momentarily I had forgotten his interest in the river.

"Hello there, Caleb!" he called out jovially, pulling a black muffler down from his mouth to let the words out.

"How are you, Doctor Condon?" We clasped mitten-covered hands. "What're you doing down here? Not catching a boat for Portland?"

The minister laughed, his breath sending a great cloud of steam into the air. "No, Caleb. This is my first chance to see the river with ice on it, you know. How is Mary?"

"Fine, thanks. You want to come and see us. We're in the old Barstow house."

"I know. I've been meaning to pay a call. But," he grinned sheepishly, "I've been spending a lot of time along the river and in the hills. Matter of fact, if I don't attend a little bit more to the parish, I'm afraid I'll be sent out by an outraged congregation, I'd deserve it, too!"

I remembered that Thomas Condon had become intensely interested in the geological formations of the country. Indeed, it was rumored that he was going to write a book on the subject. Already he had discovered fossil bones of a tiny prehistoric three-toed horse, so small that it could have been held in the palm of a man's hand. But his greatest interest, aside from his work in the Congregational Church, was the Columbia.

Thomas Condon's reference to "an outraged congregation" was pure invention. He was loved by everybody, within and without his church. Dan Handley, a good Roman Catholic who would one day be buried with the dignity he deserved, made no secret that his will contained a bequest of five hundred dollars for the Congregational Church "out of regard for its pastor in Dalles City, the Reverend Thomas Condon."

"Where you heading for now, Caleb?" Condon enquired.

I confessed that I had in mind heading for the Umatilla House bar. Condon grinned. "Well, I can use their stove, anyhow. I'll join you."

The bar was crowded with men fortifying themselves against the cold, but we found an unoccupied table near a window that looked out over the river. Condon rubbed an elbow across the frosty pane. "Are you going to work for the Oregon Steam Navigation Company, Caleb? Seems to me that's what you had in mind."

"Yes. I got word a few weeks ago that I'm to be purser on the *Wright*. I'll start as soon as the ice breaks up."

"Good." The minister looked out at the still, white stream. "Outside of myself, I think you're as gone on the old Columbia as anybody in town." He turned his pale blue eyes upon me, and asked seriously, "What part of it impresses you most?"

"I think the Gateway, up by the mouth of the Walla Walla." I laughed at the memory of myself caught naked in the pilot house of the new *Wright*. "Maybe it's because I'll never forget how it looked on my first trip up the river. No steamboat had been up that far and those big rocks were pretty forbidding to me."

"A river a thousand feet deep ran through there once." Condon's statement seemed to trouble him, as if his geology and his theology had for the moment clashed. He added: "I've been trying to measure the gap at Big Eddy, but so far I've succeeded only in coming near to drowning. I'd like to get that gap measured and I'd like to sound some of those holes the current has whirled into the channel." He fastened my gaze suddenly. "Do you know what causes those holes?" he asked.

"Why—erosion," I ventured.

Condon snorted. "No, sir. The Columbia *plucks* out that jointed rock and heaves the fragments clear over the rim. I've got a piece at home I'm sure had been tossed a hundred feet."

When I had finished my drink we struggled together along the length of the main street before I left him to take my own path up the hill. "Give Mary my best," Condon said, "and tell her I'll be seeing her soon." He reached for my hand again. "As soon as the weather opens up I'm going to make a trip down the river. Didn't you tell me your mother and father were buried at The Cascades?"

"Yes."

"I'll stop there," he said, and then went trudging along the street.

By the following spring I had quite forgotten his promise until one day I received a letter from him written on the stationery of the Palace Hotel in San Francisco. When he had come up the Columbia to take his post at Dalles City he had possessed no interest in geology. On this first downriver trip it was as if he had seen the lower river for the first time.

"I had never dreamed such beauty could exist in nature," he had written. "Our steamer went from barren, rolling hills into a lush green with a swiftness that took my breath away. I was particularly interested in the ancient water-marks on the rock banks, hundreds of feet above the deck of the steamer. Unquestionably it means that there was gradual elevation of the mountain chain and, at the same time, an erosion by the river. In brief, Caleb, the heights got higher and the depths deeper. The peculiar columns of basalt which give such a weird touch to the beauty of the gorge must have been caused by local seismic disturbances, or perhaps volcanic activity. Frankly, I was relieved when the boat reached Portland. Somehow I felt that I had no right to be in that ancient channel. It was like walking into God's room in God's absence.

"After leaving the gorges, the Columbia did not interest me so much. I felt that it had grown tired, contemplating its end in the great Pacific. Yet when we reached Astoria to transfer to the *Brother Jonathan* it had gathered itself into a final fury, apparently ready to lash out at this last adversary.

"It was tremendously rough going over the bar and almost all on board were ill. I was among them, I am frank to state, but I did manage to hang to the taffrail and look back at the river's mouth. I left it with genuine regret; I saw the river dissolve into the gray ocean and almost cried. You may depend upon it, I will be back soon to the mother of civilization in the Northwest country!

"As we went out, the land seemed to close, and I understood then how Captain Vancouver decided that there was no Great River of the West. Through this understanding, my admiration increases for Captain Gray, steering for what seemed a line of breakers and finding that for which mariners of all nations had been searching for two hundred years.

"Here in San Francisco—an amazing and ungodly town, Caleb! —I am still fascinated by the memory of the Columbia. It is curious how, although it reveals so obviously how much greater it used to be, one is still awed by it. But I remember once meeting an actor, too old for dramatics at last, who had been a great Richard Third. The power was still there."

The boys at the wharf boat would have been amused by Condon's references to "local seismic disturbances" and his comparisons of the river with an actor. I might have read it to them except for a postscript which the minister had added. That postscript caused me to keep the letter entirely to myself. It said:

P.S. At The Cascades I visited the graves of your father and mother. They are in excellent shape, as is the one of James Sinclair beside them. The carving on the head-boards is very legible after these six years. I spaded the corners of the mounds a bit, and placed some wild berry sprigs which the cold weather has preserved way beyond their season. I said some prayers; also I remained there for a respectful time and did some thinking.

Yrs,
T. C.

". . . After these six years," Condon had written, and I had to count back in order to convince myself that it had been no longer than that since the massacre at The Cascades. I had been too occupied and too young to think of time; and yet if I had been aware of time I would have thought that those dim, terrible days and nights of the Indian attack had occurred much longer ago. So much had happened to the river and to me. I was a young man, eighteen years of age and married; a man of parts, with an interest in a gold claim and a job promised with "the company."

As for the river and the settlements along it, they hardly resembled the Columbia and the settlements of the quiet days when the *Mary* and the little *Hassalo* plied the waters of the middle river from The Cascades to Dalles City. The Oregon Steam Navigation Company had only begun, yet already the rush of men and supplies to the mines and towns of the interior was taxing it. The whole lengths of the portage roads were lined with freight on both sides of the track, open to damage and a prey to thieves. Freight damage and loss in a single month, all occurring along the portages, was amounting to from five to eight thousand dollars a month—yet so great was the rush, and so anxious was Ainsworth to accommodate it with the equipment available, that the leaks could not be stopped. Men and freight were wanted up the river; the gold dust had to come down or be worthless. And an upriver trip could net ten thousand dollars for passengers and eighteen thousand for freight—with another two hundred dollars thrown in by the party who operated the bar concession. The downstream trips would bring fifty thousand, a hundred thousand, sometimes three hundred thousand of the yellow cargo, to be transferred at Portland to the *Sierra Nevada* or the *Brother Jonathan* and sent south along the rugged coast to the Golden Gate.

CHAPTER

2

At last there came the day I had dreamed about ever since Mike and I sat on the bank of the river, in the shadows of the block-house at The Cascades, and launched toy boats into the white swirls. It was April 12, 1863—the day that Lawrence Coe was to initiate me into my duties as purser on the *Colonel Wright*. A purser is not a captain, but Coe had read to me that part of Ainsworth's letter which said: *I'd like to give the boy a pilot's job, and I know he could handle it. But we have a reputation to build, and we cannot put on men too raw in the pilot house. Naturally, I hope, there will be new boats—and new captains to command them. Meanwhile he can learn a lot from Captain Stump.*

"Stump?" I said. "Is Len White transferring to another boat?"

Coe shook his head. "Len is leaving the company."

I couldn't believe it; and then I recalled the gentle argument of White and Ainsworth in Galbreath's whiskey shop in Walla Walla. "You mean Ainsworth finally lowered Len's salary?"

"That's it. You see, Thompson and I could afford to pay Len five hundred a month—but the new company can't set wages like that for a captain. Not yet, anyhow. Our expenses are too great, keeping up with the rush, and we've got to put still more money into the pot to win out."

I had to admit that three hundred a month was a good salary for a man. Len White's five hundred a month had been a half-believed legend all along the river. It was hard to imagine Len White stepping down from the wheel of the *Colonel Wright*, but

I knew that he was stubborn and that his fabulous salary had been a matter of particular pride to him.

"You'll like Tom Stump," Coe had promised me. "He was one of the best on the Sacramento."

Now, on this April day, the sun was streaming down into the gorge, and the ice had long since drifted downstream. Out in the channel the river was not yet boiling as mightily as it would in the months to come. Coe stood waiting for me on the steps of the Umatilla House.

"Cap' Stump is having breakfast," he told me. "I want to introduce you to him, and then we'll go down to the wharf boat and I'll show you the ropes."

As early as it was, business was brisk as usual in the Umatilla House. Dan Handley saw me coming across the lobby and extended his big paw over the desk. "Well, young one—I hear you're the new purser on the *Wright!* Congratulations. I had a notion you'd be winding up on the boats that night you came in here with Coe and White."

The Umatilla House had changed with the town. There was fresh wallpaper in the lobby, and new chairs ranged along the walls. The stove which I had thought so grand had been exchanged for one even more ornate, with isinglass doors and a graceful stag molded into the iron sides. The chimney lamps had given way to a great chandelier suspended from the center of the ceiling by an iron chain and supporting no less than a dozen wicks in bases of brightly polished brass.

The lobby was jammed, as always when a boat was in, with soldiers, deck hands, roustabouts, prominent citizens, miners and stockmen. Whatever they were and wherever they were going, they were filtering through the lobby of the Umatilla House. The talk was lively, but it centered on only two subjects: gold and the steamboats, inseparably. The *Idaho* had brought up so many prospectors. The *Wright* had brought down so many thousands in gold dust.

I followed Coe through the crowd and into the dining room. My glance at once fell upon the angular Len White, sitting straight at a table, his elbows driving like pistons as he sliced into a platter of ham and eggs. Across from him was a small man with alert black eyes and a clipped beard.

"I want to say hello to Captain White," I told Coe.

The agent nodded. "That's Stump with him."

As we bore toward their table I tried to overcome my astonishment that White and Stump would be breakfasting together. After all, Stump had come up from California to take White's job at a lesser figure.

When White saw me he leaped to his feet and stretched a long arm. "Sit down, sit down!" he invited. "How's the wife?"

Lawrence and I joined the table, and Len introduced me to the new captain of the *Wright*. "Meet Tom Stump, Caleb—and the Lord save you. I suppose you heard he's taking over on the *Wright?*"

I looked at Captain Stump. He was as brief in physical appearance as Len White was extended. But I liked him instantly. "How do you like our country, sir?"

"God damnedest rainiest section I've ever seen," said Captain Stump. His face and hands were tanned a deep brown from the sun of the Sacramento and I could imagine that the cold drizzle was a shock. "It rained when I got into Portland. Rained all the way up the river, and now it's raining here. They tell me that's all it does."

Coe laughed. "You'll get scorched plenty on the upper river run. It may rain occasionally down below, but a drop of water in the summer up here is pretty rare."

"Any man that would steer a boat on that upper river for three hundred dollars a month hasn't any right to be kicking," mentioned Len White with a wink at me.

The little captain nodded good-naturedly. "I can get along on three hundred—and you'll wish you had."

"Like Hell I will. I'm going to build my own boat."

"Make it good," said Stump, "because the O.S.N. will be taking her over the first thing you know."

They railed at each other while Coe and I ordered coffee, as both of us had had breakfast at home. When Coe had drained his cup he turned to me. "Let's let these boys argue it out. You and

I'll go down and take a look at the books."

I told Len White I hated to see him leave. "Don't worry," he said. "I'll be around. Maybe when I build up my fleet I'll have a captain's berth for you. And I'll pay you five hundred a month, too! A decent captain oughtn't to take a cent less." Stump never flicked an eyelash, but continued to attack his corn-meal mush and syrup.

Coe and I walked out into the sunlight. The *Wright* was at the Deschutes landing, but the agent maintained his office at the town landing. Moored alongside the wharf boat was the familiar outline of the *Idaho,* smoke flattening over the stack in the quiet air. She looked lazily asleep, but the landing was a hive of activity, with cases piled high on the wharf boat and the portage cars headed east to the *Wright*.

"The passenger fares are easy to figure," Coe told me. "I've written them all out and you can tack them in your cabin. It's sixty dollars from Lewiston to Portland, plus meals and beds a dollar each. If anybody is broke and wants passage free and they seem all right, let 'em have it. You'll get to know the ones that ought to have it. It's a company policy and Ainsworth likes to have it remembered."

He opened the door into his office aboard the wharf boat and led the way inside. It was a litter of records and papers. They burst from a half-closed roll-top desk and scattered on the floor. They seemed to have flown on the walls and stuck there, but closer observation showed these to be schedules of rates and diagrams of the accommodations on the various boats. Coe handed me a sheet on which he'd neatly penned the rates of freight per ton measurement.

"You'll need this to check your freight accounts."

I looked at the sheet:

Portland to Dalles City, 121 miles	$10
Portland to Fort Walla Walla, 217 miles	$20
Portland to Lewiston, 401 miles	$40

I must have looked startled, for Lawrence Coe laughed. "Seems steep, does it? Well, I suppose the rates are a little high. Fact is, we charge ten times as much to move a ton of freight up the Columbia than it costs to move it along any other main water course in the whole country. Might even be higher on some cargo—because on everything except lead and nails and such-like solids we figure by measurement. Forty cubic feet to a ton. You want to get that straight, Caleb, because otherwise you'll be wondering how a boat that's 150 tons net register can turn in the cash for a couple or three hundred tons of freight."

He pointed out the doorway to a wagon bed which lay ready for shipment up the river. "That wagon is going to Walla Walla. Now we measure that just like she was all set up and ready to hitch the mares to. You take the full length, height and breadth and carry 'em out the full size, the biggest way of the piece, to get the cubic contents. See what I mean?"

"But the wheels and the tongue are tied to the bed."

Coe looked at me a little wearily. "That's got nothing to do with it. It's like I told you—you measure the width of the bed. Then you measure from the tip of the tongue to the back wheels. Then you lift up the tongue vertical and measure the height. Multiply them all together and you got your cubic measurement. And every forty cubic feet is a ton."

I was flabbergasted. "You mean there's nothing deducted for vacuum?"

"Of course not. That's how you can get three hundred tons on a hundred and fifty ton boat. You'll hear the story that the company hitches mules to a mounted cannon and measures in the mules, too. But that's not true. At least I've never done it."

I could hardly believe my ears, and for several minutes I thought that Coe was making a fool of me. But when he showed me some sample calculations and entries I quickly discovered that he was telling me the truth. I must have let my shock get away from me, for Coe said, "The company's got to do it, Caleb, and you might as well get that through your head. We started with a handful of insignificant steamboats and look what's happened. Before we get through with our plans we'll have spent three million dollars. We got to have new portage roads and new warehouses. If the men don't get upstream and the gold don't get down, they'd all raise

Hell—and we're doing it, aren't we? So we got to charge what the traffic will bear."

Lawrence Coe spat meditatively at a corner. "A company's in business to make money. We don't pretend to be running any philanthropy. But look at the good we're doing! We're the missionary that's dedicating new regions to settlement and transforming the wilderness. We're reaching out and bringing remote sections into the civilized world. We're even saving the lives of a lot of these miners by getting their grub to them when they need it."

I looked at Coe, astounded. I don't know whether I was more amazed at what he had told me, or at his unsuspected gift for touching his work into poetry. Of his sincerity there could be no doubt, and while I was still gasping a little at the freight charges and measurement methods, I had to admit that the agent was largely right.

"I guess the interior wouldn't be worth much without the boats."

"Worth much?" exclaimed Coe. "It wouldn't be worth a tinker's damnation. Why, a bunch of little independent steamboat owners couldn't have done what Ainsworth and Jake Kamm and the rest are doing. They can put the money into new boats—and now all the different portage interests won't be throttling the Hell out of each other all the time."

He glared at me, as if daring me to deny one small word of his argument. "And maybe you think Ainsworth didn't have a job rigging up the company. Some of those stockholders were pretty, trying to play both ends against the middle. They were just thinking of themselves, but Ainsworth kept thinking of the O.S.N. That's where he had the drop on them. He had a bigger idea than they did and he could spot a dirty trick as far as he could see it." Coe drew a deep breath, and intoned solemnly, "You're working for a real company now, Paige, and don't you forget it."

Thus Coe sent me up the portage road that afternoon with my mind filled with admonitions to respect the O.S.N. and my pockets crammed with facts and figures necessary to a functioning purser aboard the *Colonel Wright*. But all he'd said did not mean as much to me as the simple fact that I was going to be on the river.

I had not had enough experience with Ainsworth, perhaps, to have instilled into me the regard for "the company" that was in Coe—that, in fact, was in almost all the O.S.N. people I ever knew, from the deck hands to the captains. It was not simply his oft-spoken regard for "the boys." It wasn't his statement that flew from boat to boat up the river. "If we have to cut costs, we won't begin on the crew." It grew out of an admiration for what he had built, built against conniving selfishness more than with co-operation. Later it was fostered by the fierceness, the utter ruthlessness with which he stamped out competition. For we were all working together and we knew that what hurt "the company" would hurt us—but more than that, we were proud of our boats and men and we wanted no rivals on the river.

But none of these things had come to me yet as I rode the portage car up toward the Deschutes where the *Wright* was moored. All I knew, and all I cared about, was that I was at last a part of steamboating on the big river.

CHAPTER

3

WHAT few misgivings I had harbored about the purser's job on the *Colonel Wright* were melted that first spring. It was a pleasant duty—almost too easy—and Captain Tom Stump was an eminently satisfactory master under which to serve. "You collect the money," he used to tell me when I'd ask advice, "and I'll get her up and down river." The relief pilot, the mate, the engineer, the crew, he ruled with the iron hand of a swift water man. But I think he considered the purser's office beneath his notice. He disliked the goings-on of the agents and the freight offices, the continual hullabaloo between portages. Naturally, he connected the purser with these. After all, the purser had one foot ashore. He was the one to act between the shore business of "the company" and the steamboat. Stump's fight was with the river, and he loved it. His charge was the boat herself, and he took good care of her.

Once there was a mix-up in cargo and freight for which the owner had paid extra for fast service. Lawrence Coe had ordered the *Wright* to leave two hours earlier than usual. When Stump got the news he stormed into the agent's office.

"What's this—sail two hours earlier?" he demanded.

The disturbance took Coe completely by surprise. "What's wrong, Tom? We're in a jam and I didn't think you'd mind."

"Mind?" yelled Stump. "Have you looked outside?" The captain waved an arm toward the window. "That damned sun would be right square in my eyes."

This display of temperament nettled Coe. "Look, Tom, my job's to get the freight moving. That's what I'm here for."

"Who takes the *Wright* up?" Stump demanded. "It's not Ainsworth, is it?"

"No."

"It's not Jake Kamm or Lawrence Coe or Ladd or any of the stockholders, is it?"

"No."

"And it's not the fellow who's got a burr under his tail about his freight, is it?"

"Nobody said they—"

"Who takes her up?" demanded Stump, his voice rising.

"You do, Tom."

The little captain drew himself up as tall as possible. His mouth, trembling with indignation, made his beard waggle. "Then, by God, I'm not taking her up until that sun is two hours more along!"

The purser had no such problems. My work was routine, but never boring. The passengers themselves preserved the purser from that fate. Yet I think I could have made those forty hours from Deschutes to Lewiston and back again if there had been no passenger aboard. I never got over the thrill of the three blasts—the two—the final single blast on which followed, almost immediately, the explosion of the gangplank as the deck hands swung it aboard and dropped it to the foredeck. Inevitably, there would be the last straggler, his carpet bag banging against his legs as he ran, one arm signaling in frenzy toward the wheel house. If we were not too far out toward the mouth of the Deschutes, Captain Stump would bellow an order to reverse and wash it down the speaking tube with curses. Then we'd bring the red-faced and embarrassed late-comer over the side.

It was always pleasant to feel the deck's tremble as the *Wright* caught the first shock of the Columbia, and her boilers let out power to breast against the current. It never failed to take me back to the morning when, naked as a jaybird except for Len White's blanket, I had first felt that tremble in the *Wright's* timbers.

For the first hour of the trip, if the wind was not too strong, most of the passengers would stay on deck and I'd spend the time answering the questions of the newcomers. My cabin was my office and I transacted business from a ledge which fitted into the doorway. Few of the strangers, making their first trip, wanted to know about the country, or the *Wright,* or the size of Walla Walla or Lewiston. Their questions were almost always of how much gold had been brought down so far, and where I thought the best claims had turned out to be. Some would show me their clothes and equipment, enquiring if I believed they had been wrongly advised by the storekeepers at Portland.

Eventually, weary of asking questions, or impatient for the end of the journey, they'd drift into the saloon to identify and classify their fellow passengers. It was then that I'd hurry to get my accounts in shape, and go to the wheel house to stand with Tom Stump. He taught me much that was to come to use. He knew I wanted to be a river captain and rarely in the wheel house did he open his mouth except to discuss some point of piloting or point out how, at this season, a current or a channel had changed. He was not as daring as White. I doubt that he could have made that first trip with the *Colonel Wright,* for he was too careful to be possessed of the gambler's instinct to play a hunch. But once he knew his water I think he was a greater pilot, for he bettered White's time as a rule, and without straining the boat or demanding too much from below.

Except for my time with Stump in the wheel house I enjoyed the dining periods most of all. The purser sat at the captain's table, and across from us were four or five chairs into which the waiters guided people of importance—Army men, or merchants, or bankers, or ladies going inside to join husbands who were doing well. Once in a while we got a journalist, for they were beginning to be sent to Oregon for their papers, or we drew some distinguished-looking but discreet individual whose mission was never revealed. These latter annoyed Stump. He had a habit of looking at our table companions with his piercing glance and demanding, first off, what they were and why they were going into the interior. Whenever he encountered a man who preferred to keep his business to himself Stump would retire into his own shell and refuse to carry on any sort of conversation whatsoever.

We ate at the first table, which was the best, although the rest were well enough served. Ours and a few other tables sported a white cloth while those with bandana coverings indicated to the Indians, the Chinamen, and the cattle drivers where they should receive nourishment.

Our table, like the others with white cloths, was set with the new silver serving dishes which were a part of the swift new affluence of "the company." They sat on little stands, under which burned alcohol lamps, bearing hunks of beef and pork roast; or, on occasion, a huge baked Columbia salmon, pink against the silver.

It was pleasant, when Tom Stump was off watch, to walk about the boat, passing the time of day with the passengers, or observing the bustle of the steward and the waiters, who, between meals, were forever filling the lamps with oil or polishing windows or (their most heartbreaking task) cleaning up the continual litter of careless miners and cattlemen.

Little landings had sprung up here and there along the banks since the *Wright* had made her first trip up the river, and whenever a white flag appeared or a man stood waving on the landing, we would nose the steamboat in. Sometimes he would be a passenger, but more often he handed me a letter or a package to take upstream.

The *Wright* had never had enough space for fuel; now with heavy cargoes our stops for cordwood were more frequent than of old. The company had contracted with settlers to provide stacks of wood at stipulated spots along the bank, and it was short work for the deckhands to throw a load on the foredeck.

Every stop provoked the curiosity of the passengers who streamed out of their cabins, or the saloon, and even left their meals, whenever the boat landed. Crowded close to the rail, they'd have given the *Wright* a list if she had been anything but flat bottomed. And fortunate was the lone traveler who got aboard at some isolated spot without a thrust from a self-styled wit at the rail.

There were always card games in progress in the men's cabin. Stakes were highest on the downstream trips, when there would be pokes of gold on the table and men would play with tense, hard lines to their mouths. Sometimes when a man had won heavily he'd give me the money or the dust to keep in the purser's safe until we reached the portage. It was for this reason that I never slept without the weapon Lawrence Coe had given me at The Cascades. Yet as long as I was purser on the *Wright* there was never any thievery attempted and I never saw a fight in the men's cabin over cards.

The landing at Lewiston, the terminus of our trip—as Ainsworth had promised Seth Slater—always carried with it an element of surprise. In my mind's eye I saw it as on the day when the first few tents were being erected and Slater was keeping one eye on his stock of whiskey and picks. Now there was a boat landing. There was the obvious beginnings of a street. A double row of shacks and canvas-topped dwellings straggled parallel with the high bluff. When the boat came in the whole town rushed down to meet it.

It was the stop at the mouth of the Walla Walla I liked best, where I could recall most clearly the night Mike and I suspiciously followed Cut-Mouth John to the settlement. At the Wallula landing were the wagons to take passengers inland to the town, and a row of government wagons to transfer stores from the *Wright* to the fort. It was a long stop, with passengers to get rid of, and mail, and supplies for the merchants in Walla Walla, and great quantities of dressed meat for the fort.

At least every third trip Mike would ride down in the stagecoach to meet me. But he never came aboard, for he was as touchy as ever about his leg and afraid he might encounter some old friend —or enemy—from Dalles City. He would get out of the stagecoach before the boat landed, then loiter behind the agent's shack until I came ashore. There we'd have a half hour's talk and he'd report on how Ben Guiness and Tom Ludden were getting on with the mine.

On our first July trip he met me with two heavy leather pokes. "There you are, son. It's your part of what we got out so far."

Unbelieving, I hefted them. By now I could make a fair estimate of pokes, but I dared not believe these carried what I guessed.

"Mike, you're surely giving me more than my share."

"Not on your life, my bucko. There's three thousand in those bags and every grain of it's yours, fair, square and accordin' to agreement."

I looked the Irishman in the eye. "What about Cut-Mouth?"

"Well, I gave him three hundred dollars in dust and I got plenty of Hell for it, too."

"Why?"

"Seems like money goes to Cut-Mouth's head. He ain't like he used to be. Not at all. He's got to usin' fire-water when he can get it, and he swells around and gets into fights. Two or three miners have been threatenin' to cut his throat. The Indian agent says I better not load him up with any more dust."

"But that's not fair," I objected. "We've got to give Cut-Mouth something whenever the claim produces."

"We will—only I got to be careful with that agent. You never know what the Hell an Indian agent can think of next."

I asked Mike how Guiness and Ludden were making out, and Mike began to swear. Already the ex-soldiers were complaining. "They say they do all the work and ought to have a bigger piece of the proceeds. They've gone back in, but I bet they try a shenanigan this time. I bet they make a cache outside of town for themselves, the thankless bastards!"

When the whistle blew and I had to get back to the boat I took the pokes into my cabin and put them in the safe. Then I sat down on the bunk to think. I was surprised because I felt no elation. Three thousand dollars was a fortune to me. I had never owned more than a few dollars in my life before my salary from the navigation company began to come in. I could not even conceive of the sum in terms of purchasing power or visualize it in coin or bills.

Yet I was not happy about it. On the contrary, those pokes of dust weighed as heavily on my mind as they had in my hands. I felt that they had trouble in them, vague yet unmistakable. I didn't like what gold had done to Cut-Mouth John even though I believed he should have his share. And I feared that Mike was going to have real trouble with Guiness and Ludden.

But there were three thousand dollars in dust in that safe that belonged to me. I remembered what Mike had said up there in the hills when we discovered the claim, about how people would bow and scrape and I'd have a wonderful sense of power. But somehow I did not like the idea of people bowing and scraping; and the only time I had a sense of power, of being master of my fate, was in the wheel house of the *Wright,* trying to outwit the river and feeling that I could.

I looked at the safe and in my mind's eye I could see those leather bags lying behind the iron door. There would be other such bags coming out of the claim. Mike would bring them to me at the landing, or send them down by the boats, and one day I would be rich.

I lighted a stogie and lay back on the bunk, trying my best to be pleased. But no pleasure came. It was not satisfying, this thought that you would be rich because you had found a piece of ground in which there was gold. The thing that would be satisfying would be to have people say, "There is the greatest captain on the river," and to know it in your heart and still be humble when you faced the river.

"Yet," I thought, "Mary will be glad."

Mary would be happy when she knew of the bags of dust. For this was the big diamond in the mountain, the jewel we had talked about that night by the side of the bubbling creek on Kiessling's farm.

It was July when Mike Shea handed me that first gold dust from the mine, and the river had never been more beautiful. On the day we swept down into the Deschutes and made fast to the home landing, the rolling hills had not yellowed and there were patches of bright green everywhere. The sky was faultless, and the river, ruffled only by the current, reflected deep blue as if it were a lake.

I got my gold dust onto one of the portage freight cars, and instead of riding down with the passengers on a bright plush seat, I stayed with the cargo. When I piled off at the landing Lawrence Coe saw me.

"Well, Caleb, what you got there?"

"Fellow got sick," I lied, "and we put him off at the Wallula landing. He asked me to leave this at the Umatilla House for him."

The explanation sufficed, and I took my new wealth across to the hotel and delivered it into the safekeeping of Dave Handley. "It's mine," I said, "but I'd rather not have anything mentioned about it."

Handley winked. "So Mike finally came through, did he?"

CHAPTER

4

When I first began making trips on the *Wright,* Mary came to the Umatilla House to wait for my arrival. But in the summer, when the mines had opened up again and the traffic and cargo were tremendous, the boats were sometimes delayed. I'd warned her not to risk the chance of a wearisome wait.

But this July day of 1864 was still and she had heard the whistle of the *Wright* clear from Deschutes. As I climbed the hill back of town I saw her walking to meet me. It was not unusual for her to do this, and yet as I watched her now I grew uneasy. When we met she held me close, wordless, and when I had greeted her with a kiss, she held back her head and looked at me oddly.

"Mary," I said, "is there anything wrong?"

She laughed, but there was nothing of the wholehearted Heinrich Kiessling in it. It was tight and strained. She took my arm and started up the path, but I stopped and faced her.

"Something is wrong, Mary. What is it?"

She shook her head. "No, Caleb. Honest." And she took my arm again and pressed me toward the house.

It was always good to be home, much as I loved the river. Mary had transformed the place. The floors were as spotless as the deck of the *Wright* after a scrubbing. She'd ordered lace curtains from Portland and trimmed every window. Even the furniture we'd bought from Max Vogt had Mary's touch, with antimacassars for the backs of the covered chairs, and a cushion for the rocker. No one would ever dream, now, that the house had been lived in by worthless Nick Barstow.

Inside the house I stepped toward the south window to look up along Military Road toward the McNulty house and the clapboard cottage of John Storrs, the conductor on the portage road. Then, crossing the room, I gazed down toward the town. The latter was not a pretty view, for the backs of the stores were not well kept and we were not high enough to see the river. But when I reached home I liked to have a look from the windows to get my bearings.

I turned to Mary. "Some day I want a new house on that hill east of town."

She was in the center of the room, not moving. I went to her and grasped her by the shoulders. "Look here, darling. You've been acting queer ever since I set eyes on you. What in the devil is wrong?"

She tried to look into my eyes. Suddenly she put her head on my shoulder. "I'm going to have a baby, Caleb."

I almost fell to the floor. "Are you sure?"

She nodded against my shoulder. "While you were gone I fainted—out there in the yard. When I came to, I was frightened, so I went to see Doctor Bryan."

I held her close. "You poor darling. I—I'm sorry I wasn't here."

Mary drew away from me and met my glance. At last a tiny smile was illuminating her face. "Are you glad, Caleb?"

"Glad? Of course I'm glad." I sat down and drew her onto my knees. "I think it's wonderful—the most wonderful thing that's ever happened."

"But Caleb, I don't like being alone so much. You don't know what it's like."

I tried to tell her that she'd get used to it. I tried to make her see that I couldn't stop working on the boats when I was in line for a better berth. But it was little use. She'd been thinking during this last trip of mine, and would not be argued out of the notion that I should come ashore for keeps.

"You're not feeling well," I told her finally. "You need some rest, and then you'll see—"

"Caleb, I wish you would not be a fool on top of all your crazy taking to the steamboats. You don't know how it is to sit here alone.

I have been used to my sisters, and to my father who knew what a home was for and came back to it at night time. There are only a few women who can have time to come and see me, and the rest I would not see if they did come to my door. And when I go down town to buy food the sidewalks are crowded with dirty men coming out of saloons, and the talk is always about the steamboats—the boats you are so crazy about while I am staying here!"

"Mary, I never dreamed you were so unhappy."

She seemed to recoil at the words. And then she fell at my knees, all in a heap, sobbing. "Caleb, it isn't that. I am happy when I think of you and how I am in love with you and how you say you are in love with me, whispering it into my ear when we are alone together in the dark at night. But then you have to go to the boat and sometimes I hear you humming to yourself after you have left me and are going down the steps."

"But you knew I wanted to be on the boats. And you said that if I came back to you whenever I could, it would be all right."

She pressed her eyes with her apron as I drew her to her feet. "But I didn't know how it would be. I was only saying foolish things because I could not think. I didn't know how it would be to live alone, because always I have had my sisters, and before that my mother. It is so cold in the winter here when the wind howls up the river, and when summer comes it is so hot that I cannot have a baby, even, without fainting when I go outside."

I made her go into the bedroom and I lay beside her on the bed until she fell asleep. Then I went softly out of the house and trudged up the Military Road, and on past the fort, until I reached a ledge of scab rock from which I could look down at the town and the river in the dusk.

There were the scattered houses below me, connected by a maze of paths through the sage and the prairie grass. There were the two rutted roads from the town. Beyond were the close-packed buildings, the Umatilla House standing out from them all. I could see them through the clear evening air. The disreputable shacks to the east, Madam de Bilk's place, and The Golden Rule. I could see Tom Miller's hardware store, and Maxmilian Vogt's where Mary and I had bought our furniture. I could see the red brick front of the Waldron building where Judge Wilson and Doctor Bryan had their offices. I did not need to count the flat roofs of the saloons, for I knew that now there were thirty-six of them, all going strong.

I told myself that it wasn't very pretty to Mary. It was not like the Kiessling ranch there on the creek that ran through the green valley. Yet it was alive and exciting—and it was held together by the great broad ribbon of the Columbia.

"You could leave the boats," I whispered. "Mary is really right. You have money, and you will have more, and you don't have to stay with the boats. You can do something in the town, and every day you can watch the boats come in from downriver. You can drop into the Umatilla House and talk to Eph Baughman and Tom Stump and DeWitt Van Pelt and the rest. They can tell you the news of the boats and it will be just like being on them."

But I knew better. It wouldn't be like being on them, not by half. I had seen Mike Shea get away from the life he loved. I knew that even now, with his gold mine, he wasn't happy, that he wouldn't have been happy with two good legs under him. A man had to do what he wanted, and here above the river I was sure of it.

There might come a time when the country would get to be like the East. I'd heard of New York and Boston and Chicago and all the great cities with their thousands of people, with so many doing things they did not want to do, because they could keep themselves alive in no other way. But this was Oregon, new and broad, and to be had for the asking. It was not a place for a man to be false to himself.

There drifted up from the landing three blasts of a whistle. Then two. After a long silence there was one blast, and clearly I heard the scraping of the gangplank on the gunwales of the *Oneonta*, up from The Cascades.

I started down toward the Military Road, then struck along in the prairie grass to avoid the white dust. In a few moments I was at the door of the house, quietly so as not to wake Mary. I went into the bedroom and looked at her, sleeping. "Your child is inside her," I thought. "It's no longer just you to be thinking about. From now on it's Mary and the child."

But it was no good. Even as I stood there, aching for Mary in her loneliness, wanting more than anything in the world to make her happy, to make her glad to be having my child, I knew that it was no good and that I would stay with the river.

She opened her eyes and I knelt down beside the bed. Smiling drowsily, she reached up and put her fingers through my hair. "I'm sorry I was so cross," she whispered. "I think that you were right and I was tired."

I knew that she did not believe it, yet I was so desperately selfish that I caught it up. "I know, Mary. It'll work out all right. You'll see."

CHAPTER 5

To Mary the steamboats had no meaning. It was a long time before I got this through my head. I would come home when the *Wright* had landed and, sitting down to the table with her, plunge with words into the world I had just left. Or, if we took supper at the Umatilla House, I was sure to be drawn into it again, for we would always meet someone from the boats. When this happened, Mary would lapse into silence, and gradually I saw that it was a protective silence. She had nothing to do with that world and wanted none of it. Passively now her resentment worked, and this was more marked as her pregnancy grew.

In the first year of our marriage I tried to include her in the world I knew. It would take a little while, I thought, and presently she would be as fascinated by the river as I. But gradually I saw that my efforts made her all the more resistant, and I soon found that she was happier if I pretended I had forgotten all about the steamboats the moment I entered the door. As this deception increased I began to experience a feeling of guilt whenever I was home, as though I were playing a rôle to which I had no right; as if, in acting a husband, I was an impostor.

I do not mean to say that Mary consciously fought against what she knew was my life. I do not mean to say that she was selfishly unconcerned. It was only that she somehow feared the river and had come to defend herself against it instinctively. Mary had always been like that, and I might have seen it if I had not been blinded with love. "When is it," she had said on the bank of Kiessling's creek, "that you are going to stop going away and settle down?" That was the thing that was in the Kiessling blood and would always be there. It would be in the blood of our child, so that perhaps the river would mean nothing to him. There were two kinds of people who had come West. There were men like my father, who had come with hope and without fear. And there were men like Heinrich Kiessling who had come because he was forced to come and he knew of nowhere else to go.

Mary was pure German, as her mother and father, as her grandmother and grandfather before her. And in me there was Welsh and Italian and God knew what. I was too likely to grow impatient as she became most serene. And whenever my spirits rose she seemed to grow afraid.

Those months just before the baby came were not pleasant ones. I was too inexperienced to realize what Mary was going through. I knew nothing of what it might be to be carrying around a kicking weight inside you; to be nerve-strained and half nauseated and darkly depressed. I think that Doctor Bryan would have taken me aside and told me had he thought of it. He didn't know that I was mistaking Mary's moodiness for resentment. Ainsworth had at last intimated that I was ready for a captain's berth, and I half believed that this was rankling Mary. The thought that she could not rejoice with me was a bitter one to harbor.

It did not help matters that our son was born while I was bound for Lewiston at the wheel of the *Wright*—in command of her, because Ainsworth had transferred Tom Stump to the *New World*.

The baby came two weeks earlier than we had expected, on April 15, 1865. It was on the day that Lincoln died, as we learned later, and that was how Mary always referred to the date. ". . . on the day Lincoln died, just six days after Lee surrendered."

It was the year that the *Brother Jonathan* struck off Point St. George, bound up from San Francisco with two hundred passengers aboard. And Brigadier-General George H. Wright was not among the nineteen who reached Crescent City in the only boat that had been put over.

When I returned to Dalles City from that first voyage as captain of a river steamer my son was already five and a half days old, and had been christened by Reverend Thomas Condon.

My foot had scarcely touched the gangplank when the boys on the landing, waiting to unload our freight, set up loud cries of congratulations. And Coe had come up on the portage train to give me the news.

"Congratulations, Captain!"

For a moment I thought he was congratulating me on completing my first voyage in command, and I simply thanked him and started down the gangplank.

"What's the matter with you?" Lawrence Coe demanded. "Don't you want to know whether it's a boy or a girl?"

I felt all the color draining out of my face. "You mean—Mary's had the baby?" I stammered.

"Sure as Hell and high water, and it's got a handle on it."

I grabbed Coe by the arm. "Look, Lawrence, let's get the passengers aboard the train and go down without waiting for the freight. I didn't know it was going to be so soon, and Mary—"

"Sure," he said. "Come on."

I took a lot of guying on the way into town, for the word quickly got around among the passengers. They sang songs all the way down, and yelled ribald comments, and one miner who had struck it rich and was full of tanglefoot began passing his bottle through the car. I had little stomach for their fun. Coe assured me that Mary and the baby were well, but I was filled with regret that I hadn't been there when the boy was born.

"What does that matter?" Coe said. "They don't need the old man around."

"But Mary would want me to be there. Damn it, why did it have to be early?"

Coe roared. "Steamboats run on schedule, Caleb, but not kids."

When we reached the town I leaped to the ground before the train had stopped and went streaking up the hill with the laughter and cheers of the passengers following me. By the time I got to the cottage I was wet with sweat and my boots and trousers were covered with the dust I had kicked up in the flight.

Martha Danby met me at the door. "Well," she said, "it's about time! A pity you couldn't be here for the christening of your own child."

This difficult reception did not seem to me to be fitting for a father, despite my embarrassment at having missed the event. And I was nettled because the baby had already been christened.

"They're not running any flying machines overland, Martha, so naturally I'm a little late. But I don't see why you couldn't wait on the christening part."

"Mary wanted it done with." Mrs. Danby was speaking in a subdued voice. "She's asleep now, and don't waken her. You can tiptoe in and see the baby if you want." A note of pride crept into her tone. "He's right smart."

Gently I slipped into the bedroom. Mary was lying with one arm flung across the pillow, her face paler than I had ever seen it. She seemed pinched in the cheeks, too, and beneath the coverlet her body was amazingly slight. I forgot Mrs. Danby's warning and knelt down to take her in my arms.

"Mary—Mary, I'm sorry I wasn't here when it happened," I whispered. "Was it awful, darling?"

She opened her eyes, moved her head to study my face, and then she smiled slowly, as though resigning herself to my shortcomings. "It wasn't bad," she said. "Except for you not being here, it wasn't bad." She looked toward the other side of the room. "Have you seen him, Caleb?"

On the table there was a basket lined with a sheet which lapped over and hung to the floor. I got up from the side of Mary's bed and peered into the basket. What I saw there startled me. There was a great mass of folded blanket; from beneath it were two wrinkles of flesh in the shape of half-clenched hands, and between them an ugly pygmy face with eyes closed and mouth half open.

"Isn't he sweet, Caleb?"

"Do they—is that the way they always look?" I asked.

Martha Danby's voice cut at me from the doorway, "And what's wrong with the way he looks? If you looked half as good when you were five days old it was better than you look now."

I went to the foot of Mary's bed. "I didn't mean that, Mary. But he's so small he—he scared me."

Mary stirred slowly beneath the coverlet. "I named him Henry," she said, "after papa."

"Henry?" I repeated the name dully. We had never discussed a name for the baby, yet I realized now that all along I had believed it would be a boy and that it would be named Caleb, just as I had been named Caleb, after my father. My disappointment must have shown on my face, for Mary said, "You don't mind, do you? You don't mind not helping to choose his name?"

"Of course not. Heinrich will be mighty pleased."

I stood there awkwardly, and finally Mary said, "How did it seem at the wheel of your own ship?"

"Fine," I said.

I could think of nothing more to tell her about it.

CHAPTER 6

When the baby was six months old, Mary wanted to visit her father and sisters. They would be anxious to see the baby, she said, and besides she had not been home in a long time. "The harvest will be in," she told me, "and I would like to see how papa has done." So we set a date when she and Henry would go upriver, and I wrote Heinrich Kiessling so that he could meet the boat at Wallula.

When the *Wright* steamed past the mouth of the Walla Walla, Mary's father was on the landing with Sidonie. Beyond him I saw the familiar buckboard with the two brown mares, the same vehicle and team by which Mary and I had escaped a charivari on our wedding night.

I turned the wheel over to the pilot and went on deck to join Mary and the baby. She was fairly dancing with joy at seeing Heinrich and Sidonie again, and her eyes were moist. She kept waving her handkerchief and shouting at her father and sister eagerly. It made me ashamed to think that I hadn't suggested that she visit her family before this.

I relieved her of the baby and followed down the gangplank to where Heinrich and Sidonie stood. The old man gave her a swift hug, and then came over to look at the baby as Mary flew into Sidonie's arms.

"How are you, Caleb?" he asked, slapping me on the shoulder. "How is it now to be a father?" He looked at Henry, who blinked back at him in the sunlight. "Who is it that he looks like?"

"A little like you, I think, Heinrich."

"So?" Kiessling was pleased, and he studied the small face again. "Maybe he does. Babies do not look like anything much, so maybe you are right." Nevertheless I could see that he was swelling with enthusiasm for his grandson. He looked up at me. "Your letter did not say—are you staying with us also?"

"I'm afraid I can't, Heinrich. You see, the boat has to go up to Lewiston and be brought back again."

Sidonie came over, tilting her hoop so that her skirt did not catch on the splinters of the wharf boat planking. She pecked my cheek in sisterly fashion and then scooped Henry from my arms. "Isn't he darling! Else and Hulda are terribly jealous because I am getting to see him first."

Our visit was brief, for as it happened the freight for Walla Walla was light—and from the decks my passengers were already glaring, wondering by what right the captain was dallying with his family when they were impatient to reach Lewiston and the gold streams beyond.

"On the down trip after next I'll expect to pick you up," I told Mary. "You're not to stay longer."

She laughed happily. "You won't be lonesome, Caleb. As long as you have that old boat there, you won't miss Henry and me."

I bade her goodbye, shook hands with Heinrich and Sidonie, and rejoined the *Wright*. When I reached the wheel house the Kiesslings and Mary were arranging themselves on the wagon seat, Mary between her father and sister, the baby still held tightly by Sidonie.

Mary waved at me as Heinrich swung the team, and I answered from the pilot house window. As the *Wright* swung to port I heard Henry's wail. The whistle had frightened him out of his wits. It was odd to be in the wheel house, standing out toward the channel, and hear the new raw voice of your child. And it turned out to be hard to be leaving Mary and the baby somehow, leaving them not at home, but in a place which was not home to me and yet was home to them.

Unmistakably, Mary was happier than she had been for a long time. She was glad to be going back to the Kiessling ranch, to be seeing her father and sisters again. The knowledge made me feel shut out and strangely alone, and I did not want her to stay there too long. I did not want Henry to be growing up away from me, so that in time he too would want to be going to see his grandfather and his aunts as happily as his mother. It was selfish and foolish, but I could not help myself. I could not feel differently. There was no place for me to go back to, ever, except those two sunken mounds at The Cascades.

When I had returned from Lewiston and landed at Deschutes I did not go home to the empty cottage but took a room at the Umatilla House. When I had registered at the desk and returned the pen to the half raw potato which Dan Handley neatly replaced every morning, I found I did not want to go to the empty room. Aimlessly I sauntered down to the wharf landing to watch the loading of the *Oneonta* bound for The Cascades.

I glimpsed Eph Baughman at the wheel house and decided to go aboard to talk with him. But when I reached the top deck I saw that with him was a prettily dressed woman. I had gone too far to retreat when I recognized Victoria Hunt.

"Caleb! . . . Caleb, I would have known you anywhere!" As she held out a tiny gloved hand I smiled inwardly at the deceit. She had not known me in the Umatilla House that night she had been with Kirt Inge.

"Why not?" My voice was not as light as I had tried to make it. "It hasn't been so long."

"It's been four years at least, Caleb. Or is it five?"

Eph Baughman cleared his throat. "So you two know each other?"

"We're old friends," Victoria laughed.

Baughman grinned at me, as an older man gallantly leaving the field to a younger. "You'll pardon me, won't you, Victoria? I have to see Lawrence Coe. Don't overlook my table at supper time, will you?"

"You can't keep me away, Captain Baughman!"

I looked at her, drinking her in from tip to toe, like a man out of a desert come upon a spring.

"Do you like my outfit?" Victoria asked. "The ladies of Dalles

City are quite shocked," she added with obvious satisfaction. "But they don't realize that the styles are changing. You see, I have a lady who writes me from London, and another who tells me what they are wearing in Paris."

I could well imagine it, for she was dressed more grandly than even the women of the theatrical troupes which were beginning to roam the country, playing in saloons or dance halls or muslin houses, wherever the semblance of a stage could be arranged. Her dress was a patterned silk, the first foulard I had ever seen; and her traveling coat was soft English cloth.

"You must be doing well," I said.

She flushed and turned the conversation to me. "I hear wonderful things about you, Caleb. You're in command of the *Colonel Wright* now—the youngest captain on the river! And you're married and have a baby."

"Yes," I said. Then, searching for something to say, "Are you —are you going downriver?"

"And on to Portland. I wish you were captain of the *Oneonta* instead of the *Wright,* so that we could talk. Don't you think you could persuade Captain Baughman to trade places with you for one trip?" It was said casually, lightly, but it warmed my blood.

"It can't be done, Victoria. I wish it could."

Then, before I had a chance to say any of the things I wanted to say, ask any of the questions I had failed to muster courage for, Eph Baughman returned to the wheel house. Vicky and I stepped out onto the deck. The first whistle sounded, a throaty scream above our heads. Victoria clutched my arm. "It always frightens me," she said. "I should be used to it, but I'm not." She did not stand away again and I caught the delicate scent of perfume. "There'll be another blast," she said, still holding my arm.

"We'd better go below," I told her. "Eph is getting ready to pull out."

Vicky's tone was petulant. "Then you refuse to be shanghaied? And it's been so long since we've talked. You've made a very handsome man, Caleb, do you know it?"

"You—you—" I stammered, "have made a very pretty young lady."

"Thank you, Caleb. That was what I was fishing for!"

We went down the companionway to the main deck, crowded close, Victoria tilting out her small hoops. Above us the whistle screamed again, twice. "They'll be taking in the gangplank," I said, stepping down onto the deck. "I'll see you when you get back."

She nodded, but did not move out of the companionway. And when I reached the wharf landing she was not visible as the *Oneonta* pulled into the stream and went west with the Columbia's current. I watched the vessel disappear behind Crates Point, stayed until there was only the black plume joining the fading trail of the paddle-wheel.

I turned on the landing to go up toward the town. Beside a stack of wooden cases stood Kirt Inge. I was sure he had been watching me, but when our glances met his eyes did not waver. He smiled in friendly fashion and asked after my health. There was no way to read behind his eyes, and he did not offer to walk up the street with me.

CHAPTER 7

THE following week, when at the Wallula landing I stopped to take Mary and the baby home, there was a tearful scene. This time not only Sidonie accompanied Heinrich and my wife and son, but Else and Hulda as well. Mary looked amazingly happy; the baby was as brown as a berry. But no sooner had the whistle of the *Wright* sounded, signaling our departure for Dalles City, than all four girls burst into tears. Even old Kiessling became somewhat lugubrious while his daughter engaged in a babble of damp farewells. "Sometimes I wish that you liked farming instead of the steamboats, Caleb," he said. "I think Mary and the boy would be happy on the place."

"You've got three fine daughters there," I laughed. "Surely they'll be marrying men who'll want to farm."

Heinrich shook his head sadly. "Else is keeping company with a storekeeper in Walla Walla, and Hulda is serious about a young prospector who has struck it rich and already is talking of living in Portland."

"What about Sidonie?"

The old German's eyes lighted a little at the mention of her name. "I think that Sidonie will wait until someone comes who will want to run the place." Heinrich looked at me from out sun-crinkled eyes. "I am not so young now, Caleb, and it is not easy to think of leaving the place with no one to till it."

I felt extremely uncomfortable, and was grateful that the time was short. Obviously Heinrich wanted to urge me directly to give up steamboating and come to the ranch with Mary. I was convinced that he and Mary had discussed it and the idea made me faintly resentful.

But I was glad enough to have Mary and young Henry back under any circumstances. I installed them in the best deck cabin and as soon as the *Wright* was into the channel I turned the wheel over to the pilot and went below to join them. The cabin was warm, and the baby, disturbed by the sudden heat and frightened by the vibratory noises of the *Wright,* whimpered steadily. When I tried to comfort him he set up an even louder commotion.

I turned to Mary ruefully and she said, "After all, Caleb, he does not know you very well yet. You are on the boat too much for him to get acquainted."

I laughed, and took her in my arms. "We'll get acquainted," I said. "Give us time. It's wonderful to have you back again."

"Did the house seem lonely?" she asked.

"I didn't stay there. I took a room at the Umatilla House."

She looked at me with that queer smile of hers, the smile she used when she seemed to say that there was no changing me. "That is the kind of a life you would really like, isn't it? Being on the river all you can, and just stopping in at the Umatilla House between trips?"

The remark nettled me. "I wish you wouldn't keep saying things like that, Mary. Men have their work. They try to do what they like best, and they've got to be able to give it all their attention without—well, without having it thrown up to them."

Mary put her hands on my shoulders. "I'm sorry, Caleb. I shouldn't have said that. But I've wished so often that you could do something that wouldn't keep you so much away."

"Good Lord! Suppose I was a sea captain. Suppose I had to take the *Oriflamme* to San Francisco, or a schooner to the Orient? Most of those men have wives, and children, too. They're away for weeks and months."

She looked into my eyes a long time before she answered. "I did not mean that you are away in body only. But sometimes I feel you are with the river even when you are home, at the table, even. It frightens me sometimes."

"Frightens you?"

She nodded dumbly, groping for words. "Because, I think, it makes me feel so much alone. It makes you feel so alone when the one you love most is with you and yet isn't with you, either." She stopped. Then: "Oh, Caleb, I don't know how to say it! I just know how it hurts, and when I was home this time I kept always thinking how good it would be if we were on the farm, and you in the field, coming home each evening."

"Yes," I said. "Your father mentioned the same thing to me. I suppose you talked about it."

"Of course," Mary answered, missing the bitterness in my tone. "Papa said how nice it would be, and so did Else and Sidonie and Hulda. I think it is fine of my sisters not to be jealous, to want you to be there to have the farm when—when Papa is too old." Her eyes grew suddenly round with foreboding. "Papa is not as well as he was, Caleb. It was not mentioned when he was around, but Sidonie told me how three times he has fainted dead away in the field and how he cannot get his breath sometimes after supper is eaten."

"I know, darling. But—" What good to try to say that there was my work, and there was Heinrich Kiessling's? Or to say that there were our lives to live—Mary's and the baby's and mine, together—and there was Heinrich Kiessling's?

"It isn't the little farm now, either," Mary said. "Papa has bought more land. More than a thousand acres he has got besides what he had." She added proudly, "He is making money now."

I tried to think of something that would distract her. The baby was still fussing, the cabin stifling. I held her close to me again. "I know how you feel, Mary. We'll see what we can do. I suppose you're right. I suppose I can't go on being a steamboat captain forever." Gently I sat her down on the edge of the bunk. "Try to get the baby to sleep so that you can go below for supper with me, won't you?"

"I don't know as I should leave him alone."

"Nonsense," I said. "He'll be all right. . . . Did you see Mike in Walla Walla?"

"No."

The quickness of her reply flicked me. "Surely you rode into town with your father or the girls while you were there?"

"Just twice."

"Why didn't you look up Mike? You know he would have liked to see you and the baby. He'll know you were there and he'll think it's odd you wouldn't even try to see him."

Mary's mouth drew into a thin line. "I don't know Mike well, Caleb."

"But I do. He's the best friend I've got. He—he raised me."

"Caleb! You should not talk such foolishness. Mike Shea did no such thing. He did nothing for you at all. Martha Danby has told me what he did for you—letting you go ragged while he stayed in saloons and—and worse—instead of looking for a job. You would be better off now if you had never met Mike Shea."

"Better off?"

"You would have some—some feeling for the things I am trying to tell you about. As it is, all you think of is the river and the steamboats, and—"

I stood before her, feeling the heat rise in my face. "Look here, Mary. I might have been better off, as you call it, if my parents had lived. But they didn't. Mike Shea resigned from the Army and took me over. He resigned from the Army because of me. And he was the one who wanted to look for the diamond in the mountain. If it hadn't been for him we wouldn't have found the gold mine. As for my thinking of the river all the time, I thought about it even before Mike Shea took me—and he never wanted me to go on the river. Time and again he tried to discourage it."

Mary got up from the bunk. I had raised my voice to such a height that I'd frightened the baby. "Please, Caleb . . . I'm sorry I said what I did. But, after all, there was no reason why I should have seen Mike, and you shouldn't get so angry about it."

"I think there was every reason in the world why you should have at least let him see the baby. Mike's sentimental. He's Irish. He'll think it mighty queer that you came to town and didn't let him see Henry."

"He'll think nothing of the kind," said Mary. "From what I

heard, he couldn't have thought much of anything. They say he's drinking up the gold dust as fast as it comes out of the mine."

"He's been sending me my share."

"You can't be sure of that," Mary said. "They say that the two men he got to work the claim are robbing him. He's almost always drunk, Caleb, and they give him only what they think he will take without argument."

I went to the stand and poured myself a glass of water from the pitcher. "I suppose I should check into the mine myself," I said. "I don't imagine you saw Cut-Mouth John, either, did you?"

Mary did not answer for a moment. "He—was killed, Caleb."

I set down the tumbler. "Killed?"

"He killed himself, they say. Or maybe it was an accident."

"What do you mean? An Indian doesn't commit suicide."

"They think it was an accident," Mary said. "Or else he was crazy from drink. He—he jumped out of the second story window of one of the stores."

When I left the cabin I did not go to the wheel house immediately. I walked to the rail and stood watching the glistening red paddles of the *Wright,* coming over at me, and down into the river, dripping with water, leaving the short rows of waves behind. I felt ill, physically ill, and I could not bear the thought of going up into the wheel house, although it was my watch.

I remembered Cut-Mouth John, proud and straight on his pony, the night he had led Mike and me into Steptoeville. I remembered what he had told me about the mission at Waiilatpu and of what Narcissa Whitman had taught him. And then Mike's story, later, of what the gold dust had done to him. I had seen the young Nez Perce braves, naked to the waist, laughing at the wind as they rode pell-mell over the sage. I thought I knew what Cut-Mouth had been, and what he still might be if Mike and I had left him alone.

As long as the white men were coming, it would really have been better for Cut-Mouth to have held fast to the gods he knew from the brown breasts of his mother. There had been no way for Cut-Mouth to realize that Narcissa Whitman, too, was aware of only what she had been told as a little child in a comfortable house far east, in a place unlike anything that was beyond the Stony Mountains. I thought bitterly that nobody has the right to tell of God until they know a little something of what He has created upon the earth.

CHAPTER 8

"It's going to be dog eat dog on this river," Coe was fond of warning me. "As long as the harvest is on, there'll be other companies trying to get the river."

He was right; there was periodic competition for the rich prize of the Columbia River traffic. Sometimes a rival company succeeded in running for a time. Others would hardly begin before, often mysteriously, their boats were withdrawn. The steamboat *Maria* was brought down the coast and around over the bar from Fraser River by a new company called the Independent Line. But she was quickly condemned by the government on a technical charge. She'd been meant to connect with the *Dalles City* on the middle river, and with the *Spray* on the upper river. Even cut off as she was by the loss of the *Maria*, the *Spray* was a money-maker; but it was not long before Ainsworth bought her, put Charles Felton at her wheel and made her one of the company fleet.

There was the tiny *Cascadilla*, weakly powered, which had a short life between Deschutes and the Walla Walla. She had been built by three hopeful men, and later Len White bought her. We would pass him on the river, never failing to give him a couple of blasts. I always fancied his look at the old *Wright* was an envious one, and it was not long before "the company" had bought him out, torn the engines from the *Cascadilla* and put them into a new hull.

Not all rivals were easily conquered. The Peoples' Transportation Company sprang up with sixty-five stockholders scattered along the Willamette River and with the *James Clinton*, the *Relief* and the *Enterprise,* they made money. They were encouraged to have a try at the Columbia and built three steamers to pit against the Ainsworth line. Their *E. D. Baker* was a fast boat and could outstrip our *Wilson G. Hunt* on the run between The Cascades and Portland. But in the expansion they'd contracted sixty-five thousand dollars in debts and faced a reorganization. It was at this auspicious moment that O.S.N. suggested a way out—the *Iris* and the *Kiyus* on the Columbia in exchange for our company's three boats on the Willamette, with seven thousand dollars to boot. And the Peoples line was to stay off the Columbia and the Snake!

Shippers did not accept the rates without a murmur, and when one rival line was squelched another was sure to make a further attempt to scuttle us. Joe Latourelle interested a few Portland men in a line of steam schooners to carry freight between there and Dalles City. But their only vessel on the middle river was soon swept over the rapids and with her went their dreams of vanquishing the Ainsworth crowd.

It was not always luck, or a stronger financial position, or greater influence, or better men, which kept the O.S.N. supreme on the great river. For, as Coe had pointed out, "the company" was continually investing more in the service. When the new boats and the new portage roads were not enough, they scoured the country for additional steamboats ready to go into commission. They brought them from the Sacramento and the Fraser, from Puget Sound and the Gulf.

There were those which reached the Columbia not without strange adventures on the way. I never saw the *New World* without remembering Tom Stump's tale about her struggle to fulfill her destiny in the building of an Empire. Stump had been on the Sacramento River when she arrived, jammed to the stacks with miners attracted by Sutter's discovery.

"That was the first damn steamboat to be launched with her steam up," Tom Stump told me, "and there was a Hell of a good reason for it, too. Bill Furness built her, back at New York for a fellow named Brown, but before she could be delivered she ran afoul of the sheriff for debts. Cap' Ed Wakeman was in command of her, and sheriffs have got to be built smarter before they can get ahead of him."

Stump chuckled at the memory of Wakeman securing permission to get up steam before the launching. "So as not to let rust accumulate, he told 'em. But he had it all arranged for the engineer to have a full head of steam. All of a sudden he cuts the hawser and down she goes, with the sheriff and his men! He takes her down the bay to the narrows and when he gets there he runs close ashore and steps out of the wheel house.

"The sheriff jumps right at him with a pistol and says, 'I am the sheriff of New York City and County, sir, and this vessel is in my charge.'

" 'The Hell you say,' Wakeman yells. 'I'm the master of this vessel, afloat on the high seas, and don't get in her way!' "

With that, according to Tom Stump, the crew appeared with pistols, knives and cutlasses, and put the law into a small boat with a pair of oars for company.

"So she gets on her way, and runs into Pernambuco at night, and gets out again. She gets chased into Rio de Janeiro by a British frigate that knew she was without clearance papers and a lawful prize. But the *New World's* too fast for her, and gets into Rio. Well, Wakeman steps out of his cabin with the tin box that's supposed to have her papers and he manages to fall overboard right in front of the officials. Of course when he comes up he's lost the tin box! Maybe that consul is diving for it yet—but anyhow he sent Wakeman on his way with his sympathy and, so help me God, a letter explaining, to whom it might concern, what had happened to the ship's papers!"

On to Valparaiso the *New World* had gone, where she was held in quarantine for eight days. Then on to Callao where she found that news of her escape had reached the Pacific. Wakeman ran into Panama under cover of darkness, and anchored behind the Island of Tobago.

It was this part of the *New World's* story that tickled Stump most. "Wakeman puts on a disguise and goes ashore and finds out two things—there's only one man can seize the ship and only ten soldiers to enforce his order. Second, the whole damned town was full of people willing to pay three hundred dollars each for passage to California. So Wakeman don't make any more bones about it. He admits the name of his vessel and where he is going—and his eager passengers offer to cut the throat of anybody who tries to stop him."

On to San Francisco with two hundred passengers had sailed the *New World,* landing at San Francisco in July, 1850. At once she'd gone to work on the Sacramento, until she was bought by Ainsworth to run on the Columbia. She was a fine packet, the *New World,* and somehow she seemed to carry with her the swagger of her escapades. Two hundred and twenty-five feet long, twenty-seven at the beam, nine feet hold, she had a walking-beam engine forty-six by a hundred and twenty-one inches. There were thirty-five staterooms and a hundred and eleven berths, but she had plenty of speed as she proved when she made a round trip between Portland and The Cascades in less than seven hours' running time.

The schemes of the head office in Portland, the conferences, the sly, optimistic plans of rival companies; the acquisitions of new vessels, the improvement of the old, the continual struggles to keep control of the portages—all these never really worried us on the boats. True, they filled our minds and we gossiped of them incessantly, but our lives were wrapped inside the hull of the vessel to which we were assigned. "Let the boys do their job," Ainsworth would say, standing in his long black coat on some wharf boat crowded with freight, "and we'll take care of the rest of it." And the word would float up and down the river, from landing to landing and deck to deck. "I hear Peoples is putting on a new boat—biggest on the river." Then the answer: "What do we care? You know what Cap' Ainsworth said the other day? 'Just let the boys do their jobs,' he said, 'and we'll take care of the rest of it.' "

Not all the boys were loyal—some would go overside to dream of a boat of their own, or to take a berth with Peoples or whatever rival company seemed likeliest. But in the end they found themselves in the O.S.N. once more, or, without a berth, went to San Francisco or Seattle or shipped on ocean steamers. But they never forgot the river, and, given a choice, all would have come back to it.

I have seen them, wandering up the river between their deep water voyages, looking at the channel hungrily, longing for the feel of the nose against the rapids, for the swift trip back. Wishing for the echo of the whistle against the basalt cliffs, and the sight of the moon's brightness lighting up the canyon.

But there were those who stayed. Gene Coe, Van Pelt, the Gray brothers, Sampson. Felton, McNulty, Miller, Wolf. And there were others coming along, for the future years. Every family of size along the river had at least one boy "on the boats"—Gore, Winslow, and the greatest of them all, Jim Troup. And down along the Willamette, from Wilsonville to Champoeg, were still younger boys who would bring their family names to ring along the great river of the West. Graham, Zumwalt, Riggs, Geer, McCully, Kruse, Vicars, Senn, Jones, Cunningham, Hoey, Ives, Vaugh, Epperly, Galbraith, Short, Coulter, Evans, Epler, Golding—good pilots, with clear eyes and firm, strong hands, and a set to their shoulders that unmistakably pegged them. For the steering gear that John Gates had invented wasn't yet on all the boats, so that a man held out against the river with his two hands and his shoulders and sometimes a curse or a prayer.

Some of the pilots were growing up on the "wood boats," the flat-bottomed barges with their squaresails on a mast and their cargoes of cordwood from the lower river. It was good training to wait for the west wind up the gorge and pilot a wood barge against the current. The barge men came to know every eddy and every rock in the river, and not a few of them graduated into the pilot houses of boats they had been furnishing with fuel.

The names of the river men were the names that you heard on the wharf boats, in the Umatilla House, at the garrison, even in the lonely miners' camps. And the stories you heard were of what Ainsworth had said; of how Eph Baughman had looked when Jim Troup towed him off; of the latest amount of gold dust the *Tenino* had brought down from Lewiston, and the number of passengers the *Idaho* had taken aboard at the Deschutes landing.

Those were the names and things that overshadowed everything in Dalles City. The rest, good or bad, was taken for granted. The gossip of men and women who were slipshod in morals, the killings that sometimes occurred on Front Street or behind the shacks on the east edge of town. The thievery against drunken miners in Madam de Bilk's saloon. Such matters were taken along with the tolerance of Thomas Condon, the open-heartedness of Dan Handley, the good-natured meddling of Doc Bryan, or the wisdom of Judge Wilson. It was a tolerant town, too young and busy to have yet turned back upon itself.

Relationships such as seemed to exist between Inge and Victoria were taken casually along the river, and I never once heard theirs discussed. All I had learned about Victoria I had got from Ed Danby, and he himself knew very little for she had kept entirely to herself. Shortly after Mike and I had fled the town, Victoria's mother died. Apparently she had come to have small control over the girl, and when she died her sister was powerless as well as unequipped to care for Victoria. At any rate, she had almost immediately given up the attempt, and moved to Portland.

Victoria was sixteen then, and precocious even for a girl who had been raised on the frontier. "Inge paid Mrs. Hunt's funeral expenses," Ed Danby told me. "But nobody thought anything about that. Inge does that considerable. He's always helpin' out, one way or another. I reckon maybe it helps him sometimes when he gets into a particular sort of jam. . . . Then the next thing you know, Victoria blossoms out as quite a lady with fine clothes and a house of her own up on the hill."

This the town regarded as wholly the business of Kirt Inge and Victoria, and there was an undercurrent in Ed Danby's tone which was trying to tell me that I had best not regard it as mine.

Ostensibly, Kirt Inge was nothing more dangerous than a sharper. It was up to the townspeople to beware; there was no law against a man who quenched the miners' burning urge to try their luck across a table. The fact that Inge owned The Golden Rule, that he had set up an establishment like it in Lewiston, was ignored.

True, there were stories about him that, could they have been proved, would have got him a hanging, or at the least an order to leave town by the following sunset. Outside of Lewiston and Walla

Walla there were two shebangs which some suspected were owned by Inge. These road-houses were headquarters for cut-throats and thieves without a visible leader. Miners outfitting in the town were watched and descriptions of their equipment taken down. Then on the trail the unfortunate prospectors would be confronted with "officials" who possessed bills of sale for their outfits. If the miner resisted the dispossession it was likely to be the final event of his life.

There were other curious happenings. A miner with thirty thousand in gold dust left his diggings for Lewiston but never appeared there, although the weather was open and he knew his way about. More curious yet, no trace of his outfit was ever found, although a short distance from the trail were discovered the charred bones of his pack mules.

Neither was it unusual for a stranger in Dalles City to be fleeced by the purchase of a lot in a fraudulent town-site in the interior—by means of a map which showed schoolhouses, town parks, even a railroad. And horse stealing was an everyday occurrence, and few stolen animals were ever recovered.

Such things went on, were accepted, and even after the formation of vigilante committees arrests were not many. No vigilante committee was free of members who were either directly or indirectly connected with the criminals—and sometimes a member of the committee was the criminal himself. It was not easy to ascertain whether a plea for leniency sprang from a charitable heart or a black one.

That there were leaders for this web of lawlessness everyone knew. As to who they were, almost every citizen had suspicions. Yet few wanted to make an outright accusation, not simply because he might be wrong but also because, on some tomorrow, he might feel the sting of lead.

Whether Kirt Inge held interests in such shady enterprises was never certain, but many felt that he must. And there were many who valued his friendship, with its attending power, more than they valued good government in the town. His connection with The Golden Rule, and of some of the more disreputable shacks east of town, Inge made small effort to hide. The women who colored the streets of Dalles City on cool afternoons were all known to Kirt Inge, and frequently he met the new ones at the boats, escorting them uptown for drinks. The hardier ones he assigned to the mining camps, sending them along the trails in men's clothing, with revolvers at their belts. No trails were too strenuous for such women —and when they returned to civilization they had to filter through the portages where they reported to Inge or his henchmen.

For such open industry, Kirt Inge suffered no malice from the town. The miners and the cattlemen—and, not infrequently, respected citizens—required respite from their labors. It was better that someone bring a semblance of organization into such matters. It was well known that what few disorganized females drifted up on the river boats were sure to cause trouble. They quarreled among themselves, and slashed with knives, and stole gold pokes, and doped drinks. But those who were brought up the river by Inge were orderly and business-like, and I always suspected that it was this service which protected him in his other enterprises, those distant deals which, occasionally, involved thievery and the shedding of blood.

He was a handsome fellow, dark, and with finely bred features. It may have been that only his false hand twisted him into what he was. Inasmuch as my own features are broad and heroic, my education small, my background limited, I do not think it would have hurt me so much to lose a hand, to have had to carry, forever, a tight black glove from beneath my sleeve. But to Kirt Inge, so perfect, that flaw could easily have turned him into something he wouldn't otherwise have become.

What cruelty he had came, I think, from that. I expect that this was why he trafficked in women on the river. Perhaps there was always in his soul the bitter feeling that women might recoil from the sight of that set, frozen hand; that its touch, against flesh attracted by his face and smile and voice, might make them shudder. And so, in revenge, perhaps, he made the flesh of women his business. He watched them fawn and laugh, because they wanted the market he controlled—and then he drove them into the shacks and onto the trails, and he levied against them when they came out at the last.

There was no question of his attraction, either with men or with women. Jealously, I have never understood why Victoria was so attracted. I have tried many times to understand it, but in the end I have always given up because I have known only two women in my life. When Ed Danby confirmed my suspicions, I tried to rationalize the affair. I supposed that in her loneliness and youth, when her mother died, Victoria had been easy prey to Kirt Inge. She had no father, not since that day I would never forget, when I saw his riddled body slump to the hewn pine floor of Bradford's store. I tried to make myself believe that perhaps there was something deep in Kirt's eyes, something that welled up from her dimly remembered past, that reminded her of her father. But of course I was being a fool, a jealous fool.

CHAPTER

9

NOT until a year after my talk with Victoria aboard the *Oneonta* did I see her again. But a hundred times within that year the memory of her face arose in my mind to disturb me. Often, as I stood at the rail of the *Wright* on my off watch, gazing at the river forever swirling toward the sea, I would grow vaguely uneasy, without knowing why, as if something real and important had become lost to me; and I would struggle to find it among the racing, plunging memories that were mine since the day I had started in search of the diamond in the mountain. Then, suddenly, the face and figure of Vicky, sometimes as I had glimpsed her in the dining room at the Umatilla House, and sometimes as she had talked with me on the deck of the *Oneonta,* would come to me.

It was not strange that we had never met since then. She appeared rarely with Inge, and was seen alone only when she made the trips to Portland. Whether these journeys downriver were temporary escape into a world unaware of her place, or were business trips for Kirt Inge, no one knew.

It was at a town social that I met Victoria again. The social was held, like every reputable affair in town, at the Umatilla House. It was a benefit for the missionary fund of the Congregational Church. That winter Mary and I had begun to attend some of the town's entertainments. I refer to the ones which the townspeople themselves arranged, for the performances of the theatrical troupes which wandered up the Columbia were usually produced in the saloons and unattended by women. But Dalles City was beginning to have a little leisure, and had gradually managed to build up recreations of its own.

The sight of people amusing themselves with games and dances opened up a whole new world to me. At The Cascades the social activities of the ladies had been, as I remembered, confined to quilting bees. The relaxation of the men consisted of hunting and fishing, and even these were for the purpose of eating the game or salmon. As I grew up with Mike I am afraid I gained the impression that the alternate recreation of men was drinking hard liquor and telling lies to each other across the table of a saloon. And later when we had lived at the Danbys' I had never seen Martha Danby venture outside the house except to "buy vittles," as Ed put it, or attend church.

Womanlike, Mary took to the socials and the balls like a mallard to water and air. I never felt quite comfortable attending them, but I figured they would help Mary to accustom herself to both the town and my absences, and I will not say that I didn't enjoy them. We went to the basket socials that the Reverend Condon liked to arrange, and we looked forward especially to Dan Handley's "open houses" when the whole town, apparently, would crowd into his hostelry to gossip and sample the mild punch served in great cut-glass bowls. Occasionally we attended a dance at the garrison, but they were rough-and-ready affairs, with the men naturally outnumbering the ladies three-to-one. Mary found these tiring, and I never relished the idea of having her waltzed to exhaustion simply to provide officers with entertainment.

I received a pleasure from these town functions which went beyond the fun of them. The business of being a family man, of being a river captain with a wife and son and a definite place in the community, was still new to me. And going to the socials was a part of it. Life seemed at last to have taken definite shape for me, and the consciousness of this fact was good.

So, whenever I came up from the Deschutes landing on the portage road, and strolled through the lobby of the Umatilla House before going home, I would look for the notices of town meetings or the placards announcing a social or a ball. The dates were always set well ahead, for men whose businesses ranged up and down the river had plans to make and schedules to meet. If the date occurred on one of my nights ashore I would tell Mary the news, and we would arrange with Martha Danby to come to the house on that night to care for Henry.

I think that the reason I remember so clearly the printed placard which announced Thomas Condon's social is that there followed it a train of circumstances which were to affect my whole later life. It was a white placard, tacked firmly to the dark mahogany front of the Umatilla's lobby desk, and on it Bill Hand of *The Mountaineer* had lavished great care—no doubt due to the fact that he admired Condon as much as the next man and wanted to help out the Congregational missionary fund. The type was large and curlicued and there was a border of flowers around the whole.

COME ONE! COME ALL!

A SOCIAL FOR THE FAMILY

GAMES! A MOCK TRIAL!

50¢ 50¢ 50¢ 50¢

All the money goes to
the Missionary Fund of
the Dalles City Congre-
gational Church, the Rev.
Thomas Condon, Pastor.

HAVE FUN AND HELP
THE HEATHENS

Umatilla House — January 18th.

Aside from a mention in *The Mountaineer,* that single placard was all that was necessary to bring a crowd to the Umatilla House on the night of January eighteenth. Bill Hand would simply set up his big type, smear it with ink, hammer out a single impression on white cardboard with his wood mallet, and tack the finished job in the Umatilla House.

For the social I hired a buggy from Bert Patterson, because the streets were ribbons of mud and Mary had just bought a pair of blue silk slippers with satin rosettes of which she was very proud. From Patterson's I called for Martha to take her up to the cottage. The good woman always sniffed when we asked her to keep Henry, pretending that she thought it sinful for us to leave him for our own pleasures. In truth she loved the duty.

After saying goodnight to young Henry, who was always particularly affectionate when he knew we wanted to get away, and settling Martha Danby comfortably, we were almost too late to find a good spot from which to watch the fun. Such affairs were held in the dining room, the tables taken out and the chairs ranged in two rows along the walls.

Condon saw us and came hurrying across the big room to meet us. "Mary, how are you! And is this scallawag behaving himself and making a good husband for you?"

He seemed to be everywhere at once. No one who entered the door missed his attention, and yet he made not a single motion as pastor of his church. He was attempting to curry no favor. The rough-looking stranger, who had wandered in out of loneliness on his way to the mines, got the same sort of greeting as the best supporter of the Dalles City Congregational Church. Tonight he was neither minister nor geologist, but a simple man who liked people.

The feature of the evening came first—a mock trial, and the prisoner was the man in Dalles City who, almost since the semblance of law and order showed itself, had peered down at prisoners and done the judging.

"Ladies and gentleman," announced Dan Handley from the center of the floor. "You are a jury tonight to decide upon the fate of a man charged with chicken-stealing. Now will you all stand up, ladies and gentlemen of the jury, to allow the judge to take his seat?"

At this point, Condon, wearing a powdered wig after the English fashion, and a long black robe, took his place at the improvised bench.

"And now," boomed Dan Handley, his brogue thick with mirth, *"bring in the prisoner!"*

When Judge Joe Wilson was brought in, the crowd roared in good natured approval and settled down to enjoy itself hugely. At least half the male population in that room had been sentenced or lectured by Joe Wilson, and the other half knew it. All were highly entertained at the picture of him badgered and maligned by Vic Trevitt as the prosecuting attorney, and defended by another saloon owner, Tim Baldwin, who gave a fine performance as a lawyer with neither faith in his client nor heart in his work. Masterfully it was developed that the culprit had been stealing, not chickens, but horses; and in his address to the jury, "Judge" Condon adjured them to ignore both the facts and the law and to vote "as your consciences dictates." As one, the crowd joyfully gave an immediate decision: "Guilty!"

The mock trial over, Condon, with Handley's ready assistance, began organizing groups of men and women into games. Soon there were under way games like Consequences, Hunt the Slipper, Catch the Ring, Twirl the Trencher, Compliments, and half a dozen others. Condon and Dan policed them all to see that losers received slips of paper with the "forfeits" written on them.

It was a queer sight, under the bright lamps of the Umatilla's dining room. The overcrowded room had long since become warm and stuffy, and most of the men were in shirtsleeves. They looked oddly disheveled in comparison with the women, all of whom had worn their best and even kept their shawls with them. In one corner was a laughing circle of men and women seated on the floor, passing a slipper around while a worried looking fat man tried to determine where it stayed to rest. In the center of the room was another circle playing Twirl the Trencher with a huge wooden plate. The place rang with confusing shouts and laughter as the slower-witted were caught at failures and were handed forfeit slips by Handley or Condon.

Usually I tried to dodge the games, but tonight I was dragged at once into a game of Ribbons. Mary was placed in the center of a ring while each of us held the end of a ribbon in hand. The other ends were gathered up and united in Mary's hands. The game was that we were to let go the ribbons when she shouted *"Pull!"* and yank them when she shouted *"Let go!"* It seemed so simple as to be childish, and yet it was astonishing how many forfeits were won—and I was the second or third to step out. Immediately I was pounced upon by Condon who handed me a slip of paper on which was written: "Kiss the candlestick." There was a number in one corner of the paper and I knew I would have small chance to escape my fate when forfeits were called after the game.

It was, of course, the forfeits which really furnished the entertainment. The games, while enjoyed, merely set the stage for the series of embarrassing didoes of the losers. I stood in a sweat with my slip of paper, watching men hop around the floor on one leg, or go through the pantomime of singing a song, or imitating a leopard, or—comparatively simple—kneeling to the wittiest, bowing to the prettiest, and kissing the one they loved best.

The next thing I knew, Dan Handley was calling out: "Number fifteen. Kiss the candlestick. Cap' Paige, I think you got that one—and here you are!" He was handing a lighted candle out to me.

I took it, enquiring how I was to kiss the candlestick when there was none. The crowd began to laugh, and I realized then what my forfeit really was. I must hand the candle to one of the ladies, whereupon she would become the candlestick. With the laughter ringing in my ears I felt like the fool I must have looked. In a panic I glanced around the room. Out of that blur of faces I saw one whose mouth was not parted in mirth, but only curved in a gentle smile that was somehow vaguely familiar. And then I saw that the face was Victoria Hunt's. I walked straight to her, put the candle in her hand, and kissed her on the lips.

I had not walked halfway across the room before everything went silent, before every vestige of laughter had stopped. And that sudden silence angered me. Not for the world would I have turned from her then.

I took the candle from Victoria, extinguished the flame, and slipped it into my pocket. Then I walked toward the lobby of the Umatilla, conscious that every eye was on me. I heard Condon's voice in forced joviality, "Now let's see, folks. The next forfeit. Number sixteen."

I had intended to wait for Mary in the lobby while soothing my embarrassment with a stogie. But to my surprise she was standing just beyond the door, her face aflame. When she spoke it was with a bitterness that was like a blow. "I was never so ashamed in my life, Caleb!"

"But—but why?"

"Why?" Her eyes flew wide in amazement. "Everyone—everyone knows that she had no business coming here. And of all the women in that room to pay your forfeit with, you choose her!"

"I've known Victoria since we were children," I retorted hotly. "And as for her having no business at the social, you must have been listening to a few narrow-minded women who ought to keep their mouths shut!"

"Then it doesn't matter to you that you—that you humiliated me in front of all those people?"

I was dimly conscious of a group of loiterers in the lobby. I thought how stupid it was for Mary and me to be shouting at each other in front of them. And yet I was angry, too. I was angry at myself for being a fool, and I was angry at the women who had told Mary about Victoria and Inge.

"Come on," I said. "Let's get home."

Mary shook her head. "I'll not go home now, Caleb, and have them thinking we quarreled because you picked her out to kiss."

"I don't give a damn what they think," I said. "And you can stay as long as you like." With that I flew past the grinning loiterers and into the street. Burning with rage, I sloshed across the mud and thrust through the swinging doors of the Mount Hood Saloon.

Trevitt had left the social after his part in the mock trial and was doing honors behind his bar. "Well, sir," he said, "did the games get too all strenuous for you?" His accent was as broadly Southern as ever, and his manner, so smooth and gentlemanly, was faintly irritating. "Will you have a drink on the house, Captain?"

I thanked him with what grace my mood allowed, and asked for rye. He poured out the whiskey with a meticulous, unerring hand. "Every time I see you, Captain, I think of that disastrous wager I made with Captain White!"

I managed a laugh and raised my glass. "To your better luck, then!"

Trevitt bowed, and excused himself to serve a customer at the far end of the bar. I stood there, sipping my rye. I had somehow never learned to throw it down like Mike, sending it in a neat curve clean past my throat and into my stomach. As I touched the glass to my lips I grew conscious of someone beside me, and I saw slip over the bar a hand gloved in black kid. I knew at once who stood beside me, even before I raised my eyes to the back mirror.

"How are you, Paige?" said Kirt Inge.

I turned, and with an effort held out my hand. "Very well, thanks."

His good hand moved across the one which lay so stiff and still on the bar. His grip was firm and friendly, but his palm seemed cold. "Glad to see you again." He nodded toward the tables. "Let's sit down, shall we?"

When Inge seated himself he rested his gloved hand on the table, just as he had on the bar. He did it with a careful, hunching motion from the shoulder, not touching his left arm with his other hand. I wondered why he didn't leave it beneath the table, and then it occurred to me that Kirt Inge was half proud of this thing that marked him. It was curious how there was no passing sympathy in you when you saw it, how your ignoring of it came from a repugnance rather than an effort to put him at ease. It was not the false hand. It was what he did with it. It was the way he carried it, like the talisman of his own evil.

I studied his face. It was perfect enough, too perfect. The eyes were dark and alive, the thin-bridged nose was straight, the mouth good. It showed no dissipation and yet it revealed no innocence, either. It was like a drawing of a vain man by a timid and dishonest artist.

"I understand you're married now." There was something faintly patronizing in his tone, almost as if I were a child. Yet I was twenty-two, and he not more than thirty-five.

"Yes," I said, "I was married in Walla Walla about two years ago."

He ordered a drink by signaling the bar, then settled back in his chair so that the black-gloved hand slid away from me. He seemed to expect more.

"I'm with the O.S.N. . . . Captain on the *Wright*."

"I know." He waited until the drink came, tossed it off, and pushed the glass away from him. "I hear you and Mike got a gold claim, too. I hear you got a couple of fellows working the claim for you. That's smart. There's going to be plenty more money made off these monkeys without digging for it. Let somebody else do the digging, is what I say. Have another drink, Paige."

"One more. I have to get back to the Umatilla House. Mrs. Paige is still at the social."

Inge smiled. "I looked in at it. I'm not much of a hand for socials. You seemed to be having a good time—when I looked in."

"Yes," I said. I heard the clink of glasses as Trevitt's bartender set down the drinks Inge had ordered.

Suddenly Inge said, "Vicky tells me you two knew each other as kids."

Her name on his lips irked me; and, unmistakably, his eyes were saying that nobody could have Victoria while he lived. His eyes said that she was his. They were more than the eyes of a jealous man; they seemed to be saying that he enjoyed the futility of other men desiring her.

He picked up his glass and motioned for me to take up mine. He didn't toss down his drink this time, but sipped it, waiting for me. "I always thought a lot of Victoria," I heard myself saying. "I knew her mother. I've wondered how she was getting along."

Inge's eyes had been fastened on the brown circle of whiskey in his glass. They raised now quickly and fastened on mine. He brought the glass away from his face. "I wouldn't wonder too much about it, Paige. She's getting along all right." Then he added slowly: "Friends of mine get along all right in Dalles City. Why don't you bear that in mind, Paige?"

A red curtain dropped down in front of my eyes. I felt blood rushing into my head, into the very ends of my fingers. I knew I had to get out of there. I jerked up from the table, and it tilted toward Inge, spilling the whiskey. When he stood up there were dark streaks down his trousers.

"You crazy son of a bitch," he said quietly, "what's wrong with you?"

I half turned, then swung into his face with all the force my incensed brain could send into my fist. I struck full on his cheek and mouth, sending him sprawling, rump first, solidly onto the floor. He was up in an instant, that false hand swinging slowly, like a pendulum, his right hand clenched above his waist. Then Vic Trevitt jumped over the bar with a pistol in each hand. He walked slowly toward us, pointing one weapon at me, the other at Inge.

"This here is a gentleman's saloon. Whichever one of you delivers another blow this side of the door is going to be powerful sorry."

I looked at Inge, his face twisted with pain and anger. "I'll be just outside," I said, and stepped backward toward the doorway. Outside, I walked down off the boards and waited.

Inge came after me, deliberately, his face a mask, the black glove slowly swinging. I was too filled with hatred to feel that I should not hit a man so handicapped. I would have killed him then and there if I had carried the pistol Lawrence Coe had given me.

He walked on through the saloon, the dozen men inside forming a curious and discreet ring behind him. These stopped just inside the doorway and Inge came out into the night. I waited until he had stepped into the street, and then made for him again. I saw his good hand grab his left arm just above the elbow. I saw him turn quickly, and then there seemed to be a terrific explosion that made silver slits in the darkness that enveloped me.

The next thing I knew I was on my hands and knees in the dust. I was looking at a pool of blood that was fed from somewhere above me. There was a horrible roaring in my head, a maddening noise that drove me to my feet.

I looked at Kirt Inge through a haze. I heard Vic Trevitt say from a great distance, "Inge, another one like that would kill him."

I tried to shout out that inside that black glove was a hand of hollow cast metal. But no sound came out of my throat. A warm wet sheet of blood oozed down over my eyes, and I fell into the dust again, biting my lips to keep from screaming with the pain in my head.

CHAPTER 10

When I opened my eyes I was looking into Mary's face, quite close to mine. For a terrible moment I believed that I was lying in the street and that she had heard of the fight and hurried over from the Umatilla House. My head was aching in throbs, and when I tried to use my voice I could not.

"Don't talk," Mary said quickly, putting her cool fingers over my lips. There were tears welling up in her eyes as she bent over and kissed me. "Doctor Bryan said you were not to talk. And I am supposed to tell him that you are awake."

I saw then that I was in our bedroom. Beneath my palms, suddenly with feeling, were cool sheets and not the mud of Front Street before Vic Trevitt's saloon. Mary ran into the other room and came back with her shawl. "Don't try to move, Caleb. Don't try to get up. I will get Doctor Bryan." She started out of the room, then ran back and held my head in her two hands, crying openly now. Her hands were hurting my head. "Oh, Caleb, I have been so frightened."

She hurried out, and I heard the front door close. I heard her feet on the porch and down the three wooden steps to the path. Then I must have dozed off again, for when I opened my eyes she was in the room and a man was with her. A round ball of a man with a black beard through which red lips showed in a full crimson blob. He had a way of resting his stubby hands palm-down on his paunch, looping the thumbs over a prodigious nugget chain. He stood there studying me awhile before he turned to Mary. "I'll want to make a rather thorough examination, Mrs. Paige, if you don't mind."

"Yes, Doctor. I'll be right in the other room if you want me."

When Mary closed the door, Doctor Bryan sat down beside the bed, his hands still resting on his paunch. "How's the head?" he asked.

"It aches," I managed to tell him. "I wish you'd give me something to make it stop aching."

Bryan slid around in his chair. "You got to expect that. You'll be all right. That was a real blow, son. I was mighty afraid of severe concussion."

"How long do I have to stay here in bed?"

Doctor Bryan chuckled. "You can get up any damned time you want. But if you try to get on your feet now I think you'll change your mind fast enough."

"You told Mary I wasn't supposed to talk."

He wagged his head slowly. "You haven't been married long, Paige. I thought I'd better see you before you did any talking." He paused a moment. "I guess I might as well introduce myself in my true colors, because you'll find them out sooner or later. I'm an old fool. Always meddling in other people's affairs. Not content to stick to the practice of medicine, as such." He drew an asthmatic breath. "To get to the point, you got hurt in a saloon brawl. Now that's all right. It happens quite occasionally in this fair city where some of our best people engage in the sport when their tempers are a bit sharped up with forty-rod."

He raised his hands off his stomach and waved them at me. "Now I don't want you to get excited over what I'm going to say. Be bad for your head. . . . You see, I got to know your wife when the baby was born. She's a sweet girl, and you ain't been married very long. I got to wonderin' if you could handle the situation. So I just made sure you wouldn't go blabbing your head off the minute you came to."

"I don't know what you're getting at, Doctor."

"You remember the brawl, don't you?"

I nodded.

"And you remember what it was about?"

I looked at Bryan. He nodded again, as if I had admitted the cause for my quarrel. "I accidentally tipped over the table in Trevitt's and Inge called me a son of a bitch," I said.

"Now, look, son. I wasn't born yesterday. Besides, everybody in town knows by this time that the fight was over a lady." He pursed his lips, then went on. "Naturally your wife knows about the fight. But I told her it was a matter involving a lady's honor. That was the best way to put it, and you take my word for it. I was afraid you'd deny a lady had anything to do with it."

"But I don't see—"

"It's a terrible thing, Paige, when a woman gets her confidence in a man all built up and then feels it go out from under her. So I figured to give her the pills sugar coated, right at the start. And I wanted you to know, both of us being males, what the story was."

His meddling nettled me, and yet I had no choice but to accept it. And I could not help but be amused at his obvious sincerity.

"There are things she may find out besides what I told her," he went on. "So my advice is that you feed them to her gradual. This lady that brought on the business between you and Inge is pretty well known in Dalles City." He looked at me hard, to see how I was taking it. I must have been grim, for he stood up slowly, and when he spoke again it was in a different tone. "Well, there you are, son. I told you I was a fool and meddlesome. But I don't make any extra charge for that sort of thing. It comes with the pills." He broke into a great, infectious laugh that to many of his patients must have constituted a cure in itself.

"I appreciate what you're trying to do," I said. "But Mary will understand."

He shook his head at me sadly. "I'm relieved to hear you say that, son, because it goes to show that I was right in deciding to meddle. Every doggoned young husband figures his Mary or whatever her name is will understand. Then he finds out that she's a woman, by Harry, and she don't understand a God damned thing where other women are concerned. That disappoints him and makes him mad—and then Hell can pop."

His insistence made me laugh, but I quickly stopped when a streak of pain shot through my head. "Anyhow," I said, "I want to thank you."

"That's okay, son." He shook a finger at me. "And let me tell you something, don't go harboring any resentment against Kirt Inge. Don't get the idea you'll pay him back for this. He'd have beat you to death with another blow or two of that iron mitt of his if Vic Trevitt hadn't been standing in the doorway of the Mount Hood Saloon sort of fondly fingerin' a couple of weapons."

He reached down and took my wrist, pulled out a giant silver watch. While he counted my pulse he hummed to himself, and finally he let my wrist drop with a grunt. "I don't know now why you ain't dead—but you aren't even close. Just lay quiet a couple of days, then take it sittin' up for a day or two."

He started across the room, stopped halfway, and turned: "Remember what I told you about Inge. You don't look like a philanderer to me, but if you got even a slight notion that you can stake a claim to anything Inge wants badly you might as well go on up to the cemetery and start diggin' yourself a hole." He ran out of breath and drew in another great gust. "Dalles City," he said, "is a Hell of a fine town to mind your own business in. You're a river pilot. It's a right healthy profession and I'd stick to it."

He opened the door. In the other room I saw Mary jump from her chair and come toward him with wide questioning eyes. "Is he going to be all right, Doctor?"

Bryan patted her shoulder, and let out a modified version of that laugh. I judged it to be the one used on women patients so as not to scare them completely out of their wits. "Your husband is as tough as an ox. He's going to live a long time—if he's careful not to get too rambunctious whenever he hears an opinion expressed in a saloon."

For the next three days, whenever I tried to get out of bed I grew so dizzy that I could not stand erect. Mary waited on me hand and foot, serving me food, bringing me water, and, most humiliating of all, performing all the duties of a paid nurse.

Never once did she bring up the encounter with Kirt Inge or mention Victoria Hunt. It was as if I had fallen into an illness the source of which we did not know. She could not have failed to realize the nature of my quarrel with Inge, and following as it did upon my performance at the social, the situation must have embittered her. Yet whenever I attempted to admit I had been a fool, whenever I tried to tell her I was sorry for the humiliation my temper had caused her that night, she would change the subject or quietly put her hand over my mouth.

I could not stand this evasion; and when at last I was sitting up and feeling equal to it, I made up my mind to have the thing out. "Look here, Mary, why is it you don't want to talk about my trouble with Inge? Is it because you feel that—Victoria Hunt is in it?"

"Wasn't she?" asked Mary suddenly, fastening her gaze on mine.

"If that's the reason," I said, "I don't like it. I don't want us hiding any part of our life together."

For a long time Mary did not speak. "I—I just don't like unpleasant things, Caleb. I would rather forget it."

I took her hands. "All right, then. But we must really forget it. Bury it deep." In a wave of sudden relief, I could laugh. "But I wouldn't have been hurt if he hadn't hit me with that damned pig-iron hand."

Mary looked at me soberly. "It would not have helped, Caleb, even if you had won."

True to our mutual promise, we said no more about my fight with Inge. Yet I was not eased by the closing of the subject. I could not rid myself of the feeling that there was more I should have told, more we should have discussed. I tried to salve my conscience with the thought that Mary was right: it had been nothing more than an unpleasant incident. I tried to tell myself that there was, actually, nothing more for her to know. And yet a gnawing, premonitory feeling persisted in my mind.

In the months that followed, that feeling persisted. It haunted and changed me. I fancied that I could see the change in my face when I looked into the mirror. It was not the faint lines around my eyes, not the beginning furrows in my forehead. It was an evasive change that had nothing to do with time, nothing to do with the slowly healing scar that stretched from my hair to the outer corner of my right eye. It was something that grew from my realization that I was hating Inge because he had possessed Victoria Hunt, because he had let me know plainly that I must never possess her.

Beneath that was the knowledge, too, that I would one day have to meet Inge again. Despite what Doctor Bryan had said, there is something a man has to face at some time in his life: the cowardice inside him, in the blood from the days when men were inferior and fleeing, with no real place on the earth's great face. Some men get through a lifetime without discovering that it is there, and it is only these men who, in reality, know no fear. They know no fear because they have never been faced with it. The fear of facing a mountain or a river or the sea is nothing to the fear of facing another man. It is nothing to be beaten by them for they are superior and a man is vanquished with honor. But to be defeated by another man is to risk the jeers of humanity which knows, deep in its heart, how puny it is. I would have to meet Kirt Inge again, not simply because I hated him, but so that I might live with myself.

CHAPTER 11

In the spring, when the mines opened and prospectors were starting upriver again, I stopped off at the Wallula landing and let Pat Henley, the relief pilot, take the *Wright* on up to Lewiston.

I wanted to see Mike Shea.

I had not heard from Mike in months, and I had been worrying ever since Mary told me she believed that Guiness and Ludden were bilking him. It was not for my own share that I feared, and I was fairly convinced that Mike would be better off with less money to throw around. But if Guiness and Ludden had really decided they were deserving of more gold they might do anything to get it. If Mike, during one of his sprees, should be accidentally killed, then Ben Guiness and Tom Ludden would be that much richer. In the six years since gold had been discovered beyond the junction of the Snake and the Clearwater I had seen plenty of what it could make men do.

When I had completed my overland journey from Wallula landing I found that Walla Walla had changed almost as much as Lewiston and Dalles City. The muslin shacks and hewn log dwellings had given way completely to whipsawed lumber buildings. There were few recognizable landmarks. One of them was Galbreath's and it was there I found Mike after making the excellent guess that he would patronize his old friend rather than some of the newer liquor merchants.

He wept when he saw me, holding me off at arm's length while he blubbered, and I could not believe his tears were entirely alcoholic.

"You've changed, bucko! Yes, sir, you've changed. But then I guess we all do that." Suddenly he saw the pink scar beneath the brim of my hat. He reached out and took my headgear off. "Who in the Hell done that?" he cried.

"A little accident on the boat," I said.

"Oh, so that's it?" He looked at me again, as if he weren't quite sure I told the truth. "Sit down, Caleb. Sit down and have a drink and tell me about yourself."

"There's nothing much to tell, Mike."

"How's Mary and the young one?"

"They're fine." I added a well meant lie. "Mary wanted to be remembered to you."

"Did she now?" said Mike, pleased. "I don't see old man Kiessling in town much any more. He's ailing, they say." Mike paused for a long time, studying me. "Caleb, it's good you're here. Since Cut-Mouth took himself off I ain't had an ear I could trust. It's like I told you all the time, we shouldn't have given that damned redskin any. Gold ain't good for them."

I smiled. "Some people say it's not good for anybody."

"Well, it didn't do you any harm. I've heard more'n one say how you been just a-workin' along on the boats when our gold mine was comin' in."

"That was so I could save what you sent me, Mike. I reckon you've saved some, too?"

He hiccoughed and his face flushed up redder than normal. "Saved some money?" he repeated. "Oh, I got a little laid away. I'm fixed all right, Caleb." He stopped, then leaned toward me over the table. "I'd be fixed better, and so would you, if those God damned bastards we got to work the claim had been honest. They been cheating us, Caleb—and now they've skipped out."

"Skipped out? Are you sure?"

"I know it."

The news was a relief. If Guiness and Ludden had fled the country Mike's skin was safe. If they were finished, if they'd decided they had all they wanted, they wouldn't be plugging him in the back for the rest.

"That's fine," I said. "We don't care how much they stole. It wouldn't be worth going after them to get it back. The thing to do now is work the claim right. Look, Mike, you've got so you can get around all right on that leg, haven't you?"

"Say!" Mike lifted his peg in one swift movement atop the table. "This damned thing works better than the one I had there before, bucko! Only, I still wish I had a boot on the end of it, damn me!"

"Mike, why couldn't you go up and work the claim? That way you'd be sure of not losing what you ought to have. It would be good for you to get up in the hills, away from town."

I expected Mike to hem and haw and make excuses as to why he couldn't leave town and go up into the hills. But I didn't expect the look of stricken sheepishness that came over his broad face when I mentioned the idea. For a long time he did not speak, but just sat twirling his whiskey glass in his blunt fingers. Finally he looked up at me, drew a long sighing breath and said, "There's no more gold in our claim, Caleb. That's why Ludden and Guiness lit out."

For a moment I couldn't believe him. It somehow had never occurred to me that eventually the claim might run out, that within that area of ground we had staked out six years before there might eventually be no more gold dust. But as I sat there it filtered into my mind that this, naturally, would have to happen. Within a given area—no more gold, no more timber, no more feed for the cattle. The country had seemed so vast, so profligate, and God so good.

"No more gold in the claim?" I asked, dully.

"That's it, bucko," Mike said. "Not many of them have run out yet, but ours ain't the only one. Of course, there's probably more claims to stake. I might do that—I might go up there and find another claim."

I looked at Mike. He had grown more red in the face, more fat in the middle, and there was gone from his eyes all the fine fire I had seen when I had first known him on the bank of The Cascades. He would never go after another claim—never would he seek again a diamond in the mountain—and he knew it as well as I. He knew it, and all he asked now was that I pretend that I didn't know it.

"Sure," I said, after a while. "There're more claims coming in. I hear about them every day on the boat. You'll find another one."

He raised his eyes. "Me? Wouldn't you come in, too?"

"No, Mike. To tell you the truth, I don't give a damn that the dust has run out."

He searched my face and saw I meant what I said. Then: "You're a funny one, Caleb. I really think you mean that."

I did mean it. Despite the lax management of Mike, and the cupidity of Ludden and Guiness, I had received almost fifty thousand dollars in gold dust out of the hills. All I had done for it was to make a rough journey with Mike and Cut-Mouth at a time when I possessed not a cent in the world, no future, and had nothing better to do. And as a result of it, I had been forced to raft down the Clearwater and so gained the attention of Ainsworth and "the company." For that series of accidents I had become comfortably well off, and a captain on the river. Cut-Mouth John had split open his skull. Mike had lost his leg and sat here before me with his fire quenched and, I suspected, his dreams gone with his money.

Yes, I was glad that the claim was through—glad for myself and glad for Mike, in a way.

Now the other pilots could not say to me, even good naturedly, "How's the capitalist?" And I would never again be torn between the idea of staying with the river and the possibility of going ashore. I knew what I would do now; I would build a fine house in Dalles City with my money—and stay with "the company" as long as Ainsworth wanted me.

It would be better for Mary, too, I told myself. She had had the quixotic notion that a gold claim was like a wheat farm, producing better if you attended it, and that it would produce forever. I had never told her how much money it had brought me, because I had been afraid the knowledge would make her unhappier when I stayed with the boats. I had not wanted her to know that I was really independent of them.

I did not go out to the Kiessling ranch from Walla Walla. I was still too conscious of the pink scar on my forehead. Mary was so close to her sisters that I could not be sure how much she had confessed in her letters to them, and I did not care to face Sidonie, especially, with the mark Kirt Inge had left upon me.

But I was almost happy as I took the stage out of Walla Walla, bound for the Wallula landing. The only thing that worried me was what was going to happen to Mike, for I was sure he had spent his money as fast as he had got it. If it hadn't been for the Irishman I could have forgotten completely I had ever discovered gold above the Clearwater. But Mike, his peg leg hidden beneath a table at Galbreath's, was drinking his heart out, wanting to come to Dalles City to see Lottie Moore, and Bert Patterson, and the rest of the cronies he did not realize had forgotten him.

CHAPTER 12

ONE afternoon, a few months later, when I brought the *Wright* into the landing at the Deschutes, I saw Victoria Hunt on the shore. I could not imagine what she was doing there, why she had come up from Dalles City on the portage train when there was no boat scheduled for the east trip until next day. When I went down the gangplank she was standing at the foot of it, waiting.

"I want to talk to you, Caleb," she said.

I looked at her, eagerly hoping. "Is there anything wrong?" I said.

Victoria shook her head. "No. But I've wanted to see you since —since that night at the Umatilla House. I didn't know how to arrange it. I couldn't very well come to your house."

I glanced at the portage train where the passengers were climbing aboard, the stevedores busily hoisting cargo onto the freight car. Already the driver was cinching up the harness on the mules, preparatory to the heavy haul back to town. "We'd have no chance to talk on the train," I told her quickly. "If you don't mind the wait, I can have Pat Henley tell Patterson to send out a buggy."

She seemed uncertain, and I added: "It'll make us quite late getting in. Maybe if you'd rather not—"

"Let's do, Caleb," she said.

When Pat came down the gangplank, hurrying with his bundle of extra clothing to catch the portage train, I told him to stop by the livery stable and send up a driver and buggy for me. His glance at Victoria was fleeting and impersonal. "Sure thing, Cap'n! I'll have it started right out," and he waddled off toward the tracks.

I took Victoria's arm and we started along the low, sandy flat which edged the lower side of the Deschutes. There was a path, faint now, but still visible, which had led to the old Trevitt toll bridge in the days before the *Wright* was on the upper river. Wordless we followed this until we reached a broad moss-covered rock and there we sat down, well above the mouth of the little river, below us the white, shallow swirls noisily shutting out the sound of the mule-driver as he urged the portage train to town.

I had kept my hat well down over the scar on my forehead, and as I sat with Victoria it was with the scar away from her. But she reached up and turned my face.

"I knew it was there, Caleb. I saw it one time when you were in the lobby of the Umatilla. I am glad that it is not—not as bad as it was. It was so red when I saw it—but it is only going to be a little white line." She stopped a moment, and dropped her hand from my face. "I wanted to tell you how sorry I was, but I couldn't. Kirt was with me."

I sat there, half rigid, my palms against the warm dry moss on the rock. Victoria's voice sounded strange and muted against the plunging Deschutes. The scent of violets that she wore was heavy in the still air. "Is that what you wanted to see me for? To tell me that you're sorry for my scar? It doesn't bother me—but it does make me remember what happened."

She turned suddenly, searching my eyes. "Caleb—Caleb, you're not going to hold it against Kirt, are you? I mean, you won't make trouble again?"

"Are you in love with him?" I had never meant to ask that. I hadn't meant to ask it, but she answered quickly, "Yes," and the monosyllable was like a knife stab when she breathed it.

Then she went on, in a different voice, a slow monotone, as if she were thinking aloud: "Sometimes I think I'm not. Sometimes I tell myself that I couldn't be. That's because I'm afraid of him."

"Afraid of him?"

"I don't mean that he treats me badly. He—he's always been good to me. Yet somehow I'm always afraid." She looked up at me.

"It's hard to tell you what I mean. I think I'm afraid because he can be so ruthless about everything but me. I'm always wondering what he would do if he decided he no longer wanted me."

"You said you were in love with him," I muttered dully. "It could be that it's because he's the only man you've ever known. He took you up when your mother died. You weren't more than sixteen."

Victoria smiled oddly. "He's taken care of me, Caleb. Do you know what would have happened to me if he hadn't?"

Her question startled me. It echoed my defense against Mary when she had criticized Mike Shea for the way he had brought me up. "I know," I said quickly. "It wasn't easy. Especially for a girl it couldn't have been easy."

"You still don't know what I mean, Caleb. You said he was the first man I had known. That isn't true, you see."

I slid down from the rock and faced her angrily. "You're talking nonsense. When I left town you were in pig-tails."

Victoria nodded. "In pig-tails, and with my school books under my arm. But after you went upriver I refused to go to school any more." She stopped, her eyes almost pleading. "Caleb, why must you be so—so much like a conscience? Don't you understand? When my mother died everyone in town knew what I was. Kirt told me he planned to put me into The Golden Rule—and I would have gone, don't you see? But he didn't do that. He could have used me to make money, but now I do nothing but cost him money." She laughed up into my eyes, but there was no mirth in the sound. "Isn't it funny, Caleb?"

Hotly I pulled her to her feet and shook her like a child. "You were a kid without a father. Your mother didn't know how to bring you up in a town. Why do you want to talk like a whore?"

She smiled slowly, half fearfully, half in pity, and as I looked into her dark eyes all my anger seeped out of me, leaving me weak and trembling. "I'm sorry, Vicky. It's—it's none of my affair."

She nodded, looking down at the river. "That's what I really wanted to say, Caleb. I wanted to tell you I was sorry you got into trouble with Kirt over me—that you shouldn't worry about me any more." And then suddenly she clung to me and burst into tears. "It's so hard to say that, Caleb. I don't really want to say it. You're the only friend I have. They are all nice to me in Dalles City, but they know what I am and they aren't friends."

Her body was small and hard against me. Her soft wet cheek was brushing my lips. "You mean Kirt doesn't want us to be friends? Is that it?"

"He's strange, Caleb. He's had a hard life, and his hand—" She broke off, at a loss for words. "He wants all of everything, Caleb, don't you see? People used to make fun of him, and he never wants it to happen to him again. I think he would kill anyone who made a fool of him now. He's had things his own way for so long that he couldn't bear to go back. And if you and I tried to be friends there might be talk, and he wouldn't stand for that."

"We were friends before we knew Kirt Inge," I said. "I haven't let anyone run my life, and I won't begin now."

Vicky shook her head slowly. "You've got to begin now. You've got to begin, just as I did, Caleb. You've a wife and son and they'll run your life for you."

We went back along the path to the sandy flat. A scolding crow screamed down at us, following us from tamarack to pine clear to the boat landing. And when we reached the landing the black, unpleasant bird perched high and squawked at us unmercifully. While we waited for the driver we exchanged almost no words. We talked about the way the river looked as the sun slid down behind the hills, and about the *Wright*, and I told Victoria of the plans Ainsworth had for "the company." But in reality we exchanged no words. What we said was only meaningless sound to drown out our thoughts. I was relieved when I saw the mare and buggy beyond the trees that lined the portage road. Patterson had sent out a single-seater driven by a disreputable looking loiterer he had hired from in front of the livery stable. He drew up beside us and lifted his hat. "You wanted to drive back to town, Captain?"

"Yes," I said. "I like to drive myself. Do you mind riding in the back?"

It was plain that he minded considerably. There was no cushion on the bed of the buggy and the road into town was rutted after the long winter rains. Sourly he handed me the reins and climbed over the seat. I helped Victoria into the vehicle and took my place beside her.

The mare was spirited and we made brisk time through the leafy, darkening arches of the Deschutes grove. Then suddenly we were in the open again, with the night surrounding us endlessly and the smell of sage rising on the damp night air.

As the lights of the town loomed ahead, Victoria whispered, "It would be better if you let me out just before we get into town."

"I don't like to do that, Vicky. Why don't you take Bert's man and the buggy? I can walk into town."

"It would be hard to explain the buggy. Whenever I want a buggy Kirt orders it for me."

I drew the mare to a halt. "I'm damned if you're going to walk into town," I said. I turned to where Bert's man had been holding on uncomfortably. "Will you take Miss Hunt where she wants to go? I'll walk along to the stable and pay for the buggy hire."

Vicky's hand touched mine in the darkness. "You won't forget what I said?"

"I'll try to mind my own business, Vick." I jumped over the wheel into the road. Then I began walking toward the town behind them. I passed the shacks clustered where the road widened into Front Street. It was a quiet hour among the rough board hovels that surrounded Madam de Bilk's. It was quiet for The Golden Rule, just a little way beyond. But ahead were the lamps of the saloons, burning high, throwing yellow streaks onto the dark mud of the street, and already there was the dull drone of talk, as if from a thousand bees.

I interrupted Bert Patterson in the act of sitting down to a plate of beans in the back room of his livery stable. "Well!" he said. "When the Hell did you start getting so fancy as to refuse to ride down from the boat behind the mules? Have a plate of beans with me?"

It suddenly occurred to me that Mary would be waiting with supper that had been ready for more than two hours. "I had some business with a party, Bert. Your man is driving her home."

"Oh . . . it was a *her* you had business with?"

"See here, Bert!" I said soberly. "You ought to clean the horse dung out of your mind at least as often as you clean it out of the stable." I paid him for the buggy and handed him an extra silver dollar. "But I do have reason for not wanting anything said. Will you give this dollar to that fellow and tell him to keep his mouth shut?"

Bert was instantly contrite. "Sure! I never say nothing, Captain. And neither do the fellows I got workin' for me."

Feeling cheap and sneaking, I hurried out of the stable. My state of mind was not improved by the knowledge that I dare not tell Mary the real reason for my tardiness. The truth would not be worth the unhappiness it would cause her.

When I reached the cottage she was standing on the steps, and I could hear Henry calling to her complainingly from inside the house.

"Caleb? I've been worried about you."

I kissed her quickly. "We had trouble with the boiler coming down. I thought I'd better stay around until I was sure Jake had it fixed for the next trip up."

With the lie stinging my lips I could not put my arms around her as we entered the house. Instead, I hurried inside to greet Henry—whose eyes, I knew, would not be questioning.

CHAPTER 13

THE gold claims did not all peter out at once, and as here and there one was finally exhausted, there was no panic along the river. Chinamen bought up the dead claims and continued to work them —getting gold, too, because they were willing to work longer than the whites; and they knew how to live on what they earned.

Most of the claims held up, and occasionally a new strike was made, farther over toward the Bitter Roots, drawing fresh hordes of prospectors from downriver. Already Dalles City had petitioned the government for a mint of its own so that the dust would not have to be shipped clear to San Francisco; and, sure enough, the stone walls of the mint began to rise.

There was, of course, something deeper than simple optimism for the lack of panic as the gold rush slackened. By now the towns along the river had sizable populations and established businesses. If the people had lost a little of their rugged bravado, they were drawing new strength from feeling themselves a part of the United States of America. The overland mail had begun to connect us with the East, forming a much closer link than the old pony express into Sacramento. With it came new topics, national topics, which we could discuss before they became dead issues. We talked about Mexico and the problems it posed. And while the men let go their vigorous opinions on the street corners, or in the Umatilla House or Vic Trevitt's Mount Hood Saloon, the women were properly horrified when the Emperor Napoleon notified the Pope that he could not longer guarantee his support. Or, while they pressed leaves in oiled paper, they prattled pleasantly of Queen Victoria's mourning.

But neither the men nor the women regarded events outside the United States in anything but the most theoretical light. We believed too wholeheartedly in the future of America to be distracted from our own part in the fulfillment of its destiny. Naturally, however, the talk on the steamboats became more varied than of old. Once it had been confined to the movements of the troops and to speculations about the Indians. Later it had been talk only of gold. But now whenever I was off watch and sauntered among the passengers, or went into the dining saloon for supper I might hear a discussion of Gatling's new battery gun, or a typing machine that in some way printed letters on a sheet of paper when you pressed upon keys which represented the letters of the alphabet.

We even began to have culture along the river—poets, in fact, like C. H. Miller. Usually, like Miller, they were something else first. Miller had been a pony express rider, an Indian fighter, a lawyer, and almost anything else you could name. Both he and his wife wrote verse (I always thought hers the better), which sometimes appeared in *The Mountaineer*. He was a queer fellow, even on the frontier, and after a while he grew tired of the jibes he had to suffer, and left for San Francisco where he called himself Joaquin Miller. I understand that he became a great favorite there, and then he went to England to try his effect. He created as great a furor there as in San Francisco, but I do not know whether it was due to his poetry or his discovery that Britishers could be shocked and amused by a man who had been raised on the rivers. As far as I know, Miller was the nearest thing to pure genius that we ever had along the Columbia. We had no Mark Twains, or Bret Hartes, or Ambrose Bierces, like San Francisco. It wasn't that Dalles City wasn't big enough. I think it was mainly because there was no audience for them. We got few Easterners out West on a "sightseeing tour." Those Easterners who came to the Oregon country were there for some purpose: to hunt gold, or raise cattle or grain, or profit from those who did. They had no time to listen to poetry or essays, and would have had no patience with a literary clique if there had been one.

Our pleasures were less subtle—like the socials in the Umatilla House, or the annual ball of the Jackson Engine Company No. 1, or the donation parties of the churches; or the aspect of some particularly obnoxious character at last getting his carcass ventilated in front of Tim Baldwin's saloon. The killings were naturally the most interesting of all our entertainments. They always produced an amazing number of eye-witnesses, every one of whom vied with the others to give the most dramatic account. Old Billy Saunders boasted that he had never missed a gun fight in Dalles City since before the War. As he was always in one or the other of the resorts where the killings were most likely to occur, nobody had reason to doubt him.

The O.S.N. had been bringing no produce downriver—we had brought nothing downstream except the gold and the miners who wanted out. There had been a few farmers, like Heinrich Kiessling, who wanted to use the boats to get their grain down to market. But the rates were too high for farm products—and, on the other hand, farm products were a nuisance to "the company."

But when, here and there, a claim gave out there were those who said that quiet times were coming for the Columbia. It was Jim Troup, Captain of the *Almota,* who convinced Ainsworth that we should build bigger boats, designed to bring down the wheat that was being raised in ever larger quantities in the interior.

Jim Troup's father had been a steamboat man before him, and in young Jim there were rolled into one man all the best attributes of a white water captain. Ainsworth, always careful, put him off by saying that a boat bigger than the *Almota* could never navigate the John Day or the Umatilla. And Jim Troup always answered, "You build one. I'll take her through."

Eventually, the larger boats were built. But I must be careful not to make it appear that they were built at once. So fast was "the company" growing that if it had not been for young Henry, I would never have realized the time these events actually consumed. I had taken the *Wright* when the boy was a wrinkled mite with a thatch of black cradle-hair. Thereafter I was always astonished when I returned from upriver, for there would be some marked change in him. The black hair rubbed away and left him startlingly bald. Then he began to grow a red fuzz which presaged Mary's coloring. He grew fat and round and utterly phlegmatic—phlegmatic, it seemed to me, but Mary and Martha Danby pointed out that he was simply, providentially, "a good baby."

And one day I came home from aboard the *Wright* to find that he could struggle, step by step, across the room to Mary's arms.

His growth was not so noticeable after that, but I began to take a greater interest in him. It gave me a queer, soft feeling to have him run across the floor to me when I came home. On the downriver trips I began to anticipate it, standing there in the pilot house, imagining his soft hand against my face, and smelling the cleanness of his smooth cheek.

When he could walk a greater distance I would sometimes carry him down the long path into the town, set him carefully on the board walk, and take him over to watch things at the boat landing. It had never occurred to me that Mary would dislike this, but one day she said, "Why do you always want to have Henry down at the landing?" I knew then, from the tightness of her throat and the look in her eyes, that she had long forborn to ask that question.

"Why," I answered, "I think he likes to watch the boats. He's got so he isn't a bit afraid of the whistles when they go off."

"Caleb, I'd just as soon you didn't do it when he gets a little older. I—I don't want him to—well, to be brought up like you were. I'm sure you don't either."

"Of course I don't," I agreed. "And I can't see that he is. He's got a mother and a father, and a home. But I see nothing wrong in letting him know what goes on, and while we're on the subject, I don't see too much wrong with the way I was raised. I haven't turned out to be a drunkard or a horse thief."

Mary was quickly contrite. She said she hadn't meant to hurt my feelings. "My feelings aren't hurt," I told her. "But I'm damned if I see anything wrong with taking him to the boats. It doesn't follow that he'll turn out to be a steamboat man, if that's what is worrying you."

We went over that ground a good deal after that, increasingly as Henry grew older. For, like all the rest of the kids in the town, he took a natural interest in the boats. He couldn't very well do otherwise, and he got so that he could tell a boat by her whistle, long before she rounded Crates Point. He began to know how many buckets there were on any given paddle wheel on that part of the river. When he was seven years old he got into a fight with the son of an officer from the fort. The other boy had said that the *Colonel Wright* was the slowest boat on the river now.

I thought this amusing and was secretly proud of his defense. It pleased me to tell him that I might be commanding a new boat which would be as fast as any of them. But Mary apparently felt that I should have punished him for getting into the fight with the officer's boy. Embarrassed at my lack of knowledge as to a father's natural duties, I took Henry into the backyard and gave him a lecture. And when I had finished I added, "Son, it's just as well that you don't talk about steamboats around your mother. She don't give a hang for them."

The moment I had given that advice I could have slit my tongue. In those surprised eyes I could see that Mary had never once intimated to him her real feeling about the boats. The news came to him as a shock he could not quite absorb.

"But aren't *you* a steamboat man?" he asked.

"Yes." I tried to laugh the subject away. "Yes, but that doesn't mean your mother has to like boats. A lot of ladies don't care much about steamboats. I—I guess they're sort of afraid of them."

It didn't work too well, that explanation. After my slip, the boy began to sense his mother's feelings when he had not sensed them before. Often I caught him looking at me in a strange, new, critical way; and he stopped asking me about the boats or talking of them. I tried to believe that he was only taking my advice, but something told me that it went deeper than that. Unwittingly I had let him sense that chasm between Mary and me, and he was trying to decide where his sympathies must lie.

A little while after he got into a fight with the officer's boy, Mary took him again for a visit to the Kiessling farm. Heinrich had been failing fast, and Else and Hulda had married and left, as the old man had predicted. Only Sidonie was with him now, and a hired man.

Mary went up to Walla Walla for three visits within a year, each time that Heinrich suffered a spell and Sidonie wrote her in alarm. I guessed that the old man was on his last legs and finally suggested that Mary stay as long as she pleased. I was afraid that she might not be with him at the end, and that if she were not she would regret it all her life. I tried to get her to leave Henry with Martha Danby, not only because I thought that Heinrich's spells might have a bad effect on the boy, but because, too, I did not like to see him so much away from the river. I did not want him to come to feel that the Kiessling farm was where he really belonged, and I was strengthened in my feeling because I was certain that Mary, unconsciously or not, believed that he did belong there.

But she would not hear of leaving him with Martha while she visited upriver. "I'd be worrying about him," she said. "And papa would never forgive me if I didn't bring him along."

CHAPTER 14

STRANGE new smells began to be borne on the river winds—the smells of tar and oakum. There were new sounds, too—of mallets and adzes flailing in swift arcs against solid timbers. Not the timid sounds of men building houses, shelters against adventure and the elements, but the brave sounds of men building boats.

And as quickly as they were finished they were slipped into the river and started on their maiden voyages. The *Okanogan,* the *Spray,* and the *Nez Perce Chief* followed the *Tenino*. They were upper river boats, to take the miners and their supplies over the last of the water miles. But downstream, too, the shipbuilders were busy knocking together the *Iris* to follow the new *Idaho*. On the lower river the inrushing hordes found more than the *Belle* to take them eastward. They boarded the *Carrie Ladd* and the *Jennie Clark* and the *Mountain Buck*.

From everywhere shipbuilders made their way to the Columbia and were taken up gratefully and set to work. They came out of the West, from San Francisco, and Puget Sound, and British Columbia. They followed the sun from Maine and the Great Lakes and the Mississippi and took up their draw-knives and caulking irons. Many a man who came to the river to ply a profession weakened and joined the search for gold, but never the shipbuilder. He wanted only a boat to build, solidly and well. Only a poem to write. Only a picture to paint. Only music to play. And only a ship to build. Let the rest grub for the gold and die in their souls for it.

Master of them all was John Holland, clear from New Brunswick, a man with coal black hair and glorious mustaches and unswerving eyes that could spot a bad plank at a quarter of a mile. He would range up and down the river, from the Deschutes to Portland and back, watching the new boats. The keel, the stem, the knees, the ribs, the planking—every nail, every snake-like strip of oakum, every rivet in every boiler, had to pass those keen eyes. And if Holland did not like it, then even Ainsworth wouldn't pronounce it good.

He had the preoccupied air of a man who has come to a place to do a certain job and neither knows nor cares what is around him. He never seemed to belong to the river. To him the Columbia was only the medium which would carry the boats he designed and built. If the time came when there were no more boats to build on the river he would leave—leave for anywhere, to build whaling vessels in Puget Sound, or trading ships at Sitka far north in Russian America. He belonged to no country by the time we saw him, but rather to the waters of the world. He belonged to no era, but to an art that is timeless.

Added to the burden of passengers and supplies were new cargoes which, brought together by the skill of Holland's men, would create the new boats of the Oregon Steam Navigation Company. Strewn along the portage roads, sidetracked momentarily for mining or military goods, would be the boilers, the steam engines, the iron fittings for the giant paddle wheels. And then John Holland would come roaring down, giving the agents Hell for the delay, enquiring how the company was to function without new vessels and how new vessels were to be built without materials.

There was no time to lose. At Portland the steamers from San Francisco were dumping off gold-crazed miners a thousand at a time. Out of the cargo holds were lifted the cases of shovels and picks with which to get the gold; up were lifted the boxes of food to feed them, the casks of whiskey to make them drunk, the clothes to keep them warm. And from everywhere were coming those to bleed them—the gamblers, the shysters, the thieves, and the murderers, all pressing for passage up the Great River, all clamoring for suckle at the full breasts of a new country.

No time to lose. The gold was being taken from the mountains. The gold was coming down, and with it those who could not wait to spend. Down the river it must come to be loaded aboard the ocean vessels and headed for San Francisco's mint. The waterfront of Portland was a chaos of men and supplies going up for gold and rich-loco miners on the way out. Freight wagons, creaking under overloads, lined up for blocks to wait their turns.

No time to lose, roared John Holland, with Captain Ainsworth at his back. Gone were the lonesome days of the Columbia when only the little *Mary* and the *Hassalo* breasted the troubled currents between The Cascades and the Deschutes. Was it for this that the Columbia had been waiting? Was this why it had roared its way for so many millions of years, now in this channel and now in that, pushing great blocks of granite and basalt, searing its bed deep and wide? Perhaps, I used to think as I stood at the rail of the *Tenino*, perhaps it had once served another great purpose which had been forgotten, or lost to the memory of man. Perhaps it would serve still another purpose long after the *Tenino* was a rotting hulk and I had been laid beside my father and mother and Jim Sinclair at The Cascades.

So great was the pressure that at last the portage roads proved inadequate. No matter how many or how fine the boats, the portages were the weak links in the chain. John Holland had done all he could, and Ainsworth went to work. Up from San Francisco he brought a pony locomotive that had hauled sand from the excavation for a new hotel. He learned that two single-drive locomotives had been built for the Bolivian Railway and that the Bolivian Railway could not pay for them. These came by ship along the coast, and were set down in Portland for delivery up the river.

Swiftly the tracks were laid along the old portage roads—some were wood rails strapped down with metal, others were real iron rails brought up from California. And on them ran the first locomotives to be seen in the Northwest. Ainsworth was proud of them, and the people along the river were proud of Ainsworth—and "the company."

Nothing had had greater effect on us than those little engines.

We hadn't been half as excited about the first pony express from St. Joseph to Sacramento, or the telegraph line that put it out of business a year later. Neither had affected the river greatly. Oregon had got into the Union the year Mike and I lit out for Steptoeville. We'd read the Emancipation Proclamation in the *Statesman*. But these happenings were remote and mysterious; Ainsworth's tiny locomotives were something that belonged to us. We began to feel that our land amounted to something and was more than merely an outpost about which every Senator and Congressman made windy speeches but so few had ever seen.

There were things that we had begun to know. We knew that the land was rich, richer than any land anywhere, and in more things. It was rich to Heinrich Kiessling whose vision was wheat. It was rich to Dorsey Baker, whose ambition was to be a merchant and a banker. It was rich to Ainsworth whose dream was in transportation. It was rich to the thousands who saw wealth only in gold. And this was not all. We were not through. The look of the land was good, and there was a lot of it. There was timber and acres for the plow and fish and game and minerals.

There was still more than this. There were the people who had come in, ready for anything. A man with an axe and a plow could build a home for himself. A man with a pick and a pan could grow into a millionaire. Anything was possible, and we began to sense it. The feeling sprang from man to man, like a communicable disease. It was a fever in our blood.

We were a long way from the East and the South and the wide plains and even from California. It did not matter. We had a great broad land and we were sufficient unto ourselves. Let them stay in their cities. We were building cities of our own. Let them destroy each other, fighting among themselves. We were erecting an empire beyond the mountains. Those who would come were welcome; but let the rest ask for what we had, and we would get it, and send it out and down the river.

There was no limit to our ingenuity, and the world was beginning to know it. Not all our schemes worked, but that was a secret we kept to ourselves. We knew about the men like Amos Crawford who built a barge with a tread-mill on which cattle were to walk themselves upstream to market. We knew that the vessel was swept ashore and that the cattle devoured the feed and then escaped.

But Crawford had made the attempt, and we did not laugh at him. We knew that we lived in a land where anything might turn out all right, where everything was worth a whirl.

CHAPTER 15

As Henry grew older, and Mary more accustomed to the trip upriver, they took to visiting the Kiessling ranch more and more. It was apparent that old Heinrich would never be well. He had worked too hard and too long; he had expected too much from his square, solid body, because it had always given him so much. Now it had broken, and yet Heinrich held stubbornly to life.

Mary made his condition the excuse for her frequent visits, and she was sincere in this. She grew to fear the idea of her father dying while she was away, and each time she returned to Dalles City she was convinced that she would never again see him alive. Yet unconsciously these visits were bringing her closer to the old place, and farther away from Dalles City and her life with me.

It was during one of her absences that I did something I had dreamed about doing for a long time. I bought five acres of land on the hill south of town. It overlooked the river; on clear days you could see the mists rising from Celilo Falls past which the portage road meandered.

There I wanted to build a house for Mary and Henry and me. I wanted to create a place that would be our own, a place in which Mary might grow to feel at home. In my mind I visioned an elaborate dwelling, for I still had the money from the mine; and I had bought a few shares of stock in "the company" which had risen tremendously with the fortunes of the river. "The company" was hatching millionaires all along the Columbia, and although I was far from that category, I had added several thousand to my stake from the claim, and I was getting five thousand a year as captain.

I did not tell Mary I had bought the land, but I began to talk of building a house. Families were settling down in Dalles City, and whenever one of them started a new dwelling I would be sure to call Mary's attention to it. But I could arouse no envy in her, and no desire for a place of her own. "It would be foolish to spend so much money on a big house," she would say. "This place is good enough for only the three of us."

"But I think we ought to have a house that Henry can grow up in and feel it's his own. You can't understand that, because you had it."

"Then why not buy this place?" Mary would want to know. "You could get it for a little money."

I was ashamed to say that I wanted something much grander than the Barstow house. I wanted a great house with three stories, and a cupola, and a drive into the grounds. I wanted a place for people to drive by in their buggies and say, "That's where Captain Paige lives."

So a year passed, two years, three, and I didn't build the house. The *Colonel Wright* was outmoded, and still we stayed on in the Barstow place. We were there when Ainsworth told me that they would have to dismantle the *Wright* and replace her. We were there when the *Blair Anthony* was built for the run from Dalles City to The Cascades and I was given command of her.

It was good to be on a run which would take me out of the bleaker stretches of the river and bring me again to the scenes of my boyhood at The Cascades. It seemed to me that the river had reached its full birthright. The boats were perfect, the men as solid as they come. Passengers from Portland to Lewiston were passed from boat to boat and captain to captain, taken up the often treacherous passages with infrequent discomfort. They took the *Wide West* now, with the solemn-faced Wolf in the pilot house, and John Marshall at the throttle. And at the upper Cascades, if I did not receive them aboard the *Blair Anthony,* they were in better hands aboard the *R. R. Thompson* with John McNulty in the pilot house. And at Dalles City they went to the beautiful *Harvest Queen* and

Jim Troup. The *Harvest Queen* was a huge, beamy boat that lost nothing in beauty because of her utility. And Jim Troup could take her through Hell Gate and John Day and the Umatilla Rapids as easily as I had once taken the little *Wright*.

The *Harvest Queen* was the realization of Troup's dream—a big boat that could carry a real cargo of grain yet give the passengers every comfort. For the flow of gold had lessened appreciably in the intervening years since Mike's claim had run out, and Ainsworth had seen that increasingly "the company" would have to depend upon the grain for freight. The mint, which had been rising slowly and solidly, was ordered stopped by the government. It was plain now that Dalles City would not need a mint. So the four stone walls were sold to a private citizen who put a tin roof over them and used the building for a warehouse.

But the glory of the river grew rather than lessened. The *Harvest Queen* had not been the first of the grander steamboats. Before her was launched the *Daisy Ainsworth,* her engines and hull built for speed, her cabins for elegance. Brussels carpets covered the cabin and stateroom floors. Glittering chandeliers lighted her from stem to stern. Silver plate and linen from New York City made the buffet and dining room tables resplendent. And when she was launched, in April, 1873, Ainsworth himself took the wheel for her first testing time. She was "the *Daisy*" to every man and boy along the river and when they spoke of her they put into the name all the affection Ainsworth would put into the name of the favorite daughter for whom she was christened.

The *Daisy* was a hundred and seventy-five feet long, and more than two hundred feet over all. Her houses extended clear to the gunwales to hold the increasing freight and there were fifteen staterooms. She had a twenty-one foot wheel with twenty buckets and with three hundred tons load she could make better than twenty miles an hour.

Every gear was meshing on the big river now. "The company" was in its stride. As elaborate as the *Harvest Queen* was, she went only to Wallula, for at that point there were the *John Gates* and the *Almota* to take passengers on to Lewiston, while the *Harvest Queen* stood by for her cargo of wheat.

At Wallula a new sign of progress met the passengers now—for Dorsey Baker had built a narrow-gauge railroad from Walla Walla to the river. The tall man with the deep-set eyes, the questioning fellow who had stood in the wheel house of the *Wright* on her first trip upriver had seen a vision of his own when the little steamboat breasted the outflowing current of the Walla Walla River where it flowed into the Columbia.

The narrow-gauge into Walla Walla was not the only way our passengers could turn, however. They might take the stage to Pend Oreille Lake and connect there with the lake boats that carried Wells Fargo letter-express further into the interior. From the lake boats they could make connections with Missoula, and from there filter deeper into the wide land beyond the Bitter Roots. For only thirty dollars they could climb aboard a thorough-braced Concord and try their luck in a wilderness that Mike and I had never dreamed of as we sat on the bank of The Cascades seventeen years before.

Naturally Walla Walla had changed with the fortunes of the country. Now it boasted The Stine House, a hostelry of brick made twenty miles away in the tiny stagecoach station of Weston where a suitable clay made a kiln possible. But the lime had to come from San Francisco and cost eighty dollars a barrel by the time it reached Walla Walla. The glass for the windows came from France, clear around the Horn, and citizens proudly spread the rumor that every window in the place was worth four hundred dollars.

The Stine House was in grand contrast, however, to the rest of the town. Walla Walla even yet sprawled indolently on either side of a Main Street which was still as dusty as the Indian trail it followed. The town got less rainfall than we on the river, and the streets were made impassable in summer by the continual grind of the wheat wagon wheels. Straw covering helped a little, but not much, and the scraggly locusts—the only tree which would grow in the light, dry soil—grew tall but unprotective. We in Dalles City joked about Walla Walla and called it the town of one-story houses and two-story trees, but they in turn poked fun at us because our buildings along the river were built on stilts.

I have a menu of a very grand dinner which Walla Walla gave for Doctor Baker. It is printed on white satin, with a gold border, and it is in French which I do not have the education to guarantee:

Menu of
Dinner
Given in Honor of
DOCTOR BAKER
By the Citizens of Walla Walla at
The Stine House

Potages

Green Turtle, a la Anglaise — Raviloa, a la Neopolitan

Poissions

Salmon, a la Cambridge — Oyster, au Coquille

Rotis

Chicken — Loin of Beef
Turkey, Cranberries

Salads

Oyster — Russian

Hors D'Ouvers

Boudin of Fowls, a la Richiliu
Filet de Boeuf, au Chartreuse
Marriande of Chicken
Fricandeau with Puree of Green Peas, a la Macedoine
Scallops of Sweet Breads, a la Dupelles
Godiveay, au Moduc
Matelotte of Eels, a la Bordelaise
Macaroni, a la Polanise
Fruits d'Amour

Legumes

Mashed Potatoes — Browned Potatoes
Sweet Potatoes — Cauliflower
String Beans

Patisserie

English Plum Pudding — Russian Charlotte

Jelly

Panachee Pineapple

Fruit

Oranges Peaches Pears Grapes

It was a splendid affair, that dinner, to which some of the steamboat captains were invited; and in one corner of the menu there is written in fading pencil on the white satin the initials V. H.

The initials are, of course, those of Victoria Hunt. The hours we were together at that elaborate dinner were among the few that were without guilt on my part and fear of Kirt Inge on Vicky's.

Mary and I had gone to Walla Walla together, but when we rode out to the Kiessling place we found Heinrich in one of his low spells and Mary decided not to attend the dinner. Being a representative of "the company" I did not feel I could absent myself as well. I rode back into town and presented myself at The Stine House; and by a queer turn of fortune I found myself seated next to Victoria Hunt. She, too, was without a companion, for Inge was detained in Lewiston on some mysterious business and had failed to meet her in Walla Walla. We both knew that he could not possibly get downriver until the next day.

I had seen her often since the day she had waited for me at the Deschutes landing—to tell me that I must forget her! But they were furtive meetings calculated to deceive Inge as well as myself. Sometimes I would be on the wharf landing when a downriver boat sailed and I knew that Victoria was going to Portland. Sometimes I would hire a saddle mare from Bert Patterson when I knew that she was driving along the river. I learned that it was her habit to take a Sunday afternoon walk along a path that skirted the fort. I took care never to miss a social or a ball where I believed she might be and I might have a chance to talk with her openly.

I think that in the beginning I sought these meetings with Victoria out of stubbornness. I was irked by Mary's attitude when I had kissed Victoria to pay my forfeit after the games at the Umatilla House. I rebelled against the sudden silence of all the people in that room, a silence that seemed to say that I should have nothing to do with a girl who was, outside of Mike Shea, my oldest friend along the river. And I was still smarting under the warning that Kirt Inge had given me. I was well to do, and a captain on the Columbia, and too young and spoiled to bear the thought of being barred or driven.

I am sure it was this foolish stubbornness rather than a growing loneliness that kept driving me toward Victoria. Yet there was the fact that I felt less and less a part of the lives of Mary and young Henry. It was not only their long visits to the Kiessling place that left me alone; it was more Mary's refusal to let me take her and the boy into my own life. And Victoria Hunt was a part of the river and all my memories along it.

At first I did not realize her mortal fear of Inge. I did not take it seriously even when she confessed it to me, even after that night when she had hesitated to drive into town with me from the Deschutes landing. When I saw at last that her dread was real, and that through it ran a regard for Inge that was deeper than fear, I tried to keep away from her. I told myself that she was in love with him, and that she liked me only for a youthful idealism and perhaps because I reminded her that she had once been a little girl in pig tails and untouched by life. I told myself, too, that I had a wife and child, and that my attraction to Victoria was unfair to them.

But there was no use. Victoria Hunt was a part of the river and all my memories of it. I could no more fight against my yearning for the sight of her, for the look of her eyes and the sound of her voice, than I could stop my love for the Columbia and its boats. And the reason I could not fight against them was because, in the end, I did not want to. In the end I said to myself that nothing mattered except that we be together. It was easy to rationalize this feeling when at last I reached it. Mary wanted Henry to be raised without a feeling for the river and the boats, and to me this seemed selfish and unfair. She wanted nothing of me as a river man, and unless I was a river man I was lost—as lost as Mike without the Army.

These and a hundred other reasons I could conjure up in my mind as I stood for long hours in the wheel house of the *Blair*

Anthony. Sometimes they sufficed, and at other times they seemed weak and invalid. During those other times I would think back to my first days with Mary, I would remember that night in the wheat field, and the sweet excitement of the wedding at the Kiessling ranch, and would decide that I had been selfish and cheap, and that I must forget Victoria, even forget the river a little, and try to be a better husband and father. During these periods I would become fired again to build my grand house on the hill, telling myself that there everything would be different. There Mary would change and grow to love the river and the town. There Henry would grow up to know some of the things that I knew and felt were good. There I would become fixed in mind because at last I would have roots.

And this was the way it went, with nothing settled, with my inward thoughts as disturbed as the river, and Victoria never really forgotten. By the time of our meeting at The Stine House I knew I would never forget her. Never before had we been together where there were people, where we could be taken for a man and a woman with a right to be together. It had not been possible in Dalles City, because of Mary, because of Inge—and because of a growing sense of morality that was settling over the town as families grew and life became more ordered. But in Walla Walla we were among mostly strangers; and those few at the Baker dinner who knew us could see that we had been thrown together quite by accident. After dinner, at the dancing, it was easy to explain that Mary had been kept at home by the illness of her father, and that Inge was detained upriver.

Soon I abandoned everything except the pleasure of being for the moment free, and in the company of Victoria Hunt. The gay lilt of her talk, under the yellow flames of the lamps in The Stine House, amazed me. Her mind darted at everything and she commented on all that it encountered. Unlike Mary or Martha Danby or hundreds of women in Dalles City, she had not been circumscribed by the duties of a housewife. And unlike the women at The Golden Rule or the shacks below it, she had been no prisoner chained by the nature of her sinning. I told myself that she was wilful and vain, yet I could not deny that she was more clearly perfect than any woman I had known. Unwillingly I compared her with Mary. I knew that Victoria would never ask a man to deprive himself of the thing he loved most in the world. She valued freedom too much herself, and she wanted too many things too keenly, to possess Mary's fault.

As I danced with Victoria in the crowded ball room of The Stine House I was flushed with the importance of the occasion and excited by the music. Victoria seemed to float in my arms. Suddenly I thought how wonderful it would be to be able to go everywhere with Victoria, openly. I began to wish that I had never met Mary Kiessling on the main street of Walla Walla. I felt that if that had never happened I would now be Victoria's husband. I felt that something had gone wrong with my life when Mike and I got into trouble with the Southern sympathizers that night on Front Street in Dalles City. For if that had not happened Vicky and I would have stayed together. There was no other way my life should have gone.

On the day the *Daisy Ainsworth* was launched I was thirty years of age. It seemed old to me, and I did look more than thirty. There were deep wrinkles at the corners of my eyes not altogether from squinting at the sun on the long afternoon trips downriver. The scar on my forehead, though it had shrunk some and lost its color, did not lessen the look of years.

But it was not so much my looks that made me feel old as what I had seen transpire along the river. It seemed to me a lifetime since I had witnessed the massacre at The Cascades; in reality it was less than two decades. Yet in that time the empty river had filled with life and spilled that life along its banks in a dozen places. In that time a bloody war had been fought, a President assassinated. Johnson and Grant had followed, weak and pale beside the man who had freed the slaves. The old and broken Atlantic cable which Mr. Harrington had so proudly described in the two-room school had been forgotten, and now a new one, which really worked, replaced it. We had bought Russian America, although nobody knew why.

But those were vague and distant happenings beyond the Stony

Mountains. If they touched us at all we hardly realized it, for it seemed to us that our destiny lay only along the great river. It was not by the national events that we reckoned time and progress. It was by the appearance of Baker's narrow-gauge, or improved portage tracks or a new building on Front Street, or—most important of all—a new steamboat on the Columbia or the Snake. It was not a Black Friday in New York that moved us, for we were self-sufficient; it was the news that Custer had come to death beyond the Bitter Roots, or that Chief Joseph had at last given up all hope of saving the land for his people.

There was one piece of news which we might well have heeded and yet did not. We should have heeded the growing web of steel rails in the East, and, most of all, the locomotives heading West to span the continent. But there were too many who still remembered that heartbreaking distance across the plains and the mountains. There were too many like myself who could not imagine a river without commerce.

CHAPTER 16

THE *Daisy* was launched in April, 1873, and that summer I began the house I had planned so long in my mind.

I arranged it to be a surprise for Mary. I had long since stopped trying to persuade her that we should build the place. Not for at least a year had I mentioned it. But I had grown more determined to have it, and I believed that if I could make it a reality while she and Henry visited the Kiessling ranch then she would return and accept it.

When they had gone upriver I rushed the construction with every ounce of effort. When one of Mary's letters indicated that sturdy Heinrich seemed to be improving, I told her that the weather in Dalles City was stifling and dusty and that she should stay as long as she wanted. I got carpenters up from Portland—twice the number necessary, for I wanted the house to go up in a hurry and yet be well built. Even in frame it was one of the biggest in Dalles City and whenever I came ashore from the *Blair* and saw the progress, I was awed with what I had started. The plans were for two and a half stories, with five gable windows, and a porch all around. In the center of the roof was thrust a windowed cupola from which one could see all up and down the river. And there was a carriage house in identical architecture. It looked more like the house of a banker than a young orphaned steamboat man, and the boys on the boats made great jokes about it. They called it "Paige's Folly" and "The Dalles City Jail" and accused me of putting on style and planning to retire ashore and raise vegetables. When I wrote Mike Shea about it, his scrawling reply, which came after an interval of a month, was filled with a combination of awe and disgust.

But I was more pleased than not with their taunts. The new house had begun to fill my mind. I would call it "Celilo Haven" because from it you could see the mist rising from the falls. It seemed to me that all my life I had been working toward this and that when it was finished my life would have begun to take shape at last.

Dalles City was only beginning to have elaborate dwellings, and so there were almost always some curious citizens climbing through the scantlings or viewing the whole structure from the discreet distance of the road. If I happened to be on the premises I would proudly invite them to see every inch of the place. The only roof I had known was that little cabin on The Cascades, and the cottage Mary and I had rented. This house was tangible proof that I had come a long way and belonged on the river as surely as Ainsworth or Nick Sinnott or Joe Wilson.

One late afternoon as I stood watching the carpenters, a carriage rocked its way up the newly laid drive. It was not a rented one from Patterson's stable, and I did not recall having seen it before. It was a two-horse private coach, with a driver on a box, and it was so brightly new that the sun's rays flashed back from the black enamel.

I went forward to meet it, standing self-consciously where the steps of my porch would be, ready to greet my visitor. The carriage stopped and I looked through the opening to see Victoria Hunt. She was smiling mischievously at me from beneath a bonnet of purple velvet held to her head by a velvet band strapped beneath her chin.

"You can't be the only one to be showing off, Caleb Paige! How do you like my new carriage?"

"It's very grand," I told her.

"I think so, too. It came up yesterday on your own *Blair Anthony* —and Robert just got it set up. Aren't you flattered that I came to see your house on the maiden trip?"

"I really am," I admitted. I opened the door and helped her to alight. Her hand was soft and cool in mine and she held my fingers firmly. Then she stood looking at the place, not relinquishing my hand. "Caleb, it's going to be wonderful."

"Would you like to go through it?"

"Oh, not now. I'm afraid I'd rip my petticoats on nails and things. Just let me look, and you tell me about it."

Robert, a ratty looking individual strangely out of keeping with the fine carriage whose box he occupied, was watching us narrowly. I slid my hand from Vicky's and, in some embarrassment, lighted a stogie. "Well," I said, "there's a big sitting room, in the front there. You get through it by a little hall. And the dining room is on the west side, and there's a kitchen and pantry back of that. The woodshed is part of the house and really opens right into the kitchen. . . ."

I described the place room by room, clear to the cupola, and Victoria stood, seemingly entranced. When I'd finished she said, "I'm not just curious, you know. I'm going to build a house of my own at The Cascades."

"At The Cascades?"

"Not a big place, like this."

"But why The Cascades?" I asked.

She looked at me in astonishment. "It's beautiful down there—so green and cool in the summer. And it still seems like home to me."

I reminded her of the time I had first come to Dalles City and found her already a confirmed town dweller. "You said there was nothing but trees at The Cascades, and you were very superior about it."

Victoria laughed. It was a laugh like the dust of silver tossed into the air. "I remember. What an unpleasant thing I must have been." I wondered if she really believed that she had changed. She must still know that she was play-acting, that she could not hold herself from sweeping onto a stage which she herself had set—like coming this afternoon in the new carriage to surprise me with the news that she was going to have a house at The Cascades.

"Of course," she said, "I won't use the house much except in the summer, when it's so warm here. And on the holidays I may open it for parties. It's such an easy jaunt down the river that I'm surprised no one has thought of it before this."

The thought of a cottage downriver, simply to escape the summer heat, had occurred to no one else in Dalles City. It was understood that Europeans maintained summer villas if they were rich, and that Eastern society women went South in the winter. But along the middle and upper Columbia people took the weather as it came. Weather was something which might interfere with work, but it was not a thing you escaped.

Victoria's eyes were amused as she watched me. She was enjoying herself immensely, and I could see that already she was anticipating the talk of all the practical housewives when the news got around that she was building a retreat at The Cascades. Her superiority flicked me. "A new gift from Inge?"

"Caleb. . . ." She reached out and shook me gently by the lapels. "Caleb, please don't. Here I come up the hill to offer to help you, and you fly into one of your silly moods."

"Help me?" I repeated.

She nodded. "Have you ordered your furniture, or are you going to wait until Mrs. Paige gets back?" She had a trick of mentioning Mary as if my wife were someone we knew only vaguely. "You won't have half enough furniture from the old place, Caleb. Besides, it won't look nice in this house. Wouldn't it be wonderful if you could have everything ready for her and Henry when they get back?"

"After my next trip I'll go see Max Vogt and have him fix me up."

Victoria made a little sound of horror. "Caleb! You *can't* have Maxmilian Vogt select your new furniture! You'll have whole new suites to buy—and rugs and pictures and bric-a-brac. You ought to go down to Portland and have a store there order it from San Francisco. I'm going down tomorrow—why don't you be there, too, and let me help you select the things?"

I said nothing, and Victoria read my face. "I'll keep it a secret. Mrs. Paige might not appreciate having the things selected by—another woman. But I do know what's fashionable, Caleb, and you'll get all the credit for having done it nicely."

CHAPTER 17

THE thought of having Victoria aboard the *Blair*, of traveling as a passenger with her to Portland on the *Wide West* was exciting.

She was among the earliest aboard the *Blair* next morning, arriving in her carriage even before the omnibus from the Umatilla House, a gaudy vehicle with hand-painted scenic decorations which was one of Dan Handley's proudest improvements. Except for Robert, Victoria was alone; she let herself out of the carriage and walked easily and gracefully up the plank while he followed with a carpet-sack and a trunk-like box. She wore a turban hat with small white feathers spreading over one side of the crown, and a gray traveling cape.

I suppose she came early because the sight of a woman boarding the boat alone was likely to make onlookers gape. Once aboard, she could mingle with the passengers and her lack of a companion would not be noticed.

Impatiently I waited in the wheel house, my watch open on the ledge of the window. When at last I could blow the final whistle and take the *Blair* into the middle of the river it was with a quixotic sense of rescuing Victoria and taking her into a new life.

I had already arranged for a relief captain to take the *Blair* back up the river so that at The Cascades I could continue to Portland on the *Wide West*. I was looking forward to the voyage on the lower river boat aboard which I would be without duty, but I was deeply disappointed in the weather we encountered. A short way below Memaloose Island there began a slow drizzle of the kind that threatened to be steady—one of those week-long precipitations that earlier settlers so wearily recorded in their diaries: *Rain. . . . Rained again today. . . . Rained most of the day.* And, finally, beginning passage after passage with the exasperated entry, *More rain!*

When we transferred to the portage train I took a place beside Victoria and delightedly she pointed out to me the site for her house. It was on a slight knoll, just above the road where I had once found young Kyle with the arrows sticking in his back. As she pointed it out to me, all the horror of that moment swept back into my mind—but obviously the dark green shadows of The Cascades brought no oppressive recollections to Victoria. All the way down the portage road she rattled on enthusiastically about her house and how pleased she would be to get away from Dalles City in the hot months.

"See how cool it is!" she exclaimed. "And when we left Dalles City it was scorching."

I remarked that it was not only cool, but wet.

"It is a pity, Caleb, that you have that Italian blood in you. You're either tremendously enthused or blue as ribbon." I had once told Victoria what little I knew about my antecedents. She had the average Nordic's contempt for Latin characteristics and whenever my reactions displeased her she would blame it on the mixture in my veins.

At the lower landing we scurried with the rest of the passengers, hurrying through the soft rain for the shelter of the *Wide West*. With Victoria I took a place at the rail under the top deck so that we could watch this part of the Columbia which I had so seldom seen. But I could not long be satisfied with seeing only one side of the stream. Noticing my discomfort, Victoria laughed and said, "Caleb, why don't you go up to the wheel house with Captain Wolf?"

"Are you sure you don't mind staying in the ladies' cabin?"

"Of course not. Please go up."

With Wolf I watched the awesome passing panorama of the lower Columbia, and not even Condon had prepared me for it. I was amazed at the narrowness of the channel for several miles below The Cascades, for through the long years the rock material had been pinching in and was, I could see, still attempting to throttle a river that was too great for it. All the lower aprons of the cliffs were soft and disintegrating, and with a blast of the *Wide West's* whistle Wolf could produce miniature landslides, sending down tiny streams of crumbling volcanic rock that lost themselves in the gray waters. Everywhere I looked were pits and ridges, swales and divides. Everywhere I looked were the scattered remnants of once great trees, giant firs half buried in the always shifting rock, or mauled into weathered strips of bark and fiber. Wolf told me that higher, on the flat above the river, there were springs and lakes which constantly appeared and disappeared.

As I watched from the windows of the pilot house I could literally feel the constant shifting of the strange land that had once been the center of a volcano, a weird gorge of andesitic and basaltic lava, jumbling and rumbling into some settled shape far into time, refusing to be held by the threads of pung vegetation or the cloth of forest.

Swiftly we left Table Mountain and the sweeping front of Red Bluff, swept down beyond Mount Wauna towering gaunt into the misty rain clouds. Quietly, borne on the stream, urged by the Columbia's eagerness for the Pacific, the *Wide West* skirted the wide mouth of Tanner Creek and was dwarfed below Mount Hamilton.

And then, dead ahead on the Washington side of the river, I saw Beacon Rock. I knew it at once, and when I called out its name excitedly, Wolf laughed, "Yep. That's her. Funny damned thing, ain't it?"

I nodded. "Thomas Condon described it to me."

"I reckon he's the only man that's been to the top of her. How in the Hell he did it, I don't know. She's eight hundred feet high and the base don't cover more than seventeen acres."

Up from the very edge of the river the jointed pillars rose in almost perfect horizontal columns forming an eerie monolith that had stood there before either the Columbia or the Cascade Range, and that still stood after an eruption had blown surrounding rock into a smoking flow.

I saw petrified trees below Beacon Rock. In the mouths of creeks I saw glistening through the rain the rays of quartzite pebbles. I saw great vents through which lava had once poured. And before I had assimilated the wonder of them, we were abeam of a jagged pinnacle that reared itself two thousand feet above us, its flank skirted with sliding talus.

And then we came into a country of sparkling waterfalls whose names Wolf called out to me, one after the other, as we sped down on the current—Horsetail, and Oneonta, and Multnomah, and then Mist Falls, so fragile and slender that half way in its thousand foot drop to the Columbia it disappeared and joined the blowing rain.

We passed Latourelle Falls, then, and Bridal Veil, and ahead loomed Crown Point which Wolf called the guardian of the gorge. Beyond it the Columbia widened into a low green land and now the stream was dotted with little islands. But still towering over us was Rooster Rock and the forbidding face of Angel's Rest. And across on the Washington side were visible through the lifting mist the rolling brown hills.

When at last we had maneuvered into the mouth of the Willamette and were breasting our way up toward Portland I turned to Wolf. "Good God, what a stretch of river!" I said. "If I had this run I'd go over it in bed in a nightmare, after every trip."

"Don't you like it?" smiled Wolf.

"I—well, I like it, but there's something about it that's uncanny, too."

Wolf nodded sagely. "Things go on back there in the gorge, no question about it. But, Hell, you don't have the rapids to buck like you do on the middle and upper stretches."

That was true enough, I thought; but a captain on the run through the gorge had something else to buck. He had the threat of those shifting banks, and the hazards of those great spires that edged into the white edges of the river. And when he went down between those walls he was pushing himself back through a corridor of time. He became something tiny and pink and raw which as yet had no real place in that part of the world which was not yet ready for him.

Preoccupied, but dimly realizing that we were nearing a landing, I left the pilot house to Wolf and went below. Victoria was standing at the rail, and as she heard my step on the deck she turned. "Did you and Captain Wolf have a nice visit?"

"Visit? I was watching the gorge. I've never been on this stretch of the river much. It's always wonderful to me." I saw that she held a book against the rail. "Don't tell me you stayed inside the ladies' cabin the whole trip down?"

Victoria laughed. "I'm reading *St. Elmo*. I'm sure it's more exciting than the river. And, Caleb, I met a lady in there who had a book of poetry. It's called *Leaves of Grass* and it's the most scandalous thing you ever saw. It's amazing that it could be printed. I hope I can buy it in Portland." Suddenly she stopped and looked up into my eyes. "Caleb, you're going to take me to supper tonight, and buy me champagne!"

I felt my blood warming at her glance, at the touch of her hand on my sleeve. "I suppose we should celebrate, at that."

"I've brought my very finest dress along. We'll have roast duck at the hotel—and you must ask them to bring the champagne in a silver bucket."

It was so like the old days, when she ordered me around and outlined what grand business we were to act out, that I laughed. But the laugh turned a little bitter in my throat, and I said, "You are a beautiful lady, and I am falling in love with you—but all the fine fellows in Dalles City are in love with you, too." I was using the half-drowsy singsong with which Victoria used to set the stage as a child. "And there is one fellow named Kirt Inge—"

"Kirt Inge has nothing to do with this!"

She flung the words at me, suddenly and petulantly. Her cheeks had paled. Quickly I took her hand. "I'm sorry, Vicky. You could as well remind me that I've a wife and child."

For a moment she did not answer, and then she said quietly, "Why should I, Caleb? Why can't two old friends be together without . . ." Her voice drifted into silence and she looked at me, wordless and helpless.

"All right then!" I said. "Two old friends together, Vick. And nothing of Dalles City."

"It won't work. I've something better than that—because, you see, old friends have memories, and memories mix things up. Let's pretend—" She recognized her lapse into the old way, and smiled ruefully. "Let's pretend that you and I have met for the first time, here on this boat."

"Good," I said. "Good enough!" But my heart knew that it was a dangerous pretence.

We had our fine dinner in the hotel—Victoria splendid in dark red silk that cupped her small, firm breasts and caressed her tiny waist, then billowed down around her so that she seemed to float whenever she moved. Over the dark red, her shoulders and her small oval face were like the faintly shimmering tip of a flame. She had done her jet black hair in a way I had never seen—pinned up at the back, parted in the middle at the front and drawn above her ears. The ends were made into finger puffs at the top of her head. I knew that it was daring, for when we took our table every woman in the room was looking at Victoria's coiffure. Most of them were frowsy in comparison; or, if they had made an attempt at fashion, wore the long ringlet over their shoulder, so that they gave the impression of having all studied the same wood-cuts in the same ladies' paper.

As Victoria's escort I felt boorish and awkward. I wore the suit in which I'd piloted the *Blair Anthony* to The Cascades although I had sneaked out of the hotel before supper and invested in a new shirt and scarf, and a pair of boots to replace the ones so long scuffed against the standard at the boat's wheel. Most of my discomfort grew from the fact that I was in a strange town—a metropolis, in fact—while I was a man who had lived upriver all his life. I felt exactly as I had when Mike Shea brought me into Dalles City for the first time.

But as I grew more accustomed to the dining room (it was certainly no finer than that of the Umatilla House, and the silver was not as good as Ainsworth put aboard the boats) and began to look around, I noticed that every man in the room was envious of my place with Victoria. It was plain in their eyes when they glanced our way; and the eyes of the women held that half wistful, half piqued look they reserved for a female they cannot help but admire.

With the champagne I grew less reserved and uncomfortable. I felt gay and carefree, and superior to all these men and women who did not pilot a steamboat, and have a fine new house in Dalles City, and enjoy the company of Victoria Hunt.

By the end of the supper I was giddy enough to need fresh air, and suggested to Victoria that we take a carriage ride. She was delighted with the idea, and sent up to her room for a shawl, and when we were inside the carriage she said, "I never knew you to talk so much, Caleb."

"It's the champagne. I'm not used to it. What did I say?"

Victoria laughed. "Don't you really remember?"

"No. I hope I wasn't making a fool of myself. You see, I—"

She put her cool fingers against my lips. "No, Caleb. You weren't making a fool of yourself. You were talking about the boats, and how the river looks in the early morning on the way to Lewiston. You should see your face when you talk about those things, Caleb."

I turned to her in the half-light of the carriage. "Why?"

"You're—you're beautiful when you talk like that."

I thought that she was making fun of me and my cheeks grew hot.

"I really mean it, Caleb," she said. "But I know you don't like it."

She was right. I felt stupid and silly and a little resentful that a woman should take such an advantage. "Where shall we drive?" I said.

Victoria drew closer to me, like a thrilled child. "Anywhere . . . I heard the waiter tell someone that there was a boat in from San Francisco. Shall we go down to the river and see it?"

I sat up most of that night, staring out of the window of the hotel and smoking stogies endlessly. The champagne still prickled inside my head and every nerve was taut. At first I was angry with myself because I could not go to sleep, but gradually I began to enjoy watching the changes in the night. I had seen the night changing on the river, and on the prairie, and in the mountains above the Clearwater. But I had never watched it change over the street of a town. Just below me was the tarred flat roof of a saloon and I watched it grow lighter after midnight, saw it take on just before dawn the dull sheen of worn silver. And the cobblestones of the street were never the same for an hour in succession and never echoed the sound of a hoof or a boot twice in the same way. There was more silence in the night of a town than in the night of the open, I decided. In the open there was no silence at all, but a steady muted symphony of moving leaves, and a million small things crawling, and the soft wind in the grass. There below the hotel window there was none of this—there was only a dead and empty silence occasionally broken, not by nature, but man. Only once, toward morning, was there a silence like that I knew; it came from the cobblestones and the wood of the buildings, the silence of rocks and forests.

Before dawn a thick gray fog rolled up the Willamette and pushed sidewise onto the town. Then I tried to sleep, taking off my coat and waistcoat and flopping on the bed. I didn't succeed, only half dozed, my mind still tramping over the last few hours like a man who has lost something and gone back to find it.

When the sun began to yellow the fog I got up, took a towel, and went down the hall to the men's bath. I had heard the chamber woman cleaning the tub at midnight, and no one had used it since. It was smooth and gleaming and smelled faintly of strong lye soap.

The scrubbing took the place of rest, and in half an hour I felt new again, although there was still a small nagging bubble of champagne in my left temple. I went down to the hotel bar, took a whiskey, and followed it with a cup of black coffee. If I had known how long I would have to wait for Victoria I would have followed the bitters with something considerably more substantial than coffee.

She appeared in the lobby at ten, not a moment later, announcing that she was famished for breakfast. "Famished!" I ridiculed. "I should think you'd be skin and bone. Do you know what time it is?"

"Of course. It's ten o'clock. I never am up before nine."

I blinked at the luxury, and wondered how she would feel when she was old, with only a little more time, and recalled that she had wasted an hour every day in dressing. Yet perhaps in the end she'd win, I told myself. Perhaps she'd grow old less quickly with such care. I'd seen her mother, weighted down beyond her years. I knew that Mary had lost the freshness she had once possessed. I had not thought of it before, but maybe Victoria was right—maybe it was as sinful for a woman to let drain the charms God had given her in her youth, as sinful as some claimed it to be to pamper them.

After breakfast I hired a carriage and we started on a round which wearied and dazzled me. At the breakfast table Victoria had me draw a sketch of the floors of the new house. When I finished, she studied them a moment, then said, "I can see it all, just as it ought to be."

I think I have never seen such a display of energy as I witnessed the rest of that day. Suddenly Portland seemed to me to be a town made up entirely of furniture shops, and certainly we visited all there were. At first Victoria tried to gather my ideas of how the house should be furnished, or of what Mary preferred, but at last she gave this up and went about her business as if I were not present. Most of the merchandise already in stock she spurned in high disdain. The shop owner would hopefully show her his wares, and then, realizing how difficult and adamant this customer was, reach for the catalogues which showed what could be ordered from San Francisco.

And late in the afternoon, when we had made the last purchase, and Victoria settled into the carriage seemingly as vital as when she started, she said, "Oh, Caleb—I've spent an awful lot of money for you! I forgot to ask how much you wanted to spend. Do you mind awfully?"

"It's all right. I wanted something nice. I can't tell you how grateful I am that you've helped me." I looked at my watch and found to my astonishment that it was after five. "Look," I said, holding out the timepiece. "We haven't bought a thing for your own place—and you planned to take the boat upriver tomorrow."

Victoria laughed. "I'm in no hurry. I'll take the next boat." She touched my arm. "Can't you stay over, too, Caleb? It's been so nice, and I sort of wanted you to help me decide some things about my place."

"I'm sure you did," I chided her. "You never let me open my mouth about my own."

"That was different," she answered slowly. "I—it didn't seem quite right for us to be planning that together. I'd rather just pretend I was doing it for your wife."

"I'm afraid I can't stay," I said quickly. "I'll have to report aboard the *Blair* for her next trip up."

"I wish you didn't. I really wish you didn't, Caleb." She sighed, quickly, cutting her sigh short as though she wanted to regret nothing. "But we've got tonight, haven't we?" She laughed up at me. "Champagne again?"

"Champagne," I said. "But not so much for me as last night. I'll be damned if I want you calling me beautiful again!"

She was searching my face, amused, and then suddenly all the mirth went out of her eyes. They became sober and eager and somehow frightened. The next thing I knew I held her in my arms and was pressing against her cool cheek with my lips.

"Caleb . . ." she whispered. "Caleb, darling, you mustn't." I kissed her mouth into silence, holding her slenderness fiercely, wanting to encompass her with myself, put her forever within me so that wherever I was I would have Victoria Hunt.

"Caleb, please . . . people are looking into the carriage."

I sat back, holding her close with one arm. "It had to happen," I said. "There was no way out of it. I've wanted you like that ever since I met you with Eph Baughman. I think I've always wanted you, Vicky, even when I was too young to know what was wrong with me."

The *clop-clop* of the carriage horse on the cobblestones drifted back to us, and we listened to it until it became meaningless and wild. "Remember the colored book you sent to me when you left?" Victoria said slowly.

"You actually remember that?"

She nodded against my shoulder. "I even remember the verses from it. '*At noon she would work with her needle sometimes, Or else a small drawing would make; Now and then when the weather was pleasant and fine, She a sketch of the landscape would take.'* I cried when I got the book."

"I thought you were a heartless little girl," I said.

We talked like that, trying to believe that we were the Caleb Paige and the Victoria Hunt who had pretended. But the carriage was taking us to the hotel, and we did not want to face it that this was no pretence.

I had the sense of being carried along, of being unable to alter the course of my life at this point. It was like striking downstream into a rapids on the river, watching the nose of the boat line up with a rock. You knew that there there was a place where a turn of the wheel could save you, where the rudder and the wheel and the very current which pressed you on would combine to bring you out of it. You knew that ahead lay disaster and that the sure way of safety was to reverse the paddles, yet you let yourself go on.

At the hotel I went directly to my room. I thought of leaving the hotel, of taking up a room somewhere else until the boat should sail on the morrow. As I paced across the room I caught sight of myself in the mirror. "You're lying," I said aloud. "You're trying to lie to yourself. You don't want to keep away from her—but you've got to. There's too much between you and Mary now, and this would break it. Even if she never knew, it would break it, because once you take Victoria you'll want her again, always, forever."

Then, protectively, my brain no longer seemed to function. I had nothing except an overwhelming desire for Victoria. Like a man in a trance I opened the door and walked down the hall to her room. I opened it, and there facing me she stood, one bare arm outstretched from her peignoir as though she had been reaching for the knob.

She came forward and lifted her face to mine. The cashmere rustled against me, like the crackling of the white flame of her body.

"I was coming to you, Caleb," she whispered.

CHAPTER 18

It was bitterly cold next day when, promptly at eleven, Wolf blew the *Wide West's* whistle for the lower landing at The Cascades. Earlier, as I had left the hotel in Portland and made my way to the river, the fog repeated itself. Observation Rock had been half obliterated in the mist, and the fog had hung in patches all the way upstream.

There was no let-up at The Cascades where the trees and underbrush were bright with a wet sheen. The six-mile trip on the portage train was like traveling through a dank cavern, for the trees on either side of the track were weighted and arched by the fog. I had been depressed all the way up on the *Wide West,* and The Cascades, with its memories of my parents, had never lightened my mood.

The *Blair Anthony* had her steam up and was waiting for me. I went directly to the pilot house, not mingling with the passengers, not even greeting Davidson, the purser. I was glad that Pat Henley, the pilot, was asleep in his cabin, and that the relief man had already gone ashore to take the portage train back to the lower landing. I wanted, more than anything else, to be alone, to do some thinking; and I was anxious to blast the signals and hear the gangplank clatter aboard, for I could think best at the wheel of the boat.

As we pushed our way toward Dalles City the fog patches persisted, some so thick that they would smother the nose of the *Blair*. I found myself, as usual when the weather was bad, bend-ing all my thoughts to the river. I cursed the lack of a clear day, for I had wanted a little respite in which to clear my brain. Last night was still like a dream, and I wanted to examine it in the light of day. I wanted to see where I stood when my blood had cooled, and the mists had cleared. But the mists, literally, were persisting.

"Good morning, Caleb. Have a good time down in the city?"

I started, not recognizing a voice that should have been as familiar as my own. Pat Henley stood in the doorway, ready to take his watch.

"It was all right," I said. Then I added, feeling utterly foolish for doing it: "It was just a business trip. Wanted to get some furniture for the new house."

Henley took the wheel and squinted through the frosted glass ahead of him. "This is damned early fog. Wouldn't be surprised if we had a Hell of a winter. The last two have been mild, and things usually average up." He turned and looked at me oddly. "Do you feel all right, Cap'n?"

"Why, yes. Why?"

"No reason. Except you seem quiet."

I'd never been given to much talk in the wheel house, but I knew what Henley meant. He'd sensed, without quite realizing it, my preoccupation. "I'm sort of hungry," I told him. "Didn't have any breakfast. I'll be more normal after dinner."

I didn't, however, go near the dining saloon. I sauntered aft and stood at the rail, watching the buckets, until a tail wind began to whip upstream, throwing spray at me. Driven to it, I went into the men's cabin and sauntered to the poker table. Four men were playing draw and I was on them before I realized that the one facing me directly was Kirt Inge. When I saw him I was so surprised that I went guiltily cold all over. But this passed at once when he raised his head, looked squarely at me and nodded once. I returned the greeting in kind, my lips compressed.

I wondered whether he had embarked at The Cascades, or had been aboard the *Wide West*. It could easily have been the latter without my knowing it, for I had bought a cabin and kept to it all the way to the lower landing at The Cascades. I was certain that if he had been to Portland he knew more than I cared to have him know. Even if he had taken to the river at The Cascades he must be speculating about my absence during Victoria's journey.

The men at the table with him were strangers; I could see that the game was irritating to Inge. They played carefully and slowly, and the stakes were not large. I imagined that he had hoped for a better opportunity. I watched the game awhile, solely because I did not want Inge to think that I was keeping out of his way, and finally I turned to leave the cabin. I heard Inge saying, "You gents are about even now. Would you mind if Captain Paige sat in on a little session with me?"

I turned back to meet Inge's gaze. "Are you willing, Paige?" he asked.

"My poker isn't the best," I told him slowly.

"If the stakes aren't too small, I won't be bored. As for your bein' rusty, it's a game of chance, you know." His voice was bland as butter, his eyes as impassive as always. The black gloved hand rested awkwardly on the green felt of the table.

"I'll play until my watch," I said, and sat down.

Inge held the cards in his good hand, looked at me questioningly and I nodded. He began the deal, his one hand blurring the card ends.

I was glad for the relief of the game, for I had no desire to go to my cabin during my time off watch. Yet I could not rid my mind of the feeling that he was trying to get at something, that his invitation was a prelude to a plan that lurked behind his tightly drawn face. But gradually I took a grateful interest in the cards, glad to have my mind diverted.

We played steadily for perhaps an hour, and Inge scarcely won a pot. This struck me as strange, and certainly it was unnerving, for I was not a good poker player—I knew only the rudiments of the game—and I had heard that Inge possessed uncanny luck together with, it was sometimes hinted in Dalles City, an acquired mechanical talent.

But at the end of an hour the luck began to run his way, slowly at first, with a hand here and there, and then steadily. He looked up at me and his mouth twisted into a mirthless smile. "I got a feeling it's my turn now, Paige," he said. His good hand paused as he drew in the cards for the deal. "But you've been running all right, too. Like to make a real bet?"

"Gambling isn't my line," I said.

"You'd take a challenge, wouldn't you?"

"That depends."

He gave the cards that lightning one-hand deal, set them in the center of the table for my cut. His smile was set now, and he began to deal. Slowly I picked up my hand, card by card, and found that I had received four aces from the deal. A feeling of relief swept over me, not at the hand I'd drawn, but because those aces seemed to mean that Inge wasn't gunning for me. I'd been afraid that he wanted to draw me into big stakes, take me with some trick I couldn't fathom, and of which I would dare not accuse him. I'd wondered, too, if perhaps he were not trying to maneuver me into an accusation so that he would have an excuse to shoot me down for the insult.

Those four aces settled my mind. I studied his face, but I might as well have attempted to discern an expression in a wall. His eyes took in the room, then he leaned across the table and said in a slow, even voice: "Paige, I need ten thousand dollars." He paused, leaned back. "Ten thousand dollars, Paige, against my leaving Dalles City for good."

I wondered if I'd heard aright. He said it again, "Ten thousand dollars against my getting out of Dalles City—*alone*. Wouldn't it be worth that to you, Captain?"

My inclination was to knock him out of the chair. But I was in command of the *Blair* and in no position to get into a brawl with a passenger over a card table. And I held four aces in my hand.

"All right," I said.

He leaned harder against his chair back so that it creaked in the stillness. In the chairs along the wall of the cabin men were reading, or dozing with hats over their eyes and mouths open. A far table held a four-handed game. But none was aware of the strange wager Inge and I had just made.

His eyes met mine. "Cards?" he said.

I had opened my mouth to stand pat when a strange shadow seemed to flick across his eyes. It could have been no more than an interruption of light from the cabin window, but so impassive was Inge that even that shadow startled me. I knew that some way he had me trapped—and then, out of my memory struggled up a tag end of a story Mike Shea had told me about a gambler. "The dealer gets himself a bobtailed flush, see?" I could hear Mike's voice, plain in my ear. "Say the nine, ten, Jack and Queen of clubs."

That was it—that was what Inge held across the table, and there was a way for him to fill it. He'd fill it whether I stood pat or drew one card.

"Cards?" said Inge again. His voice seemed to come from a great way off. The smoke of his stogie was thick beneath the lamp, dulling the green felt on the table. I was trying to think what Mike had told me, how that bobtailed flush would be filled. And suddenly it came to me. I knew that on top of that deck were the King and the eight of clubs. If I stood pat on four aces, Inge had the King to fill his flush. If I drew one card he'd have the eight.

And yet I could be wrong. Suppose Inge was playing it straight? Suppose he didn't know that I had four aces, and that the two cards on the deck were equally unknown to him?

"Cards?" Inge said again, his voice edged with impatience.

I took the chance. I tossed down two cards, one of them an ace. "Two." I watched Kirt's hand peel them off, and I drew them up. They were the King and the eight of clubs! I raised my eyes. Inge's face was underlaid with a dark purplish cast, but there was still not the movement of a muscle, nothing in the dead eyes.

I spread my three aces.

Inge said, "You win, Paige." He got up slowly, and I with him. "It will take me a little while, of course, to arrange things to get away," he added ironically. Then he walked out onto the deck.

When I returned to the pilot house I found Pat Henley leaning between the spokes of the wheel, his eyes actually bugging from his head.

"God damnedest fog I ever see for mid-afternoon," he said,

standing back, one hand on the wheel. "Take her over and you're welcome, Cap'n."

I took the wheel in my hands and looked out. We were at the broad curve in the river, just before the *Blair* would come abeam of Memaloose Island. Henley had been bearing toward the Washington shore, heading for the deep channel. Normally I could have seen the flat shore which marked the mouth of the Klickitat beyond and to port. But now I could see scarcely beyond the nose of the *Blair Anthony*. Until I had reached the wheel house I had been unaware that the fog was persisting. It must have been rolling in over the rail when I emerged from the men's cabin and made my way above, yet I wasn't conscious of it until I opened the door of the pilot house and saw Pat Henley getting his head between the knobs of the wheel, trying to pierce through the fog patches by the sheer force of his Irish will.

I set my feet apart and tested the rudders. I was grateful for the Gates gear that made the big wheel easy in my hands, but I reflected that in the old days, when the *Wright* was first built, I could have known where we were by the feel of the current against the rudders. As it was now, I could easily be fooled. I had to watch the openings in the fog patches sharply, so as to verify my feeling, based partly upon instinct and partly upon the element of time, that we were about to come abreast of Memaloose, the old Indian burial ground.

To starboard an open place appeared in the fog, and through it I saw the white sloping sands, dotted with sage, of Memaloose. I pushed the wheel a little to port, took out my watch and laid it on the ledge of the pilot house window and there I held it while the seconds ticked off, and the minutes, and finally I let her come back —and watched through the fog to catch the sight of the Klickitat's flat mouth.

Darkness was hurried by the fog, and on the forward deck I got a glimpse of one of the boys coming up from below, shielding a taper, on his way to light the *Blair's* lamps. In my mind I followed him, through the dining room, and the ladies' cabin, and then into the men's cabin. I could see him going along the deck, knocking at cabin doors, asking if light was wanted. I smiled at the thought of him, bringing light all over the boat except to me, except to the captain, who needed it most.

Actually a lamp in the wheel house would have reflected against the windows, made it more difficult than ever to see outside. Navigating the Columbia in that thick rain-fog was like navigating the river at night, and nobody but a fool attempted that unless his cargo was only cattle.

I did not mind. Rather I was thankful for the darkening wall outside. It forced me to keep my mind on the river. It made it impossible for me to think of anything else. Somehow I sensed that they were all clamoring to get inside the pilot house with me, those thoughts of Mary, and the house I'd built, and Kirt Inge—and Vicky. But they couldn't gain entrance. They couldn't gain entrance, because the *Blair* had to be taken upriver to Dalles City and the fog mist was thick outside.

I did not hear the door of the pilot house open. If the weather had been clear, if the wind had been howling up astern, clearing the river of mist or rain or smoke haze, I would have known when the door opened. I would have heard the howl, and felt the bite of it at my legs. But with the fog patches there was no wind. There was no sound beyond the decks except the sound of the current, and that was in my ears always, even above the throb of the engine below me.

No sound of wind, no draft against me as I stood at the wheel—and yet I began to feel that someone had entered the wheel house. I knew that someone was there, in the darkness, and at the same time I knew that I must not turn, that if I turned now I would never again get my face toward the river. Someone had crept into the wheel house and was watching me, was waiting to see if I gave a sign that I knew he was there. The skin on my back began to crawl, and beneath my cap I could feel the cold sweat forming on my forehead.

I knew why he did not shoot, or plunge a knife into my back. Outside the fog was thick, and as yet he could not see me clearly against the windows of the pilot house. He would have to come closer, and before he came closer he wanted to be sure that I did not know he was there.

With the greatest difficulty I kept from turning, for I wanted to know if I was right, or if my mind was only playing tricks. I might turn, I thought, and find nothing in the darkness—and then I could laugh, sheepishly, and tell myself that my nerves were shot to pieces and that I must ask Ainsworth for a holiday. But I had to know. The night was creeping in fast over the edges of the basalt cliffs; unopposed by the weak sun, the fog mist was thickening. I could not stand there with even a part of my brain wondering what was lurking in the pilot house. Three minutes, two, would mean disaster for the *Blair*.

I had been letting her have full steam, because the current whipped hard against us at that point and I felt sure of myself. But now I decided to bring her to half, yelling it through the speaking tube. I hoped that in reaching for the speaking tube I could get at the revolver—at the weapon Lawrence Coe had given me—always on the window ledge. But most of all I hoped that half-ahead would save us, for I was sure that whoever was in that pilot house was going to kill me. In my mind I could see the wheel spinning. I could hear the splintering of wood as the *Blair's* nose struck and the paddles exploded into a thousand pieces out astern.

I took a deep breath, so that my voice would not shake, and reached for the tube in the darkness. *"Half speed. . . . Half speed."* I spoke it slowly, distinctly, and the engineer's voice squeaked it back at me, like an echo, through the tube. Then I hung the mouth of the tube on its rack, and as my hand came back I brought Coe's revolver with it and held it against the wheel.

I was sure now that Kirt Inge was there, at my back. He had never meant to leave Dalles City. He had hoped to bilk me of ten thousand dollars by cheating at poker; and now, rather than welsh, he was going to kill me.

The thought of Inge being there, squatting somewhere in the blackness, waiting to find his target, made me forget all my caution. I spun around, one hand on the wheel, the other clutching Coe's pistol, and fired at a shadow that seemed deeper than the rest.

Almost at the same instant there was a gurgling scream, and a flash of flame against the darkness. Then there was no sound except the engine below me, and I turned back, trembling in every fiber, to take up the speaking tube and order full ahead.

Pat Henley, whose cabin was in the Texas behind the wheel house, heard the shots and the scream. Almost instantly he was in the doorway, without a coat, and shirtless, his white wool underwear looming against the night outside.

"Cap'! Cap', what's up?"

Before I had a chance to answer he was lighting the lamp, holding it below the windows so as not to impair my vision outside. I glanced down at the floor. It wasn't Kirt Inge who lay there. It was Deb Snyder, a deck hand!

The ball I had sent into the darkness had caught him full in the throat, and the floor around my feet was glistening wet. In one outstretched hand lay a pistol, and the other arm, broken in his fall, was stretched grotesquely under him.

Pat Henley crossed himself, then stared up at me, his face white. "Mary, mother of Jesus!" he said. "What was between you and Deb?"

There had been nothing between us, I thought. And then, realizing I hadn't answered Pat, I said it aloud.

CHAPTER 19

AINSWORTH was at Dalles City on the first possible boat after he had heard of the death of Deb Snyder. I had expected him, and I met him in Larry Coe's office at the wharf landing. He shut the door and we stood there in the little room, facing each other. He wasted no time in preliminaries.

"This hasn't happened before on the line," he said, looking straight at me. "Do you regret it?"

"I can't very well regret it, sir. The man was going to shoot me in the back. He was endangering the lives of the passengers as well as mine."

"Was there any reason why he should have wanted to shoot you in the back?"

"None that I know of," I said.

He looked out of the window at the river, saying nothing for a moment. Then: "All right, Paige. Maybe this will teach the deck hands they're not to try to pick up extra money on the run. We pay them good wages." I looked at him. There wasn't the ghost of a smile on his face. "I'm sending Snyder's widow a check for two thousand." With that he went out of the office and boarded the *Blair*. I took him downriver to The Cascades, and did not encounter him again on the trip.

With the town I was not to get off so easily. Since the first steamboat had ruffled the waters of the middle river there had been no killings on the boats, and while everyone along the Columbia recognized the right of a captain to put down mutiny with whatever heroic measures necessary, there was plenty of talk about the death of Snyder.

His reputation was neither good nor bad; and he had not been with the O.S.N. Company long. Still, he had been a deck hand, and as a class they were a happy, friendly lot; and the mystery of why Deb Snyder was in the pilot house intent upon killing me had never been fully explained. I think that Pat Henley suspected, yet he never mentioned why he believed Deb Snyder had been paid to murder me. "He was a queer one," Pat would lie cheerfully when he was asked about the matter along the street or in the Umatilla House or Vic Trevitt's saloon. "A queer one, Deb Snyder was, God rest his soul. Probably got the idea some way that Caleb Paige was against him—though why I wouldn't know, for on the whole river there isn't a softer hearted captain with his men."

Surely no man ever had more on his conscience than I when, a month later, I went to the Deschutes landing to meet Mary and the boy. All the way to the Deschutes on the portage train I wondered how much of my guilt was showing in my eyes. I wondered what a man could go through without having it written upon his face, to be seen there by those who knew him best. I stood there on the wharf landing half fearfully, watching for the black plume of the *Harvest Queen,* waiting for the signal of her landing. But when I saw Mary at the rail, holding in the reckless young Henry, I knew at once that she suspected nothing. That she had heard of Snyder's death I could see at once, and it obliterated any other feeling she might have had.

I stood at the foot of the gangplank, waiting, and Mary and the boy were among the first to land. Mary came hurrying down the plank and scarcely waited for my kiss before crying, "Caleb—Caleb, I heard you were in trouble."

"It's nothing, Mary," I said, leading her and the boy away from the crowd.

Her blue eyes went wide. "You—they said you killed him, Caleb."

"If I hadn't, I wouldn't be here now."

Henry's hand tugged at my coat. "Did you kill a man, Papa?"

Mary hushed him with a horrified sound. She held close to me as we walked to the portage train. "Have you been well?" she asked. "You look so—so gone."

"Naturally I haven't liked the Snyder business."

"Caleb, will it cause you any trouble? They were talking about it even in Walla Walla. And on the boat. What did Captain Ainsworth say?"

"I've seen him. Everything is all right."

When we were settled in the portage train with Henry between us, Mary said, "I suppose you haven't been home at all? I suppose you've been living at that old Umatilla House?"

"Yes," I admitted. "I—it's lonesome at the house when you and Henry are gone." I looked at her and managed a smile. "You wait," I said. "Wait until we get to town. I've a surprise."

Mary looked at me oddly. She had never liked surprises; she liked everything to be planned. "What do you mean, Caleb?"

"You wait." I reached over Henry's legs and patted her hand.

"I rode a horse at Grandpa's," said Henry.

"Did you, son?"

"I rode all over the ranch—and I brought in the cows."

Mary smiled. "He does so enjoy himself at papa's."

"Heinrich's getting better?"

Her face clouded. "He'll never be really well, Caleb."

Henry was worn out from his trip on the *Harvest Queen*, and now, lulled by the rhythmic swing of the portage car, he went sound asleep against Mary. She drew his coat up around his legs, and said in a low voice, "Are you sure there won't be trouble about the—the deck hand?" She looked at me oddly. "Caleb . . . you don't seem sorry that you did it."

"I'm not. Oh, I wish it hadn't happened, naturally. But the man was trying to kill me. It was either him or me, don't you understand?"

For a moment she said nothing. "It's frightening that he wanted to kill you, Caleb. He must have believed he had some reason."

"Certainly he believed he had a reason," I answered. My guilt edged my tone with impatience, and I added quickly, "I mean, he probably decided that he wasn't being fairly treated. He may have been angry at the company, and wanted to take it out on me." The words turned weak as water; I hated the lie too much to give it any force.

"Let's forget this Deb Snyder business," I said.

She nodded, holding Henry closer against her. "All right, dear. I do think it's best—the less we say about it, for Henry's sake. Only . . . please do be careful, Caleb."

I tried to analyze the tone of that plea, to fathom if Mary had heard more than she was letting me know. It would be like her to say nothing, even if she knew what lay behind Deb Snyder's attempt to do me in. I wished she would come out with whatever was on her mind. I felt in the devil's own fix, for certainly I had no wish to make her unhappy—or, if you will, paint myself unfaithful—and if she did not already suspect the truth I did not intend to give her any clue. On the other hand, if she knew the truth, or had guessed at it, I wanted her to let me have it.

I struggled all the way into Dalles City, and once or twice I was on the verge of confessing that the reason Deb Snyder was after me was because Inge had paid him. And that Inge was jealous because Victoria Hunt and I had been in Portland together. Then it would be over, and done with. There'd be nothing on my mind and nothing between us. I didn't want to be moving into the new house with this thing in the shadows. I wanted the new house to be the beginning of a new way of living for Mary and me.

But I didn't make that confession to Mary. I was afraid of it. I knew too well what might happen, before even we'd had a chance to start again. No, I decided, the way to do would be to wait—wait years, if necessary, and then say to Mary, "Once I was very foolish. . . ." And after the years had passed there might be no reason to tell her at all. It might be better never to tell her; for, after all, it would concern a Caleb Paige who had nothing to do with the Caleb Paige she would know then, older and more settled and forgetful of his youth.

Then suddenly the portage train was abreast of the Umatilla House and chugging slowly into the station by the landing. I roused Henry, and held out a hand for Mary.

"We'll take a carriage," I said, and when we stepped from the portage train I left Mary and the boy while I went across the street to Patterson's and hired an open buggy.

Mary protested. "I'm not really tired and it's so short a way."

"It's a longer way to where we're going," I laughed, helping them in beside me.

Henry was quite impressed by my control over the mare. "Can you drive a horse, Papa?" he enquired.

"Your father is a very versatile fellow," I told him jocularly. "I'm afraid you don't appreciate me." My spirits were rising at the thought of their witnessing the house for the first time. Deliberately I took the most devious way, driving first the length of the main street, then cutting up toward the hill.

"Where are you going?" Mary wanted to know when she saw I wasn't heading for the cottage.

"To show you the surprise."

"Caleb, I wish you wouldn't be so maddening. What is it you are so mysterious about? We ought to get Henry home. He's dead tired after the trip and should be in bed."

"We won't be long," I told her.

Piqued at my stubbornness, she lapsed into silence and this was what I wanted; I was afraid she might lead me into letting the cat out of the bag before we reached the place. On the upper road I reined the mare south and topped the rise. Now we could see the house, and the drive, and the poplars and alders in the front.

Mary exclaimed, "Who would be wanting to build such a big place 'way up here?"

"It isn't so far," I said. "Dalles City is going to grow, you know."

"But who built it?"

"Some fellow here in town. I can't think of his name." I let the mare saunter abreast of the place, then turned her suddenly into the drive.

"Caleb, what are you doing? They may have moved in already."

"I don't think so. Wouldn't you like to see it?"

The sound of the buggy wheels on the gravel of the drive was pleasant in my ears. The house loomed big and proud with its gables and its cupola on the top. The gray sides glistened, and from the place came a clean odor of paint and newly planed wood.

Just in front of the porch I drew in the reins, looped them over the whip-socket and leaped down to the drive. "Come on," I said, holding out my hands. "Let's go in!"

Mary looked at me, her eyes wide with unbelief, and then she looked up at the house. "Come on, Henry," I cried. "Let's go inside before it gets too dark. The lamps aren't in yet."

Mary's wondering gaze had returned to mine. "Caleb—Caleb, you haven't . . ."

"Indeed I have! It's yours. Every bit of it yours and Henry's!"

She just sat there, saying nothing, and it suddenly occurred to me that I'd given her a pretty big surprise to take all at once. Perhaps, I thought, I should have broken it to her a little bit on the portage train.

"Come on," I said, taking her hand. "I'll show you inside."

Like one in a daze she came onto the porch with me, watched me unlock the big door with its frosted glass picture. "Look at the cow," Henry said. "Look at it, Mamma."

"That's a stag, son," I laughed, and swung open the door. "We'll name him Buck! I'm sorry the furniture isn't here, Mary. I ordered it from Portland. Everything just for this house, all figured out the way it ought to be. There'll be a big lamp hanging here, and portieres between the hall and the sitting room. . . ."

I took her from room to room, explaining the wood work, and what the furniture would be—as nearly as I could recall it from Victoria's flying journey through the stores. Downstairs, and upstairs, room by room we went, poor Henry's barrage of questions drowned out by my own enthusiastic monologue.

Then I took Mary to the window of our bedroom upstairs and showed her how it looked out over the yard and toward the river. "There's still a better view from the cupola. But the stairs haven't been put in yet. The workmen will be all finished by the end of the week, and the furniture—most of it, anyhow—ought to be here by then. We should be able to move in by Monday or Tuesday."

I turned to her. "Well, what do you think of it? I haven't given you a chance to say a word. Of course, we can make changes if you—"

"Oh, no, Caleb. It's—it's very nice." Her voice sounded small and light, not at all the way I had expected. "It must have cost a lot."

"Not a dollar more than it's worth. And I should have done it long ago instead of letting you be cooped up the way you were."

She looked at me, her eyes oddly lost, and then turned her head toward the window again. A hundred yards beyond the carriage road was the edge of the deep channel of the Columbia, and far across in a blue haze was the north shore.

"Oh, Caleb . . . !" It was a sobbing little cry, as she turned swiftly, her eyes filled with tears. "Caleb, why did you do it?"

For one scant, foolish second I thought that she was sobbing for joy, and then like a blow in the face I got the truth in those frightened, bewildered eyes. I could only stand there witless, not knowing what to say or do.

"Caleb, I—it's hard to say, to tell you what makes me feel this way when you have tried so hard to please me."

I nodded slowly. "I know," I said dully.

"But you don't, Caleb," she said. Then, very slowly, like a small child unsure of her words: "It—it just seems so wasteful, Caleb. I could be as happy in that cottage as I could anywhere in this awful place with everyone thinking of the river and gold, and the children running loose on the wharf landings—and my own husband having to—to kill a man. Why should you think you could change it all with a fine big house, Caleb?"

I did not answer. I turned and went down the stair, and Henry's voice drifted after me. "Don't you want to live here, Mamma? Mamma, are we going to live here?" I went out and down the steps and climbed into the buggy and waited.

From the buggy I could still hear Henry's voice, echoing in the big empty house; and then I heard Mary cautioning him not to talk on the way home, "because Papa does not feel well."

As wordless as the puzzled Henry I drove down the hill to the rented cottage. It looked pitifully dejected and snubbed. I reached into my pocket and handed Mary the key. "I'll take the buggy to Patterson's. Do you want me to light the lamps for you before I go?"

"No, I can manage." She got out of the carriage and helped Henry down. "You won't stay in town tonight, will you?"

"Of course not. But I don't want to keep the mare and buggy all night."

She reached out and touched my arm. "I'm sure I will like the house, Caleb. I am sorry for what I said. It was only that at first it seemed so big and strange."

I sat motionless until she took her hand away, and then I slapped the mare's rump and started down the hill to Front Street.

CHAPTER 20

When I drove into Patterson's an oddly familiar figure hobbled out of the manure-smelling shadows to greet me

"So there you are, you crazy nickel-plated galoot!"

It was the unmistakable roar of Michael Shea, and never had I been more glad at the sound of a man's voice! "Caleb, God damn you, I chased up to your tepee and nobody was there. Then they told me you built yourself a castle on the hill and I hired a rig and went up there. Nobody was there, neither—so I just came back here to wait until you brought Bert's rig in."

I jumped down from the buggy seat and grabbed his thick arms. In the half-light of the stable's single lantern, Mike's face was haggard and worn. There were great bags under his bleary eyes, and his mouth was trembling like the mouth of an old man. Time had not done well by Mike Shea, and a pang of regret shot through me for not having searched him out oftener since last we had talked together in Galbreath's.

"How in the Hell are you, Caleb?" he bellowed, pounding me hard on the shoulder.

"Fine as a frog's hair," I told him. "When did you get in?"

He grinned. "I came down on the *Harvest Queen*, same trip as your missus and the boy. My God, I couldn't believe that kid was yours, he was so big. But I reco'nized Mary—and I guess it's been a while since I been in Dalles City, at that." He added quickly, "I steered clear of your family, don't worry."

"But why, Mike?"

"I just figured I'd better," said Mike cryptically. "And anyhow, I got something to talk with you about, bucko. I was goin' to wait 'til you got the missus and the kid home and then sneak you outside alone."

"Come on down to Trevitt's. I'll buy you a drink and you can talk your head off."

We went to the back room where Bert lay lazily on a battered Army cot and paid him for the buggy hire. "You mountaineers keep out o' trouble," he said, thrusting the money into his breeches without rising. "The Irishman's got the old glint in his eyes—an' I bet that there peg leg is hollow so he can hold twice as much liquor as he ever did before!"

I saw Mike wince, and I slipped out into the dark of the stable to let him follow. At the wide doorway Mike held my arm. "We better not go to Trevitt's," he said.

"Why not?"

"It just ain't a good idea, that's all."

"But why, Mike?" I thought he was still thinking about his peg leg and I was scheming how to get a couple of drinks into him so he'd forget about it.

He looked at me queerly. "You mean you ain't heard what's being talked?"

"Talked? I don't know what you mean."

The big Irishman sighed patiently. "Look, you idiot, you killed a deck hand deader than Hell, didn't you?"

"Yes, but—"

"Well, they're after you."

"Who?"

"The deck hands. Who'd you think?"

I laughed and tried to get Mike to walk on toward Trevitt's Mount Hood Saloon. "You're crazy. I've been making trips all month on the *Blair* and nobody's looked at me cross-eyed."

Mike stood stolidly with his feet wide apart and his big fists on his hips. "Look here, you probably never got out of the wheel house or the dining saloon. How in the Hell do you know what the deck hands are talking about? Not all of 'em are after you, maybe —but enough of 'em to shoot you so full of holes that nobody could tell your phiz from your rear end. I just happened to get wind of it on the wharf landing at Wallula, so I hopped aboard the *Harvest Queen* and came down. I did a little card playin' below deck on the boat and made a few gentle enquiries. Some of those boys ain't very much in favor of captains shooting deck hands. They figure it wouldn't be healthy to let one get away with it."

"Mike, you're talking a lot of foolishness," I said. "I had to shoot Deb Snyder, and even then I wouldn't have shot to kill if it hadn't been so dark I had to take a wild chance. Ainsworth knows it, and so does everybody else on the river with any sense."

Mike drew a long breath and his eyes were like little slits as he grew indignant at my stubbornness. "Look, Caleb, don't it occur to that thick skull of yours that somebody might be eggin' them on?"

"What makes you think that?"

"I don't think anything. I know what I'm talkin' about. I suppose you ain't got the faintest notion who the bucko might be."

"You mean—"

"The gent who cracked your head open with that phony hand, and paid Deb Snyder to kill you."

I said nothing; Mike took my silence for disbelief. "If you're not convinced," he said, "maybe I could think of another reason why that gent would want to have the boys stage a little hangin' bee on a certain captain. Oh, I hear a thing or two in Walla Walla, bucko! The boats still go up the river, even if you ain't taking the *Wright* up there any more."

"That's all right, Mike. But even if what you say is true, there isn't any reason why we shouldn't have a drink at Trevitt's. I can't be hiding out because Inge is trying to incite some deck hands to a hanging."

"No," agreed Mike, "you don't have to hide out. But also you don't have to stick your head into the noose by bein' around the streets at night when deck hands are loading up on Dutch courage. This thing will probably blow over in another month and then you can forget it."

"Mike," I laughed, "I think it's all blown over right now. I think it's all in your head." I shook him by the shoulder. "Damn you,

Mike, did you come down here just to take care of me?"

"You *need* takin' care of," Mike said, abashed. "And anyhow I haven't forgotten what you did when those damned Disunionists were after me—or about the raft, either."

"You're full of blarney, Mike. The only reason you came to Dalles City was to see Lottie Moore. I knew you couldn't stay away forever. She's still around, Mike, and pretty as ever."

Mike's face twisted so suddenly that I thought he had been stricken. "I've seen her," he said, his voice guttural with bitterness. "I saw her when the train got in. She was walkin' down toward the Umatilla House and she saw me comin' up the street. I know she saw me and I know she recognized me, because I saw the look of her face when she seen this God damned leg. So I just slipped into the entrance of the Umatilla House and waited. I knew if she wanted to talk to me she'd stop." Mike paused and looked at me fiercely, as if I were responsible for all the vagaries of all the women in the world. "She just walked past," he said. "She went by like I wasn't there—because she figured I hadn't seen her."

I tried to argue him out of it, although in my heart I knew he had things right. "You were always a damned fool about that leg, Mike. Lottie probably never saw you at all. I think you've got her wrong. Even if she's still good looking, Mike, she's not as young as she used to be. I'll bet she'd be ready to go up to Walla Walla with you and settle on a farm. Remember Cora Leeds? She did that, over in Canyon City. Married Bill Heppner and they got two kids." Mike's stare was so pitifully hopeful that I kept on. "Cora makes Bill a fine wife, too, they say."

"That's a funny thing now," said Mike, almost eagerly. "That's just what I been thinking about, off and on. Caleb, if only I could get down to Portland and get one of those wood legs that you could put a boot on, it wouldn't be bad. You'd hardly notice it, and a woman wouldn't be ashamed to be seen around with me. I'm all right every other way, damn it all. I'm just as good a man in bed as I ever was!"

On the strength of that boast I almost got Mike in Vic Trevitt's, but after a moment's consideration he decided against it. "Here's what we'll do," he said. "I'll go on down to Trevitt's and buy a bottle and we'll come back here to Patterson's."

I refused to hide in a livery stable during this process and told Mike that I'd compromise. "I'll go with you to buy the bottle, and then if it'll make you any more comfortable I'll come back here with you."

I still believed that Mike was imagining things, but I no longer wanted to discount his belief that the deck hands were after me. He'd jumped aboard the *Queen* and come down to warn me of trouble, and if it made him feel any better I was for it. Lottie Moore's avoidance of him had cut deep, and now if I discounted his help poor Mike would have his feelings hurt beyond repair.

We were not halfway to Trevitt's when we heard a commotion up the street, near Madam de Bilk's, and I turned to see a knot of men forming a darker clot in the shadows of the desreputable shacks beyond.

I felt Mike's hand on my shoulder. "That's them now," he said. "We'd better get to the boat landing. They won't touch you on the *Blair*."

I shook my head. "If there's going to be any more trouble, I don't want it to be on the boat."

"Then for the love of Mary let's get our backs up against something," Mike said, and started me back toward the livery stable.

They saw us in the half light of the street, and I heard one of them shout, "There he is—I told you he'd be bringing the buggy back to Patterson's." They crossed the street and began moving up the walk toward us, and when we reached the entrance of the stable they were perhaps half a block away and I could hear distinctly the dull monotone of their mutterings.

"They're all drunk as skunks," Mike said. "Have you got a gun?"

"Yes, but—"

"By God you'd better get ready to use it. I'll get Bert's rifle and tell him to douse his lamp."

We dodged into the stable and I stood in the darkness against one of the stalls. Mike slid back to the rear room and I saw the crack of light as the door opened. It was almost instantly extinguished and I heard Bert's alarmed, "What's up, Mike?" Then came the soft tap of Mike's peg leg on the manure-matted boards of the stable, and I felt his shoulder against mine.

"Stick tight," he whispered, "and let them make all the moves."

Out of the darkness the wide doorway of the livery stable began to loom lighter; and then, just as my eyes were accustomed to it, the opening was darkened by a mass of men. I could not tell how many there were, for they stood close together, pressed into one hulking giant.

The mumbling stopped and out of the silence came a voice, "We saw you go in there, Paige. Somebody was with you. We want you to come out alone—and if you don't, we'll come after you."

Mike's big hand touched my mouth.

"You'd better send him out of there, Patterson. Because we're comin' in and shoot him down in the dark like he shot Deb Snyder."

"Hell, I thought we was goin' to *hang* him," enquired a very drunken voice. A roaring laugh went up from the dark mass there in the doorway.

Suddenly Mike boomed out beside me, "Captain Paige ain't coming to the orders of a bunch of drunken deck hands. And if you set foot through that door there's enough of us here to blow you to Hell."

This was considered in a moment of silence, then: "He's a-lyin' to you, Pete. There's only two of them in there, and maybe Bert Patterson. If Bert gets his nose into this we'll burn his God damned stable down." The man raised his voice. "Did you hear that, Bert? We'll burn your God damned place down, that's what we'll do."

"I'll talk to them," I said to Mike, and started forward.

He sent his elbow into the pit of my stomach. "Don't move, you damned fool!" he whispered hoarsely. "They mean business." Then aloud he flung at them again, "Did you lizards get that straight? Cap'n Paige ain't coming out to your orders—and if you step in here you'll get drilled, singly or all at once, whichever way you like it."

There was more muttering within that dark mass, and from behind the crowd came an enquiry as to whether the men up front were scared. "What the Hell did we come here for, anyhow? You'll fool around until we're jugged. Get the son of a bitch out o' there and let's string him up."

Suddenly the men at the back of the mob began shoving forward, thrusting half a dozen from the pack and spilling them into the darkness of the stable. One sprawled so close that his outstretched hand touched my boot and I let the back of his head have the heel of it. I saw a spurt of flame, and then I heard Mike's gun explode, and the mob moved back into itself again.

I had not fired. Consciously I had fought against pulling that trigger again in the darkness. Bert's horses were kicking up a lively fuss, letting out screaming whinnies and splitting the stall planking until the whole place rang with their din.

I drew a deep breath and shouted, "Now get on your way, before we let you have it right!" I put into that bravado threat all the authority I had learned on the boats, for I knew that in that instant, if ever, they might waver. If they came again now it would be all up with me. Not one word more would work, nor one more shot more into their midst. I stood waiting, the sweat pouring down my nose and salting my dry lips.

They stood outside the stable, mumbling angrily. Every second was precious, for surely those shots would bring some curious out of the saloons and the Umatilla House at the corner.

And then, almost as if at a signal, they melted into Front Street's shadows. In a great burst of relief I turned in the darkness. "Mike! Mike, they've given it up!"

There was no answer. I put out my hand and encountered nothing. *"Mike!* Mike, what's happened?" With a sickening fear I remembered that flash which came out of the mob the moment before Mike's weapon had answered. *"Mike! Mike, for God's sake!"* I got down on my hands and knees, searching wildly in the damp straw.

He was whispering when I found him, belly down and head toward the street. I turned him over and took up his head, yelling at the top of my voice for Bert Patterson.

But Mike's whispering was growing fainter, and I bent to catch it. "Don't put me down there without a decent leg, will you, Caleb?" He said it again, running all the words together in one gasping breath. Then that great, crazy, stubborn head rolled in my arms and Mike sighed, as if he were afraid I hadn't heard.

Quickly I answered him. "One you can put a boot on, Mike. The finest—the finest God damned leg they've got!"

CHAPTER 21

WHEN Bert and I had put Mike on Bert's cot in the back room, I rushed blindly out of the stable and through the straggling crowd drawn into the street by the sound of the shots. I knew in my mind that Mike was dead, but there was a wild hope in my heart that there might be still the breath of life in him. I struck out as fast as I could go for Father Bell's cottage at the edge of town, and I brought him back, perspiring in his black robe, at the same pace—for the old man was as anxious as I that Mike make his peace before he died.

But Doc Bryan was there before us. He shook his head at the wheezing, red-faced priest.

"I want to wait two days before the services," I said.

The old man was surprised. "Two days? Did Mike have some relatives who would like to be here?"

"No. No—but there is something I have to get for him. Something that will have to come up from Portland on the boats."

I got Mary and the boy out of town the next morning, for after the deck hands had left Patterson's livery stable they had taken out the remainder of their feelings in smashing windows in the new house. I knew that as long as their talk ran high it was not safe to leave Mary and Henry in the cottage alone, and I was determined to make my trips on the *Blair Anthony* as though nothing had happened.

Father Bell arranged everything for Mike's funeral, and I resented so his sticking to the rule of his faith that I let him do it gladly. It seemed to me that he owed Mike something, and that certainly Mike should be given the dignity of having a priest worry about his burial. There was only one thing that I did, and that was the thing Mike had asked me to do. I ordered an artificial leg up from Portland, a carved leg with a metal joint at the knee, and a wooden foot. From Max Vogt's I bought the finest pair of boots in the place. I bought a new suit, too, at Max's, and a pleated shirt and black tie; and I took them to Sol Bender's, the upholsterer and undertaker, so that he could fix Mike up.

Then I went to The Golden Rule to see Lottie Moore. I knew that she'd heard of Mike's death, but I pretended that she hadn't. "Mike always liked you," I said. "I thought perhaps I ought to be sure you knew."

The biggest floral piece at Mike's funeral was from Lottie. I heard later that it cost her more than a hundred dollars, and I knew how it would have pleased Mike to have the most expensive offering come from Lottie Moore. There was a wreath from The Golden Rule, too, ordered from Portland at the same time as Lottie's—and except for Lottie's it was the most pretentious of all the floral offerings Mike Shea got.

Of course, Father Bell had not blessed the ground where Mike rested, and no priest after him would be blessing it.

But Mike Shea had shed his own blood on the manure rotted floor of Bert Patterson's livery stable for a man he loved. I think that whatever ground his big bones found, at the last, would become as holy as any of God's earth.

CHAPTER 22

GRADUALLY the feeling among the deck hands subsided. Yet I knew somehow that Inge was along the river, or that he would return soon, and when I got ashore I was never relaxed. Whenever the *Blair* docked I took up the old pistol Coe had given me and put it in my side pocket. I formed the habit of walking along the street with my right fist clutched around it.

With Mary and the boy gone, I did not use the cottage but took a room at the Umatilla House. The furniture for the new house arrived and I left it in the company warehouse. I had not even repaired the windows the deck hands had smashed. I visited the place only once; and then only to see what damage had been done. When I looked at it then it had been only wood and paint and there were no dreams in it for me.

My life became a routine, restricted thing. The moment I debarked from the *Blair* I walked into the Umatilla, had supper, smoked a stogie in the lobby, and then went upstairs to bed. In the morning I would have breakfast and step aboard the *Blair* for the trip downriver. Every Saturday I wrote Mary, and every week I received an answer in a stilted style which told nothing of how she felt. All I could gain from her letters was that she was not discontented with her exile and that Henry was having a fine time on the Kiessling ranch.

All the remainder of that summer I did not see Victoria, but I had heard that she was at The Cascades in her new house. Curiously, I had no desire to see her now. The death of Mike had numbed me, and the anger of the deck hands had made me feel much less secure as a river captain. I wanted more than anything else to be let alone. There was only one man in the world now with whom I wanted to talk. That man was Thomas Condon, and he had left his parish at Dalles City to become a teacher of geology at the University.

In early October I got a letter from Mary which began: *What I have been fearing has happened. Papa died at two o'clock this morning. The end came very peacefully, in his sleep. . . .*

It was on that day that Lawrence Coe walked up to me as I stood at the Umatilla House bar and said, "Two hundred cattle are being driven into town tonight for shipment to Portland."

I knew immediately what that meant. The *Idaho,* the reserve boat, was too small to handle two hundred head of cattle. They were putting the *Idaho* on the passenger run and ordering the *Blair Anthony* downriver with the cattle. It would be a night trip, so that the beef could reach the Upper Cascades and be loaded on the lower boat by mid-morning.

I looked out of the window. The pane was black as pitch. "It's a fine night to be making a cattle boat out of the *Blair,*" I said to Coe.

Coe shrugged. "Maybe the sun was shining down at Portland when the order went out."

"Tom Stump would tell you where to go if he thought the boat would be in danger."

"You're not Tom Stump," the agent grinned. "The cattle will be loaded by midnight."

"I'll be there."

"There'll be a light on the Upper Cascades landing," Coe said.

All that afternoon the snow sifted down, until the street was covered except for the wet-brown trails of the wagon wheels. At five o'clock I went down to the wharf landing and watched the big river swallowing up the white flakes. Aboard the *Blair Anthony,* below decks, was the sound of hammering. They were setting up the bulwarks for the cattle, shielding off the engines, bulkheading at bow and stern. It would be strange to be piloting the *Blair* downriver with no passengers, with her cabins ghost-like, and that milling herd of animals below. But it pleased me to be taking the beef down toward the coast, just as it had first excited me to be taking gold dust out of Lewiston. The time was past when we needed cattle in the interior; now we were furnishing food for the outside.

At midnight I met Pat Hanley on the wharf landing and we went aboard the *Blair* amid the lowing of the frightened herd. "I had the divil's own time gettin' away," Pat confided to me. "The wife didn't want me to go."

"She ought to be used to being a steamboat widow by this time, Pat."

"Sure. It's a queer thing that she got a notion this trip was bad luck."

"Bad luck?"

The pilot nodded. "You know what fancies a woman will be gettin'. 'It's bad luck, Pat,' she says. 'It's bad luck to be takin' cows on the *Blair* in the middle of the night. I can feel it in my bones,' she says to me, 'and if you're set on goin' I want you to wake up the children and say goodbye to them.' " Pat swore in mild amusement. "Well, I humored her. It's the only way to do. But it is a Hell of a night, ain't it?"

The snow was flicking softly against the windows of the pilot house. It whipped up horizontally from the west, not falling to the deck, but sweeping on up the river into the vast blackness astern of us.

I slid her easily into the current. Soon Crates Point was passed and I took the long crossing to avoid the sand bar that reaches out like a finger from Cayuse rock. And when I was in the channel current I knew it was going to be a job. Feeling, straining against the darkness, dizzy with the white flakes which streaked at the wheel house over the feeble lamp on the foredeck, I found the channel along the Washington shore and watched for the rocky headland that marked the mouth of the Klickitat.

I had never seen a night so black. If it had not been for the lamp on the deck I would have sworn the snow itself was black. It veiled the river and blotted out the shore. But I went with the current, getting back to midstream, back alongside of Memaloose Island to where the narrow passage dares a pilot to make it safely. My heart rose in my throat as we neared this first real test. There was no time for doubt, no margin for hesitation. I shoved the wheel to starboard, thinking: "Not every man could take her down tonight. Troup, and Stump, and McNulty. I've got to do it." And then Memaloose, where lie the Indian dead, slipped past like a dark wraith. Alone in the pilot house, all the curtains drawn against the aft lights, I watched for the Mosier rocks, frothing the surface, clutching up only a few feet and reaching down in broad pillars that would be like tearing teeth on the bottom of the *Blair Anthony*. Past them we sped, on through the tortuous channel which lies between the shore and the island called Eighteen Mile.

I was feeling easier now; I was getting hold of myself, but there was still the strain of working against the driving snow. And when we got into the long reaches, the wind roared up the canyons against the current to make up a quick, nasty chop so that the nose of the *Blair* slopped incessantly.

With the current I let her slide past the Bingen divide, and with every mile the wind grew stronger, the chop more insistent. When we reached the mouth of Hood River a real sea was kicking, so that the *Blair* was difficult to handle. By the time we had come abeam of Mitchell Point I would have given anything for a patch of daylight, for even a moment's let-up in the driving snow.

I heard the wind howl as the door of the pilot house swung open, and felt Pat Henley's shoulder against mine. His pipe smelled cold and strong in the darkness. "She's a bitcherino, ain't she?"

"I'd give a lot to get a glimpse of Underwood Mountain," I told him.

"Hell! We're lucky if we get a look at White Salmon Hill. Unless we get a *damned* good look at it right on the starboard bow. That was Mitchell back there. Did you get it?"

"Yes. Seven miles to Shell Rock and Wind Mountain."

Pat grunted and reached for his tobacco pouch. There was a sudden flare as he lighted his pipe, and his round good-natured face, illuminated in the glass, was set eerily against the black channel.

Not a shore light had I seen since leaving Dalles City, and I did not expect to see one until we reached the upper landing at The Cascades. What few settlers had chosen the river bank were long asleep in their cabins.

Now the gorge seemed to narrow, for the rock cliffs were rising ever higher. I began to sound the whistle, listening for the echo, calculating the distance. Sound travels at one thousand ninety feet per second when the temperature is at thirty-two degrees. Sharp, short blasts—then count the seconds, one-two-three-four-five . . . the echo reaches us.

With every blast of the whistle the cattle below would grow more frantic, but I heard their noises only faintly. My ears were tuned to the echo, my mind was set on the fleeting seconds. I could see nothing of the shore lines now, and when we should have been abreast of Wind Mountain even that great crumbling sentinel was blanketed by the blizzard and the night.

I could not help but wish that Tom Stump or Len White could be in the pilot house. They would be proud, I thought, of their teaching. And yet, had one of them been there, I would willingly have relinquished the wheel to him. For the strain of getting the *Blair* down increased rather than lessened. Each mile that we put safely astern had no relation to the mile ahead, and the nearer we got to The Cascades the greater was the force of wind against us.

"I'll bet Doran is sweatin'," said Pat after a long silence.

I could imagine the engineer, watching the compound steam engine, the driving arm, the boiler gauge, his red hand on the throttle, his ear ready for every signal from the pilot house.

"It would play Hell," Pat said, "if them cows busted things down and got into Doran's machinery, wouldn't it?"

I laughed, more to relieve my tight nerves than in amusement. "You think of the damnedest things tonight, Pat."

The chop was so high now that it was necessary to call for a little more steam from below. She was banging so hard that when Pat and I exchanged words at infrequent intervals our voices shook in our throats. "We ought to be gettin' there," Pat said. "I'll go below. Maybe I can spot something and signal you from up forward."

With my eyes I tried to tear out a piece of that maddening blackness. "It seems to me we ought to be off Herman Creek, but if we are we should be picking up that light Coe was talking about."

Almost continually now I blew the whistle, trying to check our position in the channel, marking the quality of the echo, attempting to tell whether it sprang back from basalt or the soft cushion of thick pines. Dimly below me, under the weak forward lantern, I could see Pat Henley.

I was working into a bad spot and I knew it. The darkness and the wind had made me unsure about our position. I felt that we were near Herman Creek, and yet I did not want to slow down in the chop; unless we had headway she was hard to handle, and if ever I needed control of the *Blair Anthony* it was now.

I saw Henley turn and lift his face to me. I saw his mouth open wide in a shout that was lost on the wind. With pulses racing I peered ahead—and saw a light. With what tremendous relief I picked up that wavering yellow spot in the vast darkness I could never describe. Perspiration began pouring from my face in rivulets; my shirt was wet and clinging underneath my coat. My knees were like paper. I began talking there in the pilot house, in crazy relief. "We made it, old girl! We made it—and I'll bet they've been wondering down in Portland and back at Dalles City!"

I had hardly shouted into the darkness when my blood froze in horror. That light was not right. The realization swept over me in an instant, and was all the more paralyzing because I did not know why I believed it was not right. All I knew was that we were wrong—but not how or why. In a frenzy I spun the wheel to bring her back to the Washington shore, but even as I did it I knew I was too late. I was lost, lost and I knew it. And even in that swift moment of retribution I had time to curse myself for a fool. I had laughed at the river before the lines were fast ashore.

The human frame can withstand no dread more violent than that which shudders through a man when a boat strikes, when he knows that the ship beneath his feet is lost. All my life I had been seeing the power of the Columbia. Always there was a consciousness that disaster could lie in the next white rapids, or might strike from the shifting base of the next basalt cliff. A current faster than calculated, a sudden gust of wind down the hillside, a trick from the rudder, one of those or a hundred other things could in the next ten seconds mean the loss of a boat and of life. And in those awful seconds while I spun the big wheel I knew there could be no retraction, no repair. There flashed into my mind the whole picture of the *Blair Anthony*—I saw her proud and whole upon the river, her black plume trailing back, her paddles turning majestically. I saw the glittering chandeliers in the main cabins. I saw the green pattern of her Brussels carpets. I saw the silver on her tables in her dining saloon. I saw the shining metal of her compound engine.

We struck hard. We struck so hard that I was thrown against the wheel and my right fist burst through the pane of glass. She seemed to leap, as if she were trying, with me, to get over it and down the stream to safety. In one swift glance below I saw a cloud of white lift over the forecastle, taking the lantern with it so that when the wet cloud subsided I could not see Pat Henley.

A hundred different sounds swept up to me as I ran across the tilting floor of the wheel house. The ripping of the forward planking, the grinding squeals of twisting beams and frames, and then from out astern the splintering of the paddle buckets. As I gained the door the *Blair* was lifted by the bow again and set down more solidly, so solidly that I saw the door frame twist before my eyes and it took all my strength to escape onto the deck. But that sticking door saved my life, for just as it gave outward the *Blair's* stack crashed overside, smashing the rail and ripping like cloth at its rivets; and its broad base, torn from the metal column, came rolling down the deck exuding a warm wood-breath.

I half fell down the companionway and made my way forward. We had swung around now. The heartless current was pounding us from above, and the wind waves were smashing clean over the port rail, the two forces meeting midway on the foredeck and throwing a crest so high that the capstan was hidden. I knew that if Pat Henley had not run back when the *Blair* first struck he was lost now. All around us were struggling dark splotches, for the cattle in their panic had broken their hastily built corral and plunged into the river. What few were still aboard sent up frightful moans from below.

I ran back along the deck and knocked into Bill Doran. The engineer was wet to the thighs and the voice that came out of the blackness at me was more hurt than frightened. "Sweet Jesus, Cap'n what did you do?"

"Where's Pat?" I yelled. "Have you seen Pat?"

"No—I just got up through the grating. All Hell's busted loose down there—"

"The boats," I cried. "Get the deck hands and get a boat down!"

As I started aft I heard the hissing of ashes as they were floated out of the boiler. The hot smell of them whirled on the wind. When I reached the stern I saw a shambles. The paddlewheel of the *Blair* was a mass of twisted wood and steel. The deck was soft and springy beneath my feet and I knew that the whole stern was broken. She was open end to end and a good part of the river was rushing through her. I thanked God that Bill Doran had got out and I prayed that the fireman had been as quick.

But there was no Pat Henley on the lower deck.

When I got back forward against the wind I saw Doran and the fireman and the two deck hands struggling to get a boat free from twisted davits. Urging them to speed, I made my way to the upper deck again, thinking that Henley might have returned there in search of me. But the wheel house was empty; the snow was swirling in and had drifted in a little pile in one corner.

I went to Pat's cabin in the Texas. The door was jammed solid, but I could see inside through the window. The gimbal-mounted lamp on the wall was still burning dimly, showing me the two pictures nailed over Pat's bunk. One was a colored print of the Virgin Mary, the other a photograph of Pat's modest cottage with his wife and two little girls standing self-consciously on the porch.

I began to feel a queer detachment now. It was as if all the damage had been done and there was no hurry to leave the *Blair*. Pat Henley's cabin looked so quiet and orderly, that as I stood there I no longer heard the sounds of the *Blair* being disintegrated by the river. I had an overwhelming desire to go through that part of the boat that wasn't flooded, to walk through the dining saloon, and the men's cabin, to look into the staterooms. I knew that the *Blair Anthony* would never float again. But she had been a brave boat; she had been the only one of them to try the Columbia in a night blizzard; and I wanted to have another look at her, carefully, so that I would always remember. Then I recalled the wheel house, with the door awry, the little pile of snow in the corner, and nobody at the wheel.

Suddenly a hand touched my shoulder and I jumped. It was Bill Doran. "For God's sake, we got to get out of here!"

I followed him down the companionway to the lower deck. The men had the boat over the side and they were holding her with lines at bow and stern. Almost all the sounds had stopped now, or were drowned by the rush of water below us. The only light aboard was the one that showed dimly from Pat's cabin above us. It was a little yellow square of light across which the snow streaked endlessly.

The five of us dropped quickly into the boat and each took up an oar. For what seemed minutes we were rushed downstream, battered by the current and the wind and blinded with the snow. But at last we got control and began heading obliquely for the shore.

Wet and shivering, I left the rest with the few settlers at the upper landing who had been brought out by the tumult of the frightened cattle, and made my way to the wharf boat. There was a dull pain in my right hand and when I looked at it I was surprised to find it covered with blood. I had forgotten I had plunged it through the wheel house window when the *Blair* struck. The knuckles were in ribbons of flesh and I could hardly close my fingers.

When I reached the wharf boat I searched it from end to end for a lantern whose flame had gone out. But there was none anywhere, and I followed back along the edge of the river to discover what beacon I had used. At last I saw it, blinking in the wavering branches at least six hundred yards from the landing. I pushed through the wet, white-covered brush until I reached the light. It hung on a lower branch of a scrubby pine half of whose roots had been eaten away by the river. Peering out into the channel I saw that the light lined up almost perfectly with the falls!

The portage train was not in commission at that time of night, for the *Blair* naturally had been expected to arrive safely and tie at the upper landing until morning. I ordered the crew to get themselves warm at one of the settler's cabins, then I started down the portage track toward the lower landing.

The company watchman was half gone with sleep when I knocked at his door. He blinked at me, holding his candle high. "Cap'n Paige! I didn't figure you'd be around here until morning. Got in all right, eh?" He was frightened, for he had seen my wet clothes and the look on my face.

"Did you set a light on the upper landing, like you were told?" I asked.

"Yes, sir. I put it there. Six o'clock it was, and I made sure to fill it."

"You should have made sure it stayed there."

"Stayed there?" The poor old man fought against his drowsiness. "I set it right in the notch on the wharf landing, sir. And I made sure it was full."

"It isn't there now. Someone moved it—and I ran the *Blair* aground and lost a man and two hundred head of cattle. Hereafter if you get orders to set out a light, stay with it until the boat gets in."

I turned in the wet snow and left him standing, his candle aloft and his rheumy eyes blinking. I didn't mind giving him something to think about for the rest of the night. It was the captain of the boat who was responsible for her—not the company watchman. We didn't make night runs with cattle, and a watchman couldn't be expected to stay with a light he'd set out. The man who'd wrecked the *Blair Anthony* was Captain Caleb Paige. There was nothing that could happen to the watchman for the loss of a boat; and if he missed some sleep with thinking it would do him no harm.

"I don't know how it could've happened." I heard him behind me. "There ain't nobody around here would do a thing like that."

He had followed me out into the snow in his bare feet and woolen underwear. The candle trembled and went out. From the darkness his squeaky voice pleaded, "I would of stayed there if I'd had any idea—but there ain't anybody would do a thing like that."

"No strangers around that you know of? Nobody with a grudge against the company?"

"I know everybody around here and there ain't anybody with anything against the boats. And there ain't any strangers—except Miss Hunt that built that house opposite Bradford's Island."

"Is she there now?"

"Yeah. She came down last week with a friend of hers. I've seen him around, but he ain't exactly a stranger, and he's been in Portland most of the time."

"Is his name Inge?"

"I don't actually know. That sounds like it might be it."

I whirled away and started in the direction of that little knoll above the portage road, opposite Bradford's Island. I walked faster and faster, heedless of the cold against my wet clothes, forgetting the pain in my hand. And as I walked there welled up inside me a hatred fed by a dozen springs.

There were no lights in Victoria's house.

It had the odor of new paint, and around it the snow stood in mounds on the earth which had been thrown up for the excavation. Softly I unlatched the door and stood in the deeper darkness inside. From somewhere in the house I heard a voice, a muffled whisper, then the scratch of a sulphur match. From the next room there grew a gleam of light; it splashed along a wall of flowered paper and reflected into the room in which I stood.

As my eyes became accustomed to the shadows I looked about me. The room was in curious, shocking contrast to the rugged setting of the house itself. Glowing ghostlike was the gray marble face of a fireplace shielded with a brass-bound iron screen. The table in the center of the room was huge and covered with an embroidered, tasseled cloth. On it rested an elaborate china lamp with a hand-painted shade hiding the tall chimney. The chairs in the room were gilt, and the rug beneath my feet felt deep and soft.

"Who's there?" a voice called out. It was Inge. It was Inge and I felt my skin crawl at the sound of it. My blood began to pound through me, and my injured hand felt as if it were bursting at the knuckles. Slowly the light began to fill the room, and I drew Coe's gun in my left hand.

Inge came in, holding the lamp high. He was stark naked; there was black, curl-matted hair from his throat to his groin. The false hand was gone. There was only the stump of his arm, ending round just below his elbow, and there were red marks where the false hand had been strapped.

He could not yet see me in the darkness, and I called out, "I've got a gun. Put the lamp down and come outside, Inge."

At the sound of my voice, Victoria rushed in from the other room, her face white. She wore the cachemire peignoir I remembered. She started toward me, then stopped behind the table. The cachemire rustled in my ears as it had on that other night. "Caleb—Caleb, please don't bring trouble."

"You're out of this, Victoria," I said. "I want him to come with me."

Inge set the lamp down. He began to be aware of his nakedness. He kept rubbing the stump of his arm where the false hand should have been. "What the Hell do you want here?" he said.

"I've come to kill you. This is the last time I'll ask you to come outside. If you don't come now, I'll shoot you down where you stand."

"Caleb!" Victoria ran at me, getting herself between me and Inge. "Caleb, you've got to listen."

I pushed her aside, away from the revolver. "The *Blair* is out there breaking to pieces. Pat Henley was lost when she struck. Mike—Mike Shea would be alive now if it weren't for Inge." I reached behind me and opened the door. As my fingers closed stiffly over the latch a streak of pain shot clear to my shoulder.

I stepped out into the snow, and when Inge followed I thrust the revolver at him and marched him toward the bank of the river. As we headed down the slope I got out of my coat and let it slide off my injured hand. With it I dropped the gun, and when we were at the river I called Inge's name.

He turned, looking for the revolver—and then suddenly he lunged, the stump of his arm straight at my face. It struck me in the mouth like a block of wood, and when I tried to smash at him with my right hand it fell weakly against his chest. While his fist and the stub of his arm flailed at me I reached out with my left hand for his throat, not trying to stop his blows, not feeling them. I felt his throat in my fingers and brought my knee upward in a thrust that made him scream. Then I dragged him to the edge of the river, dragged him by the throat as if he were a sack. There I lifted him up with strength that came from madness and hatred. I lifted him and flung him at the rocks that split the channel between Bradford's Island and the shore. I heard his back bone snap as he struck. I watched him slip broken from the dark rock and be swept into the white whirl.

I stood there weakly, and then turned, half staggering, to see Victoria running toward me. I clutched at her shoulders, held her from her flight. We stared at each other wildly and I said, "You're free," not knowing why I said it. "You're free now."

Behind us the river roared and lifted and fell over the dark rocks, plunging toward the sea.

CHAPTER 23

I WAS riding from Walla Walla to the Kiessling ranch, and when the mare turned toward the line of willows that marked the little creek I saw Mary in the road. I dismounted and tossed the reins around a clump of rye grass and went to meet her, and suddenly there came back to me the memory of the time we had met by the side of the creek, when I had come to tell her that Mike and I were going to search for the diamond in the mountain.

That seemed a long time ago, that stretch of rushing years between myself and the awkward Caleb Paige who had dreamed of being a river captain. My life had been like the country along the river. It had opened out to me amid the horror of an Indian massacre, and then swept along so swiftly, bringing me so much of what I wanted, that there had been no time to think. But it was not too late for readjustments, and I looked without longing toward the Caleb Paige who had hung his clothes on a willow branch and beat the dust from them with a stick. I had no regrets, for what had happened to me thus far had been the things that had to happen if I wanted the river above everything else.

"I came to meet you," Mary said, stopping in the road. "I thought it best that I see you here instead of at the house." She looked up at me, and then with an effort she explained it. "Sidonie—Sidonie refused to have you come into the house. I couldn't insist on it, Caleb, because it's really hers now."

No, I thought, Mary would never insist on it. She would never stand up to the thin-lipped Sidonie and demand that the father of her child be admitted to the house Heinrich Kiessling had built for them both. There was no iron in poor Mary Kiessling, and that was why she had never liked the river. I should have seen that—I should have seen it once when we sat in the moonlight by the little creek.

"You might have brought the boy," I said.

"For what we have to talk about, I thought not." Mary's voice was very small and strained, and I knew that she would much rather have had me stay away than meet the facts we had to face together there on the Kiessling place.

"Will it—will it be bad for you that the boat was wrecked?" she asked at last.

"I've seen Ainsworth. He's not holding it against me. Nobody had tried to make that run at night before, and besides there was —a reason for the accident."

"I know," said Mary quickly. Her wide blue eyes became as accusing as they ever could be. "I have thought things for a long time, Caleb. I—I didn't know what to do about them."

"I don't have any excuses to make," I told her. "I—I don't want things to be over. If you'll come back with me I can promise you that there'll be nothing more of Victoria Hunt."

"But sometimes you will still want her. With her you are like you are with the river, Caleb. There is nothing you can do about it. I have known that for a long time."

I had no answer and I did not want to lie. I knew that Mary spoke the truth. Whatever Victoria Hunt was, whatever she became, I would never quite be able to forget her. And whenever we met along the river, until the day that one of us died, we would be drawn together again.

I could not answer Mary. I felt that I still loved her, but I dared not risk her bitterness by speaking now of love. I had come there to try to bring us together again, and yet deep in my heart I knew that it was not the thing to do. Deep in my heart I knew that I would only be hurting her again, and spoiling all her life instead of only a part of it. I was glad when I saw that German stubbornness in her eyes, that stolid belief that she belonged there, on the

Kiessling place, and that I would never leave the river. I knew now that I was glad, and the knowledge made me ashamed.

"I will be all right," she said quietly. "I am happy here with Sidonie—and she needs me. I do not think that she will ever marry. We can hire the work done well, and it will not be long before Henry will be able to take over for himself."

"Mary . . . Mary, I wonder if this would have happened if—if there had been only the river between us?"

Mary smiled. "I would rather have it that there is only the river between us now. I think that is true, Caleb. I never should have married you, because I always knew that you were of one thing and I was of another. I knew I should not have married you, Caleb, and you did not know it. And yet I went ahead—so, you see, it is my fault that things have happened as they did."

"Mary, please!"

"Oh, yes, Caleb. You tried hard to make me happy. And it isn't your fault that you cannot forget the boats, and that I cannot like them. It would not be right for us to go on the way we were. It would only mean trouble for you, Caleb, and it would never bring me happiness."

She stopped, and looked down at the ends of the shawl she had been tying and untying while she talked. The little creek sang along softly, and I thought how odd it was that it sounded exactly as it had when Mary and I had been so happy in this place. But when I looked up at the willows and the poplars they were bare and straggly in the wind. They had not been that way the night that Mary Kiessling had called me a *dumkopf* for stealing a kiss.

"Will you send Henry up the road to see me if I wait here?"

"Yes, Caleb. You will hardly know him, he has grown so tall and strong."

When I stepped from the train at Wallula Landing to ride the boat down to Dalles City, Jim Troup waved at me from the wheel house of the *Harvest Queen.*

"Come on up, Paige!" he called.

I joined him at the wheel and watched him maneuver the big white beauty into the channel. We cleared the Wallula Gateway and came swiftly abeam of the Twin Sisters. Ahead of us the Columbia opened out into a great wide highway to the Pacific.

Troup turned to me. "You've never handled the *Queen,* have you? Want to take her awhile?"

I could think of no words with which to thank him. But that gesture from the greatest captain on the river erased the cankering memory of the little boy who had stood on the wharf at Dalles City when I had come up from The Cascades after the wreck. His dirty face was tear-stained and when he saw me he cried out in heartbreaking anger: "They said you wrecked the *Blair!*" I knew how that small boy felt, and how he despised me.

"Are you sure you'll trust me with her?" I asked Troup wryly.

I will never forget what he said to me, then, or the news he brought. "Ainsworth's already answered that, Paige. I saw him in Dalles City and he told me that he's putting you in command of the new *Mountain Queen.*"

To hide my feelings I stepped quickly to the big wheel and took it in my hands. Beyond the foredeck the water was gray-blue with ever-moving crests of white. I felt the engine throbbing easily beneath us, letting the current take us. I heard the sound of the river, urging us toward the sea. I saw the huge brown ramparts on either side, stark and solid against the winter sky.

Ahead were the rapids to run. The Umatilla, the Hell-Gate, the John Day, the Four O'clock. I glanced over my shoulder. Jim Troup had gone below. I was alone in the pilot house, pitted against the Columbia, bound down for Dalles City. . . .

Standing there I began to feel again the great river—all of it, for that part of the waters on which I rode had in it parts of all the river that was behind me and would become part of all that which was before me. Beneath me were the snows of the Canadian mountains, and the soft ice from the long placid lakes of the north country. Beneath me were the mountain rain and the marsh fog and the mist that lies at night on the prairies. Beneath me were the swirling sands of the Grand Coulee, the stream-shredded roots of the rye grass, the bleached lost twigs of the mountain pine, and the shining scales of granite rock jutting higher than the clouds.

I rode on the turbulence of the Snake and the Salmon and the